The Prosecution of Mr. Darcy's Cousin

Regina Jeffers

PEGASUS BOOKS

Pegasus Books
3338 San Marino Ave
San Jose, CA 95127
www.pegasusbooks.net

First Edition: May 2015

Published in North America by Pegasus Books. For information, please contact Pegasus Books c/o Christopher Moebs, 3338 San Marino Ave, San Jose, CA 95127.

Library of Congress Cataloguing-In-Publication Data
Regina Jeffers]
The Prosecution of Mr. Darcy's Cousin/Regina Jeffers– [1st] ed
p. cm.
Library of Congress Control Number: 2015939374
ISBN – 978-1-941859-25-4
1. FICTION / Mystery & Detective / Cozy. 2. FICTION / Romance / General. 3. HISTORY / Europe / Great Britain. 4. FICTION / Literary. 5. FICTION / Historical. 6. FICTION / Crime.

10 9 8 7 6 5 4 3 2 1

Comments about The Prosecution of Mr. Darcy's Cousin and requests for additional copies, book club rates and author speaking appearances may be addressed to Regina Jeffers or Pegasus Books c/o Christopher Moebs, 3338 San Marino Ave, San Jose, CA, 95127, or you can send your comments and requests via e-mail to cmoebs@pegasusbooks.net.

Also available as an eBook from Internet retailers and from Pegasus Books

Printed in the United States of America

Fitzwilliam Darcy is enjoying his marital bliss. His wife, the former Elizabeth Bennet, presented him two sons and a world of contentment. All is well until "aggravation" rears its head when Darcy receives a note of urgency from his sister Georgiana. In truth, Darcy never fully approved of Georgiana's joining with their cousin, Major General Edward Fitzwilliam, for Darcy assumed the major general held Georgina at arm's length, dooming Darcy's sister to a life of unhappiness.

Dutifully, Darcy and Elizabeth rush to Georgiana's side when the major general leaves his wife and daughter behind, with no word of his whereabouts and no hopes of Edward's return. Forced to seek his cousin in the slews of London's underbelly, at length, Darcy discovers the major general and returns Fitzwilliam to his family.

Even so, the Darcy's troubles are far from over. During the major general's absence from home, witnesses note Fitzwilliam's presence in the area of two horrific murders. When Edward Fitzwilliam is arrested for the crimes, Darcy must discover the real culprit before his cousin is hanged for the crimes and the Fitzwilliam name marked with shame.

THE PROSECUTION OF MR. DARCY'S COUSIN

Cast of Characters

Characters from Jane Austen's *Pride and Prejudice*:
Fitzwilliam Darcy—owner of Pemberley House in Derbyshire, UK
Elizabeth Bennet Darcy—Mr. Darcy's wife
Georgiana Darcy Fitzwilliam—Mr. Darcy's sister; wife to Major-General Fitzwilliam
Major-General Edward Fitzwilliam—Mr. Darcy's cousin; in the original *Pride and Prejudice*, he was but Colonel Fitzwilliam

Characters Specific to this Title:
Thomas Cowan—a former Bow Street Runner; once served under the then Colonel Fitzwilliam in Spain; assisted Darcy with the investigation of the elder Samuel Darcy's demise in *The Mysterious Death of Mr. Darcy*
Bennet Fitzwilliam George Darcy—four-year-old son of Fitzwilliam and Elizabeth Darcy
Samuel James William Darcy—two-month old son of Fitzwilliam and Elizabeth Darcy
Colleen Nora Fitzwilliam—four-month-old daughter of Edward and Georgiana Fitzwilliam
Rowland Fitzwilliam, Viscount Lindale—Edward's older brother
Martin Fitzwilliam, Earl of Matlock—Edward's father
Nora Olivia Rowland Fitzwilliam, Countess of Matlock—Edward's mother
Saunders Welch—the real-life founder of the Bow Street Runners
Isaac Brock—the real-life leader of the 41st Foot during the War of 1812
Mr. Simon Rumbradge—the officer who investigates the crimes for Shadwell
Captain Roman Southland—married to Darcy's cousin, Anne de Bourgh; served under Major General Fitzwilliam on both the American continent during the War of 1812 and upon the Napoleonic front; lost an arm at the Battle of Waterloo

Chapter One

Derbyshire, 1816

Darcy watched his family through the window of his study. Elizabeth and his children and his sons' nurses enjoyed a simple meal upon the side lawn. In reality, Elizabeth and young Samuel's nurse nibbled on the cakes and sandwiches while Bennet ran circles about the blanket spread upon the ground. Lily, the girl who provided the active care of Pemberley's heir, chased the boy, with laughter bubbling from both.

Darcy could not remove the smile from his lips: His world knew perfection. He wished to join them, but how could the Master of Pemberley act with imprudence?—chasing butterflies and childish dreams on a late autumn afternoon...

As if she recognized how he longed to be one of their party, Elizabeth's head turned in his direction. A knowing smile graced her lips. If anyone told him when he was but five and twenty that a headstrong sprite of a woman would bring him to his knees, Fitzwilliam Darcy would have scoffed in the man's face.

Yet, his journey to Hertfordshire with his friend Bingley changed all that. At the outset, Darcy accepted a variety of fanciful impediments to his and Elizabeth's connection, but that was before Elizabeth Bennet took him to task. Before, the lady enumerated Darcy's abundant flaws rather than being quelled by his wealth and position.

"How could I resist?" he murmured.

His wife raised her hand in greeting, and Darcy's heart lurched in response.

"God, if Mrs. Darcy held any idea of her power over me..." he acknowledged to the empty room. "Such an infatuating beauty!"

Darcy knew he should return to his estate books, but he never tired of looking upon his wife. Even after more than four years of marriage, he always sought the rich honey umber of Elizabeth's hazel eyes, and he craved the feel of her skin beneath his fingertips: Darcy carried a constant need to know his wife's ethereal excellence.

She stood to motion him to join her, but Darcy shook off the suggestion: He held responsibilities. True to form, Elizabeth's hands fisted at her waist, and a scowl crossed her beautiful countenance. The gesture reminded Darcy of those early days of their acquaintance, and the same echo of desire that he first felt when Darcy took Elizabeth's hand in his whispered in his ear. With a shrug of resignation, Darcy nodded his agreement.

Within seconds, he strode across the lawn to where Elizabeth waited. She smiled with his approach—a welcoming smile, the type to beguile a man from his reason.

"Papa!" Bennet called, scurrying toward him, arms lifted for Darcy's embrace.

He caught the boy in mid stride to lift the child above his head and to spin Bennet around.

"Gin, Papa!" Bennet squealed with delight.

Darcy spun his oldest a second time before he set the lad on the ground.

"Go to Lily," he instructed, and the boy scampered away to where Lily offered the boy a teacake, made without fruits or nuts, especially for his son.

Without asking Darcy's permission, Elizabeth deposited Samuel into Darcy's arms.

"Thank you for agreeing to join us," she whispered as he wrapped the blanket about Samuel's small body.

The boy, some two months of age, so resembled his mother that Darcy fell in love with the child instantly. They named the boy for his father's cousin, Samuel Darcy, a famous archaeologist, whose tragic death some four years prior shook Darcy's existence.

His heart clenched in caution. At moments such as these, Darcy's instinct told him to protect those he loved, for perfection was a fragile entity. Leaning into his shoulder, Elizabeth laced her fingers around his elbow.

"How could I deny your appealing gesture?" he teased in the manner of all lovers.

His gaze swept his wife's features: A bit of color kissed her cheeks, and her eyes sparkled with a sizzling depth of excitement. Her hair, simply styled, danced with auburn highlights, and she was the most beautiful woman of his acquaintance. A fierce tenderness filled Darcy's chest.

"Walk with me," he said as he leaned close.

Her gaze held his for several elongated moments, and Darcy imagined them alone—his whole world wrapped in his wife's capable hands. She smiled with intent.

"Bennet, stay with Lily and Mrs. Prulock. Your papa and I shall return in a few minutes. Then I will ask Mr. Mace to show you the new foal."

"Yes, Mama."

His son stood so proud it made Darcy's core claim a bit of arrogance. The boy reminded Darcy of the child's revered grandfather, George Darcy.

He carried the sleeping babe cradled in the crook of his arm. Elizabeth sighed in contentment as they strolled across the groomed lawn.

"Is it not a beautiful day?"

"So beautiful," he murmured.

"Mr. Darcy," she protested, but he recognized the false disapproval in his wife's tone. "We were speaking of the weather."

"Lord save us from the English discussing the weather."

He smiled at her attempts to maintain a dignified expression.

Elizabeth displayed all the stubborn persistence she exhibited in Hertfordshire, but she conceded, "It is a hackneyed topic. Perhaps we should begin again."

Darcy paused before they entered the lower gardens.

"The beauty of which I spoke was the love of a woman worth knowing," he declared.

"I cannot believe you do not grow weary of our time together."

Darcy thought of the handful of occasions they spent apart since their joining and frowned. It was odd, but since marrying Elizabeth Bennet, he turned quite content serving as Pemberley's master. He was groomed for the role, but Darcy never felt comfortable with his duty until he married the one woman who stirred his passions.

In Darcy's estimation, his wife was the missing part of the calculation—turning Pemberley from fine showplace to a home. Elizabeth was more than his wife and the mother of his children: she was his lover, his confidant, and his best friend. She completed him.

"Trust me, my dear. For me, there is never enough of you and the children."

A clearing of a masculine throat warned Darcy of his butler's presence; otherwise, Darcy would have indulged in an enticing kiss from his wife's all-too-tempting lips.

"Yes, Mr. Nathan."

"Pardon, Sir, but a necessitous post arrived by special messenger. I thought it best to seek you out. It is from Mrs. Fitzwilliam."

Darcy's frown lines met as apprehension skittered down his spine. It was not of Georgiana's nature to speak of exigency. He handed young Samuel to his mother before accepting the thick missive from the silver salver.

"Thank you," Darcy mumbled before flicking the sealing wax from the folded over pages. Mr. Nathan bowed out when Darcy excused him with a flexing of his wrist.

"From Georgiana?" Elizabeth asked in concern. "Is something amiss with either your sister or our niece?"

His wife scooted closer to read bits over Darcy's forearm.

Darcy held a hand to signal her patience. He scanned the first page for details, but he could not immediately determine the urgency.

"Bear with me," he cautioned.

He knew his wife's deep affection for his sister. Darcy read to determine the gist of Georgiana's letter. His sister was not one to raise alarm without true cause.

"My sister and baby Colleen are well."

He heard Elizabeth's sigh of relief, but Darcy read on.

"Georgie is aggrieved of her husband's actions of late," he summarized. He flipped to the second page. "The unusual climate of this past growing season levied a heavy toll on their reign at Yadkin Hall, and my cousin took the failures very ill."

Some two years prior, Darcy returned from a business journey to Northumberland to celebrate Christmastide at Pemberley, only to discover pure chaos under his roof, including uninvited guests and the news his sister chose their cousin, Colonel Edward Fitzwilliam, as her husband. Against Darcy's wishes, the couple rushed their vows before the newly promoted major general returned to the war following Napoleon's escape from Elba.

Elizabeth shifted the child to her shoulder.

"I worried from the beginning that Edward would not take well to the land."

Darcy scowled in disapproval.

"Both Matlock and I offered our assistance, but this year challenged even the most creative estate master. My cousin never spoke a syllable of his struggles," Darcy said as he returned to the tightly spaced pages. "My God! Has Bedlam claimed Edward's good sense?"

"Tell me quick," his wife insisted.

If Darcy could place his hands upon his cousin's neck, he would take prodigious delight in throttling Edward Fitzwilliam.

"The major general left early on Wednesday last, saying he meant to examine the tenant farms. When he did not return for supper, Georgiana sent out men. For three days, my sister searched for Edward, but with no word of him. On Friday, Georgie received a simple, one-page note, saying the major general traveled to London and did not know when he would return to Oxfordshire."

"Poor Georgiana," Elizabeth sympathized. "She must be quite beside herself with worry. Your cousin acted in a most unexpected manner."

Darcy's eyes remained on the pages he held.

"I may kill him," he grumbled.

"When do we depart for Whitney?"

Darcy glanced at his pocket watch. It did not surprise him that his wife meant to rush to Georgiana's side; he and Elizabeth were of the same mind in such matters.

"It is eleven of the clock," he thought aloud. "Is it worth the bother to depart today? The earliest we might leave would be one. I will not permit you to travel by night: The roads are too dangerous."

"At least you did not consider leaving me at Pemberley."

Darcy shook his head in denial.

"I could travel quicker alone, but I am likely to be absent from Derbyshire for some time. I cannot tolerate being from you and the children so long. Moreover, Georgiana will require your good sense in how best to respond to the major general's unprecedented actions."

"Then we should…"

Darcy's exclamation interrupted his wife's planning.

"We *cannot* leave! We have Samuel's christening after Sunday's services. Everything is arranged."

"We shall simply reschedule the event. I will dash off a note to Jane and Mr. Bingley, explaining the necessity of postponement, as well as one to Mr. Winkler. Samuel will forgive our delay. Will *you* not, my love?"

Elizabeth traced a finger along the boy's chin, and his son sucked on the tip of it.

"Are you certain?" Darcy asked. "I know you went to great

measures for the celebration."

"It is nothing which cannot wait until this situation with Georgiana is resolved."

"You are a magnificently kind-hearted woman, and I am so grateful that you blessed me with your favor."

Darcy kissed her forehead and held the moment as he breathed in his wife's essence. Only her presence provided him any peace.

"Then shall we set a time of one for our departure?"

Elizabeth caressed Samuel's fluff of hair.

"We will only manage five hours of travel today, but that is still five hours closer to Mrs. Fitzwilliam."

Darcy refolded the letter and placed it in an inside pocket.

"You set the servants to preparing our trunks, and I will speak to Mr. Mace about the carriages."

Elizabeth went on tiptoes to kiss his cheek.

"Georgiana is a reasonable woman. She knew when she sent the letter we would be on the road post haste. Our sister will not act from unnatural consequences."

"I know you speak the truth, but worry always was my shroud where Georgiana is concerned."

❧ ❧ ❧

They rolled from Pemberley's doorstep at a quarter past one. Two carriages, the one in which he, Elizabeth, and Bennet rode, and the other containing Hannah, Elizabeth's lady's maid, Mr. Sheffield, Darcy's valet, Lily, Mrs. Prulock, and Samuel. Elizabeth permitted Bennet to ride with them to pacify the child for not visiting with the newest horse in the Darcy stable.

"You must mind your Papa," Elizabeth warned the boy when Murray lifted the child to the coach.

"Yes, Mama," the boy said, nodding.

Darcy knew Elizabeth considered their eldest of Darcy's nature, but he recognized how the child held as much of Elizabeth's mulish impetuousness as Bennet did the mannerisms of the Darcys.

Darcy placed the boy beside him on the rear-facing seat. From the earliest days of their marriage, he took his family with him when business necessitated Darcy's travel. Although Bennet was little more than two years of age, the boy showed to be quite intelligent, and Darcy relished instructing his child in the ways of travel and the land's geography.

"A gentleman always permits the lady to sit as such," he explained.

Bennet nodded with enthusiasm.

"Mama says some come ill, but not Mama."

Darcy chuckled.

"No, not your Mama. She is made of a *sterner* nature."

"Terner," the boy repeated with an approving grin. "I be terner too, Papa."

Darcy ruffled the child's hair.

"I could ask for nothing more from my eldest."

Elizabeth smiled at their son.

"We will stay with Aunt Georgiana. You will visit with baby Colleen. I expect you to assist Lily and Mrs. Prulock with Samuel and Colleen. As you are Papa's heir apparent, it is important for you to be kind to the babies."

The boy frowned.

"Kin I p'ay also, Mama? Wily p'ays good games."

Darcy watched as Elizabeth swallowed her mirth.

"Certainly, my darling. Your Papa and I both believe little boys should learn their responsibilities, but they should also know time each day to enjoy play."

ঌঌঌ

It took over eight and fifty hours for Darcy's party to reach Yadkin Hall. If he was not so selfish about keeping his family close, his sister's anguish would know ease some twelve hours earlier, but then Darcy's own torment would take precedence.

Darcy had come to accept his dependence on Elizabeth and his children for his concord. He often prayed that when he and Elizabeth reached the end of their lives, God, in His wisdom, would take him first. Now Darcy found Elizabeth, he did not believe he could live one day without his wife by his side.

At length, Darcy's carriage rolled into the circle before Yadkin Hall. It was a modest estate—simple in comparison to Pemberley or Matley Manor, but the house was in good repair. It reminded Darcy of a cross between Netherfield Park and Longbourn. The manor's main door swung wide, and his sister stepped into the early evening light, the major general's butler flanking her, a lantern held high.

Darcy watched Georgiana's lips move, speaking his name. It was the way with them. After their father's death, Darcy served not only as Georgiana's brother, but also her guardian.

"Go to her," Elizabeth whispered as she adjusted the sleeping Samuel in her arms. "Murray will see to our needs."

Darcy caressed his wife's cheek, and without a command to his waiting servant, Darcy released the door's latch and set down the steps. Bounding from his coach, he rushed to his sister's side, catching Georgiana in his embrace. She buried her face in his chest to hide her sobs.

How many times had he held her as such? From more falls and scrapes than Darcy cared to recall and from that fateful day when Georgiana thought her heart broken by George Wickham, but nothing of this nature. He always thought Edward Fitzwilliam the most honorable of men, but his cousin's actions befuddled all reason.

The major general abandoned his wife and child: An act beyond Darcy's forgiveness. Displeasure, of no common degree, claimed his reason.

"Come now," Darcy whispered to Georgiana.

He slipped his handkerchief into her hand.

"We will settle this inside. First, you should greet Elizabeth and your nephews."

He heard Georgiana swallow hard and recognized his sister's efforts to stifle her tears. After a long pause, she raised her chin.

"Certainly," she said in a raspy voice as she stepped from Darcy's embrace.

Majestically turning her head, his sister donned her most welcoming smile.

"Elizabeth and Samuel—I missed you both," Georgiana cooed as she caressed the child's dark auburn hair. "He has the look of you, Elizabeth."

"So says your brother," Elizabeth acknowledged as she brushed a kiss across Georgiana's cheek.

"Wantie!"

The group looked up to see Bennet rushing toward Georgiana.

Georgiana caught the boy and lifted him to her.

"My goodness!" Georgiana laughed as she kissed Bennet's cheek. "You grew so tall in my absence. And so handsome."

"I am to a'sist nurse with Amuel," Bennet declared.

Georgiana nuzzled the boy's cheek.

"You must do the same with Colleen. Your cousin will depend upon your protection as I always depended upon your papa."

Bennet's arms went about Georgiana's neck.

"Tect you and Mama too."

"Then we are blessed," Georgiana assured.

Less than an hour later, Darcy, Elizabeth, and his sister gathered in Georgiana's sitting room.

"Now, explain what occurred to drive the major general from his home."

Georgiana squirmed as she always did when Darcy confronted her, but his sister did not look away: She was maturing.

"When we first arrived at Yadkin Hall, life appeared idyllic. The days were long, but hope reigned. My husband met with his tenants and planned for a future, while I oversaw the manor. But, as you well know, the weather was not kind to those who depend upon the land. It speaks well of Edward that my husband does not shirk his responsibility, but the major general permitted his failure to…"

Georgiana caught her handkerchief to dab her eyes.

"A man who has known so much success in the military would naturally take any strife as a personal defeat," Elizabeth cautioned.

Georgiana strained to smile.

"I understand my husband's need for accomplishments…"

"I do not!" Darcy insisted. "I will never understand a man who deserts his wife and children."

As his wife often did, Elizabeth softened his words.

"George Darcy groomed you to know the land; whereas, as a second son, Edward excels at stratagems and political history."

Darcy wished to remind his wife that he was well recognized for his love of history and for his financial maneuverings, but he swallowed his words. It was not the time to permit his pride center stage.

"What precipitated the major general's withdrawal?"

Georgiana's forehead scrunched up in confusion.

"In truth, I hold no definite cause. The evening before Edward's disappearance, my husband worked late in his study, only briefly appearing in the nursery when I visited with Colleen. Although the estate books are never a pleasure that Edward would claim, he did not appear worried by his accounting. I did not see him after that brief encounter in the nursery. When I awoke the following morning, Mr. Stacey brought word the major general meant to call upon several of the tenants and would return for the mid-day meal. As I explained in my letter, when Edward did not return by nightfall, I sent out search parties."

Darcy studied Georgiana's countenance. His sister withheld some pertinent facts, but he would wait for a more opportune moment to discover the complete truth. He prayed Edward did not raise his hand to

Georgiana. If so, Darcy would be forced to call his cousin out.

"Is the major general at Lockland Hall? You said Edward's message came from London."

"No." Georgiana's shoulders stiffened. "I thought my husband would either call in at his family's Town house or at Darcy House, but both households remain closed according to the messenger I sent to carry my concerns to the major general. Boyd returned without finding my husband. I possess no knowledge of Edward's whereabouts."

Darcy scowled.

"And you received only the one message?"

Georgiana fished into a pocket in the apron she donned while tending the babies. She withdrew a crumpled paper and handed it to Darcy. Grudgingly, he unfolded it to read:

My dearest Georgie,

It grieves me to know I failed you and Colleen, but it is best you return to Darcy's care. Your brother is built to protect you from harm, whereas I am built for war. I will speak to my former commander. Perhaps I can purchase another commission. When my plans are complete, I will send word. Please forgive me…

Your loving husband, E.F.

Darcy bit back the curse that sprang to mind.

"It appears I am to London tomorrow," he said through tight lips.

"How shall you know where to begin your search?" Georgiana asked. "Should we not permit my husband his way? I would not wish to force Edward to return to a situation he finds intolerable. Could we not tell everyone the major general answered the call of service? I would be pleased to return to Pemberley with you and Elizabeth."

A slight shake of Elizabeth's head warned Darcy not to accept Georgiana's wish to avoid a confrontation with her husband.

"Although I would be delighted to have you and Colleen at Pemberley, I owe my cousin an obligation. Edward holds two familial connections, and we must set his estate aright for the sake of the Fitzwilliam name," Darcy said as if nothing untoward occurred.

Georgiana's lips moved, but no sound escaped.

"What if…" she whispered.

"You will always possess a home with your brother," Elizabeth assured. "But first we must determine Cousin Edward's whereabouts. You would not wish to turn from the major general if he is suffering."

"Certainly not," Georgiana affirmed. "I desire only peace for my husband."

Darcy suspected the word "peace" held a clue to the root of what occurred under Yadkin Hall's roof, but he held his tongue. He learned long ago to watch and listen before acting.

"There are too many questions without answers. We must begin with whether Edward is in dire straits. From there, all other decisions will become evident."

Georgiana nodded her understanding.

"I shall send word to Mr. Stacey for your coach's preparations for eight of the clock, unless you would prefer to leave earlier."

"Eight is adequate," Darcy assured.

His sister's mood frightened Darcy He had not observed her so despondent since that farce with George Wickham, but after her marriage to their cousin, Georgiana seemed to put her earlier self-chastisement behind her, and in Scotland, she confronted Wickham upon the Ayrshire moors.

Now, she wished to retreat to Pemberley. Despite his natural desire to protect her, Darcy realized the truth of Elizabeth's caution: If Georgiana returned to Pemberley—if his sister abandoned her marriage, she would never leave Derbyshire again. Georgiana would rot away under Darcy's roof, never to sparkle again with happiness.

Georgiana made her excuses to tend to Darcy's wishes, and once her footsteps receded, Elizabeth suggested, "Perhaps you should seek the assistance of Thomas Cowan. The man likely knows more of the major generals' favorite stomping grounds than you."

"Yours is an excellent suggestion," Darcy said. "Now, provide me your opinion as to what occurred between Georgiana and the major general."

"When we were all in Scotland, I cautioned Georgiana that just because Edward pronounced his vows did not mean the major general could leave behind the decade of devastation to which he stood witness, but it appears she ignored my advice."

"And the major general also," Darcy agreed. "Before we recovered Georgiana from that reiver's cottage, my cousin was near mad with grief at the possibility of losing his wife. How could a man consumed by a woman not ten months prior walk away from her as if she meant nothing to him?"

"I recall your expressing concerns regarding your cousin's transition to civilian life," Elizabeth mused.

"Yes, but Edward promised me Georgiana would never know pain by his hand. He pronounced my sister his world. The major general swore, when he returned to Pemberley to discover the woman

Georgiana had become, that he felt as if God meant for him to leave his position and to claim the love of a wife and family…to know the meaning of *home*. It is all very vexatious."

Irritation crossed Elizabeth's features.

"Yet, the major general did not execute the one response that would assure his happiness: He did not trust Georgiana with his confidences. The situation with the lost crops is not the issue. Georgiana's dowry, as well as Edward's position as an earl's son, would protect the estate and the land until better times arrive. I warned the major general he must share with Georgiana the part of him he withheld from all others—to trust his wife with what haunted him.

"I told your cousin that, only when he acted as such, would he know contentment. Since the death of your father, you and your cousin served as Georgiana's guardians, and Edward clung to that mantle. He never permitted Georgiana to be the protector of his heart. Your cousin kept his wife as his *subject* rather than as his companion. Even if you convince the major general to return…"

"You are saying that if my cousin refuses to alter the manner in which he approaches his marriage, I should encourage him to relinquish my sister to my care?"

Anger swelled Darcy's heart: Anger with Edward for not recognizing his shortcomings, anger with Georgiana for rushing into marriage and anger with himself for not protecting his family. How could Darcy drive his cousin from his life in order to safeguard his sister?

Elizabeth answered in disappointed tones.

"I am saying there is no easy way to go. Either your cousin or Georgiana will know a broken heart."

Chapter Two

"Yes, Sir."

A young clerk rushed forward to greet Darcy, whose arrival set his London household on its ear. After his marriage to Elizabeth Bennet, Darcy sold the smaller bachelor Town house he purchased after reaching his majority and acquired the larger one to accommodate what he hoped would be extended family. Yet, until Elizabeth turned his world on its head, Darcy did not realize how much he would enjoy having a loud, noisy family under his roof.

"How may I serve you, Sir?"

Darcy ran his gloved fingers over his lapel.

"Mr. Darcy to speak to Mr. Cowan."

The clerk presented a proper obeisance. The man glanced at an appointment log lying open upon the desk.

"Was Mr. Cowan expecting you, Sir?" the clerk asked as he ran his finger down the page, searching for Darcy's name.

Any other time, Darcy would consider the young man's loyalty admirable, but this matter with Edward wore Darcy's patience thin.

"Simply inform Mr. Cowan of my desire to speak to him," he said with practiced authority.

The clerk glanced over his shoulder as if considering a denial.

"Certainly, Mr. Darcy… if you would care to wait."

The man motioned to a cluster of straight-backed chairs lining a far wall.

Darcy offered a crisp nod of his head. He did not observe the clerk's retreat; yet, he knew the clever fellow would inform Cowan of Darcy's presence.

Instead, Darcy assumed a position by the window to look out upon the busy London street. Cowan chose well for his offices, near enough to Mayfair to be accessible to the *haut ton*, but equally accessible to London's swelling middle class.

Quick footsteps upon the polished wood floor announced Cowan's approach.

"Darcy," the man called with a ready smile, extending his hand in welcome. "What brings you to London? And how is Mrs. Darcy? I pray your lady is well."

Darcy accepted Cowan's hand.

"Mrs. Darcy remains her spectacular self. She is in Oxfordshire with my sister. Elizabeth sends her regards."

Darcy eyed the lingering clerk.

"If you have a few minutes to spare, I have a need of your services."

Cowan frowned.

"For you I will make time."

He turned toward his clerk.

"When Mr. Leighton arrives, apologize for the delay, and ask the gentleman to wait. Be certain to provide him a cup of tea."

The clerk blushed.

"Yes, Sir. Would Mr. Darcy also care for tea?"

Darcy shook off the offer.

"I will be quick, Cowan. I realize you are engaged."

"Never too occupied for you, Darcy."

His friend directed Darcy's steps to a small, but comfortable, office at the rear of the building. The room reflected the former Bow Street Runner's simple, classic tastes. After they settled, Cowan leaned forward.

"What is so pressing, Darcy?"

Darcy removed his gloves and placed them, along with his hat, on the desk's corner.

"I have a matter of a personal nature."

After the Runner's assistance with his family's debacle in Dorset, Darcy knew he could trust Thomas Cowan.

"Without warning, the major general abandoned his wife and daughter in Oxfordshire. My sister received but one brief note declaring her husband's desire to return to his military service and instructing Georgiana to seek a homecoming with me."

Cowan's scowl deepened.

"I feared for some time that Edward Fitzwilliam would not willingly encounter his ghosts before they came to claim him."

Cowan retrieved a small journal from his desk. Opening it, he prepared to write.

"I require all the details you possess. After I determine Mr. Leighton's issues, I will set my resources into action to learn more of the major general's trail."

Despite Darcy's initial anger with the major general for running off to what was a probable drunken pity-laced birl, Darcy experienced a shiver of dread run down his spine. Perhaps something more sinister occurred: Cowan's remark emphasized Darcy and Elizabeth's private concerns.

With anxiety lacing his explanation, Darcy summarized what he knew of Edward's recent activities, belatedly realizing he lacked the details of what occurred between his sister and his cousin.

"Perhaps I should send to Witney for Elizabeth and Georgiana to join us," he suggested. "My sister could better address your questions."

In silence, Cowan studied his notes.

"I think it best we leave the ladies in the country for now. I suspect the major general sought solace in London's pitch, for it reflects his opinion of his worth."

Although he would not own it, the investigator's words reinforced Darcy's notion of the sword of Damocles above their heads.

"Would you dine with me this evening? I would know your thoughts on my cousin."

అఅఅ

Some four years prior, in Dorset, Cowan proved valuable in discovering the truth behind the death of Darcy's cousin Samuel, and they maintained a correspondence since. In fact, Darcy extended the man a personal loan to open Cowan's high purpose investigation firm. Darcy did not consider the prospect of chasing down aristocratic runaways and unhappy wives as an appropriate career for the brilliant Thomas Cowan, but the man appeared content in his choices.

"If you are up to some late night maneuverings, we should visit several of the major general's previous haunts," Cowan suggested as he cut into the fish course.

The fact that his staff set his house to order without delay pleased Darcy.

"Do you suppose our search will be so easy?"

Darcy never was a heavy drinker nor was he one to haunt the gaming hells. The false appeal of such establishments rubbed raw against Darcy's desire for control. The last time he was heavy in his cups, Darcy confessed his love for Elizabeth Bennet to Edward. In hindsight, the thought amused him, but not at the time. It surprised Darcy to learn his cousin's military service led Edward into London's seedier side often enough for Cowan to refer to the major general's "haunts."

Cowan brushed off the suggestion.

"As Fitzwilliam has been absent from his home for a sennight, I do not expect the major general will be found at the obvious places. Yet, we must start somewhere. By visiting a few select establishments, we can determine if your cousin remains in London, or if he sought a commission among one of the units making land for Africa to quash the slave trade along the Berber Coast."

Cowan's matter-of-fact announcement sent a second shudder of dread down Darcy's spine, his customary implacable nature shaken.

"You know a different Fitzwilliam than does his family," Darcy admitted. "I long wondered how the war's toll affected my cousin. The major general has known no easy dominion. Edward was always the first to defend his brother, Rowland, or me against those who would taunt a young man learning his responsibilities. He always refuses to walk away from a confrontation. I imagine my cousin's desire to protect others made him an admirable leader of men."

Darcy knew the major general and Cowan served together in Spain in '09. Darcy asked his cousin of the man when the pair answered Darcy's plea for assistance with Samuel Darcy's mysterious death, but he knew little of Cowan's side of the story.

Cowan served under me in Spain.

Edward answered Darcy's inquiry regarding his cousin's and Cowan's relationship.

Cowan was wounded at that disaster in Corunna. Sir John Moore, nincompoop that he was, possessed no idea what to do about Marshal Soult.

Darcy recalled how his cousin's sharing the details of the Spanish campaign caused the major general's shoulders to tense in a sorrowful slant and how Edward's countenance betrayed the serious darkness of the major general's thoughts. During the retelling, Edward relived each volley. At the time, Darcy thought it best if the major general, Colonel Fitzwilliam then, spoke of the horrors he witnessed, but now Darcy wondered if he did enough to assist Edward's transition to civil life.

During the siege, a volley meant for me cut Cowan down. I was the one with the epaulets on my shoulders. I was the target.

Such sadness crossed his cousin's features that Darcy half-expected to witness Edward's tears. *In our escape, I carried Cowan to the ship and tended to his injuries. Thomas has an ugly scar across his abdomen, a reminder of my poor needlework.*

Cowan's voice brought Darcy from his deep musings.

"It also made Fitzwilliam a despised leader."

Cowan's words took Darcy unawares, as Darcy could not imagine anyone thinking poorly of Fitzwilliam. His cousin possessed an easy manner, which Darcy often envied.

"How so?" Darcy queried.

"The colonel I followed was an honorable man—so honorable that he took on the impossible tasks for the sake of setting wrongs aright. Not all Colonel Fitzwilliam's men were so dedicated."

Darcy did not wish to ask the question, but the words slipped out before he could stifle them.

"Could my cousin's tenaciousness earn him enemies who acted against him?"

Had the major general met with harm? Until that moment, Darcy ignored the possibility. *Heaven forbid! Such a scheme would destroy Georgiana.* And to think of the irony of Edward Fitzwilliam surviving a decade of war only to lose his life on English shores!

"There are many former soldiers polluting the streets of London and the highways leading to the Capital. The opportunity to act against a well-recognized officer would be tempting to those who fill their guts with cheap ale."

᙮᙮᙮

Darcy kept one eye upon Cowan and the other upon the Green Dragon's patrons. With the Runner's assistance, Darcy dressed with less fashion, but even so, he recognized the unwritten "invitation" upon his back. If not for Cowan's presence, Darcy was certain someone would drag him into a dead-end alley to lift Darcy's purse.

"I want no trouble," Cowan said with a hint of warning. "I simply wish to know if you laid eyes upon the former Colonel Fitzwilliam."

"Mayhap a week or more past," a man of some fifty years admitted.

Darcy studied the fellow's features and found the man unremarkable.

"In the Green Dragon?" Cowan pressed.

It was the first mention they heard of Edward in the three hours he and Cowan searched for Fitzwilliam.

"Nah."

The man slouched in his seat. Darcy thought their informant succumbed to the tankard of ale upon the table, but Cowan caught the man's shoulder in a tight grip to straighten the stranger's stance.

Darcy held no doubt Cowan made a formidable junior officer.

The alcohol slurred the informant's speech, but he offered an explanation.

"Spotted the colonel by the docks. Old Fitz 'peared deep in his haunches."

"When was this?" Cowan demanded.

"Not be knowin. Every day the same," the former soldier confessed. "Was rainin tho. I re'ember cause Old Fitz stepped in a muddy patch and gave it no mention. Just like the colonel to ignore the storm!"

Cowan's eyes met Darcy's.

"Last Friday or Saturday. It has been dry since."

Darcy nodded his understanding, but made no comment. His educated accent would draw more unwelcome attention.

The Runner slipped a coin into the man's hand.

"Take it home to your missus, Walters. You've had enough for this night, and Mrs. Walters will welcome a bit of coin."

Cowan assisted Walters to his feet.

"Get yourself clean and then come see me. I may know of a position if you can hold your tongue and avoid places such as this."

Walters' eyes cleared.

"You mean to offer me employment?" he asked in disbelief. "Why?"

"I mean to provide you an *opportunity*. It is your choice to make the best of it," Cowan corrected. "And as to the reason—I recall your taking a bullet in the leg to save those orphans in Spain. A man willing to do for others deserves a better life than this."

Cowan turned Walters' steps toward the exit while Darcy followed close behind. When they reached the main road, Cowan hailed a cab for him and Darcy before directing Walters to the side street.

The former soldier staggered away. As Darcy watched him disappear into the night, he prayed they would find Edward before his cousin sank so low.

"Will Walters follow your advice?" Darcy asked Cowan as they crawled into the filthy hack.

Cowan responded with resignation, confessing with an accepting grimness.

"I provided Walters only enough coin to assist his recovery and not to add to his misery. I spoke to him of a moment of honor, which I pray will serve the man in reclaiming his name."

"Why?" Although Darcy held the man in admiration, in truth, he knew so little of Cowan. "I know what you said to Walters, but..."

"Let us say that, but for God's grace and Fitzwilliam's interference, I might be Walters."

They finished the night with a cursory tour of the docks before returning to Darcy's Town house.

"We will call upon the harbormaster in the morning. Mr. Belker will know if any of the ships possessed one too many shipmates before sailing. If so, we must contact the Navy and have them intercept the ship. Matlock's influence may be required."

"I would prefer not to involve the Earl of Matlock until we possess more definitive information, but I will inquire of my uncle's whereabouts in case the earl's authority proves essential to our success."

Cowan's smile widened.

"The colonel was never one to seek his father's *persuasiveness* in a matter, but it would do no harm for Belker to know the depth of your family's connections. The harbormaster responds well to bribery and to pretentiousness."

ॐ ॐ ॐ

Georgiana did not realize Elizabeth was in the nursery when she entered: Elizabeth came to sit on the floor beside Bennet's bed to rest a comforting hand on her son after the child awakened with dreams of dragons. Elizabeth sat in the dark shadows and silently observed her sister-in-marriage.

Although in obvious turmoil, Georgiana closed her eyes to listen to the soft "snore" of her daughter. Earlier Darcy's sister admitted to Elizabeth that since the major general's exit, only quiet moments with her child brought Georgiana any harmony. During the day's growing tension, Georgiana insisted they would receive word from Darcy in the late post, but Elizabeth reasoned Darcy was in the Capital less than a day.

"It is too soon," Elizabeth insisted, despite the look of hope upon the girl's countenance.

Poor Georgiana! Darcy's sister convinced her foolish heart that if Edward meant to return, he would do so when Darcy confronted him.

Over the four years of her dwelling at Pemberley, Elizabeth learned something of the girl's nature: Georgiana always professed to be a very practical woman, one who recognized how life's troubles made a person stronger; however, Elizabeth knew at her core that the girl possessed a romantic heart. Lamentably, when Georgiana married the major general, she assumed her husband possessed the same sensible nature, as did all the Fitzwilliam men. Needless to say, she erred.

Elizabeth watched as Georgiana hugged herself tightly and stared down upon her sleeping child.

Georgiana's tear-filled confession in a moment of weakness surprised Elizabeth. Earlier, the girl spoke of a most troubling incident.

"I suppose I should not say this," Georgiana whispered through a hiccupping sob. "But I know you will forgive me for being so forward. I must tell someone."

"I am as always your confidant," Elizabeth assured.

With downcast eyes, Georgiana confessed.

"It is wanton of me to say, but I miss the exquisite feel of Edward's hand upon my skin and the sound of his voice as he calls my name. I miss all the little things, Elizabeth: The gurgle of a snore when he sleeps, the way his eyes meet mine, even in a crowded room. With him, I knew the end of loneliness, a feeling, which haunted me my entire life. My mother's early passing marked me as a single."

Bitterness laced the girl's tone.

"As you will recall from my girlish confessions in those early days of our acquaintance, I fell in love with my cousin when I was but fourteen, but Edward was seven and twenty at the time, and he had a life in Town. It was the pain of young love thwarted, which drove me to foster a relationship with George Wickham, an act that nearly ruined my chances of knowing my cousin's tenderness. Lacking the sensibility of one more mature to recognize the foolishness of my choices, I sought the familiarity of Mr. Wickham's acquaintance to replace the love I thought never to possess."

At the time, Elizabeth wondered if the same could not be said of Georgiana's choice of Edward: Neither Georgiana nor the major general was prepared to know a deep, trusting love.

With a shudder of dread, the girl continued.

"Elizabeth, I must speak of what occurred at Yadkin Hall or I shall go mad. However, you must promise me you will not share what I say with Darcy. My brother would act with honor, and one of us would wear widow weeds."

"You have my word," Elizabeth assured. "If I may be of service to you, speak from your heart."

However, Elizabeth possessed no idea how far the situation at Yadkin Hall deteriorated.

As Georgiana's tears increased, she buried her forehead into Elizabeth's shoulders.

"One day, perhaps a fortnight prior, I innocently strolled into the estate chapel to say my prayers; instead, I found Edward kneeling at the altar, a gun positioned beneath his chin."

Her sister in marriage's pronouncement shook Elizabeth's customary resolve. How had things come to know such an end?

"I heard my husband cock the hammer, and pure terror filled me. Do you see? Edward thought to take his life. Here I was thinking we found happiness—that having me as his wife pleased him."

She laced her fingers through Elizabeth's, and Elizabeth held tight to both her growing anxiousness and Georgiana's hand.

"I was afraid to call out–afraid my voice might jar Edward into action. I watched in interested horror, praying my husband would not pull the trigger. Unable to say anything, I backed from the vestibule, and then I pretended to approach again, this time, humming the lullaby I sing to our child at night. I meant the song to serve as a reminder of the good things in our life. It was all of which I could think to prevent Edward's dudgeon claiming him. As I reentered the chapel, the major general returned the gun to a pocket and plastered a smile of greeting upon his lips; yet, I am no longer so naïve."

"Have you also known the major general's ire," Elizabeth asked as Georgiana hid her face deeper in Elizabeth's shoulder.

Elizabeth prompted Georgiana's response.

"I apologize for my impertinence, but I noticed earlier that you do not move with your usual grace, as if you suffered a fall, and there is the remnants of a bruise, which appears to be fingerprints, upon your arm, just above your sleeve."

"Please tell me Darcy did not observe what you did!"

"Men are not so sharp-eyed as they would like to think," Elizabeth assured.

"It was my fault," Georgiana declared. "I wished to know whether Edward was happy in Oxfordshire or not, and my shrewish tongue was too much for my husband to bear. He did not strike me, Elizabeth. I swear it is true. I stepped into Edward's path when he meant to quit the room, and he shoved me from his way. I hit the wall to the left of the hearth in his quarters. The look upon the major general's countenance spoke of instant regret, and all I suffered were a few bruises. You must not speak to Darcy of this, but I believe the incident and the one earlier in the chapel precipitated Edward's speedy exit. If Darcy knew, he would defend my honor against my husband, and I would lose one of the two men I love most dearly."

Georgiana's voice in the darkness brought Elizabeth to the present.

"I can tolerate the pain of knowing Edward's displeasure."

As Elizabeth looked on from the silent corner, Georgiana traced the curve of Colleen's cheek.

"If your Papa will simply return to us, I can bear it all."

Elizabeth never witnessed Darcy's sister so distraught.

"There is room in my heart for one more private ache. All I wish is for you, my Sweet One, to know your father's love. I can live without love if Edward would return for you. A child should never spend her life without knowing both her parents' affections."

Elizabeth felt tears forming in her eyes. Georgiana concealed her deepest pains, even from her brother. The girl suffered dearly from being the cause of her mother's death.

Quietly, Georgiana moved to where she could look out upon the night, and Elizabeth sank deeper into the shadows. In the moonlight, Elizabeth could observe how worry and pretense left its mark upon Georgiana's features. Harsh lines appeared around her sister's eyes. The girl shivered before resting her forehead against the glass.

"The major general thinks I do not know he reaches for me only when he wishes to silence my questions."

Georgiana's tone spoke of the heartache of unfulfilled dreams.

"All, which remains, is the hollowness I knew all my life."

The girl sighed in acceptance.

"Sixteen months," Georgiana admitted in chastising tones. "I had sixteen months of happiness. It is enough. I have Colleen and Darcy and Elizabeth and my nephews. It is foolish for me to think I could also claim Edward's love. I must not covet what others possess. I must make myself act with Christian forgiveness and make my marriage as tolerable as possible."

❧ ❧ ❧

"I expect you to reexamine your records, Belker," Darcy said with his best "Master of Pemberley" voice.

He favored the harbormaster with a quelling glare.

"I want to know unequivocally that no one impressed my cousin into service upon one of the ships recently setting sail from the Thames. If you ignore my request, you will know the wrath of the Earl of Matlock, Viscount Lindale, Lady Catherine de Bourgh, and even His Royal Highness Prince George, who favored the major general upon more than one occasion."

Darcy took pleasure when his exaggeration caused Belker to flinch. The harbormaster was not happy to observe Cowan enter his office.

Without doubt, as a Bow Street Runner, Cowan hounded Belker's existence, for the man held a reputation for the importation of illegal goods. When this investigation knew completion, Darcy would use his extensive influence to aid Cowan in replacing the man who used his position for personal benefit.

"As I said previously, Mr. Darcy," Belker shot a furtive glance to a glaring Cowan, "the major general was here. Saturday last. But he never boarded any ship."

"How can you be so certain?" Cowan growled.

Belker puffed out his chest in self-importance.

"Assisted the officer meself," he declared. "Some men upon the *Towson* thought the major general an easy target for your cousin consumed more than his share of drink."

Darcy did not like to think upon Edward imbibing so heavily. Whatever drove the major general from his home rested hard upon his cousin's soul.

"Certainly, some can hold their drink better than others."

Belker straightened some papers upon his desk while organizing his thoughts.

"Those from the *Towson* thought to claim the major general, but Lord Matlock's son proved himself worthy of his position. With just his fists, the major general dispatched the four men from the *Towson*. More easily than what anyone might believe of a gentleman's son, I might add."

"Explain," Cowan demanded.

Belker did not disguise his disgust, but he provided the information. The harbormaster would not cavil over a thing like principle.

"Needless to say, none on the *Towson* realized the man they discovered passed out among the crates waiting to be loaded onboard was a gentleman. The major general's clothes be finely cut, but they be filthy. On the night in question, my dockers escorted all five men to my office, and I summoned a surgeon. Your cousin had but a few bruises and cuts, Sir. Two from the *Towson* are still housed at the infirmary two streets over."

"Do you know the major general's destination when he departed the docks?" Darcy asked.

"Said he meant to find himself an inn to wait for his next set of orders. I thought him a junior officer on one of the ships, for he wore no epaulets. Thought he expected to depart soon," Belker disclosed.

Cowan stood to depart.

"Do you have a guess as to where the man took residence?"

Desiring their exit, Belker stood also.

"Can't say for certain. Most sailors avoid the inns close to the river, preferring those inland for obvious reasons. I would image a King's soldier would follow suit. If I wished to hide from those who would follow me, I would avoid the city inns."

Weariness claimed Darcy's stance.

"If you think of anything of import, please contact me at Darcy House. It would be well worth your time."

Chapter Three

"What is our destination?" Darcy asked as he followed Cowan into a let hack.

The investigator arrived on Darcy's threshold a few minutes before eight with a demand to speak to Darcy. Six and thirty hours passed since they parted, and Darcy knew relief with a possible lead to his cousin's whereabouts.

"Wapping."

Darcy did not bother to hide his surprise.

"Wapping? Surely you do not think my cousin is in Wapping."

Darcy shook his head in disbelief. As one of the three roads entering and exiting London ran through the Wapping streets teeming with the poor, Darcy often rode through the area; but none of the *beau monde* visited the shops lining the road. It was not an area for the faint of heart.

The roads built by the Romans bordered the bluff above Wapping Marsh. In the 1500s, early Englishmen founded a harbor along the red cliff. Now, filth and tenements crowded the road, frequented by sailors, prostitutes, pawnbrokers, rat catchers, carpenters, and the like.

Wapping once served as the place where pirates knew public hangings. The broken buildings followed, reaching to Limehouse, Poplar, Radcliff, and Shadwell. The streets twisted in upon themselves, often coming to unexpected dead ends—unsavory hovels. The steps of Pelican Stairs, Wapping New Stairs, and King James's Stairs led to the River Thames, which brought both life and death. The residents catered to the desires of the sailors, who swarmed the cheap boarding houses and the businesses like the Biblical plague of locust.

"I possess a good accounting of a man fitting the major general's description at an inn near Wapping. Rather than employing your Town carriage, I thought the let one more desirable for this task."

Darcy glanced out the window to the sprawl beyond central London. "How did Edward fall so far? I never thought it possible."

"War eats at a man, Mr. Darcy," Cowan offered in explanation. "The major general saw more than his fair share of death in both America and upon the Continent. So much devastation rips a man's heart to shreds."

"I do appreciate your repeated cautions, but I experience difficulty in comprehending how the major general suffered without any of his dear family being aware."

"Is it your failure to recognize the major general's pain or Fitzwilliam's plunge into remorse that you question?" Cowan challenged.

Darcy would dearly love to ignore Cowan's question, but he was not one to shun his responsibilities. Even so, Darcy's insides twisted in a stranglehold upon his heart.

"I am not certain. Perhaps a bit of both."

"At least you did not deny the possibility of your being equally at fault in this matter," Cowan observed.

"Nevertheless," Darcy asserted, "the responsibility for seeking assistance for what ails him falls upon the major general's shoulders."

Noting Cowan's scowl of disapproval, Darcy attempted to soften his disdain.

"In truth, what I do not understand is my cousin's abandonment of his wife and child."

The Runner offered no conjectures. Perhaps there were none. Mayhap only an acceptance of the madness would resolve the issue. At length, the let hack entered St George's-in-the-East parish, where the smell of fish, sweat, the river, smoke, urine, and businesses intermingled, and Darcy snarled his nose in response.

"Quite pungent," Cowan remarked, "but not as repulsive as the smell of blood upon a once-sturdy companion. That particular smell stays with a man long after they bury the body. I can close my eyes and relive the odors, the sights, and the sounds."

"I understand." Darcy swallowed hard. "I will attempt to temper my criticisms."

The coach rolled to a halt before a row of public houses. Cowan disembarked to give the driver instructions to wait.

"Four times your usual fare."

The driver looked about in apprehension.

"No more than a quarter hour, Sir. Not safe to remain a standing target."

"A quarter hour and not one second less," Cowan warned. "Come, Darcy. We must hurry."

Darcy tailed Cowan along a busy street to turn into a four-walled alley. Cowan pointed to a once brightly painted sign.

"The Sephora."

Darcy shook his head in incredulity, but he followed close on Cowan's heels as they entered the dim foyer.

"Yes, Sir?" a woman in a low-cut dress greeted them. "Do ye gentlemen require me services?"

Her smile showed several missing teeth. Cowan ignored her offer, pushing past the woman to mount the stairs, while Darcy dodged the female's grasp to follow.

"How did you know to look for the major general here?" he whispered when Cowan stopped before the third door along the hall.

"The Runners are a *corps d'elite*, guarding the main roads leading to London. One of my former associates overheard a watchman speaking of a gentleman taking housing at the Sephora. I asked questions of the innkeeper before I sought you out."

Darcy nodded his appreciation.

"Do we knock?" he gestured to the door.

Cowan dug into his inside pocket.

"No need. I have the key."

"I shan't ask how that particular fact came about." Darcy chuckled.

Cowan slid the key into the lock.

"If the innkeeper speaks the truth, the man within is rather inebriated. If it is the major general, we must carry him from here; if it is another, we will leave him to his devices."

With that, Cowan released the lock and opened the door on silent hinges. Grabbing a rush candle from a small table, the former Runner struck a flint and set the long tube on fire. Leading the way into the room, Cowan held the rush high.

The room was empty except for the bed, a small table, two straight-backed chairs, and a shaving bowl with an ewer. The stench of vomit and urine filled the air as Darcy's eyes searched the darkness for a sign of his cousin. At length, a loud snort announced that the room's occupant stirred.

"Who's there?" the man slurred. "Leave me be." He rolled to his stomach to bury his face in the single pillow upon the bed.

But Darcy and Cowan ignored the man's objections.

"My God, Fitzwilliam! What have you done?"

Even with the poor lighting, Darcy could see that blood covered the bedding. He rushed to turn his cousin to his back.

"Where are you injured?"

Darcy tore at his cousin's bloody clothes.

"We cannot remain, Darcy," Cowan coaxed. "We must remove the major general before he draws more attention."

"But he is injured!" Darcy objected.

"The blood is dried," Cowan corrected, "and a competent surgeon is not to be found in the area."

The investigator placed the quickly burning paper tube in a high vase.

"Assist me in lifting Fitzwilliam to his feet. The coach is waiting."

Darcy did not agree, but he bowed to Cowan's expertise in such matters. Together, they each grabbed an arm and pulled Edward Fitzwilliam first to a seated position and then to his feet.

"Grab his purse and pistol from the table," Darcy instructed.

Edward's knees buckled under his weight, and Darcy scrambled to wrap his cousin's arm about his shoulder. Cowan did the same, and between them, they managed to drag the major general to the room door.

"How do we maneuver him down the stairs?"

"Release him and permit Fitzwilliam to roll down them." Cowan smiled with sardonic amusement.

As they struggled to pull his cousin through the door, Darcy grunted, "It is a tempting idea."

To Darcy's amazement, Edward did not stir until they reached the main street and the coach. As they departed the Sephora, Darcy noted that Cowan slipped several coins and the room key into the innkeeper's hand. Irritated by the indignity of chasing his cousin to a run-down establishment, without ceremony, Darcy dumped Edward into the floor's muck, squeezing his cousin's long legs into a curled position.

The scene would make an excellent burlesque if the situation were not so serious. He and Cowan crawled over Edward's form to assume a crowded seat.

"We should take my cousin through the mews. I do not wish the neighbors to observe our entrance."

A wary expression crossed Cowan's features.

"Agreed."

Darcy sighed with resignation as the coach rolled forward.

"*Look* at him."

He toed his cousin's drunken form.

"Behold the second son of the Earl of Matlock," Darcy said with contempt. "No better than a common vagrant lying in the filth."

"The major general succumbed to the pain that never leaves a man: The fear that failure haunts his steps."

Bridled with resentment, Darcy frowned.

"You speak of a man I do not know. Over the years, Edward Fitzwilliam was my most constant companion. How do I justify this man's infirmary with the gentleman who claimed my sister's heart."

Darcy studied the dirt and dried blood, which marred his cousin's classically handsome features.

"I am glad Georgiana will not see him thusly. It would kill her to know her husband sought to destroy himself."

Except for the snore of an intoxicated man, they finished the journey in silence.

Arriving at Darcy House, Darcy ordered several of his footmen to carry the major general to one of the guest rooms before ordering a bath.

"I will not have that stench filling Mrs. Darcy's home," he told Cowan.

Darcy dispatched a footman to Lockland Hall for fresh clothes while two of Darcy's men bathed his cousin. Edward used every curse word concocted by man until Cowan assumed the role of commanding officer and demanded the major general act the part of a gentleman.

Darcy's housekeeper delivered coffee, which the major general consumed in silence, and slowly, a sense of order arrived.

"Where am I?" Edward asked as his conscious mind fought with his unconscious one.

"Darcy House."

Edward opened one eye to behold Darcy's uninterrupted scowl.

"I *thought* I recognized your voice." He closed his eyes again. "Please tell me my wife is not here."

"My sister and Elizabeth remain at Yadkin Hall."

His cousin blocked the light with his forearm. "It is best Georgiana not observe the failure I have become."

"Bloody hell, Edward! I never heard anything so absurd! Mrs. Fitzwilliam *loves* you, and you treat her poorly!"

Darcy gestured to Edward's nude body draped with the counterpane.

"You abuse all which you profess to hold most dear."

"You do not understand." A pang of guilt filled Edward's voice.

"Then explain it to me. Better yet, permit me to send for Georgiana, and you can explain it to her. She is the one you must trust with your secrets."

"Georgiana must hate me," Edward moaned.

Darcy recognized his cousin's plea for empathy as an empty promise. Edward's continual self-pity frustrated Darcy.

"We will discuss this in more detail later. You should rest now."

"Do not send for Georgie. I beg you, Darcy," his cousin implored.

"I will not send for Mrs. Fitzwilliam, but I do mean to send word that you are safe. Neither Mrs. Darcy nor my sister deserves to spend another hour in worry over your actions."

He could not control speaking in disappointment.

"I thought better of you, Edward."

ৡৡৡ

His cousin slept the day and night through, and so Darcy was a bit surprised when Edward made an appearance in the morning room.

"Pour coffee for the major general," Darcy instructed his footman, as he placed his newspaper to the side.

Edward's stance remained a bit shaky, but he managed to stagger to his seat. A grunt of acknowledgement followed the coffee service while the major general fought for focus.

"Do you require Murray to serve you?" Darcy asked with bemusement.

As Edward closed his eyes, Darcy imagined his cousin's head throbbed as if being struck by a heavy hammer. The thought brought Darcy an odd sense of comfort.

"If it would not be too much bother," Edward murmured.

Darcy motioned to the footman.

"A plate for the major general, Murray, but start with something simple. Some toast and a bit of eggs."

Darcy noted that his long-time servant withheld a smirk as Murray filled Edward's plate.

"Eat slowly," Darcy warned. "I want no accidents on my polished floor."

"Most humorous," Edward growled.

Darcy still required answers to the why and the wherefore of what occurred, but he breathed easier in knowing his cousin did not succumb to the terrors of London's underbelly. They ate in silence for several minutes.

"Did you manage to find another commission?" Darcy asked.

"No."

Darcy waited for the customary exchange of information, but his cousin kept his silence.

"Were none available?"

"If you must know, Darcy," Edward responded with frost in his tone. "With England at peace, military officers are as plentiful as the foreigners flooding our shores. What few officers the military requires are men a good decade younger than the likes of me."

Darcy's lips turned upward, and a swift smile graced his mouth.

"Struck down before you turn five and thirty. How remarkable!"

"I find nothing amusing in the prospects," Edward grumbled.

His cousin handed his empty plate to Murray.

"Would you be so kind to refill my plate, and this time, add some ham."

"Certainly, Sir."

"I thank you and Cowan for going to such great lengths to discover my whereabouts." Edward sighed as he nodded.

Darcy's expression closed.

"You must know Mrs. Fitzwilliam would plead for my assistance."

Edward placed his fork on the plate's edge before meeting Darcy's gaze.

"I never meant to hurt Georgiana, but she deserves a husband who does not know failure."

"That is the sorriest excuse I ever heard!" Darcy exclaimed. "In all the years you spent in service to King George, I heard of your valor. Never once were there rumors of cowardice or of surrender in the face of danger. Yet, when you meet the trials of a mundane life, you run away from your responsibilities."

"The crops failed," Edward said in remorse.

"Everyone suffered this year," Darcy asserted. "Even Pemberley. You are not God. Those who toil the land cannot control the weather."

Something flashed deep in Edward's eyes, and Darcy felt compassion for the man for the first time.

"What am I to do?"

Experiencing an odd sense of a lack of control, Darcy turned to regard his cousin: It was customary for Edward to offer the advice.

"You return home. Economize. Ask your tenants to make necessary changes in how they treat the land. Say a prayer for God's intervention. Apologize to your wife and begin again."

However, before the major general could agree, a loud knocking overrode the quiet of Darcy House's tall foyer. Darcy scowled but reined in his unsettling thoughts.

"Who could that be? Other than Cowan, few know I am in Town."

A familiar voice answered Darcy's question.

"Where is my son?" the Earl of Matlock's voice demanded.

Darcy presented an expression of pity upon his cousin. His Uncle Martin sounded more than a bit irritated.

Within seconds, Darcy's butler made the necessary announcement.

"The Earl of Matlock—Mr. Darcy."

Darcy rose to greet his mother's only brother.

"Your Lordship," he said with a bow of respect. "I was not aware you were in Town, Sir. I would have called at Lockland Hall if I knew."

The earl shot his son a mutinous glare.

"Rowland came to London on business last week. When he arrived on Lockland Hall's threshold, the staff informed Lindale that Mrs. Fitzwilliam searched for her husband in London. Lindale sent an express to Matley Manor, and the countess and I set a course for Oxfordshire to discover the error in the matter."

For a moment, the major general's and the earl's gazes locked in a silent battle before Edward spoke.

"I apologize, Sir, for causing my mother to worry. Mine was a foolhardy decision. I will call upon the countess later to express my regret for my actions."

The earl's dark eyes flashed with irritation.

"The countess escorts Mrs. Fitzwilliam and Mrs. Darcy to London later today. I thought it best to come ahead in case Darcy failed to locate my wastrel son."

Darcy preferred for Edward and him to ride to Witney that afternoon and to permit the major general and Georgiana to resolve their differences without further interference; yet, Darcy knew his uncle's nature was not one easily appeased.

Matlock would catalog each of Edward's faults in minute detail. Being reunited with his wife and children was the only good Darcy could acknowledge from the change in plans.

"Why do you not join us, Your Lordship?" Darcy said as he gestured for a footman to supply the setting. "I suspect this might require a great deal of explaining."

For the next hour, Edward offered an explanation to each of the earl's accusations while Darcy attempted to soften the angry words spoken by both. It always was so. Matlock never recognized Edward's strengths, only his second son's faults.

Darcy did not approve of Edward's self-absorption: In fact, he found the squalor into which the major general sank deplorable; however, he knew his cousin did not abandon his honor. Edward would suffer for his moments of self-pity. Darcy intervened to allay the earl's most recent attack.

"At a minimum—all of which the major general may be accused is drinking too heavily and exercising poor judgment."

The irony of those words would long haunt Darcy's logical mind for as if he announced the next act of a Shakespearian tragedy, a second knock upon his door changed the room's tenor.

He looked up to find Thomas Cowan framed by the open door, a painful expression upon the man's features. Behind him, two cleanly dressed men created a formidable wall.

"Cowan?" Darcy remarked in curiosity. "What brings you and your acquaintances to Darcy House? I thought upon this day you were to search for a certain lady's lover. I did not realize you meant another social call upon my household."

Recognizing Cowan's wariness, Darcy waved away his servants.

"It was my purpose, but Mr. Richards and Mr. Parker," Cowan gestured to the men behind him, "called upon me this morning. It seems word of our visit to Wapping reached the ears of those of Bow Street via the Thames Police."

A sharp unease settled in the pit of Darcy's stomach; he realized Cowan symbolically placed himself between the Runners and the major general.

"Why would the Thames Police have a care for my cousin's presence in Wapping?"

Darcy's first thought was of a report of Edward's altercation upon the docks, but Cowan's expression cautioned of more shocking news.

Extending his arm in Darcy's direction, Cowan handed over a folded newsprint.

"What is amiss, Darcy?" the earl demanded.

Darcy unfolded the paper and scanned the page for something of significance, which would affect his cousin, but nothing unusual jumped from the page to draw his attention.

"I fear I do not understand, Cowan."

His friend pointed to the lead line: "Murder Most Foul."

"*Murder?* A murder in Wapping?" Darcy whispered into the silent room.

His nerves remained tense.

"Murder?" the earl expelled in exasperation. "What murder? This is ridiculous. What could a murder in Wapping have to do with an earl's son?"

The earl was on his feet and storming toward Cowan when Darcy stepped between the irascible Matlock and the former Runner.

"We should listen to what Mr. Cowan has to say, Sir," Darcy cautioned.

Falling into the familiarity of their military roles, Edward asked, "What is the issue, Sergeant?"

Cowan smiled with the major general's slip. "During the past sennight, Sir, two gruesome murders occurred. All of London is astir with fear. Saunders Welch sent Mr. Richards and Mr. Parker to escort you to No. 4 Bow Street."

Matlock blustered, the earl's face turning red with anger.

"You think my son holds knowledge of this murder simply because he had too much to drink one night. With that type of logic, half of London should be under suspicion!"

"The innkeeper at the Sephora testified that Fitzwilliam stayed with him for more than a week, and the innkeeper has yet to observe the major general sober," Cowan explained. "The innkeeper also provided a statement that the major general returned to the Sephora covered in blood on the night of the first murder."

Darcy attempted to reason with the Runners sent by Mr. Welch.

"We spoke to a dock overseer of an altercation involving my cousin and several crew serving on the ship *Towson*. The sailors meant to impress the major general into service. You were with me, Cowan, when the harbormaster, Mr. Belker, described the incident."

"I gave Mr. Welch my statement, Darcy," Cowan assured, "but as the *Towson* set sail, it will be difficult to question the ship's captain or his men."

"Even those in the infirmary?" Darcy asked.

"Even those in the infirmary," Cowan confirmed. "They sailed with another ship to rejoin the *Towson* in Dover."

"What proof then?" Matlock demanded. "If you, Darcy, and this Belker fellow describe a fight, what proof would draw a shadow across my son's name?"

"Could you produce your sword, Sir? The one from your uniform," Richards asked.

While the others argued, Darcy scanned the news story for details that might be connected to the major general.

"It says here a man, his wife and child were killed by a military-style sword. Their throats slit, even the child's."

Edward glanced to Cowan and Darcy.

"I have no idea of the sword's whereabouts. It was not among my things when I awoke this morning. I assumed either Darcy or Cowan retrieved it when they carried me from the inn."

"We gathered your purse, the watch Uncle presented you upon your enlistment, your gloves, and the Queen Anne pistol you carried," Darcy admitted, but I took no notice of your sword Did you, Cowan?"

"No, Sir, but we hurried our perusal of the room because the carriage would not wait more than a quarter hour. We could have overlooked it."

"This is preposterous!" Matlock exclaimed, appearing black with rage. "My son spent more than a decade in the King's service in both America and upon the Continent. For God's sake, he was with Wellington at Waterloo! Fitzwilliam received his latest commission at the hand of the Prince Regent!"

"You possess little choice, Sir," Cowan cautioned. "Mr. Welch means to question any suspect. Concerned with the outcry, the Home Office offered a reward in the case. It would be best to make your statement."

"Did the major general wear a uniform when you rescued him?" Mr. Parker asked.

Cowan answered before Darcy had time to form a response.

"Why would the major general's *clothing* be of interest?"

Darcy recognized what Cowan wished him to know: Edward's uniform could be used as evidence against the major general.

"I ordered it burned," Darcy swore, although he knew his household staff washed his cousin's filthy clothing. "Fleas and lice polluted the garment. I would not risk the life of my servants or of my infant children with the prospect of typhus or worst. We destroyed my cousin's items as quickly as we could remove them from his back."

"Was there evidence of blood upon the items?" Parker asked.

Darcy did not wish to lie, but he knew that even in a drunken state Edward could not commit willful murder. The deaths of war haunted his cousin, but Fitzwilliam would not lash out at an innocent family as part of his anguish.

"I cannot say for certain. My cousin's clothes were caked with mud and dried dirt and human feces. I did not recognize blood as part of the stains."

"We should depart," Cowan suggested in a tone of false calmness.

Edward shot a look of panic to Darcy.

"Surely there is another means for the major general to respond without creating a public spectacle," Darcy concluded.

"I will escort my son to Bow Street," Matlock declared with authority. "Fitzwilliam and I will follow you in my coach."

Richards and Parker looked to Cowan for assistance.

"If you hold no objections, Sir, Richards and Parker will follow you. They have very strict orders," Cowan explained.

"I mean to go with you also," Darcy assured Edward. "We will clarify any misconceptions, and then you will return to Darcy House to reunite with Mrs. Fitzwilliam and the countess later today."

"My God!" Edward exclaimed as his anguish returned. "What will Georgiana and mother think of this shame?"

Chapter Four

"Tell me what you know of these murders," Darcy insisted.

He and Cowan followed Matlock's coach in Darcy's Town carriage.

"In truth, not much more than what I read in the newsprints."

"I am only aware of what you shared a few moments prior," Darcy admitted with a flare of unease. "I rushed from Derbyshire to Witney when I received Georgiana's missive and then traveled on to London. I barely glanced at a newsprint in well over a week."

Cowan's expression hardened with practiced authority.

"The Vaughn family from the first murder ran a bakery near Wapping. Vaughn was until of late a mate upon a German sloop. The authorities identified no motives for the Vaughns' deaths. Nothing appeared missing from the bakery shop. A locked box held what was likely the man's take for the day."

"Who discovered the bodies?"

He and Cowan had but a short journey to Bow Street, and Darcy meant to possess as many details as possible before Welch questioned Fitzwilliam.

"One of the Vaughns' suppliers called early on during the middle of the night. The man claimed he found the door to the shop unlocked, but he could rouse no one, and so he hailed a night watchman. The sentry entered the establishment to discover Vaughn's body behind a storage room door. Mrs. Vaughn and the child were on the third storey in the child's nursery."

"What of the sword?"

Cowan frowned.

"It was my understanding the authorities found the sword, but Richards and Parker acted as though they still searched for the weapon."

Darcy's heart gave a little stutter.

"You think they practice some sort of duplicitous means to trick the major general into an incriminating admission?"

The shadows of doubt darkened Cowan's eyes.

"I would despise to consider such a possibility, but a healthy outcry for the authorities to know an end to their investigations exists."

Darcy recognized Cowan to be rare among those employed by the various parishes and magistrates: Thomas Cowan held a heightened sense of honor.

"And the second murder?"

"An older couple several streets from the first," Cowan recounted. "Owners of a tavern. Well respected in the neighborhood. As with the first incident, their throats were slit, but the tavern owner's head was bashed in. It was the only major difference in the events. The newsprints are calling the culprit the 'East Side Slayer.' Both attacks were very violent crimes, executed by someone quite angry with the world."

Darcy considered his words before asking,

"Someone…such as my *cousin*?"

Cowan's tone was full of pity.

"This questioning will not go well for the major general. Fitzwilliam's leaving his young wife to come to London, where he spent more than a week drinking away his sorrow will prove incriminating. As you expressed on more than one occasion, the public will not understand how a man of Fitzwilliam's reputation would desert his wife and child for no apparent reason. In addition, the major general's fight with the impression gang will exacerbate the situation. It is not often one man can fight off four well-trained abductors. Your cousin's expertise at fighting and killing will play against him."

Trepidation laced Darcy's tone.

"Then I must be present to protect the major general."

Cowan weighed his response.

"You must manage the earl's ire and protect your cousin while divining the truth. It will require all your wit. Welch will bar me from the session."

"I understand." Cowan's warning hung heavy in the space between them.

"While you are within, I will determine if Welch's men possess loose tongues," Cowan assured.

৯৯৯

Welch waved his hand in dismissal of the earl's most recent objection.

"Richards tells me you hold no idea of the whereabouts of your sword. Is that correct, Major General?"

Edward glanced to Darcy. It took all of Matlock's influence for Welch to permit Darcy's and the earl's presence.

"My cousin did not recall seeing it in my quarters when he discovered me at the Sephora."

"Did you carry it with you when you departed Oxfordshire?" Welch asked in speculation.

Edward spoke with earnestness.

"I dressed in my uniform after I departed Yadkin Hall. I did not wish to alert Mrs. Fitzwilliam as to my plans to seek a new commission. I reasoned my rank would prove beneficial to my purpose, but I failed in my search. With the current peace, my skills are no longer in demand."

"And what skills would those be, Major General?" Welch asked succinctly.

Darcy wagged his head to warn his cousin to guard his response.

"What any officer does," Edward said with an unnatural strain in his voice. "Make critical decisions. Take raw farmers and tradesmen and turn them into skilled soldiers."

Darcy was grateful that Edward did not mention "killing," but Darcy's muscles flinched when Welch asked his next question.

"You never responded to my previous question. Did you wear your sword with your uniform?"

"If my recollections are to be trusted, then yes. Such matters are instinctive after so many years of service."

"Yet, you are not certain. Am I correct, Major General?" Welch pressed.

Scowling, Edward expelled a sigh of irritation before favoring the Bow Street leader with a quelling glare.

"Permit me to answer all your questions at once, Welch. Mrs. Fitzwilliam did not know of my plans to depart for London. I acted upon impulse. Unfortunately, I overestimated my usefulness to the military. Afterwards, I buried my bruised pride in more drink than I should, and I possess only sketchy knowledge of what occurred after the first day. As I customarily wear my sword with my uniform, I will make the assumption I did so on the day I departed Oxfordshire. Perhaps, you should ask General Leigh-Hunt. He was my contact regarding a possible commission."

Welch gestured to one of his men to record Leigh-Hunt's name, but before the Bow Street leader could ask another question, Darcy interrupted.

"It is my understanding the authorities found a sword at the scene of Mr. Vaughn's murder. Mayhap you could produce it and permit my cousin to identify whether it is his."

Confusion crossed Edward's features, but he followed Darcy's lead. It was the way of them: a mutual trust in the other's honor.

"My weapon was engraved at the tip—a gift from my brother, Viscount Lindale."

Welch chastised with a faint hint of pique.

"The blade discovered at the Vaughns' address was missing the bottom three inches. The attacker broke it against the door behind which Vaughn's body was established."

Matlock found his voice.

"If the culprit left the sword behind at the Vaughn household, what is this nonsense of a second attack? What weapon do you name, Welch?"

Welch bristled, and Darcy suspected the man planned to use the secreted information to manipulate the major general.

"The Thornes' murders hold some differences," the Bow Street leader admitted, "Yet, we are certain there is a connection between the crimes. The attacker is the same."

The earl did not display the slightest relief: Bridled with resentment, Matlock expressed his opposition.

"Then what is the status of this investigation? It would appear Bow Street holds no jurisdiction over the Vaughns' attacks, and I am assuming none exist for the second one."

Darcy cringed. From what he knew of Saunders Welch, the man held a pronounced pride in his accomplishments and was not receptive to criticism of the Runners, a name the organization did not officially recognize.

"It is my understanding, Uncle, that there is some pressure from the Home Office and Lord Sidmouth," Darcy offered in explanation.

Darcy watched in relief as Matlock heeded the warning in Darcy's tone. Rather than continuing with his confrontational stance, the earl spoke with more control.

"It is important to discover the truth, Mr. Welch; yet, I know concern for my son's reputation. I realize you showed great restraint in this matter; I am also aware if the major general was anyone less than my son, he would already be in custody."

"Several others were jailed, questioned, and released," Welch admitted.

Darcy spoke before his uncle could continue.

"And will my cousin join those who know such close scrutiny?"

Exercising the perfect stall, Welch shuffled through a stack of papers on his desk.

"It would be unconscionable of me to permit the major general his freedom simply because Fitzwilliam possesses influential family and friends. Neither the Home Office nor the public would approve. If nothing less, the Shadwell police and those of the River Thames Office should possess the opportunity to ask their questions. I will have Richards and Parker escort the major general to Shadwell. "

Darcy nodded, more from acceptance than because he did not expect this outcome. His cousin's breathing shallowed. Darcy regarded their small gathering for several elongated seconds.

"If charges are brought, I assume the major general would be housed in Shadwell."

The thought of such a scheme sent Darcy's heart reeling.

"Shadwell claims dominance in this matter, but as the son of an earl, if incarcerated, the major general would be detained at New Prison."

With intent, Darcy kicked his uncle's ankle to warn against the protest upon Matlock's lips. Welch continued matter-of-factly.

"A coroner's inquest already sat for evidence in the Vaughns' incident."

Darcy asked the question resting on all their lips.

"And the verdict?"

"Willful murder by persons unknown."

࿇ ࿇ ࿇

Matlock insisted upon accompanying his son to Shadwell, while Darcy collected Cowan to return to Darcy House. He informed the former Runner of what he discovered during the questioning under Welch's direction.

"We must learn more of the testimony of those involved. Is there a means of reading the full coroner's inquest?"

"I will see to it," Cowan guaranteed.

Cowan made a notation in his ever-present journal.

"At a minimum, we can read parts of the inquest in the newsprints. I was thinking while you were with Welch that between your and Matlock's households we can retrieve several of the postdated papers."

"Excellent idea," Darcy reasoned.

"If possible, we should question the witnesses ourselves, especially if the authorities decide to detain Fitzwilliam."

Cowan's comment rested uncomfortably between them.

"From what little I know of this uncanny chain of events, I would say my cousin would make an excellent defendant in the case. He has no recollection of his actions, which eliminates the major general's opportunity for a viable defense. In addition, when was the last time so many wardens, magistrates, and police entities took an interest in the same case?"

"Only once prior: The Radcliff murders back in 1812." Cowan explained, "Each force is highly territorial in its authority."

"I am depending upon your expertise," Darcy admitted. "I pray you can commit to the task of freeing the major general. Between the earl and me, you will be suitably rewarded."

Cowan offered a grim smile.

"I would serve my former colonel without payment."

"I possess no doubt," Darcy insisted. "But I would not have you lose your practice while assisting my family."

Before he could say more, Darcy's coach rolled to a halt before his Town house. Murray set down the steps, and Darcy led the way into his home.

Thinking only of organizing their search, when he entered the foyer, Darcy did not expect to be greeted by a boisterous "Papa" and tiny arms circling his legs.

"What, ho," he said with a laugh as he scooped his eldest from the floor and tossed him in the air before catching Bennet to him. "Have you been a good boy?" Darcy asked before placing a kiss upon the child's forehead.

"Yes, Papa."

The child was the perfect image of a mischievous imp, and that particular fact brought a large smile to Darcy's lips.

Elizabeth appeared at his side to reach for their son. She offered Darcy an upturned cheek. It was odd: the knot, which held his stomach prisoner since his arrival in London, relaxed its grasp when he gazed upon his wife's fine countenance.

"You were to follow Mrs. Prulock and Samuel to the nursery," Elizabeth reprimanded the boy.

"But Papa home, Mama," Bennet protested.

Elizabeth caressed the child's dark hair.

"Yes, my darling. Your Papa is home; but he has a guest at the moment. However, we will both come to the nursery later to see what new letter you learned."

"Pomise?" Bennet insisted.

Darcy chucked the boy's chin.

"We promise."

Elizabeth handed the boy off to a waiting maid before spotting Cowan standing in the shadows.

"Thomas, is that you?" she said with a girlish giggle that had Darcy doing a double take.

Elizabeth opened her arms, and Cowan readily accepted the embrace. Despite the foolishness of his response, a twinge of jealousy shot up Darcy's spine.

"It has been too long, Thomas Cowan," his wife chastised in that feminine way to which all men succumbed. "I hoped you would join us for Christmastide at Pemberley."

Cowan smartly set her from him, but the Runner clung to Elizabeth's hands.

"I should have done so, Mrs. Darcy," he said with an easy laugh. "My Aunt Adelaine did nothing but complain of her aches and ailments throughout the observances."

"This year then," Elizabeth confirmed.

"If it is your wish, Ma'am."

It amazed Darcy how his wife conquered a man of Cowan's worldly experience.

"It is settled," Elizabeth declared. She smiled with obvious fondness. "You may bring your aunt if you wish. She and Mrs. Bennet would make excellent company."

Darcy enjoyed the raised eyebrow indicating his wife's amusement. She wrapped her arm through his and strolled along the main hall.

"We hoped the major general would return with you. Is your cousin at Lockland Hall? The countess and Georgiana are taking tea in the green sitting room and awaiting your news."

Darcy caught her arm to bring his wife to a halt.

"Things are much worse than we thought," he whispered. "The Shadwell police question the major general regarding a crime of great magnitude."

Elizabeth swayed and clutched at Darcy's arm.

"Surely you jest," Elizabeth protested.

Darcy's grasp tightened upon her arm.

"It is no bit of sick bemusement I practice."

Elizabeth glanced to Cowan, who nodded his confirmation. "

"What do you require of me?" she asked.

Darcy smiled with satisfaction. He and Elizabeth faced more than one tragedy together: It was a heady realization to know his wife's absolute loyalty.

"I am certain both Georgiana and the countess will know great distress at what I must convey. Your perfect sensibility will be tested."

"I should see to learning more of the details of the crime while you inform your family of what occurred," Cowan said in soft tones. "Should I wait until morning to bring you my report?"

The Runner spoke in a cryptic manner.

"It will likely be in the wee hours before I finish."

"Whatever the time, you come to us at Darcy House. I will instruct Mr. Thacker to prepare a room for you," Darcy confirmed.

Cowan nodded his agreement.

"I will instruct Thacker to expect me to enter through the kitchen. I would not wish to alarm anyone."

"Please see that Mr. Thacker destroys Fitzwilliam's uniform," Darcy instructed.

Cowan shook off the idea.

"I will see to it personally. No reason to involve more innocents than necessary."

"Darcy is that you?"

The Countess of Matlock appeared in the corridor.

"Why do you delay paying your respects? And where is the earl and Edward?"

Elizabeth released Darcy's hand to rush to his aunt's side.

"We were on our way, Countess," his wife assured. "I delayed our entrance by renewing my acquaintance with Mr. Cowan, and, as customary, Bennet demanded to greet his father. The boy has Mr. Darcy's temperament and could not be dissuaded." She extended her hand in Darcy's direction. "Come along, Mr. Darcy."

Darcy glanced to Cowan, speaking in a secretive tone.

"I will anticipate your return. Perhaps, by then, Matlock and Edward will have proved all this a bit of madness."

"As Aristotle said, no excellent soul is exempt from a mixture of madness." With that, the Runner made his exit.

Darcy joined his wife and his aunt.

"I am troubled by your silence, Darcy," the countess observed.

"I mean only to tell the tale once, Aunt," Darcy cautioned as he escorted Nora Fitzwilliam into the room where Georgiana sat wringing her hands.

Darcy's sister rose to greet him, but he motioned her to return to her seat, as he assisted his aunt to one nearby. Expecting the worst, the countess clung to Darcy's fingers. Frankly looking upon the Countess of Matlock, Darcy realized how age left its mark upon her skin, and Darcy wondered why he had not noticed time's approach previously. He turned to discover Elizabeth moving a chair closer to Georgiana.

Darcy did not choose to sit.

"I suspect I should come straight to the point."

He noted Elizabeth caught Georgiana's hand in hers.

"My message to Yadkin Hall precipitated a more appalling twist to the major general's story."

"Has my husband met his demise?" Georgiana asked through trembling lips.

"No," he said with emphasis, and resisted adding, "Not yet." Darcy swallowed hard. "Thomas Cowan and I discovered Edward in a less than upstanding inn in Wapping."

"Why would..." the countess began, but stifled her words when Georgiana paled. "Continue, Darcy."

Darcy recited a concise tale.

"Cowan and I carried Edward from the Sephora and brought Fitzwilliam here to sleep off the sin of too much drink."

Darcy still could not condone what the major general did in the name of foolhardiness.

"When I sent word of recovering my cousin, I thought Edward's drunken indulgence the extent of the major general's errors. However, when the major general joined me earlier today to break his fast, we had several unexpected callers. The first was Lord Matlock, whose purpose in calling at Darcy House you are aware."

He paused to gather his resolve.

"The other callers were Thomas Cowan and two gentlemen from Bow Street."

"Bow Street?" the countess gasped. "What rationale would bring Welch's men to Darcy House?"

Darcy glanced to his sister: His pronouncement would crush Georgiana's spirit.

"More than a sennight prior a very violent murder occurred in Wapping. Less than a week later, a second scene of brutality happened.

Bow Street wished to speak to the major general regarding the incidents."

"Do the authorities think Edward held news of the crimes?" Georgiana asked with a flicker of hope.

Darcy slanted a glance to Elizabeth, warning her to brace Georgiana's composure.

"I fear not," he said in somber tones. "Edward is a suspect in the crimes. Both families met their deaths at the hand of a man with knowledge of a sword as a weapon of death. Their necks were slit. The sword in question belonged to a military man, and Edward's sword is missing."

"My husband..." Georgiana whispered through the emotions.

But it was the countess who finished the thought: "...is not capable of such brutality."

"Certainly not," Darcy assured. "But there are many questions to be answered.

Fitzwilliam's actions placed him in a precarious position. In addition to the missing sword, there are reports of an excessive amount of blood upon the major general's uniform on the same evening as the first murder. Witnesses spoke to the authorities of Edward's dishevelment."

"A logical excuse must exist for the coincidence," Elizabeth reasoned. "What explanation did the major general offer?"

Darcy appreciated his wife's quick intelligence: Elizabeth abandoned her initial shock to divine a rational solution.

"My cousin holds no memory of what occurred. Fitzwilliam imbibed too much to offer an explanation; however, Cowan discovered a possible one: Several men upon the docks attempted to impress Edward into service to their ship, and he fought with them."

From the expression upon his sister's and the countess's countenances, their thoughts and emotions remained a jumble. Darcy recognized the feeling: His head and heart fought each other for dominance.

True to form, his aunt's features tightened with annoyance.

"Darcy, I think you should start from the beginning. Tell us everything that occurred since you arrived in London. Omit nothing. Somewhere in this story lies a reason the Bow Street authorities would think Edward involved, as well as a solution to prove him innocent."

However, before he could begin his tale again, Elizabeth asked the obvious.

"Where are Lord Matlock and the major general? I cannot imagine you leaving them at Bow Street without your influence to support the earl's."

His wife was the one person Darcy trusted with his innermost thoughts. She was correct: If his cousin were in difficulty, Darcy would never walk away from Edward.

"As the crimes occurred in Wapping, Shadwell controls the investigation. Matlock and two Runners escorted Edward to Shadwell to respond to their questions."

"If Shadwell held jurisdiction, why did Bow Street insist upon speaking to Edward?" Elizabeth asked.

"Evidently, the crimes were so heinous even the Home Office took an interest. Lord Sidmouth offered a substantial reward for apprehending the person behind the murders."

Georgiana grappled with what Darcy shared.

"Will my husband return this evening?"

Darcy knelt before her and captured his sister's hands in his. Despite the room's warmth, they were cold.

"Georgie," he spoke in soft tones. "You must know if I could give you such assurances, I would, but I cannot. This is a serious situation. If Matlock cannot convince the Shadwell magistrate a mistake occurred, it is possible Edward will be placed on trial."

Tears streamed down Georgiana's cheeks, and Darcy dabbed them with his handkerchief.

"You must prevent this," his sister said in the same manner as she had when she was a little girl begging for Darcy to repair her favorite doll.

He was unable to refuse her then; neither could he do so now.

"I will do my best, Georgiana."

Darcy stood to face his aunt, who stiffened with his pronouncement that her son might know imprisonment.

"The countess has the right of it. As I repeat my tale, Elizabeth, please record what we must still discover: such a list will assist me in ordering my thoughts. Do not hesitate to ask any questions which cross your minds. Somewhere in my story is a solution to this madness."

Chapter Five

"How long do you plan to remain from our bed, Mr. Darcy?" Elizabeth said from the door of the front sitting room where he took refuge to wait either Cowan's reappearance or the return of Matlock and Edward.

Darcy cast a deliberate survey over her petite frame. Bare toes peeked out from under her cinched gown and wrapper.

"I did not wish my discontent to disturb you," he said in excuse as he extended his hand to his wife. "After four years of marriage, I thought you would enjoy the freedom from my attentions."

Elizabeth advanced slowly, a bemused smile upon her lips.

"One would think a woman of my most excellent taste would find a mere 'Mister' a most trifling companion."

Her eyes sparkled with mischief.

"However, I am quite fond of the warmth of your feet against my…my *cool* ones."

"*Cool* are they?" Darcy chuckled. "I would name them *frigid*, especially upon a cold winter's night in Derbyshire."

Elizabeth slipped her hand into the one Darcy offered and settled upon his lap. She snaked her arms about his neck.

"Then I suppose it may be noted only my feet are cold. My heart, Mr. Darcy, warms nicely to your nearness," Elizabeth whispered.

"I missed you beyond reason," Darcy murmured as he claimed her mouth.

"I admit I know relief to hear it," she sighed, and Darcy's desires spiked.

After all the months Darcy spent in Hertfordshire fighting his need for the former Elizabeth Bennet, it was Elizabeth's vulnerability, which brought out Darcy's ingrained protective nature. His role in life was to stand strong for his family. Certainly, Elizabeth softened his hard edges, but she would never remove Darcy's drive to secure those he affected. Without thinking, he tightened his embrace.

"You and the children are the essentials in my life."

Darcy nuzzled Elizabeth's neck.

Unfortunately, before she could respond, a sharp rap on the main door announced the return of his family. Darcy lifted Elizabeth from his lap, caught a shawl from the back of the settee they shared, and draped it over her shoulders just as Murray ushered the earl and Edward into the room.

Their expressions spoke of exhaustion. Elizabeth rushed into Edward's welcoming embrace while Darcy supported his uncle to a chair. Like his countess, Matlock's appearance said the earl aged dramatically since his breakfast call at Darcy House.

"Thank God, you returned to us," Elizabeth said as she caressed Edward's cheek.

His cousin tightened his embrace about Elizabeth, but he spoke to Darcy.

"Neither the earl or I expect my freedom to continue for long. For now, a magistrate could not be discovered, who would order the arrest of an earl's son based on so few facts."

"It cannot be!" Elizabeth declared. "The absurdity of the situation must prove itself."

Matlock accepted the glass of brandy Darcy handed him.

"The Shadwell officers were more knowledgeable of the case than was Mr. Welch. They asked the same questions under different guises. Fortunately, Edward kept his wits about him and fended off each accusation with sensible aplomb."

Elizabeth shot Darcy a warning glance to stifle Darcy's natural curiosity.

"Although I am certain Mr. Darcy is most desirous to know every detail, I believe Mrs. Fitzwilliam requires your attention before all others," she instructed the major general.

"Will Georgiana welcome my return?" Fitzwilliam asked in concern. "I bring more shame upon our household."

"Only your wife can answer that particular question," Darcy said with caution; although he had yet to abandon his objections to Edward's desertion, he would bow to his wife's unspoken warning. "My sister assumed her previous quarters in my house."

"And Colleen?" Edward sighed in resignation. "Is my daughter in the nursery?"

"With Bennet and Samuel," Darcy affirmed.

Edward set Elizabeth from him.

"I would take pleasure in looking upon my child's countenance. Thank you, Darcy, for tending to Georgiana and my daughter." With that, his cousin bowed from the room.

Matlock struggled to his feet.

"I should return to Lockland Hall to assure the countess of Edward's safety."

Darcy braced his uncle's stance.

"Aunt Nora set her sights on remaining at Darcy House until Edward's return. She accepted my mother's previous chambers. Join your countess. I will have your carriage sent around to the mews."

The earl's eyebrow rose in curious bemusement. As Darcy's wife, Elizabeth should reside in Lady Anne Darcy's former suite.

"Then I will bid you a good evening."

"Murray." Darcy knew the footman waited outside the door for additional instructions.

"Yes, Sir."

"First, see Lord Matlock to the countess's suite and then make certain the earl's carriage is sent around. If His Lordship or the major general requires a tray, please address my family's needs. After they are settled, you may retire. Mrs. Darcy and I will wait for Mr. Cowan's appearance."

"As you wish, Sir."

Matlock nodded his gratitude before following the footman.

"This encounter took its toll on both the earl and the countess. Did you notice how the lines have deepened around my uncle's eyes?" Darcy observed.

"I believe they were there all along," Elizabeth countered. "But you only took notice because of the strain our family knows with this madness."

❧ ❧ ❧

Edward stripped away his boots, breeches and coat before he crawled into the bed beside his wife. He regretted causing his wife even one second of distress. Before seeking Georgiana's comfort, Edward stood looking upon the perfect features of his child, so much like her mother, but a bit of his mother also. The experience brought tears to Edward's eyes, realizing belatedly how his child would never think of him with pride.

Now, as he paused to gaze upon his wife, Edward recalled how he arrived on Pemberley's threshold for Christmastide expecting to greet his sweet young cousin, but instead discovered a full-fledge woman, who encouraged his regard. He should have taken his lust elsewhere—should have permitted Georgiana to claim the affections of a man who deserved her devotion. Recognition of that particular cowardice brought a profound sadness to Edward's battered soul.

"How have I unhinged your composure?" he pleaded upon discovering Georgiana upset with their aunt's, Lady Catherine de Bourgh, plans for Georgiana to know a Season. With Darcy's absence from Pemberley, Edward stood firm against Her Ladyship's manipulations. *"Tell me what you truly desire, Georgiana. Whatever it is, I will move the heavens to make it so."*

To his promise, his sweet 'Georgie' presented him a chagrined smile. *"If anyone could fulfill my dreams, it would be you,"* she insisted. *"But I am no longer a little girl. A new doll shan't satisfy me."* Then she rose on tiptoes to kiss his cheek before she scurried away; at the time, Edward could not remove his eyes from the gentle sway of Georgiana's hips or deny his desire to discover what would satisfy her.

Two days later, he found his obsession with his young cousin beyond his control. When Georgiana sought him out on her brother's behalf, Edward permitted his emotions free rein. The images of he and Georgiana had grown into a fixation. Earlier, he made a quick reconnaissance of Pemberley House to locate all the kissing boughs the ladies hanged for the Christmastide celebration, and then he fantasized, throughout Mr. Winkler's sermon, about sliding his lips down the slender column of Georgiana's neck. Edward could not explain how everything changed between them, but it had, and he was never the type of man to walk away from a challenge.

When Georgiana delivered the message that Darcy wished to speak to him, she stepped beneath the mistletoe, raised her chin, and offered an invitation with her eyes. As if drawn to her, Edward, too, stepped into the circle of the mistletoe's magic.

Georgiana's warm breath brushed Edward's cheek as he lowered his head to caress her lips with his. Edward was aware of Georgiana's innocence, and it was difficult to go slow, but Edward meant not to frighten her. A slight graze. A series of small kisses, planted at the corner of Georgiana's lips. He could feel it all again: the soft nibble on her bottom lip—his purposeful slowness, enflaming his desire.

Reluctance abandoned, Edward edged Georgiana into his embrace before cupping her chin, lifting her mouth to his. A tender pressure, his tongue sliding along the seam of her lips. A parting. And then he deepened the kiss. The pure pleasure of holding Georgiana thusly within his arms sent him reeling.

He made himself end the kiss, but Edward did not withdraw. His mouth hovered above hers.

"Georgie, I would kiss you again," he rasped. *"But if you do not wish it, you should leave this room immediately."*

"I shall stay," she said on a husky exhale, making Edward's heart soar.

Georgiana wrapped her arms about his neck and lifted upon her toes to meet his mouth. With a groan of satisfaction, he kissed her a second time: An intimate exchange between a man and a woman in the first throes of love. He did not come to the moment without experience, but Georgiana's kiss spoke of excellence.

Edward's practical mind told him her response could not shake his very being, but it had. Years of war branded him as part of the unclean, and Edward thought at the time that Georgiana's goodness would wipe away the dissipation. However, even his wife's perfection could not remove the horror ingrained upon his very soul.

"Edward?" Georgiana's eyes fluttered open in that familiar sleepy manner, which always touched his heart.

"Yes, my love."

She reached to caress his cheek, and he turned his head to kiss his wife's palm.

"Are you well?" Georgiana asked in true concern. No words of recriminations for what he put her through. No questions regarding the madness he brought to her door. Just the love Georgiana freely offered him.

Edward caught her hand to kiss Georgiana's fingertips.

"I am now," he whispered. "Gazing upon you always brings me peace." Georgiana was the only steady, unwavering reality in his life; yet, even knowing the chaos he brought to her threshold and the regret which followed, Edward could not say for certain he would not do it again.

"Tell me you will forgive me, Georgiana. I am flawed, but I promise to mend my ways if you will welcome me as your husband." He pronounced the required words and prayed this time they would stick.

Edward waited for her response for an unnerving moment before Georgiana slid her hands about his neck and pulled him to her.

"For better and for worse," she whispered. "I am your wife, the woman who loves and esteems you above all others."

❧ ❧ ❧

Elizabeth fell asleep in his arms, but Darcy did not carry her to their shared bed until after he saw Thomas Cowan's safe return to Darcy House. Darcy felt responsible for the man risking his life in London's underbelly. When Cowan arrived, he sent the investigator to bed without asking the gamut of questions plaguing Darcy's mind.

"Matlock and his countess, as well as the major general and Mrs. Fitzwilliam, will wish to know what you discovered. There is no reason for the story's repetition. You may share what is important with us in the morning."

"Thank you, Darcy." Cowan swayed in weariness. "I will admit to exhaustion."

And so they gathered in the morning room—three couples and an inquisitive friend.

"Speak to us of your investigation, Cowan," Darcy said after their party had their fill of the morning spread. It pleased him to observe Georgiana enter the room upon Edward's arm. Although his sister still appeared pale and distraught, her expression was less taut and the lines about her eyes not so severe.

Cowan retrieved his ubiquitous journal. Darcy read several of the man's notations when Cowan assisted with Samuel Darcy's disappearance and death, but he could not make sense of the former Runner's markings. Cowan used a special symbol and letter code, which reminded Darcy of Egyptian tomb writings. Whatever his method, Cowan recorded his transcriptions in painstaking detail.

With confidence, the former Runner cleared his throat.

"Some of this will be repetitive, but I wish all to be aware of the complete details."

He paused to nod his thanks to Elizabeth for refilling his tea.

"As I mean to be quite frank," Cowan said with a blush, "I will ask the ladies' forgiveness beforehand."

He stalled briefly, as if he thought how best to explain.

"I spoke to several who viewed the situation at the bakery. It appears after the initial investigation by the officers, several hundred people trooped through the shop and house to view the ghastly scene."

Elizabeth's mouth screwed up in disapproval. An angry blush tinged her cheeks.

"The world has gone mad."

Cowan nodded his agreement.

"Later today I mean to speak to the first officer on the scene. The two men with whom I spoke last evening reside in a boarding house several doors from Vaughns' bakery. They were among those who pushed into the tight space after hearing the ruckus in the night's middle. Under the crowd's inspection, the first officer, a Mr. Rumbradge, searched the shop and the upper storey.

"Apart from the broken sword, the authorities discovered no other weapons, although blood marred two wooden rollers and a broken chair leg, the assumption being made that the attacker used them as clubs to knock Vaughn and the man's family unconscious."

Elizabeth commented before Darcy could organize his thoughts.

"Perhaps Mr. Vaughn used the items to fight off his attacker."

Cowan smiled with satisfaction. A panoply of emotions crossed the Runner's features.

"My thoughts exactly Mrs. Darcy, but the witnesses made no such connections. I will be interested to learn if the investigating officer holds opinions different from those who looked on."

"Continue."

A glumness filled Edward's tone. A familiar relenting expression, one as unassailable and compelling as Darcy ever noted, crossed his cousin's countenance.

A series of throat clearing grunts followed the major general's command, but Cowan kept his expression deliberately bland.

"My witnesses describe a blood-soaked cradle and pallet in the child's nursery, as well as blood covering the floor of the storage room where Vaughn was found. The broken sword rested beside Mrs. Vaughn's body. One of those with whom I spoke said it was as if someone purposely dropped it after killing the child. Blood covered the handle and blade."

Darcy tilted his head in contemplation.

"Were there any evident stab wounds? It would seem to me if a person carried a sword, he would use it to stab his victim rather than to use it as a cutting tool."

"A knife would serve the purpose better," Matlock observed.

Cowan flipped to a blank page in his journal to make a notation. He spoke as he scratched his note with a dull pencil.

"An excellent observation. I mean to ask the Shadwell officer that very question." Returning to the previous page, Cowan continued his summary. "The floor held a set of dried bloody footprints of a man's boots. And there were also two heavy prints in the mud outside the kitchen door."

Georgiana frowned in abstraction.

"Can we identify what type of boot by the imprint?"

"To the best of my knowledge," Cowan explained, "no match was made. It is another of my questions to those in charge." The Runner paused before cautioning "One of the problems we will encounter in proving the major general's innocence is the lack of coordination among those investigating the crimes. High Constables. Constables. River Thames Police. Shadwell Police. Night watchmen. Deputies."

"Bow Street," Matlock said in bitterness.

Cowan viewed the earl with resigned amusement.

"True. Mr. Welch often does not recognize his limits."

"Perhaps we could use the lack of coordination to our advantage," Edward suggested. "Each entity possesses limited knowledge, but if we learn what they uncovered, we could identify the weaknesses."

Cowan smiled with familiar satisfaction.

"You were always a brilliant strategist, Sir."

Darcy did not wish to think upon the lack of public safety they might encounter in their efforts to prove Edward's innocence. Five and thirty parish men, generally of advanced years, mixed with unpaid Constables and a local bench of magistrates in Shadwell. The scheme was not one he wished to maneuver.

"Were there other witnesses? I cannot imagine the streets in that section of London ever empty," Darcy suggested.

"I agree. Someone must have seen or heard part of the disturbance. With your permission, Darcy, I would send several of my men to canvas the area."

"Hire as many men as you require. Darcy and I will stand the cost," Matlock assured.

Darcy would prefer to respond for himself, but as he agreed with the earl's response, he swallowed his objection.

"Coming to the investigation late," Darcy added, "we are at a disadvantage. Moreover, I suspect many in the area will be hesitant to speak to the earl or to me; therefore, additional men appear prudent."

"Who all has a hand in the investigation?" the countess asked. "Is it possible one entity to rule Edward innocent while another finds him guilty?"

"Nothing is an absolute, Countess," Matlock grumbled. "Our son placed himself in a most precarious position." Darcy noted the stiffness returned to the major general's shoulders. "As the Home Secretary is involved, I fear whoever is charged with the crime will be ushered through the inquiry. Public outcry will demand a speedy resolution."

Darcy disguised his apprehension.

"We must operate under the assumption Edward will be charged. If he is not, nothing is lost but a bit of our personal time. Yet, if the authorities name Fitzwilliam, we will be better prepared to defend him. The legal process would provide us a fortnight at most to conduct an investigation, and the longer we wait, the more likely witnesses will depart on ships and facts will be lost among the hustle of everyday life."

"Be prepared," Elizabeth agreed.

"A calculated plan?" Edward declared. "What role do I play in this exercise?"

Before Darcy spoke the words, he knew his cousin would not acquiesce without an argument.

"You earned the dubious role of house guest. You are to remain at Darcy House until this insanity is over." Darcy's gaze locked with his cousin's; he meant for Edward to read Darcy's determination.

"Why may I not participate in securing my freedom?"

"The answer is simple," Darcy explained, his eyes narrowing in warning. "The more the residents of Wapping are reminded of your presence among them, the more likely they are to identify you as the culprit. With any luck, the man they describe as our interloper will bear no resemblance to you."

"Darcy has the right of it, Sir," Cowan agreed. "People often believe they observed what was never there." The Runner looked upon his former commander in speculation. "It is best, Major General, to permit Mr. Darcy and me the lead in this matter."

❧❧❧

They invited Officer Rumbradge for a mid-day meal at a public house on the road leading from Wapping into central London. The officer appeared comfortable with the recent celebrity of his position, a fact that rubbed raw against Darcy's sense of civic responsibility.

Evidently, he and Cowan were not the first to approach the man regarding details of the crime. With what appeared to be a congenial smile, Rumbradge attempted to disguise the fierceness and darkness in his eyes, but Darcy recognized the power the officer wielded. However, Cowan's instincts did not appear as wary, and so Darcy placed his qualms aside.

Instead of his customary cynical hardness, to Darcy's amusement, the former Runner placed his normal all-business attitude aside to build a relationship with the man, asking questions of the man's heritage and of Rumbradge's desire to serve the populace.

"I noticed your ring. It is quite striking in its design."

The officer glanced to the gold band upon his left hand.

"It was a gift from my father when I reached my majority. The small stones are the eyes of a mythical dragon. My father always claimed I would be a dragon slayer. There is an inscription inside that reads 'Forever.'"

"I would not call policing work 'slaying dragons,' but it can be fulfilling," Cowan observed.

"Yes. I know a sense of satisfaction," Rumbradge admitted, and yet his tone held a vague unreality.

Cowan took a long swallow of his ale.

"Would you mind if we spoke of the matter at hand?"

The officer considered Cowan's request.

"I suppose not. After all, I agreed to a business meeting, not a social obligation."

Darcy studied Rumbradge's defensive expression while Cowan asked his question.

"What might you tell us of the crime scene and the East Side Slayer?"

"The night watchman had some sense."

Rumbradge wiped his mouth on the rough cloth offered as a serviette. "Mr. Lester discovered the bodies and then sent for assistance. When I first arrived, less than a handful of interested citizens looked on."

Cowan sliced more bread from the loaf the owner of the Red, Red Rose placed on their table and slid it across the corner of Rumbradge's plate.

"There were five pounds in Vaughn's pocket," the officer continued, "and another thirteen in a locked box under the main counter. The baker reportedly did not trust banks. Anyway, we ruled out robbery as a motive."

The man continued through a mouthful of stew.

"Vaughn's body was in a storage room used for bowls and flour and sugar. We were not certain whether Vaughn was in the room when his attacker entered the building or whether the baker hid there."

Darcy could not imagine any man hiding while an outsider attacked his family: Darcy would meet any difficulty if someone placed Elizabeth and his children in danger.

"Could the attacker have killed Mrs. Vaughn and the child first?" Cowan asked.

Rumbradge spoke before swallowing all of his food.

"We have no means of knowing. A man of honor would never permit a woman to know such brutality."

"Men of honor," Darcy considered "are fewer these days." His immediate thought was of his old nemesis George Wickham, who raised his hand on more than one occasion to Elizabeth's youngest sister Lydia; yet, Darcy kept his thoughts to himself. Now was not the time to criticize the Shadwell authorities.

Rumbradge presented Darcy a glaring stare, as if he resented losing Darcy's full attention, before continuing his tale.

"I discovered Vaughn's missus in the nursery. I found nothing unusual in the room where the Vaughns slept so I went across the hall to the smaller room used for the child. It appeared from the number of cuts upon Mrs. Vaughn's hands that she attempted to fight off her attacker. The woman rested upon the floor in a pool of blood. The babe laid on its back in the crib, his blanket and gown covered in the child's blood."

Cowan's eyes narrowed.

"Do you have an explanation for why the attacker did not use the sword to stab his victims?"

Rumbradge regarded Cowan in surprise.

"Who said the Vaughns were not stabbed with the sword?"

Darcy could almost hear Cowan's jaw clench in frustration.

"The newspapers did not speak of anything more than the Vaughns' throats being slit," Cowan explained.

"There was more," Rumbradge spoke with confidence. "Much more."

Cowan regarded Rumbradge in a searching manner. Darcy knew the investigator's patience snapped.

"Perhaps you could provide us with your expert estimation," Cowan said through tight lips.

The officer's features settled into an unreadable expression, which made Darcy more uncomfortable.

"Based on my experience," Rumbradge claimed, "I would say the attacker entered the bakery through an open door in the private kitchen on the lowest level. He entered the storefront to discover Vaughn either removing or placing items in the storage area. I would venture the stranger took Vaughn unawares for there were no signs of a struggle. A large cut on the back of the baker's neck indicated he was struck from behind. He rested on his left side; a stab wound on the right entered above Vaughn's waist and exited through his stomach several inches above the navel.

"The attacker slit Vaughn's throat before he climbed the stairs to accost Mrs. Vaughn. There were two blood stains on the stairs to the third storey."

"Accost?" Cowan's hard, assessing gaze swept Rumbradge.

The officer lowered his voice.

"It is not common knowledge," he began, and Darcy was certain they were to learn details not spoken, but assuredly known, among those who witnessed the Vaughns' bodies after the attack. "The attacker violated Mrs. Vaughn prior to her death."

"Sexually?" Darcy whispered in disbelief. Swallowing hard, he assured the officer, "My cousin's temperament is not one to act without honor toward women."

"The woman's night gown was rucked up to her waist, and the attacker's seed remained upon her leg."

Darcy shuddered in revulsion as an image of the unknown woman formed in his mind.

"Were there other abuses?" Darcy's mouth was a grim slash upon his face.

"The attacker slit Mrs. Vaughn's gown and removed Mrs. Vaughn's left breast," Rumbradge affirmed. The officer lowered his voice further. "We never found it in Vaughn's house. We think the interloper took it with him as some sort of token of the deed."

Darcy fought for a coherent thought, but Cowan found his voice first.

"Were you involved with the investigation into the attack upon the Thornes?"

Rumbradge blinked in momentary confusion before responding, and Darcy wondered why the question discomposed the man.

"The Thornes' murders hold some similarities, but are not a replication of those thrust upon the Vaughns, making one consider whether they were committed by the same man."

"Such as?" Cowan prompted.

The officer spoke with open displeasure, but Darcy remained uncertain whether Rumbradge disapproved of the severity of the crime or of Cowan's persistence.

"The Thornes' attack came nearly a week after the one at Vaughn's bakery. As reported in the newsprints, the better-known events were the same. The throats of Mr. and Mrs. Thorne were slit, as well as that of the barmaid, Mrs. Winthrop, but as we discovered the broken sword in the bakery, we are uncertain of the weapon used."

"Were there other similarities?" Darcy asked in guarded curiosity.

Rumbradge heaved a weary sigh.

"The perpetrator attacked Mrs. Thorne and Mrs. Winthrop in a like manner as was Mrs. Vaughn."

"Including the mutilation?" Darcy clarified.

Rumbradge nodded his agreement, but Darcy studied the expression of disbelief upon Cowan's countenance. His friend's instincts were on high alert.

"The scene at the Thornes appeared arranged, as if someone meant the couple ill will and used the Vaughns' deaths as his model," Rumbradge shared.

"If the scene were arranged, the architect of the second crime must have been present at the Vaughns' house," Cowan assessed.

Rumbradge blanched.

"Even if it proved so, we would still possess several hundred possible culprits. Vaughn's bakery became a macabre spectacle."

"What was different?" Cowan asked with the confidence of a man accustomed to analyzing difficult facts.

Rumbradge's eyes dropped in unexpected submission.

"One major difference of which I should not speak."

"But you will speak," Cowan encouraged.

They remained silent for several minutes before the officer whispered his response.

"Mr. Thorne's attacker cut out the tavern owner's eyes so Thorne could not identify him."

Chapter Six

"Edward?"

His wife's summons brought Edward from his dark musings. As if he again looked upon the room, his mind conjured up the blood, splattered upon his clothes and upon his hands. Everywhere. The bodies mutilated from the sharp edge of the blade. The woman's hair mated about her face, and her child cradled in her arms.

Edward could not account for how long he stared out upon the dark garden below, the images haunting his every breath. One hour? Two? The quiet stillness became his means of permitting the war's memories to exhaust him: Standing at a window or staring into the dying embers of a fire for hours upon end as his wife's soft sigh of sleep sounded from the bed behind him.

"I am here," he said without emotion.

He was not happy to have the memory interrupted for although it was gruesome to behold, Edward knew if it did not complete its tale, the image would return when he next closed his eyes to sleep.

"Will you not return to bed, Husband?" his wife pleaded in a sleepy haze.

He turned to look upon Georgiana's sweet countenance. When he, at length, recognized her as a desirable woman, Edward thought he discovered his salvation—thought her goodness would wash away the stench of death, which clung to his body so prominently Edward often wondered why others did not smell it.

"Soon," he assured with a lack of enthusiasm. "The past few days weigh heavy on my soul, and I require time to think upon how best to proceed."

"Do you require my company?" Edward recognized the pain he again inflicted upon Georgiana's pride.

He returned to the bed to crawl across the mattress to her.

"You are a tempting morsel, Mrs. Fitzwilliam."

Edward pressed Georgiana into the pillows, as he kissed her senseless. He often practiced this romantic ruse when he wished to distract his wife from the obvious madness, which visited him nightly, and as ruses went, Edward never objected to the pleasure of enjoying her intimacies.

"And I am blessed to possess your devotion."

Georgiana sighed and laced her arms about his neck. Moments such as these were the ones, which kept him sane.

An hour later, his wife returned to her dreams, but Edward dared not to join her. His dreams held horrors no man should know, and so he refused to close his eyes. Instead, he stared at the pattern of the bed's draping, praying the dawn would arrive soon, and he could steal a few hours of restorative rest before he must face the world.

Unable to bear the weight of guilt any longer, Edward moved with care. So as not to wake Georgiana, he lifted his weight from the bed to stand beside it. Edward wished he could return to Georgiana's side. Wished he could venture sharing his personal terrors with her, but no woman should learn of the extent of man's brutality, especially from the one she called 'husband.'

It grieved Edward that he failed her. From the first time he looked upon Georgiana in her crib—he barely a teen at the time—Edward fancied himself as Georgiana's protector.

"Yet, I erred," he whispered to her sleeping form. "I pray some day you will forgive me."

In resignation, Edward retrieved his breeches, boots, and jacket. Stealing across the floor upon silent feet, he slipped into the dark sitting room adjoining his wife's quarters to don his breeches and boots before sliding his arms into his coat.

Stuffing his shirt into his breeches, Edward decided to go without his waistcoat or cravat. Having been subjected to remaining behind closed doors all day, he meant to find a few moments alone–to be rid of the shadows lurking at the edges of his mind.

Creeping down the servants' stairs, he exited through the kitchen, taking a moment to reset the latch for his return. The air remained damp and thick, but Edward gave it no care; London's perpetual fog never bothered him. He always enjoyed the way it swirled about his legs and how it provided a man certain anonymity.

He inhaled deeply before setting out across the garden path. A ride would do him well, but he would not disturb the horses, nor the men hired to tend them. Instead, Edward set out through the back streets of Mayfair, praying he could escape the darkness of his soul.

❧ ❧ ❧

He did not know how many minutes passed or how far he walked, but Edward long since left the upscale streets of Mayfair and entered a more commercial area. Where in Mayfair the streets were silent except for the occasional gentleman arriving home deep in his cups, the streets he now traversed remained heavy with life: A gaming hell open to Society's rakes. A public house closed for the evening while other businesses prepared for dawn's early opening. Street vendors arranged their carts.

A world teemed with life in the midst of the night's blackness—a crowd where he least expected to discover one. Despite his best efforts, Edward could feel his chest constrict with anxiousness. He preferred to avoid large gatherings—had purposely remained absent from the Prince Regent's many celebrations of England's victories and had yet to escort his wife to a ball or a musicale.

Periodically, Edward paused against the side of a building: He wished no surprises, wanted no one to take him unawares. At moments such as these, he considered his strife without merit. On balance, as a son of the aristocracy, he would never know the fear of losing his heritage. Nevertheless, that knowledge did little to relieve Edward's heightened fear of failure.

He fought for those who made England strong, likely served beside some of the men bringing the street to life. The thought earned a brief moment of pride. However, among the downtrodden polluting London's streets were many former soldiers.

"The streets brim with them," he whispered as he turned his steps once more toward Mayfair. "And I could easily be one of a them. One step from oblivion."

❧ ❧ ❧

"I thought perhaps I would need to drag your body from the Sephora once again," Darcy spoke in accusation.

Thankfully, his cousin lit a candle and so Darcy's voice did not come from the darkness. Being startled was one of Edward's least favorite emotions, for he never knew whether he could control the desire to strike out at whatever waylaid him.

"Where have you been?"

Edward's frown lines deepened in disapproval.

"My whereabouts are none of your concern."

He eased the door closed before turning toward the servants' stairs.

"Now, if you will excuse me…"

Darcy's cold tone stayed Edward's steps.

"Your whereabouts became my concern when my sister sought my assistance."

Of late, Edward's ire rose quickly.

"That is part of the problem, Darcy. You continue to think upon Georgiana as your 'baby' sister, when, *in reality*, she is *my* wife, and what occurs between us is *our* dealings, not *yours*. Now, I mean to seek *my* bed."

Darcy smiled that all-knowing smile, which always irritated Edward. Tonight, the gesture was a twist of the knife cutting away at Edward's soul.

"*In reality*," his cousin emphasized, "the bed you name as yours stands within a house bearing my family's crest."

"Would you deny Georgiana access to your home?" Edward taunted. "If so, then we would be welcomed at Lockland Hall."

Darcy unconsciously squared his shoulders, and Edward expected a confrontation.

"You know I would never deny Georgiana anything within my power to provide," Darcy declared.

Edward bowed in a taunting manner.

"Then you must tolerate your sister's husband enjoying her body in said bed."

Edward did not know why he spoke so familiarly. It was not of his nature to act with base instincts, but it did him well to observe Darcy flinch with the spoken vulgarity.

However, Edward did not anticipate Darcy's frustrated indignation. His cousin's quick assault found Edward plastered against the kitchen wall, a pantry shelf jabbing into his back.

"I will know of your destination this night," Darcy hissed close to Edward's cheek. "I dragged my wife and my children across England to answer my sister's plea for assistance. I turned my household on its ear in order to protect you. Now, you will speak to me in a civil tone, or we may remove ourselves to the garden for a more intimate discussion." His cousin's fists knotted Edward's lapels.

"I hold no objection to a bit of fisticuffs," Edward snarled as he bent Darcy's fingers backwards.

"You may hold no objections," Elizabeth chastised from where she and Georgiana stood upon the servants' stairs, "but I assure you Mrs. Fitzwilliam and I will tolerate none of it. You two will follow us," she instructed. "I shall not have more rumors circulating among the servants, and it is but thirty minutes before they will start their day."

With an impatient gesture, she shooed Edward and Darcy apart.

"Lead the way, Georgiana." Elizabeth lifted her candle higher to light the stairs, but before she turned to follow Edward's wife, she shook her finger at him. "You, Sir," she said with authority, "will act the gentleman and will answer your wife's questions with honesty."

In spite of his feelings of resentment for the interference practiced by his family, Edward bowed to her demands.

"As you wish, Mrs. Darcy."

A smirk of bemusement turned up the corners of his lips until a scowl of disapproval crossed Elizabeth's brow.

"Go!"

She tapped her foot in irritation and pointed to the upper storeys.

In resentment, Edward pushed past Elizabeth to follow Georgiana, but he heard his cousin in marriage.

"I am ashamed, Mr. Darcy, to think you would bring more disgrace upon the Darcy name by brawling with your cousin."

"I apologize, Mrs. Darcy," his cousin spoke with contrition. "It shan't happen again."

Edward would have known satisfaction at having his cousin brought low if he did not look over his shoulder to observe Darcy and Elizabeth intertwine their fingers at they climbed the stairs. Only a few months prior, he and Georgiana would do the same, but now the only intimacies they shared were when Edward distracted her from her questions. The thought saddened him.

In less than a minute he followed Georgiana into Elizabeth's sitting room. If Edward had his preferences, he would seek his bed. The walk wore away his earlier anxiousness, and Edward thought he might sleep for several hours before the nightmares returned. However, by the time he made his explanations to a persnickety Darcy and an all-too-subservient Georgiana, he suspected irritation would make another appearance.

As customary, Darcy and Elizabeth communicated without the exchange of words: The pair forming a united front. His cousin was astute in his choice of brides. The former Elizabeth Bennet was Darcy's other half. Despite his best efforts to forestall it, jealousy crept up Edward's spine.

He thought to find such wholeness with Georgiana, but he had yet to place his complete trust in his wife. On contrary, Georgiana fell in love with her "amiable Cousin Edward," not the soldier who saw too much of the world's evils.

Darcy conceded the floor to his wife.

"Edward, your absence this night brought Georgiana consternation," Elizabeth accused, "and plagued Mr. Darcy's sense of honor. You of all people know my husband's insensibilities when his loved ones experience disquiet. Surely you can see your way clear to set your family's temperaments at ease with an honest clarification."

Edward detected the edge in her tone. He glanced to where his wife sat with downcast eyes. He wished Georgiana would meet his with her once steady gaze. Wished his wife would declare her undying love for him. Wished she would demand Edward claim his role as her husband. Anything but to view Georgiana as the meek creature into which she retreated. When he chased her to Scotland, Edward discovered a strong, opinionated woman, but somehow when they removed to Oxfordshire, his wife regressed to the girl who he once counseled through her insecurities.

What began in hope digressed to a marriage of convenience, and again Edward placed the blame squarely upon his shoulders. He established the tenor of their joining, and his wife followed; unfortunately, Edward possessed no idea how to set things aright.

"It was nothing, Mrs. Darcy," he hissed in frustration. "I was feeling quite contained by the forced withdrawal to Darcy House. I simply required some air and a stretch of the legs." With true sincerity, he added, "It grieves me to present Mrs. Fitzwilliam pause, and by way of displacement, a like condemnation to your husband."

"A walk?"

Darcy's eyebrow rose in skepticism.

"At one of the clock? A walk for some three hours? One could circle Mayfair a half dozen times in three hours."

Edward's features knotted in disapproval.

"Who said I remained in Mayfair?" He glanced again to Georgiana's stance. It was the same one she wore after that humiliation at Ramsgate with George Wickham. It gnawed at Edward that his actions brought his wife so low. He wished to take Georgiana by the shoulders and shake her soundly, but the image of his wife's shocked countenance when he shoved her into the mantel of their bedchamber still haunted Edward's waking hours, as often as the more dire images of the war did his sleeping ones.

"We will not mince words," Elizabeth warned. "We are family, and family stands together." Her hazel gaze narrowed, and Darcy's wife faced Edward with a militant expression.

"Stands? Stands?" he snarled. "Look upon my wife! Look how she cringes in my presence. Georgiana does not stand beside her husband; she hides behind her brother's coattails."

A swallowed sob was his wife's only response, but Darcy bolted to his feet.

"How may Georgiana assume her place at your side when you effectively keep her at arm's length?"

Darcy's fists clenched and unclenched, and Edward realized his did the same.

"It was you," Edward accused, "who sought me out. I was quite content to disappear into London's filth. It is where I belong. I did not ask to return to the bosom of my family. It was my fondest wish simply to disappear from Mrs. Fitzwilliam's life."

His words caused Georgiana to slump forward in a tearful response, and Edward realized too late that he should not speak without candor. If they were alone, Edward would rush to Georgiana's side and beg his wife to forgive him. He possessed no heart to destroy her, but indifference was the only effective means to release his wife. How could he explain he acted from love, not from displeasure?

Elizabeth braced Georgiana's stance with a supportive hand. His cousin's wife was in no mood to be conciliatory.

"I thought you would speak with reason, Sir," Mrs. Darcy charged. "Thought you loved Mrs. Fitzwilliam enough to place your petty desires aside for the sake of your wife and child."

Edward wished to protest, but he bit his tongue and accepted the lady's vituperations.

"Perhaps you are correct: Perhaps, we should return to Derbyshire, taking Georgiana and Colleen with us. At least at Pemberley, your family will know love."

Her shoulders became rigid.

"It distresses me I played a role in encouraging Mr. Darcy to accept your plight to claim Georgiana as your wife."

"Returning Georgiana to Pemberley will place my sister in a state of perpetual widowhood," Darcy declared in fervid tones. "She is but one and twenty. If you insist in this insanity, Georgiana will never know another husband or more children. Her life will be an endless series of false hopes."

A yearning for all he would lose filled Edward, but he argued, "Being a wife and mother is not Georgiana's only option. Mrs. Fitzwilliam is an accomplished musician and artist. She could champion whichever charities she might wish to support. She might…"

"She might," Darcy hissed, "wither away waiting for her husband to regain his sensibilities."

Edward took a step back at the hard lash of anger in his cousin's voice.

"She might die!" Georgiana declared as she shoved to her feet. Tears streamed down her cheeks, and Edward clenched his fists to resist reaching for her. Her chin lifted in angry disdain.

"No, Georgiana," he said in true gentleness. "I want you to live. I want you to know Colleen's Come Out. To teach our daughter to love all the things you do. I will not permit my presence to destroy all the beauty you hold. I will remove from your life first. Despite what Mrs. Darcy believes, I love you. Love you so much I cannot permit the mania, which will never leave me, to touch you or Colleen. It would be more than I could bear."

His wife's bottom lip trembled, but she did not release his gaze.

"And I cannot bear to turn my back on my husband. It would rip my heart to pieces, so I suspect you must discover a different solution."

🙌 🙌 🙌

Darcy sat staring off into the shadows of his study. He insisted Elizabeth should return to her bed for a few hours of recuperative sleep. Long after Georgiana and Edward took their strife to his sister's quarters, he and Elizabeth sat in silent contemplation.

He knew how much it cost Georgiana to confront Edward's declarations. Darcy drew a short, rough breath, his temper rising with the memory of last evening's events. He watched as Edward's expression said more than his cousin's words ever would: the major general's heart was truly engaged.

Yet Edward quashed his emotions, driving them into a secret place. Although his cousin clamped his jaw tight to prevent shouting the words rushing to his lips, the major general's eyes spoke the truth. The possibility of failing Georgiana frightened one of England's finest military strategists. His cousin's feelings for Georgiana did not excuse Edward's insensitivity, but it went a long way in explaining the major general's irrational behavior.

"You are an excellent flatterer," Georgiana accused right before her exit. "But I am not so easily convinced. It would seem to a woman of little experience that a man who loved his family would cherish each moment of normalcy they shared."

He and Edward and Elizabeth watched her go, his sister's earlier devastation at discovering her husband's absence from their quarters abandoned to the realization Edward would walk away from their lives again. Darcy wished to catch her to him—to assure Georgiana he would set her life to order. The problem was he knew not how to correct the major general's errors. One part of Darcy wished to shake Edward soundly, while the other part knew his cousin ached for what Edward lost.

"Will you not fight for Georgiana?" Elizabeth accused with Georgiana's exit, and Darcy wondered if she challenged him or Edward.

His wife's eyes filled with tears, and Darcy wrapped her in his embrace, gently rocking Elizabeth fro and to.

"You should go," he instructed his cousin. "I am certain Mrs. Fitzwilliam would welcome a like gesture from you."

He turned his back upon Edward and waited to hear the soft click of the door closing upon his cousin's exit before Darcy bent to lift Elizabeth into his arms. He could not save his sister's marriage, but he could save Edward from an accusation of murder. In the privacy of their bed, Darcy explained his plans to his wife, assuring her he would do all within his power to protect Georgiana by shielding Edward.

"It must be their decision to claim their time together. As much as I love Georgiana, I cannot live her life for her. She must decide if Edward is her future or whether she means to return to Pemberley."

❧ ❧ ❧

The shadows lessened as dawn claimed the new day, but Darcy remained by the study's window throughout the brightening of the sky: There were no easy answers to the chaos surrounding his sister.

With the first streaks of light, a sharp rap at the door claimed his attention. The clock claimed it too early for visitors, and so Darcy stepped to the balcony overlooking the main foyer to observe who dared to disturb his household at an ungodly hour.

"Mr. Cowan?" Darcy's butler said with his customary disdain for anyone who ignored propriety.

Cowan shoved past Mr. Thacker.

"Where is Mr. Darcy? I must speak to him immediately."

Before Thacker could send Cowan packing, Darcy spoke from the third storey.

"What is the urgency, Cowan?"

"Another incident, Sir. The Slayer struck again. I thought it best if we view this one in person so as not to learn the facts secondhand." Cowan spoke in an insistent whisper, one meant not to disturb Darcy's household.

Darcy did not pause to consider what he might witness. Instead, he hurried down the stairs. Anything would be better than the Bedlam awaiting him in the family quarters.

"Mr. Thacker, inform Mrs. Darcy I went out on business. Do not mention Mr. Cowan's presence here this morning."

"Certainly, Mr. Darcy."

The butler held the door as Darcy led the way to Cowan's waiting coach. He climbed in before the Runner.

Cowan remarked as he followed.

"You appear to be anxious to escape Darcy House this morning." A bemused smirk crossed the man's expression.

Darcy scowled.

"What makes you think so?" He attempted to school his features to portray casualness.

"You did not ask why we should examine a scene likely to be gruesome at best if the major general is safe under your roof." Cowan smiled in mocked sympathy.

"As I had little sleep, Cowan," Darcy grumbled. "I am not in the mood for fending off the barbs of others." He leaned his head against the rough squabs and closed his eyes.

Through slitted eyes, Darcy noted how Cowan stiffened in wary curiosity.

"You did not deny my taunt, Darcy."

Darcy heard the hesitation in Cowan's voice, and he knew the man deserved a response, but all he wanted was to shut out the madness. Nonetheless, as duty called, Darcy straightened his shoulders and opened his eyes.

"I did not object to your intrusion on this fine day because I required a distraction from the situation between my sister and the major general."

Cowan paused, swallowing his initial response.

"Have things not improved with your cousin's return?"

Darcy drew a ragged breath.

"Mrs. Fitzwilliam attempts to conceal her tears, but red rims her eyes. The major general looks upon Georgiana with such desire one would think he would combust, but he keeps his wife set from his embrace." Darcy's chin jerked higher. "A man cannot sit idly by and permit his sister to wallow in misery nor can he tolerate observing his favorite cousin—his chum since childhood—destroy his one chance at happiness."

Cowan shot Darcy a swift glance.

"What do you mean to do, Darcy?"

Darcy silently kicked himself for his weakness. He thought best aloud, and he should not have shared his concerns with Cowan, but Edward was Darcy's customary confidant; and it was not as if he could discuss Georgiana's state with the major general.

"You should know, Cowan," he said in flat tones, "my cousin left Darcy House for several hours during the night."

Cowan scowled in disappointment.

"The major general's actions will confirm his guilt if his absence from his bed becomes well known. I hoped our viewing this latest crime for similarities to the two previous ones would prove your cousin's innocence, especially as the major general was no longer in his cups and was well removed from the scene. Now, the strong possibility exists the crime will confirm Edward Fitzwilliam crossed into mayhem."

Chapter Seven

"Does the blood always smell so pungent?" Darcy whispered through the handkerchief he held across his mouth and nose. He sidestepped a pool of blood, already dark and sticky. The murder occurred from eight to twelve hours prior. The fact no one questioned their right to be at the scene surprised Darcy, but Cowan simply identified himself, and those in charge permitted their admittance.

Cowan leaned closer.

"Much worse when it is mixed with the odor of gunpowder and the stench of dying flesh."

Sharp emotions surged through Darcy, and instant remorse arrived.

"I understand. My cousin knew such carnage until it became commonplace."

Darcy did not express aloud his fears that Edward possibly exacted such carnage, and neither did Cowan, but from the expression upon the investigator's face, Darcy's friend held similar thoughts.

"Cowan?" Darcy looked from where he knelt beside the former Runner to observe Rumbradge's descent from the storey above. "What brings you to this part of London so early of the morning?"

Cowan met Rumbradge's stare with a blank expression.

"I received notice of the situation. I thought it best if I viewed the scene personally," the former Runner explained.

"Although nothing was said of a possible connection to the previous events?"

Darcy noted the suspicion laced within the officer's tone, and he wondered why the man would wish to censure them.

Cowan's eyebrows lifted in skepticism.

"If citizens from the street are permitted to view the investigation, then am I not to be treated likewise?" Cowan shrugged off Rumbradge's objections with a simple question. "What can you tell me of the situation? Do we have another appearance of the Slayer?"

Although Rumbradge scowled with disapproval, the officer acquiesced.

"The shopkeeper. Two servants. One female. Both servants discovered in the shop's kitchen below. Nothing disturbed above."

"And this is the shop owner?" Cowan gestured to the man who rested face down in a pool of his own blood.

Rumbradge shot a glance about the room as if he searched for someone in particular, and Darcy's gaze followed the officer's; yet, nothing unusual caught Darcy's attention. Even so, he thought the gesture an odd one. Darcy made a mental note to speak to Cowan about the uncharacteristic feeling of anomaly, which eased its way down Darcy's spine.

When he responded, Rumbradge spoke in cool tones.

"Throats cut. The male servant struck with a heavy object. The man's head is crushed on one side."

"Was the woman attacked in a manner similar to the others?" Cowan whispered.

Darcy watched as Rumbradge closed his eyes to the image.

"Identical. This is a bloody business, and I question whether my skills are enough to solve this mystery. How do we discover a madman in a city full of the deranged? It may be best if I seek outside assistance."

The man's Adam's apple worked hard as he fought to control the swell of emotions; it was mortifying to observe Rumbradge's pride at odds with his knowledge. Darcy's censure of but a few moments prior disappeared, and he knew empathy for an overworked civil servant.

"I possess some experience—am familiar with investigations of this sort. If I may be of service, a simple word would secure my services," Cowan offered.

Rumbradge's eyebrow rose in cynicism.

"You mean to discover all our secrets in order to prevent your former commander from knowing incarceration."

Cowan shook off the man's accusation.

"I never disguised the fact I mean to protect Major General Fitzwilliam; however, know I also would consider it an honor to discover whoever exacts such brutal slaughter upon London's citizens."

"And if the major general is the culprit?"

Cowan held the man's gaze.

"I would escort Fitzwilliam to prison: No innocent should know such malice. I would say even Mr. Darcy would support my doing so."

Both men's eyes fell upon him, and despite Darcy's best efforts, a deep sadness crossed his features.

"It would destroy my sister to learn the truth of such a scheme, but I could not stand by and permit any man to suffer as these have. Keeping silent would place Mrs. Fitzwilliam and my niece in jeopardy." Darcy gestured to the corpse at his feet before whispering, "Women and children require a man's protection, not his revenge."

Rumbradge stood in stubborn silence during an uncomfortable pause.

"I pray I do not regret this," Rumbradge said, at length. "Follow me."

The officer led the way to a small kitchen where the other two victims could be viewed.

Darcy remained behind Cowan and permitted his friend to practice his analytical skills. Meanwhile, Darcy observed and listened. From their first acquaintance, Darcy appreciated Cowan's logical mind.

"The servants were killed first," Cowan remarked as he examined the steps.

"How are you so certain?" Darcy asked in admiration.

Cowan halted his descent.

"Note the dark spot on the lip of the stairs?"

Darcy turned to view what Cowan observed.

"But not on every step," Darcy stated as his mind clicked away the possibilities.

"Likely mud mixed with blood."

Cowan touched a finger to one of the marks and brought his hand to his nose. Darcy witnessed the man do something similar in Dorset when a witch's bottle broke upon the hearth.

"Has the metallic odor of blood, but also of fresh earth. I suspect whoever committed these acts entered through the kitchen. See how the marks are darker on the bottom steps. Our interloper walked through the blood below with his left foot, but not his right. The marks are on alternating steps."

Darcy's eyes followed the "trail."

"It would appear the perpetrator wears a large boot," he suggested.

Cowan smiled as he stepped before Darcy.

"Why do you assume so?"

Darcy ignored his friend's lighter tone. In spite of the morbid scene, Darcy found the experience exhilarating; mental challenges and puzzles always were a guilty pleasure for him.

"The marks display only the toe box. As the steps are very narrow, the man either climbed on tiptoe, which makes sense if he planned to surprise the shop's owner, or his boots were too large to stand flat upon the narrow steps."

"Excellent, Darcy," Cowan said with genuine approval.

"And how do we know the marks were not made by one of my men or by the night watchman who discovered the scene?" Rumbradge challenged.

Cowan presented a vague shrug.

"Easy enough to determine."

He used his ever-present pencil as a pointer.

"The marks display a cut or crack in the sole of the person's boot."

"I did not notice," Rumbradge confessed. With his right hand, the officer removed a yellow piece of paper from his pocket to mark the evidence for later investigation.

Cowan's gaze narrowed.

"I thought you wore your ring on the left hand?"

Darcy glanced to Rumbradge's hand. His friend was correct: Rumbradge displayed the "dragon" ring upon his other hand the last time they spoke to the man.

The officer dropped his hand to his side before chuckling.

"I do. I injured my left hand arresting a man in a bar brawl. Bent the ring finger backward. It swelled to where the ring cut into the skin. Thought I would wear it on the right until my hand heals."

Cowan's wariness bothered Darcy. The former Runner possessed keen instincts.

Was Rumbradge's ring significant somehow?

"Must have been several days past. Your left hand does not show the damage," Cowan noted in false contrition.

"Long enough," Rumbradge confessed. The officer self-consciously pulled the ring from his right hand and slid it onto the left. "I just didn't think of it until you mentioned it. I do not remove the ring at night when I sleep. This investigation's been so involved, I've thought of little else of late."

Cowan's gaze locked with the officer's.

"I meant no offense, Rumbradge. My mind is always taking notice of the most insignificant details. If I'd not admired the ring, I would never make the observation." Darcy's friend cleared his throat in what appeared to be embarrassment; however, the Runner did not wait for Rumbradge's forgiveness. Instead, he again pointed to the boot marks with his pencil. "I would suggest before this crime becomes common knowledge that you examine the footwear of those who had access to this area." Cowan turned to the bodies. "Were there others who viewed the servants?"

"Two of the shopkeeper's neighbors. They were the ones who reported hearing unusual noises coming from the shop to the night watchman. It seems that with everyone on alert the watchmen are asked to investigate several suspicious sounds each night. This one proved itself another bloodbath."

Cowan made a notation in his journal.

"Were there footprints outside?"

"Only at the kitchen entrance," Rumbradge confessed. "Several sets coming and going."

Cowan's nod in Darcy's direction was a silent request for Darcy's assistance.

"I will have a look outside," Darcy said. "Perhaps one of the prints will match those upon the stairs."

Slipping from the room, Darcy knelt beside the marks in the damp earth. Only two could be considered complete. With his fingertip, he touched the first one, and the dirt around the side crumbled. Both were smaller than he thought the one for which he searched would be, but Darcy followed the markings to a congested and filthy alleyway behind the narrow strip of land backing toward the shop.

Even though it was many streets removed from the river, Darcy could smell the pungent odors of the Thames as it mixed with thick smoke and the rotting vegetables found in the walled alley. The area's inhabitants depended upon the Thames and the ships bringing life and death to London's shores. The residents supplied the ships with instruments and woodworking and ropes and tackle.

Brothels welcomed the sailors for small enjoyments, while publicans relieved the sailors of what money remained of their pay once they knew their fill of the bought women. Pirates and gentlemen alike populated the streets—shopkeepers, gamblers, pawnbrokers, bakers, prostitutes, boat builders, mutineers, tavern owners, sailors and merchant navy—a cosmopolitan mix of cultures and life styles.

It was a rough life, and Darcy knew gratitude for not being born into such a world. Just briefly, he wondered if he could survived the harsh reality of life in London's East Side.

Returning to his task, Darcy discovered a second set of prints bordering the outline of the shop. Tracing the indentations, he noted how the distance between the marks shortened when they approached the single window in the back of the building, as if someone paused to peer through it. Darcy looked through the dusty grey glass, but he saw nothing moving within. The window looked upon a corner of the kitchen, where one would find the hearth.

Darcy pressed on. The buildings upon the street front abutted one another, sharing a connecting wall. A low wooden fence separated each patch of land that backed the structures. He could see bits of gardens behind several of the shops, and Darcy considered what would grow in such foulness.

A rope maker's business and one sporting clock works flanked the shop where the crime occurred. Darcy jumped the separating wall and scanned the area on the right where a full print close to the slatted fence rewarded his efforts. He bent to examine it. The fresh mud displayed what he wished to know.

"Darcy?" Cowan's voice called from the open kitchen door.

"Here!" He stood so the investigator would recognize his location. "Be careful," Darcy instructed as Cowan started forward. "There is a clear set of prints leading to the boxed alley, and a different set leading along the line of the buildings. This one appears to be of a similar shape as the one on the stairs."

Cowan and Rumbradge picked their way around several of the prints to avoid destroying the evidence to come to stand upon the opposite side of the low fence. Cowan leaned across the structure for a closer look.

"You would make a first-rate investigator, Darcy," he said with a chuckle.

"I will be glad to abdicate the title to you, Cowan."

"You might sprinkle a light coating of flour," Cowan explained to Rumbradge, "to determine the size of each print. Or even make a flour paste to capture the form. I have heard of those in America who use a cement paste, but I've not seen it done. Whatever you choose, do so before the print is destroyed by rain or by another person's foolishness. Have your men follow the trail as far as it goes. It would also be useful to ask someone to trace each of the prints. If we discover the boot's owner, we could utilize the sketches to match the footwear."

Darcy noted how Cowan said "we" and not "you." His friend carved out a place in the investigation.

Rumbradge accepted Cowan's suggestion with a gracious nod of his head.

"I will see to it."

He offered a bow of respect.

"I appreciate your keen observations, Mr. Cowan, and I will remain in touch."

Cowan watched the officer's exit.

"We should make our way through the alley. If Rumbradge's men handle the rest of the investigation as ill as they addressed it to date, the bunglers will ruin every chance at solving this crime. If evidence exists which will prove the major general innocent, we must be about it first. I am anxious to view where the alley opens upon the street and how accessible it would be in disclosing our interloper's presence."

"And I have a question, or should I say an observation, of which I would seek your professional opinion, but it can wait until we return to the carriage."

∻ ∻ ∻

Mr. Sheffield would experience an apoplexy when he viewed the condition of Darcy's boots, but their jaunt through the alley proved beneficial. Cowan approached a woman who appeared to be in her early twenties, draping wet clothing over a line of rope strung between a center pole and her threshold.

With customary ease, the Runner charmed Mrs. Dempsey. Darcy thought the situation a bit amusing until the woman began to whisper.

"Seen someone last night after two. Thought it be Mr. Tern, the clockmaker. Tern 'as himself a woman a mile down the road turd London. He be sweet on her and calls often. Tern usually returns to the 'itchen der to avoid setting lights in the shop."

"But it was not Mr. Tern?" Cowan encouraged.

"Nah. Whoever it be didnae stop at Tern's der. Kept goin."

"Could you tell where this stranger turned in?"

The woman frowned.

"Too dark and me babe called out. I's walked away and when I's returned, the person be gone."

"Did you hear of the murder?" Cowan asked.

She shivered in dread.

"Yeh. Scary tu think upun."

"Secure your doors at night," Cowan instructed. He fished a card from a pocket. He presented the woman the card and a coin. "If you think of anything else which might be of use, contact me at the directions on the card. Can you read?"

"Nah, but I's find you if'n I thinks on it. Me brother Tark reads a mite."

ન્ધ ન્ધ ન્ધ

Darcy returned to his home with the stench of the crime and the alley clinging to his senses. Neither he nor Cowan had much to say on the journey to Darcy House. They were of similar natures: thinking men. Darcy wished to delve further into Cowan's assessments of the situation, but from the closed expression on his friend's features, Darcy knew his curiosity would know no satisfaction, and so he secreted away his scattered thoughts.

"I will disembark at the corner," Darcy instructed. "I do not wish to explain more of the crime than necessary to my family."

"What will you tell Fitzwilliam?" The manner in which Cowan looked upon Darcy with something akin to sympathy brought the return of Darcy's earlier frustration.

"That I will see him drawn and quartered if he does not practice good sense in the future."

Cowan rapped on the roof of the carriage to signal to the driver to stop.

"Convince Fitzwilliam to think upon how his actions affect his daughter's future," Cowan instructed. "Meanwhile, I possess a few leads I wish to explore. I will contact you later today if I learn anything new."

"Are there facts you would care to share?" Darcy's gaze swept the street outside the carriage.

Cowan shook his head in denial.

"Too soon."

Moments later, Darcy mounted the steps to his Town house. The fact Thomas Cowan kept his own counsel set Darcy's emotions akilter. He despised unfinished games. Guilt squeezed his chest as he turned the handle to be greeted by his wife and son, who were crossing the foyer to a nearby sitting room. He did not like keeping secrets from Elizabeth, but he would not frighten his wife with the details of Cowan's investigation.

"Papa!" Bennet squealed and rushed to Darcy. He scooped the boy into his embrace, holding his son close and permitting the child to feel the protection of his father's arms. He inhaled the scent of innocence and prayed his son would never experience what Darcy observed today. He kissed Bennet's cheek as Elizabeth slid into Darcy's one-armed embrace.

"I was unaware you had business in London," his wife said in discernment.

Darcy infused lightness into his tone.

"With an estate the size of Pemberley there are always business transactions to address."

He ran his knuckle forth and back across his son's arm. The movement slowed Darcy's heart and brought him a sense of peace. Elizabeth's chin tilted in a defiant manner.

"If I translate your remark correctly, you intend to protect me from the truth of your destination."

Despite his best efforts, a frown crossed Darcy's brow before he caught his wife's hand in his grasp and brought the back of it to his lips.

"I do," he said with honed patience.

"Papa. You should not tiss Mama's 'and!" Bennet demanded in the manner of an impetuous two-year-old.

Darcy turned with a smile to nuzzle the boy's neck.

"Where should a man kiss his wife?"

"Here!" Bennet leaned forward to point to his mother's forehead.

Darcy chuckled.

"Absolutely, my son."

He followed the boy's suggestion, bending to place a kiss upon the widow's lines between Elizabeth's eyebrows.

"Any place else?" he asked the child he balanced upon one arm.

"Here!" Bennet touched Elizabeth's cheeks.

"I agree," Darcy smirked. He tilted Elizabeth's chin upward and to the left. Permitting his lips to linger on his wife's cheek, he noted Elizabeth's efforts to stifle her laughter. He whispered, "Very nice," close to her ear, as he straightened.

"You forgot ere, Papa," Bennet declared as his little mouth found Darcy's.

He could not disguise the joy of knowing his son's love. Darcy wrapped the boy in his arms, placing an affectionate kiss upon Bennet's cheek.

"The best kiss ever," he declared.

Bennet patted Darcy's cheek with the palm of his right hand.

"Better 'han Mama's?"

Darcy glanced to his wife who looked on in amusement. A raised eyebrow said she dared him to disparage her kisses.

"As you are the best of your mother and of me combined, your kiss is excellent." Elizabeth's eyebrow shot higher as she waited for his response. "However, among our womenfolk, your mother's kiss is superior. Do you not seek Mama's affection when you are sad or injured?"

"Mama kisses my 'and when I falls down," Bennet declared. "She is the 'est."

Elizabeth rose on her tiptoes to caress Bennet's cheek.

"Thank you, darling."

Tears misted her eyes. Darcy knew exactly what his wife was thinking. They lost two children prior to Bennet's arrival, and Elizabeth despaired at never knowing children. Their eldest would always hold a most revered place in her heart. His wife prayed for God's intervention in bringing them happiness.

"Pardon me, Mrs. Darcy," Lily said from behind them. "You wished me to change Master Bennet's frock before we walked to the park."

"You must follow Lily's instructions," Darcy reminded his son. "To cross safely to the park means you must listen to your nurse."

"Yes, Papa."

Darcy placed the boy on his feet.

"Then be off with you. Take a ball or a hoop, Lily. My son should exercise his legs, as well as his mind."

The girl blushed with his attention. Customarily, Elizabeth provided the instructions for the children: Men of his era avoided such details.

"Certainly, Mr. Darcy."

With the servant's exit, Darcy caught Elizabeth's hand.

"Join me while I break my fast."

He did not wait for her agreement; instead he led his wife toward the morning room. As he seated Elizabeth on his right, he instructed, "Murray, carry my apologies to Cook for my tardiness and ask her to send up a plate of eggs and ham and cheese."

"Certainly, Mr. Darcy."

The footman poured tea for Elizabeth and coffee for him.

"Would you care for another plate, Mrs. Darcy?"

It pleased Darcy that his staff showed devotion to Elizabeth's needs.

"I shall be content with the tea," his wife said with a gracious smile.

With Murray's exit, they were alone. He leaned closer to ask, "What of the not-so-happy couple?"

His wife's delicate features hardened.

"Georgiana made a brief appearance to break her fast, but she ate less than a half dozen bites before excusing herself from the table. Hannah reports Georgiana's maid brought your sister several cool compresses to relieve a headache."

Darcy reined in his simmering emotions.

"What of the major general?"

"Your cousin escorted Georgiana to the morning room, but he did not remain. Edward announced he meant to call upon the earl at Lockland Hall and then speak a second time to General Leigh-Hunt."

"The major general foolishly welcomes danger," Darcy murmured in disbelieving tones. "And Edward could pay the price for his freedom with his life. It will be difficult to prove the major general innocent if he continues to flaunt his position in Society."

❧ ❧ ❧

Georgiana squeezed her eyes shut, blocking out the memory of her husband's bitter words.

"I will see you want for nothing," Edward assured.

"Nothing except the man to whom I presented my heart," she protested.

Her husband ignored her objections.

"Yadkin Hall is not entailed, and I will gladly sign it over to you if you wish to remain in Oxfordshire. I will speak to the earl regarding the employment of a competent steward to manage the land. Between Matlock and Darcy, your future will be secure. I set aside a proper dowry for Colleen. Our daughter will be recognized as the earl's granddaughter, a lofty place in Society."

Bitter regret laced his tone.

"I am a man without a purpose, Georgiana. I pass my time in a welter of impatience because of my inability to prove myself a proper husband. I am a soldier, not a country gentleman. I bowed until I broke and other than you and Colleen, not an ounce of joy remains in my life."

Edward swallowed hard before continuing.

"I meant what I said last evening in Mrs. Darcy's quarters. It rips at my heart to view your spirit slipping away; it would be incogitable of me to turn you into a cold, dour matron before your time."

"Your life is with me and Colleen," she reasoned, although Georgiana doubted her words held any merit with her husband.

He discounted her previous pleas. Edward shook his head in denial.

"Georgie, the war claimed part of my soul. I will never be whole again. You belong at a fine estate; I do not."

"Then you mean to leave me? To break our vows?"

Her bottom lip trembled from anger and from frustration: She could not convince her husband to change his mind.

He shrugged his lack of a response.

"The world moved into a new century, Georgie. From the early years of the 1800s, I knew nothing but war. I witnessed both defeat and success, and neither is fit for mankind to know. All those men who served under me remain in my memories: They live again and die again, unchanged by the passage of time. I spent my youth in battle, and I can no longer fan the flames of normalcy."

Edward remained silent for a moment before continuing.

"I hear the stamp of their boots, Georgiana. They approach from the distance. I hear the whisper of our enemies. Feel the sweat running down my cheeks and neck. Smell the blood. Hear the cries of my men from long-ago wars. Wake to the blood-stained countenances of the soldiers I could not protect," he whispered in anguish, "They will not leave me, and I cannot chance I might harm you. How can I protect you and Colleen if I could not protect trained soldiers? It is all too much, Georgiana."

"Explain to me, Edward," she said with exaggerated patience, "how you intend to rid yourself of these horrors if you return to the current battles? Will not your seeking the familiar only reinforce the manic incidents you most fear?"

"Your softness, Wife, is more frightening than all the dismay of battle. Your smile more dangerous. The haunting sound of your voice more alluring."

Edward presented her a humorless chuckle.

"Your charms bring more harm to my heart than any enemy's bullet ever could."

Chapter Eight

"I may rip the skin from the major general's hide," Elizabeth hissed as she slid into a chair beside Darcy's.

Darcy hid the bemusement turning up the corners of his lips. Edward's practiced injustice animated Elizabeth's response.

"Then my cousin did not return to Darcy House last evening?" Having spent most of the previous night attempting to calm Georgiana's fears for the worst when the major general went missing, last evening, Darcy retired early.

Elizabeth huffed her frustration.

"Edward sent a note saying he would remain at Lockland Hall for Lord Matlock expressed a desire to know more of his son's dilemma."

"It appears my cousin means to act upon his threat to place distance between him and Georgiana," Darcy said in disgust. "How fares my sister?"

Elizabeth intertwined their fingers.

"Georgiana's eyes speak of the pain of Edward's withdrawal. I do not know if she will recover from this. How can your cousin be so cruel?"

Bitter grief darkened Darcy's eyes.

"Perhaps it is time we return to Derbyshire and permit the major general his freedom."

His mouth tightened into a straight line.

"Do you suppose we could convince Georgiana it is for the best?"

"I was thinking something similar," his wife confessed. Anger formed upon her countenance: Elizabeth's protective rage complemented Darcy's familiar sense of injustice. "First, we should ask your physician to call upon Georgiana. I am not one who believes a sleeping draught is necessary for a lady's case of nerves, but in your sister's situation, such a draught could prove beneficial. Georgiana is near exhaustion."

"I will send for Doctor Nott," Darcy agreed. "I suggest we prepare to depart for Pemberley on Monday next. The delay will provide Georgiana time to recover, as well as offer an opportunity for the major general to change his mind."

"And if he does not?"

Darcy shrugged in calm restraint.

"Then I will remove Georgiana to her ancestral home and cut all ties with the Fitzwilliam faction." Darcy prayed another option showed itself. Granted the decision would be his alone; yet, the idea of losing all connections to his mother's family caught his heart in a tight grasp.

Elizabeth's thumb stroked his palm.

"Then we shall provide Edward a strong rope to either bind himself to this family or..."

"Or one with which to commit marital suicide," Darcy finished her thought.

☙ ☙ ☙

Having slept in the familiar quarters of Lockland Hall did little to provide Edward a night's rest. He took the coward's path and sent Georgiana a note announcing he would not be returning to Darcy House. However, his resolve brought him little comfort: he missed the feel of his wife's body along the length of him. Rather than the images of war, his need for Georgiana robbed Edward of sleep.

His father and the countess argued against Edward's decision to abandon his wife and child to Darcy's care.

"You will destroy the family," his mother declared. "Darcy will sever the relationship. There must be other solutions to settle this matter."

"Darcy is likely to withdraw from all our joint investments," his father added. "It will be necessary to find others I can trust. If not..."

Edward filled in the blank: *If not, the Fitzwilliams would lose a large sum.* Guilt arrived: He made a cake of his marriage and created a financial dilemma for his father.

"I wish there were other means."

"Can you not resolve your differences with Georgiana?" his mother pleaded.

"None of what occurred is Georgiana's fault," Edward replied in weariness. "Any dearth rests upon my shoulders. I am not built to be a country gentleman. I know nothing but war, and I cannot bear to inflict my misery upon Mrs. Fitzwilliam. I assure you, Countess, this is more than a mere difference of opinion."

"You must understand," his father warned, "if you persist in this madness, there will be no turning back the clock to a simpler time. Darcy is cut from the same cloth as his father: Your cousin's temper could be called resentful, and once one forfeits Darcy's good opinion, it remains lost forever. Darcy will never welcome your return to Georgiana's side; her brother will eliminate you from Mrs. Fitzwilliam's sphere."

Edward bit the inside of his jaw hard enough to taste the blood. He made his choice, but the thought of never beholding Georgiana's countenance again tugged hard at his resolve. His wife's innocent loyalty long ago won Edward's heart.

"I am aware of Darcy's implacable nature. My cousin's temperament is too little yielding, certainly too little for the convenience of the world. Darcy will not soon forget my follies and vices or my offenses against his family."

⁂⁂⁂

The constable's arrival at Darcy House with a warrant did not surprise Darcy. By trailing Cowan through the back streets of Wapping, Darcy recognized how Edward's actions could be interpreted as suspicious.

"I fear the major general is not at Darcy House."

The High Constable frowned, as did the men who flanked him.

"How long has Major General Fitzwilliam been absent?"

Darcy knew well what the officer wished to discover, but he would not be the one to disclose Edward's absence from Darcy House on the evening of the latest murder.

"Since mid-morning yesterday."

"Not before?" the high constable asked in distrust.

Darcy preferred not to speak an untruth regarding his cousin's whereabouts, but he would not betray Georgiana's husband.

"I accompanied Mr. Cowan when the former Runner wished to view the crime which I assume brought you to my door. You may verify my presence in Wapping with Mr. Rumbradge to whom I spoke for a brief interval."

The high constable cocked his head.

"It is not knowledge of your presence at Darcy House of which we seek, Sir," he said in misplaced chastisement. "It is the presence of the major general, which remains my business."

Darcy licked dry lips.

"In my explanation, I meant to convey that during my early morning absence, the major general slept in his quarters."

"Perhaps I should direct my questions to Mrs. Fitzwilliam. In a house as fine as Darcy House, I imagine the major general's quarters are some distance from your family's chambers," the man challenged.

"This investigation left my sister distraught. I asked my family's physician to tend her, and Doctor Nott prescribed a sleeping draught." Darcy thanked Heaven for his following Elizabeth's suggestion. "Mrs. Fitzwilliam is unavailable."

The high constable's hard stare announced his disapproval of Darcy's maneuverings. There was no mistaking the man's sense of authority.

"Do you hold knowledge of the major general's current residence?"

Darcy would not bend the truth further; his family's reputation for fair dealings demanded he speak in earnest.

"At mid-morning yesterday, my sister's husband returned to Lockland Hall, the Town residence of the Earl of Matlock."

He meant the emphasis placed upon Matlock's title to serve as a warning to the high constable. Removing Edward from Matlock's home would rekindle the earl's ire.

The high constable shook his head.

"I understand your caution, Mr. Darcy, but I hold a duty to perform."

With that, the man bowed, motioned his men to follow, and then exited. Elizabeth appeared at Darcy's side.

"What is amiss?"

"The end of Georgiana's idyllic hopes."

Darcy's words came without artifice. Desperately searching for a place to know reason, his eyes surveyed the familiar room, but none was to be had. "The large gentleman with the imposing countenance is a high constable. He asked for the major general."

"Do you think the constable means to arrest your cousin?" she hazarded.

Darcy never approved of the ways of the aristocracy: Of how a man could abandon his wife and family for an all-consuming vice or of how a man could discard all morality. However, he feared Edward, a man Darcy thought to know as well as he knew himself, did just that.

"There was another murder," he admitted. "The scene was my destination with Mr. Cowan when I departed Darcy House early yesterday morning."

"It occurred while Edward was walking London's streets." Elizabeth sounded irritated.

Darcy felt another pang of sadness: His cousin's impetuous actions brought destruction to them all.

"Yes, Cowan and I hoped to discover something to prove Edward's innocence."

"But nothing denied his guilt?"

His wife's bottom lip trembled.

"All three scenes appear to be the work of the same man," he explained. "Nothing speaks Edward's name; however, the major general possessed the opportunity to commit each crime."

Elizabeth shook her head in denial.

"It cannot be so!"

"Everything changed this day, Elizabeth, and I fear I cannot set it aright for Georgiana." Darcy's voice was deep with strangled sentiments.

"You will *discover* a means."

His wife rushed into Darcy's embrace.

"You never disappointed Georgiana or me."

She stroked his jaw line.

Darcy's emotions warred: He wished to hold his wife forever, never to move from Elizabeth's warmth, but he knew he must act.

"I should go to Lockland Hall. I must be in a position to protect my sister."

He worked to remain rational.

"Please send word to Cowan of what I suspect will follow."

Darcy kissed her forehead.

"I leave Georgiana in your most capable hands."

He released her and at once felt bereft of his wife's tenderness.

"See to her, Elizabeth: My sister will require your strength."

She walked with him as Darcy rushed the corridors.

"Send word, even if the news is ill."

He paused at the top of the stairs.

"I promise."

Darcy caught her to him in a quick embrace before hastening down the stairs and into London's busy streets. It would be his duty to protect Georgiana, and that task would require him to guard Edward's future.

෨෨෨

Matlock's butler admitted Darcy without question, and he entered his aunt's favorite sitting room just as the high constable informed the major general of the officer's purpose in coming to Lockland Hall. The countess gasped and collapsed against the loose pillows lining the settee while the earl rose quickly to his feet in protest, but it was Edward's look of acceptance, which brought Darcy up short.

"You wish this?" Darcy asked into the noisy silence.

Edward's eyes remained locked on Darcy's.

"It is part of God's plan."

Darcy ignored the earl's rising ire. He stared at his cousin in stunned disbelief.

"You mean to make a sacrifice? You mean to permit the authorities to take your life as you took others during war?" Yet, Edward said nothing more. He stood straight and tall: a trained military leader.

"You will not remove my son to Shadwell!" Matlock insisted.

The high constable stood his ground.

"I have my orders, Your Lordship."

"I will go, Father," The major general said with a strange sense of finality. Edward adjusted the line of his jacket.

Matlock's cheeks turned a beet red.

"You will do no such thing! I will speak to Lord Sidmouth at the Home Office. This is a mockery of justice!"

Despite his nerves being oddly tense, Darcy spoke with authority.

"We should permit the High Constable his due, Uncle. If Lord Sidmouth agrees with you, the major general can be released in short time."

"You speak nonsense, Darcy," Matlock blustered.

As he was the only member of his family aware of the third murder, Darcy held his ground.

"Trust me, Uncle. In this matter, the high constable has his reasons."

Shock crossed the major general's countenance.

"What reason?"

Darcy kept his eyes on his cousin.

"A third incident," he explained, and before his uncle could lodge his protest, Darcy added, "I explained to the high constable you were at Darcy House when the attack occurred."

"Then there is no reason I will be kept in custody."

Darcy noted the tight fear in Edward's voice.

"It is best, Father, that no scene is made. I will go with the gentlemen and trust the British judicial system to recognize the truth."

The earl's coloring blanched white, and he swayed in place, but Matlock stepped from the way to permit the major general's exit.

"Darcy, protect Mrs. Fitzwilliam. I want no more shame delivered to her door."

"I will do my duty by my sister."

With that, Edward gestured to the high constable to lead the way. Within seconds, the sound of the door's closing behind his cousin could be heard echoing through the silent halls to where he and his aunt and uncle remained unchanged.

"You should not have permitted Edward to depart with those men," the countess sobbed. "What will they do to my son?"

"It is a dire situation, Aunt," Darcy spoke with gravity.

Matlock recovered some of his composure.

"What do you know that we do not?"

He gritted his teeth and strove to explain.

"I attended Mr. Cowan when he examined the latest scene. There are many similarities among the three incidents."

The countess asked the obvious.

"How could Edward be involved in this…this madness if he were at Darcy House?"

His aunt wrung her hands with worry.

"I spoke to the high constable of the major general's being in his bed when I departed Darcy House; however, I did not confide the fact my cousin was absent from his bed for nearly three hours in the night's middle."

Darcy released a frustrated breath and attempted to rein in his unruly thoughts. Matlock's gaze narrowed.

"How can you be certain of Edward's absence?"

Darcy scrubbed his face with his dry hands to drive away the exhaustion creeping into his veins.

"Georgiana woke to discover Edward missing. My sister feared he chose to desert her again. I searched the house for my cousin or a note of farewell. The major general returned through the servants' entrance while I searched the lower level."

"Where in the bloody…?"

The earl caught himself before his wife.

"My cousin claimed to partake of a walk."

"A walk?" Matlock demanded in incredulity.

"Yes."

Blast his cousin: Edward's stubborn streak created a living nightmare.

"The major general claimed the need to be free of our forced imprisonment."

The countess's bottom lip trembled.

"If the authorities learn of this *walk*, Edward's freedom will no longer be so easily earned."

ॐ ॐ ॐ

Darcy insisted Matlock call at the Home Office while he trailed the major general to Shadwell. He convinced the earl that Matlock's influence would best be used with Lord Sidmouth, and it would be imperative for Darcy to inform Edward of the details of the crimes, so the major general would not incriminate himself.

"Thank you for coming," Edward said with sincerity.

Darcy sat on the thin mattress of the cell's makeshift bed.

"You may hold second thoughts regarding your gratitude once you realize I will no longer risk my family's honor by lying to the authorities."

Darcy thought long and hard on his involvement in Edward's folly.

"For Georgiana's sake, I mean to protect you, but if a public trial looms in your future, I will not soil the reputation of my wife, my children, and my sister by speaking fabrications under oath. Young Bennet deserves a better example in his father than that."

"I would expect nothing less, Darcy."

Darcy shoved away the pain of seeing his cousin brought so low, as well as his continued irritation at being placed in such a position.

"Then let us prepare for the worst while praying the earl knows success."

"Where do we begin?"

"From my limited experience," Darcy confessed, "you will be first brought before a magistrate who will bind you over for trial at Old Bailey. If a trial occurs, you will possess less than an hour to prove yourself innocent. If not, you will be hanged."

"Never volunteer to offer words of encouragement to the dying, Cousin. You lack the finesse to do so," Edward complained.

Darcy's temper flared.

"I am not here for entertainment. You and I must discover the truth or my sister will be a widow."

Edward raised his eyebrows to Darcy and shrugged.

"It is not as if I can undo what is done."

"You can employ that logical mind you possess and discover the one thread, which will unravel this mystery," Darcy corrected in a firm tone.

Edward glanced about the small cell.

"It would seem I possess little choice."

Darcy laughed with derision.

"The accommodations are superior to the Sephora."

Edward's eyes glinted with guilt.

"My life has been badly played."

"Have they treated you in an ill manner?" Darcy wished he could speak with empathy, but his cousin vexed Darcy's patience.

"Other than a search of my person, no harm was done," Edward insisted.

Darcy leaned closer where they might speak in private.

"In truth I know not where to begin. I hold no knowledge of how we proceed; however, it would seem prudent for you not to answer questions without the benefit of a barrister or someone to counsel your responses. You should not freely share every detail you possess, even those, which might prove you innocent. I fear the authorities will twist the facts to find you guilty. They wish an end to this madness, and you will prove an excellent culprit. From what I know of the murders, you could be loosely tied to each."

Edward's eyes flickered to the door.

"How is that so, Darcy?"

"The broken sword. The inordinate amount of blood on your hands and uniform. Your absence from Darcy House. Your untimely journey to London. Your living rough and withdrawn from Society," Darcy recounted.

"You know I could not commit these crimes!" Edward said in a hushed protest.

Darcy broke over his cousin's objections.

"Men have been hanged on less proof. This is serious, Edward."

"I am not a simpleton, Darcy!"

"Then cease acting the role," Darcy declared with his customary rightness. "From this moment forward, you are to speak with no one but Matlock, me, or Cowan. We will find you appropriate legal counsel, who can speak to the points of law during the proceedings and advise you on what questions to answer under interrogation, but the brunt of your case will fall upon your shoulders. You will examine the evidence and refute the witnesses before the court. Every ounce of cunning you possess will be required for you to emerge unscathed."

"You appear assured I will not simply be released after they discover the error of their assumptions," Edward accused.

"The authorities released several suspects," Darcy confided, "and with each the public outcry grew. As I said previously, they want to discover a guilty party, and they want this public chorus of disapproval hushed. I am preparing for the likelihood you are their main suspect, and their efforts to find another will dwindle now that you are incarcerated."

"How much time do I have?" Edward asked in a weary tone.

"I am assuming you will soon be brought before a magistrate and possibly turned over to a grand jury's adjudication. Then a date will be determined for Old Bailey. As these crimes occurred in Middlesex, London will not claim precedence. We are at a disadvantage. Until the actual trial, you will hold no knowledge of the evidence. We must anticipate every possibility. It is essential we use every minute available to prepare your defense." Darcy held his cousin's gaze. "You will have a fortnight. A month at most."

"Likely sooner than later," Edward reasoned. His cousin's gaze drifted to the high window. "Not much time."

He paused in reflective silence.

"So often upon the battlefields I came face-to-face with Death, but I never felt vulnerable until this very moment."

Chapter Nine

He returned to Darcy House rather than to the earl's for Darcy considered it essential to apprise Elizabeth and Georgiana of what occurred.

"Thank Goodness, you returned!" Elizabeth greeted him upon his entrance. She slipped her arm about Darcy's waist and rested her cheek against his chest.

"I was so worried."

Darcy caressed the back of his wife's neck.

"It was another disastrous day," he whispered close to her ear, and he felt his wife stiffen. "Come." Darcy released her from his loose embrace. "I have several messages to address before I can ease your mind; even so, I would be pleased to know your closeness."

Elizabeth's fingers laced with his.

"Lead on, Mr. Darcy."

He closed the door to his study behind them before speaking again.

"How is my sister?" He seated Elizabeth in a chair close to his desk and poured her a short sherry.

"Still napping from Doctor Nott's draught the last time I looked in upon her. I asked Hannah to inform me when Georgiana summoned her maid. I spent the last hour with our children and Colleen."

Darcy poured himself a brandy.

"Thank you for keeping the household on course while I tended to this madness."

His wife smiled, and Darcy's heart knew the calmness he sought. Even after four years of marriage, the woman had a damnable way of distracting him.

"I enjoy it when you acknowledge my worth," she taunted.

For the first time since they shared their morning meal, Darcy felt his chest loosen its tight grip on his breathing.

"If you will permit my indulgence, I will gladly demonstrate my gratitude later."

Elizabeth blushed, as she often did when he spoke intimately, but his wife learned to challenge him with a lift of her chin.

"As yours is the most impressive offer I received today, I shall seriously consider your proposal."

Darcy knew Elizabeth held a like fascination with him, as he held for her. Their time together was the most satisfying of his life. At two and thirty, he claimed his share of God's goodness: an estate renowned for its beauty and its efficiency, two wonderful children, and a wife who met his passions with those equal to his. Only his sister's current misery brought a shadow to his existence.

He looked away from his wife's fine countenance to take up his pen, but he good-naturedly warned.

"If anyone in this household other than me offered you comfort, Mrs. Darcy, you should caution the fool that your husband is skilled with both a sword and a pistol."

Although he did not observe her reaction, he knew Elizabeth stifled her giggle before sipping her sherry.

"I shall forward your message, my husband."

He scratched out his note and waited for her curiosity to overcome his wife's patience.

"May I inquire as to the nature of your correspondence?" she asked at length.

Darcy sanded the first of his notes before retrieving another sheet of foolscap. He answered as he wrote the second of the necessary letters.

"The first is a simple note to Cowan to inform him that Shadwell took Edward into custody, and to inform the man I require his assistance as quickly as he receives my message."

He heard Elizabeth's gasp, but Darcy ignored her expected reaction. He recognized his wife's temperament: She would possess a hundred questions for him once he completed his task, but Elizabeth would not torment him until that time.

Therefore, Darcy continued to dip his pen into the ink well and to tap away the excess.

"The second is a request for my solicitor for the name of a competent barrister who might serve Edward's case in identifying points of law in my cousin's defense."

"Perhaps Matlock or Lindale will wish to find his own man," Elizabeth reasoned.

Darcy shook off the suggestion.

"My uncle will have his opinions, but I possess connections such as Mr. Cowan and my men of business, who know the law far better than the earl's or the viscount's acquaintances. My uncle used the same solicitor since I was in leading strings. We require someone skilled in defense and more familiar with the finer points of current law."

"I suppose it will not harm the major general's cause to possess several men of the law as his counselors," Elizabeth suggested.

Darcy did not argue with her diplomacy; instead, he finished the second letter and reached for a third sheet of paper.

"This time I mean to inform Matlock and the countess of my intentions to secure a barrister's services and to assure them of Edward's state of mind when I left him in Shadwell."

"Someone should send word to Lady Catherine," Elizabeth recommended. "Her Ladyship should be made aware of what occurred; learning of Edward's arrest will be hard on your aunt's weakened condition, but doubly so if she must discover the fact in the newsprints."

"An excellent point."

Darcy paused to consider his imperious aunt.

"I wish it were Lady Catherine with whom I must deal rather than her brother Matlock. My uncle knows only one form of negotiation: the demand of his subordinates to bow to the earldom," Darcy observed in proper gravity. "Admittedly, Lady Catherine is also an expert in high-handedness, but Her Ladyship also possesses the good sense to know she cannot bend the will of the government to her wishes. As a woman in charge of a grand estate, my aunt learned the art of concession."

"Perhaps after we know more of the case against the major general, you should seek Lady Catherine's advice. It would do Her Ladyship well to know you value her opinions."

Darcy belied his amusement in the look he bent upon his wife.

"No one who ever read my aunt's scathing reprimand for my choosing you as the Mistress of Pemberley would understand your devotion to Her Ladyship's tender considerations."

"Lady Catherine and I came to an understanding over the then Lieutenant Southland's pursuit of your cousin Anne," Elizabeth responded in earnest.

Darcy's eyebrow rose in curiosity.

"Will you ever share the details of that particular conversation with me?"

An indulgent, lazy smile curled his wife's lips. Elizabeth's expression was not reassuring, but her tone spoke of genuine consideration.

"You know the worst of it, Mr. Darcy. Her Ladyship feared for the future of Rosings Park."

"My aunt confided more than her fears for her estate, but I will not press you further; yet, know I mean to have the complete truth, my love."

Elizabeth pursed her lips in a pretend kiss.

"Someday, Mr. Darcy."

She reached for the dried letters to add the directions as Darcy continued to draft his note to Lord Matlock and then another to Lady Catherine. He appreciated his wife's attempt to be of service.

As he finished franking the letter to Lady Catherine in Kent, Hannah tapped on the door to announce, "Pardon, Mrs. Darcy, but you wished to be informed when Mrs. Fitzwilliam awoke."

"Thank you, Hannah. Mr. Darcy and I will call upon Mrs. Fitzwilliam at once. Please give these to Mr. Thacker to be delivered post haste." She handed her maid the finished messages.

"Yes, Ma'am."

With Hannah's exit, Darcy assisted Elizabeth to her feet.

"I fear my news will call for another draught. I pray Doctor Nott provided Georgiana more than one."

❧❧❧

It took all of Darcy's powers of persuasion, as well as much cajoling upon Elizabeth's part, to convince Georgiana to abandon her desire to rush to the major general's side.

"I know you believe it is your duty to support your husband, but it would only shame our cousin further to know his actions brought his wife so low. Edward would be devastated to realize you suffered the filth of Wapping and called upon him in a cell in Shadwell."

"But my husband must know I did not desert him," Georgiana protested.

"I am certain the major general is aware of your devotion," Elizabeth said in sympathy. "Perhaps a letter from you would better ease his troubled soul. Speak to the major general from your heart. Mr. Darcy will deliver it, will you not, William?"

In truth, Darcy held no desire to return to Shadwell, but he made his sister the promise Georgiana sought. Having left Georgiana in Elizabeth's care, Darcy returned to his study to record the basic details of the crime scenes and what evidence he expected the prosecution to lodge against Edward. Placing them in a journal he intended to share with his cousin, Darcy spent more than an hour at his desk before being interrupted by Cowan's appearance at Darcy House.

"It is as we expected," the detective said as he accepted a glass of brandy from Darcy.

A spatter of rain upon the window indicated the year without the warmth of summer had not given up its claim on London simply because the calendar read autumn. Darcy fixed his eyes upon the droplets trickling down the pane: They reminded him of the many tears his sister shed upon the major general's behalf.

"If I had my rathers," he said with interested resignation, "I would place my family in my traveling coach, set a course for Derbyshire, and never look back. I am weary of this drama."

Cowan presented a severe frown.

"The major general showed uncharacteristic poor judgment in this matter."

The hot ache of frustration filled Darcy's throat; he expelled an impatient breath.

"As much as I wish to ignore my responsibility, it appears sensible to discuss how best we might serve my cousin's cause."

"Do the authorities know of Fitzwilliam's late night stroll through London?"

Darcy shook his head in the negative.

"I instructed my cousin not to share the information with Shadwell, but I am not naïve enough to think Edward's ambulatory activities will not become known to the Shadwell magistrate. Without doubt, someone took note of a well-dressed gentleman in the merchant district. It is only a matter of time before the major general will be asked to defend himself against additional charges."

Cowan sat in silence for several elongated minutes.

"I would not wish another attack upon the City's working poor, but such an incident would prove your cousin's innocence."

"Like you," Darcy admitted, "I would prefer to find other means to name Fitzwilliam without blame." Darcy reached for the journal he began earlier. "I jotted down my impressions of the scenes we inspected in order to share them with Edward."

"And you wish me to do something similar?"

Darcy's eyes narrowed.

"Do you think this a waste of time?"

"On the contrary," Cowan assured. "Even if the effort proves fruitless in the major general's defense, the practice will provide Fitzwilliam a focus, which is more than we could hope at this time yesterday." Cowan took a thoughtful sip of the brandy. "As the prosecutors, judges, and jurors possess all the power, it will take an incalculable effort for Fitzwilliam to prevail. Although there are no victims to speak of the crimes before the court, the shear desolation of the scenes will set both judge and jury against the major general. Fitzwilliam will be expected to explain away the evidence against him."

"And as my cousin holds little memory of what he did during his drunken bouts, the journey to freedom is fraught with peril."

"Without a reservation."

A faint consternation crossed Darcy's features.

"What else should we consider?"

"Are there witnesses beyond Belker, who could speak to the major general's defense?" Cowan thought aloud.

"None of which I can think," Darcy admitted. "I suppose we might instruct Fitzwilliam to counter the testimony of the Sephora innkeeper, who will be called upon to testify to the state of the major general's bloody uniform. My cousin must impress upon the court that an alternate explanation is just as believable."

"Has the magistrate examined the major general?"

"It was expected to happen today."

"Shall Fitzwilliam be permitted to speak during the examination?"

Darcy ran a hand through his hair.

"I cautioned my cousin to hold his tongue other than what he shared previously, but I cannot say for certain. I was not in attendance, but as I received no notice of Fitzwilliam's release, I suspect he will be held over for the grand jury. The results will be the same whether my cousin put in a plea or not."

"Yet, there is much more to learn," Cowan insisted. "If the magistrate thinks the case holds merit, he is required by law not only to commit the major general to prison to await a trial, but to bind over the witnesses to appear in court. As is customary in court proceedings, I doubt the magistrate would seek a confession from your cousin."

The Runner withdrew his book to make a few notations.

"In the next few days, they will move the major general to New Prison; meanwhile, we must learn who will stand to witness in the trial, and we must secure information, which will counter their testimonies."

"I have no idea where to begin," Darcy admitted. "This is strange territory for a man trained to oversee the land."

"Then I will take the lead until you feel more comfortable, but we cannot delay. The horror of these attacks will add impetus to the authorities to bring a perpetrator to justice."

Cowan cleared his throat for emphasis.

"Have you considered the impact upon your family when word spreads of the major general's arrest? The rabble will invade Mayfair for a look upon where the 'killer' lived and to complain about the injustice of the wealthy's suppression of the poor. I imagine many of your neighbors and business associates will give you and Matlock the direct cut." His friend's tone announced Cowan's intended warning was no idle threat.

Silence coated the room. Darcy's mind raced through the possibilities.

"Are my wife and children in danger?" Anger at the thought of Elizabeth and his sons knowing fear ricocheted through him.

Cowan spoke without any hint of uncertainty.

"London is incensed by the crimes. It will be difficult to discover even one among the City's population not aware of the terror exacted upon Wapping. The interested will come to look upon Lockland Hall, much in the manner they trooped through the houses to view the crimes, to view from where a murderer rested in luxury's lap. Because you accompanied me to the homes of the victims, your name will not escape their notice. Darcy House could also be of interest. You should consider extra guards about your property, and you should caution Mrs. Darcy and Mrs. Fitzwilliam not to go out without a proper escort. A like warning should be sent to Matlock and to the major general's brother."

"That serious?" Darcy asked in disbelief.

The calm in Cowan's voice was more menacing than the sound of an approaching army.

"This will not be a simple task: Even if your cousin is proved innocent, this smear will follow your family forever. Fitzwilliam claimed feeling a prisoner in this house, and so the major general risked everything for a few hours walking about London. Now, he will know real restrictions, not only for himself, but also for his dear family. In truth, such knowledge will rip Fitzwilliam raw."

"And so it should," Darcy drawled in chilling accents. "I spent a lifetime, as did my father before me, elevating my family's name only to have a flippant decision on my cousin's part to color it with a scandal. Excuse me if my sympathy is hard pressed to make an appearance."

Cowan nodded his understanding.

"To salvage any chance of redemption, we must prove Major General Fitzwilliam not guilty of the crimes of murder."

Chapter Ten

Cowan's prediction proved truer than Darcy preferred: The magistrate held Edward over for the grand jury, and the swarm of onlookers arrived in Mayfair.

"You must limit your activity to the house," Darcy warned Elizabeth and Georgiana. "Mr. Thacker reports the servants were followed and questioned and jeered. I would not have you or the children know such censure."

"Perhaps Colleen and I should withdraw to Lockland Hall so you and Elizabeth may return to Pemberley," Georgiana suggested.

"Certainly not!" he and Elizabeth responded in perfect unison.

"We are family, and we will see this through together," Darcy assured.

Three days passed, and each day, Darcy had the argument with his sister regarding Georgiana's desire to call upon her husband. Each day, Darcy adamantly refused: He meant to do what he always did: protect his sister.

The only good Darcy could observe of the situation was the thickness of the letters being exchanged between Georgiana and the major general. Darcy bribed the guards overseeing Edward's incarceration to permit his cousin pen and ink. He prayed the major general chose to speak of the obstacles, which drove Edward and Georgiana apart. If his sister and the major general could come to an understanding, Darcy would count the trials worthwhile. It would be a mournful shame if all this misery were nothing but misery.

Today, Darcy expected the Shadwell authorities to move Edward to New Prison. If so, Darcy's access to his cousin could be severely limited. The Shadwell officers permitted Darcy to call upon the major general at all hours of the day. The interruptive changes, which marked Edward case, rubbed hard against Darcy's need for permanency, and it kept him feeling off balanced.

"You anticipated to what the Sephora innkeeper might testify," Darcy assured, "but keep in mind others of the inn's staff could also be called against you."

Edward, no longer permitted the solitude he craved, answered in a brusque manner.

"I am well aware of my role in this farce, Cousin. I shan't fail to counter whatever is spoken to my detriment."

"I would be happy to leave you to your devices and return my family to Pemberley," Darcy retorted with a faint edge to his tone. "Elizabeth, Georgiana, and the children are prisoners in my home because of the scrutiny your folly brought to my threshold. You will tolerate my need for details, or I will make good on my withdrawal."

A sound of anguish escaped his cousin's lips.

"Perhaps you should place distance between us."

A familiar tension hummed between them.

"How bad is it?"

Darcy presented his cousin a long, slow assessment.

"The newsprints carried the first of the stories yesterday. You are named in the story, along with a characterization of a military man wielding a broken sword."

"Please tell me Georgiana did not see the caricature."

Darcy's brow climbed a fraction.

"I would not permit my sister to add to her anguish."

His stomach churned in agitation.

"Edward, this madness will not know an end until you prevail. If I appear intolerant, it is because I lost the superior judgment of the one person I most trusted. "

"Tell me what I must do. I will not permit Mrs. Fitzwilliam to suffer more shame nor will I permit the countess to worry for her son's future."

Edward's half-whisper spoke of the major general's desperation. "Explain what you require of me."

"Think upon the last time you recall possessing your sword. Neither Cowan nor I is convinced the one at the Vaughns' is yours. Also, did you encounter anyone on your late night walk that might recognize you? Did you speak to a passer-by? To our knowledge, no one placed you at the third crime. Cowan is still pursuing clues from the scenes. We suspect the two men from the boarding house close to the Vaughns' bakery will speak at the grand jury. They testified during the coroner's inquest. Later today, Cowan means to attend the inquest for the third set of victims in order to learn more of the authorities' evidence."

"What of the inquiry for the Thornes?"

His cousin's expression fought to garner strength over his weariness.

The customary voice of common sense whispered in Darcy's ear.

"The authorities kept the second inquest proceedings in unprecedented privacy. Cowan thinks there is evidence at the second scene upon which the case against you rests. We spoke to Rumbradge, but the officer might have withheld information. Cowan has a man upon the search. We hope all will show itself in time."

❧ ❧ ❧

Georgiana clutched the latest letter from her husband to her chest as she rushed to her chambers. It would be foolish of her to think Edward's letters could smooth the way to a reunion, but her heart leapt with the possibilities. Each of the major general's letters professed his undying love for her and Colleen. If he would only learn to trust her, Georgiana thought they could survive this ordeal very well.

She closed the door behind her before ripping at the bit of candle wax sealing the letter's flaps. Sinking into the chair beside the window, she opened the folded-over pages to read…

My dearest G,

It grieves me to know my actions brought anguish to your brow and to your heart. When we parted, I walked away with certainty, but now I know mine were the steps of a coward. I never pushed you away because I despised our life together. Instead, I meant my withdrawal to shield you.

"Your protection, I do not require," Georgiana whispered to the room. "Desertion stings, my husband, even when done in the name of love."

I now understand the pain I inflicted upon you. The emotional trauma. The shame of rejection. The havoc wreaked by my actions.

"You forgot your Biblical teachings, my lord General. In First Corinthians, it says, 'And unto the married I command, yet not I, but the Lord, Let not the wife depart from her husband: and let not the husband put away his wife.'"

All undertakings teeter upon a critical point, one where the person launches himself into the abyss. This situation provided me the time to think on God's plan for me. Your revered mother was of the habit of telling Darcy that making plans without God's permission would always result in disaster for the Lord took such impertinence as pride at its worst.

"The prayer the Devil answers," Georgiana smiled in sadness. "Papa repeated the phrase more than once in reverence to Lady Anne Darcy."

God help her! Georgiana felt bruised and battered. A tempest of longing sprung to her chest: Longing for both her long ago family and for her current family.

Over the past few years, I admit to becoming disillusioned by the idea of God. A man who knows what I do—a man who stands witness to the world's cruelty—must question the benevolence of God. How can an ever-loving God permit good men to suffer horrendous deaths? But then I returned to Pemberley for Christmastide to find God shoving me into your embrace, and I assumed your love would save me. Unfortunately, when I was sorely tested, I faltered. I accepted a love lesser than the one you offered—lesser than the one God intended for me. I accepted my own counsel— my own pitiful self-worth, but I swear if I prevail in this matter, no one will drive me from your side again. I will place my trust in God the Father, who brought me the most innocent happiness I ever knew.

Tears rolled down Georgiana's cheeks. Her husband's words spoke of a breach in the walls he built between them. She loved Edward Fitzwilliam from the time she turned to youthful womanhood—her emotions fully engaged when Edward finally recognized her as his potential mate; yet, the major general was slower to recognize Georgiana offered more than a handsome countenance and an obedient nature.

No matter the outcome, please know, my love, you are my most precious treasure. I see you in my dreams. I hear the sweet tones of your voice as you sing a lullaby to Colleen. I revere you as the one true blessing in my life.

"My husband speaks of his love—a fact I never doubted," Georgiana murmured as her fingertips traced the familiar slant of

Edward's script. "However, I fear I may still lose him even if Darcy manages the major general's release."

Perfection will never be within my grasp, Georgie, and I executed my life badly. I wish I could remove all the grief you knew at my hand. I mean to make changes, and my resolve will play hard with both of us. I mean to share a part of me I kept hidden from the world. Everyone says doing so is the only means to a proper resolution. Bringing love back to your eyes is reason enough for me to risk everything. Please tell me this is your dearest wish. Your loving husband, EF.

Georgiana rushed to her escritoire to write her response. She doubted her brother would return to Wapping on this day, but her letter to Edward would be waiting when Darcy next ventured out. She thought it imperative that she assure her husband of her undying devotion. "Please God," Georgiana prayed as she sharpened the pen, "permit the major general to know peace."

෨෨෨

"Captain Southland, Mr. Darcy."

Darcy looked up to find his cousin's husband being ushered into the room by Mr. Thacker. "Roman," Darcy called in greeting and stood to extend his left hand to the man.

Southland lost an arm at Waterloo, and Darcy's gesture was a conscious one.

"What brings you to London? I hope you bear no ill news of my cousin Anne or of Lady Catherine."

"My wife and child are splendid," Southland said with great pride. "It is the happiest days I ever knew. Young Robert possesses his mother's fine countenance, and Her Ladyship's health continues to exceed our expectations. Although my mother in marriage is gaunter than when you last saw her, Lady Catherine remains an active force upon the estate. I am pleased that Her Ladyship claims a bit of contentment with her daughter's position. Lady Catherine is an imperious supporter of my efforts for Rosings Park."

"Has Her Ladyship disclosed the extent of her illness?" Darcy asked in curiosity.

"Lady Catherine denies even her daughter the details. Only Mrs. Darcy and Lady Catherine's personal physician know the source of Her Ladyship's frequent bouts requiring bed rest. I fear you must learn the truth of it with the remainder of the family."

Southland's lips turned upward in a teasing smile.

"All I can confide for certain is Doctor Hammrick increased the dosage of laudanum prescribed for Her Ladyship."

Darcy frowned his disapproval of his aunt's heavy medication before directing the man to a nearby chair.

"Not that I object to your company, but your presence in London piqued my interest." Darcy poured Southland a glass of claret.

The captain took a hardy swallow.

"Her Ladyship received your letter regarding Major General Fitzwilliam's dilemma. Needless to say, it took all of my dear Anne's persuasion to convince her mother to remain in Kent. Then Anne volunteered me to travel to Town to learn more of the situation."

Darcy sat across from the man who served under Edward in both America and upon the Continent. Roman Southland was a cousin to Lady Catherine's former cleric, Mr. Knight, and when Southland showed interest in Anne De Bourgh, Anne manipulated a compromising situation to trump her mother's objections. Fortunately, Anne was the wiser: She and Roman joined happily in marriage, and the captain displayed real promise in assuming the reins of Rosings Park.

"I imagine you also felt an obligation to the major general," Darcy stated.

"Aye, Sir."

The captain finished his drink, and Darcy poured another.

"If you hold no opposition, I hoped to learn of the crimes from you. As much as I respect Lord Matlock, in truth, the earl often intimidates me."

Darcy smiled by design.

"As he does us all."

"Tell me how I may be of service to Fitzwilliam."

Before Darcy could respond, a second knock at his study door brought his butler followed closely by Thomas Cowan. Darcy and Southland rose to greet the investigator. Before Mr. Thacker exited, Darcy gave his servant orders for a room for Southland.

"I did not expect you so soon, Cowan," Darcy remarked. "First, permit me to give you the acquaintance of Captain Roman Southland. The captain also served under Fitzwilliam, and he is married to our cousin Anne."

Cowan bowed his greeting.

"Cousin Anne of Lady Catherine's renown?" the investigator said with a wide grin and a moment of sublime revelation.

Southland's eyebrow rose in amusement.

"Someday I mean to know what tales Fitzwilliam shared."

Darcy completed the introductions.

"Thomas Cowan served with the major general in Spain in '09."

Southland nodded his understanding.

"The major general often spoke of you, Cowan. It pleases me to know you assist Fitzwilliam in this matter. You are at Darcy House to be part of the major general's men again, are you not?"

"Cowan is former Bow Street and extended his skills in Fitzwilliam's behalf," Darcy explained.

They seated themselves casually in a companionable arrangement.

"As you requested, Darcy, I attended the inquest for Mr. Weldon and the Uricks."

"The coroner's inquest for the third murders was today," Darcy shared with Southland. "Cowan thought it to the major general's advantage to know who the authorities called in witness."

"Third?" Southland's confusion showed.

"Permit Cowan to share what he discovered today, and then we will bring you up to snuff," Darcy insisted.

The investigator consulted his notebook.

"Rumbradge was the chief witness. He shared very much what he did when we spoke to him. The only new fact included today was Weldon knew a similar fate as Mr. Thorne."

"*Les saints nous sauver*," Darcy said in unnerving accents. "Do you mean to say the perpetrator removed Weldon's eyes?"

Cowan shook off Darcy's assertion.

"No, our murderer removed one of Weldon's ears."

"Wait!" Southland interrupted. "Something of this is all too familiar."

Uncertainty crossed Cowan's expression, and Darcy suspected it was a rare emotion for the investigator.

"Perhaps you should explain, Captain."

Slight caution balanced against certain control marked Southland's explanation.

"We…I mean those who served under the then Colonel Fitzwilliam on the American front once tracked a murderer who mutilated his victims as you described. I should have made the connection when I read the accounts of the crimes in the papers, but it is harvesting time after a wet spring and summer, and I did not attend to the details."

"Perhaps, Cowan and I should describe what we know of the crimes," Darcy suggested; yet, he did not remove his gaze from Southland.

Darcy suspected whatever notice the captain took of Edward's situation would change everything. Southland's lips twisted into a cold line.

"If you will permit a moment for me to relate a story of what occurred in 1812, you may determine whether I should continue my tale. If it is pertinent to Fitzwilliam's situation, I will elaborate further."

Cowan shifted his gaze to Darcy before nodding his permission.

Southland took a nervous sip of his drink.

"As part of King George's troops, I followed Fitzwilliam along the border between Canada and the American front. We were involved in a number of skirmishes, as well as one baffling mystery: We found ourselves chasing a ghost warrior, one who took his revenge in a most disconcerting manner."

A well of disbelief filled Southland's tone.

"We were first summoned to a small settlement on the Upper Canadian border to discover three of the village inhabitants were killed: the butcher, his wife, and the man's child."

Darcy noted how Cowan blanched pale. Southland's tale smacked of familiarity.

"The butcher's family met a gruesome death. Their throats were slit, including that of the babe's. The woman violated. Her left breast cut from her body."

The tension stretched tight between them. Cowan swallowed hard before wetting his lips.

"If you would be so kind, Captain, to start at the beginning of your tale, I am certain Mr. Darcy and I will be most attentive."

For several seconds, the silence hummed sharply in Darcy's ears, before Southland continued: Fitzwilliam and the captain at first thought the rumors of Indian Chief John Norton, a man reportedly part Scot and part Mohawk, turned against the British as true, but they were soon to learn there was more than one mixed blood Indian operating in the area.

"We discovered the British settlers were hesitant to welcome the Indians into their establishments, and so we searched for other possibilities. The then colonel was not pleased to hear his men speak of the Indian warriors as heathens, but when we came across the cruelty exercised in a series of murders, it was natural to look upon the Indian scouts and tribesmen as possible culprits. We all assumed no Englishman would act in such a vile manner, especially against women and children. Later, the circumstances proved us correct, but not in the manner we assumed: the perpetrator was of Indian birth on his mother's side, but the man's savage cruelty also knew the fighting stubbornness of Welsh blood on the paternal side."

"You know the murderer's name?" Cowan asked in anticipation.

"Knew his name," Southland corrected. "The authorities hanged Bleddyn Youngblood for his crimes. The colonel and I stood witness to the man's execution."

Darcy felt the brief glimmer of hope fade before it took root. For a fleeting moment, he thought history set upon repetition.

"London experienced three crimes mimicking what Major General Fitzwilliam witnessed upon the American continent," Cowan summarized. "Yet, from what you said, there were more than three scenes before Youngblood was caught."

"Five in all," Southland confirmed. "Cutting a swath of blood spread over one hundred miles."

"To date, our murderer has been contained to London's East Side," Darcy thought aloud.

"What we must determine is who could be committing these crimes and why he chose to imitate Youngblood while blaming Fitzwilliam," Cowan added.

"Could it be one of those who served under my cousin in America?" Darcy asked.

Southland's shoulders sagged in disapproval.

"I would dislike the idea that one of our men assumed Youngblood's persona, but I suppose the terrors of war can drive a man over the edge."

He raised the stump of his arm with the pinned over sleeve.

"God only knows the demons, which hound me since Waterloo. Do you know, Darcy, sometimes I think the arm still there? The surgeon calls it 'spirit pain.' If not for Mrs. Southland, I would not wish to know the man I became after the war. Anne and Lady Catherine made it their mission never to permit me the leisure of self-pity."

A quiet realization slipped into the menacing tension filling the room.

"The major general knows deep remorse since assuming his role as a landed gentleman," Darcy observed. "My cousin's memories of his service years served as the impetus for his abandonment of Mrs. Fitzwilliam."

Darcy paused long enough for each of them to accept the possibility Edward committed the crimes of which the major general stood accused.

Cowan broke the silence.

"We either must accept the major general's guilt or we must do what we can to prove Edward Fitzwilliam innocent. I choose the latter."

"As do I," Southland authorized.

Cowan did not wait for Darcy's confirmation; the Runner assumed Darcy would agree to what must logically come next.

"Captain, I require the names of any of those who followed Fitzwilliam in America, as well as any information you might recall so we can determine if the men are in London," Cowan instructed. "Possibly, one of the major general's former soldiers saw him in London, and the encounter dragged up the terrors of before. We must discover another possible suspect to distract the authorities from Fitzwilliam."

Darcy scowled.

"Do you expect another attack? It would seem with the news of the major general's arrest the true culprit would abandon his mania."

Cowan spoke with alarming certainty.

"A man who commits such carnage does not think in a sensible manner. He considers himself invincible. Above the law. We must anticipate another attack and be prepared to capture our mystery man in the act."

Darcy swore under his breath.

"Where do we begin? We do not know when or where to search. It is not as if we can defend all of London."

Southland cleared his throat to claim Darcy's and Cowan's attentions.

"Actually, we might know when and the likelihood of his next victims."

"Explain," Darcy said with more brusqueness than he intended. So much speculation went against Darcy's need for careful planning.

Southland drew in a sharp breath.

"If the person we seek truly has knowledge of Youngblood's rampage, he will know the pattern the Welsh-Indian practiced."

Cowan asked, "Such as?"

A sour line crossed Southland's mouth.

"It was the then Colonel Fitzwilliam who first took note of the pattern of the attacks. The second crime occurred four days after the first; the third, eight days after the second; the fourth..."

"Sixteen days after the third," Cowan interrupted. "And two and thirty for the fifth."

"The third murder occurred three days prior," Darcy worked through the dates in his head. "This would be the fourth day. That would mean we have less than a fortnight to discover a murderer before he strikes again."

Cowan grimaced.

"The situation is worse than what you imagine, Darcy. My purpose at Darcy House today was to inform you the magistrate means to convene a grand jury by the end of the week. If a true bill is brought, Fitzwilliam could be tried at Old Bailey and hanged before the authorities discover they executed the wrong man."

Chapter Eleven

When the British Army dispatched Fitzwilliam's men to join the 41st Foot, the then colonel led a simple squad of fifteen men, rather than a full battalion, a fact which proved a bit of luck in their investigation.

"British North America was a secondary theatre," Southland explained. "The real fighting remained with Wellington in Spain, which was where the army sent the bulk of the troops. The defense of the colonies never took precedence, and there were few battle-experienced regiments sent to the American front. Most of those ordered to the area arrived from the West Indies or Ireland or England. The soldiers were green, and it was Fitzwilliam's task to train them to defend the British colonies against the United States."

The captain provided the names of the fifteen men who followed Fitzwilliam along the border between Upper Canada and the American territory. Then he crossed off the names of those he knew lost their lives in later battles.

"Isaac Brock sent more than a hundred men home, many of them Welsh. Many of the 41st Foot were of Welsh ancestry. All returned to England before the colonel and I took our services into the heart of the American campaign."

Cowan studied the list.

"Thankfully, we have only nine to locate. With your permission, Darcy, I would seek the assistance of several of my former Runner associates."

"Whatever it takes," Darcy confirmed. "I will also speak to Lord Matlock regarding the additional expense."

Nodding his agreement, Cowan scratched out a note in his book.

"Now, Southland, you mentioned something of knowledge of the victims."

The captain's light brown eyes darkened.

"It was one of our men, George Ingersoll, who first landed upon the rhyme."

"What rhyme?" Darcy asked in curiosity.

"Surely you know the one: Rub-a-dub-dub, Three men in a tub; And who do you think they be?"

"The butcher, the baker, the candlestick-maker," Cowan finished.

Darcy clenched his hands in frustration.

"Not in the order of the rhyme, but certainly those were the three occupations claimed by our victims. Although Mr. Thorne transitioned from butcher to owner of a public house, I suppose that fact does not matter in the scope of the crimes."

"Upon the American front, the first three attacks involved a butcher, a baker, and a candlestick maker, and in that particular order," Southland confided.

Cowan weaved a worried sigh.

"The rhyme accounts for the first three incidents, but what of those which followed? There are only the three men in the rhyme. Did the perpetrator repeat the pattern?"

Southland abruptly closed his eyes as a shudder racked the captain's body.

"We, too, thought to know an end to the madness after the third attack, but Ingersoll recalled how his mother would say, 'Hey! Rub-a-dub-ho! Rub-a-dub, three maids in a tub.'"

"Do you mean," Darcy's words came out in a sharp whisper, "that the fourth and fifth victims were women?"

"Even more sinister than that," Southland explained. "In both the fourth and fifth crimes, the victims were three women sharing an abode. Each was abused as were the females in the other households."

"I have an unusual question," Darcy said in wariness.

"Such as?"

"Thorne's eyes were removed, and Weldon's ears. Did this Youngblood fellow remove the... the..."

Southland nodded his confirmation.

"Bedlam ruled for Youngblood removed the tongue of one of the women at the fourth scene."

"*Sanbiki no sane*, the mystic apes: *Mizaru, Mikazaru,* and *Mazaru,* carvings upon the Toshogu Shrine," Darcy whispered into the silence. "Never recognizing evil with sight, hearing, or speech. Youngblood was a learned man."

"Which means our interloper will not be easy to discover," Cowan cautioned.

"Yet we must not forsake the former colonel," Southland insisted.

"Certainly not," Cowan agreed. "We will do all within our grasp."

Darcy gazed at the pair askance.

"The task is monumental. Good Lord, how will we protect the women of London against such mania?"

Cowan collapsed in a nearby chair.

"I possess quite a few resources, but I cannot imagine the residents of Wapping will provide complete strangers the names and directions of households populated by women, especially in light of the recent murders. And who is say the culprit will not choose another of London's boroughs for his next attack? Southland says that Youngblood spread his wrath across many miles."

"And the residents recognize us as attempting to prove the major general innocent," Darcy reasoned.

"I am not known, and it would do me well to be of service to my former commander," Southland volunteered. "I owe Fitzwilliam for convincing me to return with an open heart to Anne after my injury."

Darcy thought his cousin should practice what he advised others, but Darcy did not express his opinions.

"Yet, there must be dozens of such homes," Darcy countered. "How will we induce the women to practice care?"

Cowan frowned in exasperation.

"I would say we must convince at least one of the local officers to believe our tale."

"Rumbradge?" Darcy made the logical conclusion.

"Although there is something self-possessing about Officer Rumbradge, the man is thorough in his investigations, and he possesses an inquisitive mind," Cowan confirmed.

Darcy shrugged his confirmation.

"What other choice do we possess?"

Southland wrinkled his nose in dissatisfaction. Confusion held a firm hand upon the captain's countenance.

"I hold one concern."

"Speak it, Captain."

"If I recognized the pattern to these crimes, why has not the major general? Fitzwilliam took the incidents quite hard; the carnage wore havoc upon the then colonel's sense of honor."

A tense silence fell between them. Cowan was the first to speak.

"Perhaps Fitzwilliam does not realize the similarities between the crimes because Mr. Darcy and I did not share *all* the details with the major general."

Southland shot a speculative glance to Darcy.

"Should not your cousin be made aware of the facts?"

Darcy wished he could respond with a resounding affirmation, but a part of him could not trust Edward's judgment. Could not be certain Edward was innocent.

Cowan gave a rueful shake of his head.

"Fitzwilliam's actions showed the major general irrational. My former colonel flirted with destruction even after being placed under suspicion for the first two crimes. Mr. Darcy and I kept our silence because…"

Recognition arrived upon the captain's features.

"Because, slight as it may be, a possibility exists of Major General Fitzwilliam's guilt."

"No!"

Darcy's gaze snapped to the partially opened door to find his sister framed in the portal.

"Georgiana."

He was on his feet to rush to her side; however, a lethal glare delivered in his direction brought Darcy to a stumbling halt.

"My husband," Georgiana said through tight lips, "is not capable of brutality against an innocent. My God, William, you of all people should recognize our cousin's goodness. Father thought enough of Edward to name him to my guardianship with you."

"Georgie."

Darcy edged closer to her.

"Mr. Cowan, Captain Southland, and I are talking our way through every possibility, and despite our deep affection for Edward, in the eyes of the law, the major general possessed the opportunity and the skill to commit the crimes. That fact cannot be dismissed."

Georgiana's back stiffened and her bottom lip trembled.

"Discover the real culprit, William: You promised you would not forsake Edward."

Darcy reached a hand to her.

"I will do my best by our cousin."

He would not say he thought his best would not be enough. Darcy would speak to Elizabeth later on how to prepare Georgiana for the probability of Edward being found guilty and sentenced to hanging.

His sister placed a folded over packet in his hand.

"Another letter for the major general. I would be grateful if you would see my husband receives it in a timely manner."

Darcy accepted it with a nod of agreement.

"When Mr. Cowan, the captain, and I finish our discussion, I will ferry your words to the major general."

It was the least he could do to alleviate Georgiana's qualms. When his sister made her exit, Darcy closed the door behind her.

"I apologize, Darcy," Southland said with true regret. "I did not mean to upset Mrs. Fitzwilliam."

Darcy shook off the man's act of contrition.

"I can no longer protect my sister from the world's evils. Georgiana may not wish to believe Edward guilty, but the citizens of London remain more persuadable."

❧❧❧

Edward maneuvered the single chair in his cell where he might sit in the narrow ray of sunlight cutting through the cell's shadows. He tilted his head back and closed his eyes, permitting the ray's warmth to caress his forehead and cheeks. He missed the feel of the sun and the rain and the wind upon his face.

Darcy made a second visit to him today, this time bringing news that Roman Southland joined Darcy and Cowan upon his behalf. In addition to his cousin's earlier request that Edward dwell upon the location of the missing sword, Darcy asked him to think upon several of the men who served under him. It appeared Cowan and Southland thought one of his former soldiers held some sort of grudge against him.

Edward was not foolish enough to think he made no enemies during the decade he served King George, but he could not imagine any of the men whose feathers he ruffled with Edward's no-nonsense attitude would go to such extremes.

He confirmed that the men upon the list served under him in several campaigns. If he acted as his cousin asked, Edward would be forced to relive countless battles and chilling moments again and again in his attempt to make sense of this new madness.

"As if I did not do so upon a regular basis," he grumbled.

"Think upon the sword," Edward told his weary heart.

His cousin insisted Edward's missing sword would be the key to the government's case against him, but even with the threat of loss of life, Edward could not recall the last time he saw his weapon.

"I would much rather think upon Georgiana's letter," he whispered, "My wife is magnificent. Why did I not recognized her depths previously?"

Edward's lips twitched with amusement in spite of his current misery.

"Because you were too consumed with being Georgiana's guardian rather than her husband."

A deep sigh of disappointment escaped his lips as Edward's eyes opened. With ease, he could imagine the exquisite elegance of Georgiana Fitzwilliam on their first night together: Her self-conscious curiosity. Although they knew each other all of her life, they were strangers in the ways of lovers.

It was then that Edward failed her. He skillfully brought his young wife to completion, but Edward foolishly thought he could place behind him the images of his tending to her cuts and scrapes and purchasing her a new doll for her birthday. Instead of accepting the fact he and Georgiana could use their history to create something unique in his life, Edward permitted his lust to claim her—to pretend their desires were all they held in common.

"Georgiana possesses a kind and generous soul, but I chose to ignore that very essential part of my wife, concentrating purely upon her beauty and her gentility. In many ways, I am no better than that scoundrel George Wickham."

The realization brought a groan of frustration. Edward thought to pray for God's intervention in this dilemma, but somehow he considered the act hypocritical. Although he held a strong belief in God, Edward was not certain his conscious choices were God's doing. Yet, it was tempting to place all his woes in God's hands.

"No," he said with obstinate pride. "The fault remains mine alone. I never once presented Georgiana my wholehearted approval as my wife and partner. If God had a hand in this madness, it was the placing of Georgiana in my path. For certain, it was more than Fate that brought us together. Needless to say, there were any number of young women who would gladly aligned their fortunes with the earldom, but Georgiana possessed no such motives. My wife, if given a Season, could claim a horde of suitors."

Although his poor behavior nettled at Edward's conscience, the idea of Georgiana with another brought a scowl to his expression.

"I would be hard pressed to know another woman, who loves with such pureness. The problem was never with Georgiana," he admitted. As a second son, his future was defined for him. It was only in the past five years that Edward held a hope of offering a woman a bit of normalcy: his maternal grandmother left him Yadkin Hall as part of her marriage settlements. A faint, ironic smile touched Edward's lips.

"Yet, I held myself in check, not permitting the idea of wife and children to take root," he chided, "Edward Fitzwilliam, you are a complete arse! You held perfection in your grasp. You knew the comfort of family—of awakening each morning with Georgiana's head resting upon your shoulder—of the satisfying knowledge you could follow the scent of lilacs through the manor to capture your wife in your embrace—of looking upon Colleen's countenance to observe a mix of your and Georgie's best features—of the promise of more children."

Edward went still.

"I denied my heart its peace for I feared it would know a pain beyond my bearing if I sought such contentment. Now, it could be too late."

❧ ❧ ❧

Early the following morning, Darcy roused the earl from his bed; during the night Darcy considered another ally in identifying the members of Edward's former squadron.

"We must call upon General Leigh-Hunt," he explained as he rushed Matlock through the breakfast offerings. "Edward requires the general's intervention."

Matlock's scowl deepened, a fierce look of consternation crossing his features.

"I promised the countess I would call upon our son before the authorities transferred him to New Prison."

Nerves, and something like dread caused Darcy to swallow hard.

"When did you learn of my cousin's transfer? I ferried another letter from Georgiana to the major general late yesterday afternoon. Although Mr. Cowan and I anticipated the change, Edward spoke nothing of New Prison as a certainty."

Matlock took another sip of his tea.

"The notice came late, after supper last evening. The authorities permitted Edward to send a message to his mother. I assumed a like message arrived for Mrs. Fitzwilliam."

"I assure you, no such notice arrived at Darcy House."

Darcy thought the major general should notify Georgiana first. Even if Darcy's parents remained alive, above all others, Darcy would forward the knowledge of his incarceration first to Elizabeth. Moreover,

Darcy would fear bringing harm to the health of his parents, especially as their years approached their mid to late fifties.

Darcy's eyes remained shrouded in bewilderment.

"I understand your urgency, Sir, but I fear we might require the influence of the earldom with Edward's superiors. Captain Southland arrived in London with a premise Mr. Cowan and I find quite credible. Yet, we require military records to confirm the possibility and to locate potential defense options for Edward's trial."

Matlock fixed Darcy with a direct gaze.

"That promising?"

"It is the first plausible news we possessed since this insanity began. If we are to prove Fitzwilliam innocent, we must act in haste. With the acceleration of Edward's legal entanglements, time is of the essence."

∾∾∾

"Your request is quite unusual, Mr. Darcy." The general leaned into the straight-backed chair.

"My son served England for more than a decade, General," Matlock pressed. "The major general deserves to know the support of the country he honored with his life. I could petition the Prince Regent to intervene, but I would prefer to think the British Army chose to act with credit."

Leigh-Hunt's eyebrow rose, his expression unreadable.

"There is no need for a threat, Your Lordship. It was not my intention to refuse your nephew's request. It does not serve the Army's image well to have one of our premier leaders accused of such heinous crimes."

Darcy breathed a bit easier.

"Thank you, Sir."

He fished into an inside pocket for a copy of the list Captain Southland prepared.

"The captain believes those in the first list met their demise after their service in the Americas, but if it would not be too much difficulty, I would appreciate your confirming Southland's memory. We have no knowledge of those on the second list. We hoped your sources could name whether any are in London."

Leigh-Hunt frowned as he read the list.

"I recall these men; Fitzwilliam hand chose them for reconnaissance work in the back country. Several of them volunteered to follow the then colonel."

"If you have the directions for any or all, Mr. Cowan will send his men to locate the former soldiers," Darcy explained.

Leigh-Hunt shook off the offer.

"With the war's end, I possess soldiers itching for something to do. I will send out men to question each former soldier upon your list. How long do we have?"

Darcy grimaced.

"If the pattern follows the previous crimes, the murderer will attack again on 1 November. We must search London for a man we have yet to identify and who possesses more than a hundred potential victims. However, failure is not an option: I promised my sister never to forsake our cousin." Darcy paused to emphasize his words. "You should be apprised that the authorities will move the major general to New Prison today."

Leigh-Hunt inclined his head in understanding.

"Then we must act with promptness. I will set my men in motion. No more than five days." Darcy said a silent prayer for less. "I will send word tomorrow as to my progress."

⮞⮞⮞

"Mr. Darcy, put down your pen and come with me."

Darcy looked up to find his wife not five feet from his desk. Distracted by his business affairs, he did not hear her enter his study. He returned to his Town house to address more inquiries upon Edward's behalf, as well as to respond to matters of importance for Pemberley. Just because the major general dug himself the figurative grave did not mean life did not continue its daily trudge.

"Is it important, Elizabeth?" he asked with a sigh of frustration.

"Fitzwilliam Darcy," she said with a scowl, "I am not one to make empty requests." He knew his wife fought the urge to fist her hands at her waist. The thought brought a bit of amusement to his lips.

Realizing his deliberate contrariness should not be directed at the woman he loved, Darcy offered her a gentle smile.

"I agree, Mrs. Darcy. No one could ever accuse you of idleness. What I meant to ask, through my misplaced petulance, was whether the matter could wait."

"No, Sir." His wife possessed an easy seductive mixture of good sense and youthful exuberance, and it did Darcy's heart well to look upon her.

He returned his pen to its cradle.

"Will you not provide me a hint as to what awaits me?"

In slow deliberation, Darcy rose to his feet. Unbeknownst to him, exhaustion crept into his joints.

Elizabeth extended her hand to him. She was a charming picture of femininity.

"Not even the smallest possibility."

Darcy caught her hand and permitted his wife to pull him along behind her. Whatever Elizabeth planned to distract him from his duties would be infinitely more pleasurable than what awaited him in his study. There was a time he would refuse her, but the day Darcy spoke his vows with the former Elizabeth Bennet, his priorities changed: always family first.

Entering Elizabeth's sitting room, Darcy discovered a delightful indoor picnic–blanket spread upon the Persian rug, with teacakes, fruit, cold meat, and cheese upon the plates. Wine for him and Elizabeth and lemonade for Bennet, for his children were there also.

"Papa!" Bennet scrambled to his feet.

Darcy ruffled the boy's hair.

"Did you wait for your mother and me?" he asked in a teasing tone.

A cake displayed upon the plate showed the marks of one small bite.

Bennet shot a quick glance to the nibbled-upon cake.

"No, Papa," the child said in contrition. "My insides wud not isten."

Darcy sat upon the blanket's edge and scooped his son upon his lap.

"My insides are screaming also." He kissed the top of Bennet's head. "Even so, a gentleman always waits upon a lady to be seated before he eats."

Darcy glanced up as Elizabeth filled a plate for Bennet. All his male friends warned Darcy of how marriage would bring an end to romance—that the more familiar he and Elizabeth became, the less he would find fascinating in her; yet, his companions erred. There were so many layers to his wife's personality to discover. He doubted he would ever tire of her.

"This was a most pleasing surprise," Darcy said as he placed a kiss upon the top of Bennet's head.

"You assume too much responsibility, my husband," Elizabeth cautioned with a raised eyebrow.

Darcy shrugged off her chastisement.

"The burdens are ones I accept willingly."

"Pemberley and your investments are trials you perform in gladness for they nourish your need to protect your family's name, and they define your self-worth and pride. However, this business with the major general is something beyond the pale."

Discomforted by his wife's piercing scrutiny, Darcy shifted with unease. Considering what was best to say, he watched his son pick at the soft part of the bread.

"What would you have me do, Lizzie?" he asked softly.

"Will seeing Edward punished for deserting Georgiana make you feel more noble?" His wife adjusted Bennet's position so the boy might sit between them. "One should not brood over what cannot be undone. I know you believe the major general's actions a betrayal of your trust, but doing so only eats at your conscience for not protecting Georgiana. Instead, you must change how you perceive the world. Tell me: Do you love me and the children?"

"You know my heart, Elizabeth. I love each of you most violently."

"And Georgiana? You love your sister as well?"

"Likewise."

"Then cease thinking upon this folly as infidelity. Edward's choices affect Georgiana; he did not betray you. Would you not wish for Georgiana to share such exquisite moments as this one?" Self-consciously, Darcy nodded his agreement. "Then see that Georgiana possesses the opportunity to forgive her husband's mistakes. To create her own happiness."

Darcy narrowed his gaze, his features twisting with rueful regret. A sharp, nearly unbearable ache filled his heart. He leaned across Bennet to steal a quick kiss from Elizabeth's tempting lips.

"A man possesses no skills in understanding the female mind, Mrs. Darcy; that being said, I appreciate your sharing your sensibility with me."

"Papa."

"Yes, Darling."

"I werned a new song."

Darcy smiled easily at his firstborn.

"When we have eaten our meal, I will insist you sing it for me. It will be the pinnacle of my day."

Chapter Twelve

"Thank you for agreeing to meet with me, Rumbradge."

When Darcy returned to his study after three quarters' hour with his children and another more intimate hour with Elizabeth, he sent a message to the Shadwell officer, asking the man to call upon him at Darcy House."

Rumbradge screwed up his face in disapproval.

"I was intrigued," Rumbradge admitted. "I hope you do not plan to bribe me not to testify against your cousin. Although I am far from a rich man, I cannot go against the vow I made to uphold the law."

Darcy rubbed his forehead to shove away the lingering headache, which plagued him since this ordeal began. "I expected many responses from you, Rumbradge, but the thought of bribery never crossed my mind. I could not ask a man to abandon his principles."

The officer blanched, and inexplicably Darcy's pulse quicken. It was as if Darcy should recognize something not before him. The puzzle rattled Darcy's sensibility.

"I am glad to hear it."

Darcy knew the man's pride would prevent him from saying more.

"Then why am I here, Mr. Darcy?"

Darcy gestured to a nearby chair.

"May I offer you a drink?"

The man placed his hat and gloves on a small table.

"I will decline."

Rumbradge's gaze did not falter. The man's steady stare was more intense than Darcy recalled. That particular fact multiplied Darcy's qualms regarding seeking the officer's assistance. With purpose, Darcy assumed a casual stance.

"Mr. Cowan and I stumbled upon a point, which could prove my cousin's innocence." Rumbradge's lips held a cynical expression, but Darcy pressed on. "We would ask you to join us. If we are correct, your word would go far in substantiating the truth and in freeing my cousin."

Rumbradge's gaze seemed to sharpen.

"You wish me to work for you and Mr. Cowan to prove the major general innocent and my evidence against him in error?"

Darcy shook his head in the negative.

"I wish you to seek the truth. If my cousin is innocent, it is your duty to find the real guilty party." Darcy studied the man's features, and there was something different about the man, but Darcy could not say what it was. "Will you not hear me out?"

The officer presented Darcy a curt nod of agreement.

"I suppose you should start from the beginning, Mr. Darcy. I would find it an offense if you were not completely honest in this matter. I mean to uphold the law, Sir. I appreciated Mr. Cowan's expertise with the Weldon scene, but I will not be swayed by misdirection. Just you know that, Mr. Darcy."

Rumbradge listened with a large dose of uncertainty. Yet, when Mr. Cowan arrived, the Shadwell officer agreed to accompany Cowan to Wapping to discover a means of identifying potential victims.

"If what you disclosed is true, we have an impossible task," Rumbradge grumbled as he trailed Cowan from the room.

Darcy agreed. However, they held few alternatives in the matter.

As if God sent them a bit of hope, late in the day, word came from Leigh-Hunt. One of the men on Captain Southland's list was employed in the timber trade near Greenland Docks, several miles outside of London, while a second held a position in a bank along Fenchurch Street, near where the Gardiners once resided. Elizabeth's aunt and uncle recently turned over the running of Gardiner's London warehouses to a nephew on Mrs. Gardiner's side of the family, a young man from Lambton, who apprenticed with Gardiner for the past ten years.

Meanwhile, the Gardiners established a like business in Edinburgh. If Darcy's estimations proved true, Elizabeth's aunt and uncle would soon assume a role in Society, as did Charles Bingley. Darcy would live to see the Gardiner daughters making their Come Outs and claiming gentlemen husbands.

Sharing the information with the captain, Darcy and Southland chose to call upon both men. Leigh-Hunt's message stated of the other seven soldiers they sought, one took his own life, while six were scattered across England. The general sent men to determine if any of those six recently spent time in London.

In late afternoon, Darcy and the captain sought one Morgan Pugh among the employees leaving the Cheapside bank at closing.

"There!" Southland nodded. "The one with the gray hat."

Darcy's gaze found the man—likely thirty plus years of age, but appearing older. Thin and lanky. Sharp-nosed and thick eyebrows. Not a countenance claiming trust.

Southland moved to intercept the man.

"Pugh!" the captain called.

He greeted the former soldier while Darcy looked on.

"It has been years."

"Lieutenant Southland!"

Pugh's lips displayed a broad smile, which faded when he noted Roman's pinned sleeve.

"My apologies, Sir; I did not realize."

He gestured to Roman's missing arm. Southland grimaced.

"A present from Napoleon," he murmured in that self-effacing tone Darcy now recognized as part of Southland's pride. "I still possess one good hand."

Roman extended his arm, and Pugh accepted it in a firm handshake.

"Pugh, may I present my friend, Mr. Darcy. Darcy is Fitzwilliam's cousin." Southland paused only briefly. "Mr. Darcy, this is Lieutenant Morgan Pugh."

"It is simply *Mister* Pugh now," the man confirmed. "I left the military when my father passed, and I became responsible for the family. I departed before Napoleon's first capture."

Darcy sang Southland's praises for he knew Roman would not.

"Southland achieved the rank of captain for his efforts in King George's service. He is also part of my and Fitzwilliam's family for he married another cousin. Southland oversees a great estate in Kent and claimed fatherhood, all since returning to England."

"No one deserves it more, Southland. You were always one to accept responsibility without question," Pugh said with true admiration.

"Do you have time to share a drink; I have a matter of import to discuss with you?" Southland asked.

Pugh glanced about to assure privacy.

"Is it this business with the former colonel? I could not make my mind understand such censure being placed upon Fitzwilliam's name."

Southland shot a glance to Darcy before making his suggestion.

"Come join Mr. Darcy and me for a drink, and I will explain."

Other than Southland asking of Pugh's family situation, their trio walked in silence to the nearest public house. When they settled, the captain began, "This situation with the major general is a mockery of his good name."

"I agree." Pugh glanced to Darcy. "I would think the accusations difficult for Fitzwilliam's father. It is hard to imagine an earl's son could encounter such charges."

"My cousin is bearing up well under the circumstances, but the major general is in need of anyone who may hold knowledge, which will free him," Darcy said simply.

Pugh scowled, a repressive lift of his eyebrow announcing his thoughts.

"I am confused, Mr. Darcy. If you believe I hold such knowledge, then speak so. I would be pleased to be of service to Fitzwilliam."

"Have you encountered the major general since you last served under Fitzwilliam?" Southland asked.

"Why would I?" Pugh gestured to his surroundings. "It is not as if the former colonel and I travel in the same social circles."

Despite the man's earlier declaration of support for his commanding officer, Darcy listened to the falsehoods in the Pugh's tones; even so, Darcy could not pinpoint the exact weaknesses in the man's tale.

"My cousin is not one to permit a man's station to define him; yet, that particular fact aside, as my wife's uncle is Edward Gardiner, I know for a fact Major General Fitzwilliam often called in Cheapside." Darcy noted the surprise Pugh attempted to mask.

"I was not aware of Mrs. Darcy's connection to Mr. Gardiner, whose business connections in the area are quite extensive," Pugh said in apology. "Nonetheless, I did not encounter Fitzwilliam during one of his calls upon the Gardiners."

"What of outside Cheapside?" Southland asked before Pugh had time to think upon another excuse. "Not so long past, we spoke to Private Walters: He encountered the major general near a public house."

Darcy recognized the half-truths Southland pronounced for their benefit. "No one suggested you spent time with the major general, we simply hoped you held a bit of knowledge, which would aid Fitzwilliam. Do you never leave Cheapside? Have you seen Major General Fitzwilliam upon London's streets—even at a distance?"

Pugh shifted in discomfort before taking a sip of his drink. Darcy's revered father taught Darcy the art of negotiations and how to know when to trust a man's words: Without a doubt, Darcy knew Pugh spoke without truth.

"I can say in earnest I've not laid eyes upon my former colonel since we parted upon the American docks."

Southland's expression said the captain held similar thoughts as Darcy as to the credibility of Morgan Pugh.

"Is there anything else you care to share with us? I assure you, Mr. Darcy and I are at our wits' ends. We are pursuing every possibility."

Pugh's face paled, but he remained watchful. The silence between them fell heavy with awkwardness. Finally, Pugh offered a strained smile.

"I did possess one thought upon the matter."

Southland's lips turned down, and Darcy read the captain's thoughts: Southland knew disappointment. The captain hoped not to name his former friend duplicitous.

"Please share it with us," Southland spoke as if he held no idea what Lieutenant Pugh would say.

"I am surprised it did not cross your mind, Southland."

Darcy felt a flare of anticipation rush into his stomach: Pugh knew something of the murders. Yet, was it enough to shift the focus from Edward?

"The crimes described in the newsprints are of the same nature as those we stumbled upon in Upper Canada."

"Are they?" Southland played the fool. "How so?"

Pugh's chest puffed out with pride.

"I cannot be certain, but I thought of Youngblood when I read of the second murders—of the killing of a husband and a wife and a servant. That realization led me to reflect upon the Vaughns' murders, with the baby and all."

Southland smiled as if in grateful relief.

"And you think the major general's situation smacks of that dreadful time upon the American continent?"

Pugh sported what was a deliberate blank expression.

"I am sorry to say I wondered if my former colonel chose to repeat a series of murders, which once plagued him."

The banker's lips held an all-knowing expression.

"I apologize, Mr. Darcy. I do not mean to give offense."

"No offense taken, Pugh. I prefer a man to speak with frankness, even when we do not agree."

❧❧❧

Darcy meant to accompany Southland the following morning to question Maxen Rhys, but his plans changed when Georgiana announced Matlock bribed several of the guards at New Prison so the Countess of Matlock could spend time in private with Edward. Aunt Nora asked Georgiana to accompany her.

"I will not permit my sister to attend to the countess's wishes without my attending her. I cannot imagine what tick nested in the earl's head to make Matlock think this would be acceptable," Darcy offered in explanation. "However, it would be difficult to dissuade Mrs. Fitzwilliam now that the countess extended the offer. All I can do is to protect my sister from the worst of the prison's conditions."

"Certainly, Darcy." Southland retrieved his hat and glove from a nearby table. "I understand my role in this endeavor." Darcy and the captain spent several hours deconstructing the possible reasons for Pugh's suspicious behavior.

"The then colonel chose Pugh and two others as part of his unit. We were traveling into an area where the majority of the English soldiers were of Welsh abstraction. Fitzwilliam wished to surround himself with those who possessed similar backgrounds and experiences as did the men the colonel would command."

"Perhaps the hesitation we heard in Pugh's speech was the man concentrating on the omission of his Welsh accent. I cannot imagine the Welsh tongue would serve him well in his position at the bank," Darcy offered.

"I would hope your estimation the cause," Southland agreed with a reluctant shrug of his shoulders, but it was evident from the captain's tone that both Darcy and Southland thought Pugh hid some important fact from them.

❧ ❧ ❧

Georgiana waited with annoyance as Aunt Nora sobbed in Edward's arms. She understood the countess's anguish, but Georgiana could not comprehend why her mother in marriage could not observe how the countess's actions brought more turmoil to Edward's countenance.

When Fitzwilliam entered the room set aside for their reunion, her husband appeared pale and a bit thinner, but Edward's eyes spoke of relief at seeing her.

"It is a beginning," Georgiana's heart whispered while her mind announced, "Yet, it may be too late." Even so, a hint of a smile crossed her lips in response to the conscious quickening of the pulse point at the base of Edward's neck.

Upon Edward's appearance, the countess launched herself into her son's arms, and there Aunt Nora remained as the minutes ticked by. The authorities permitted them only a quarter hour, and Georgiana could not help but wonder if she were to be honored with a few minutes of privacy with her husband before the guards returned to escort Edward away.

William evidently took note of Georgiana's agitation for her brother whispered to the earl, and Matlock rose to dislodge his wife from their son's tight clasp.

"I love you best," the countess declared as Lord Matlock guided her away from where Edward stood. Georgiana heard her husband respond, "I love you more."

Georgiana recognized the common exchange between mother and son, one heard often in the Matlock household. Despite Georgiana's best efforts, she felt the familiar twinge of envy, never knowing her mother, Georgiana felt deprived of such tenderness.

Georgiana looked on: The countess's protestations faded as Matlock led his wife from the room. Darcy, too, stepped into the passageway, and she and Fitzwilliam were alone at last.

She presented Edward a watery smile.

"Are you well?"

"I am now," Edward growled as three long strides closed the distance between them, and he caught her to him. "Good Lord, Georgie, I missed you."

A rending ache clawed its way through her veins as his mouth claimed hers. Edward's moan of anguish filled her, and Georgiana's need responded. She opened her lips so he might claim her.

Her breasts pressed hard against her husband's chest, as her arms encircled his neck. She felt as if they had been apart for years. Perhaps they never knew each other until that very moment. Edward lifted her to him before he released her lips.

"I dreamed of this moment so often."

Edward skimmed Georgina's cheek and neck with a series of wet kisses, her lips throbbing from his passion, and the knowledge she affected him brought Georgiana a private thrill. Yet she wanted more from Edward than his need. She desired her husband's heart.

"We have so little time," Georgiana whispered as she rested her head upon Edward's damp shirtfront.

"I wasted our time together," Edward admitted.

"No," she corrected. "We created Colleen together, and our daughter is perfection."

Edward broke his hold and sank onto a nearby chair.

"I disappointed you and Colleen." Her husband clasped his head in his hands.

Georgiana moved to sit beside him, her hand resting upon Edward's thigh.

"You were always your fiercest enemy, my husband. I shan't offer you absolution," she declared. "For I know your nature. If I permit you to wear the cloak of martyr, then you will do so."

Georgiana caught Edward's chin and lifted it so she might look upon his features.

"Instead, I will proclaim you the best of men. Every night and every day for the remainder of our days, I shall repeat those words to you and pray you will accept my challenge."

Edward swallowed hard, his Adam's apple working against his obvious emotions.

"I never deserved you, Georgiana Fitzwilliam."

"Do not speak in the past," Georgiana pleaded. "I cannot bear to think upon what might be."

Edward caught her hand and brought her fingers to his mouth for a kiss.

"I must bring more grief to your door," he said with deep regret. "The charges against me will be read in the next few days."

Georgiana felt the blackness rush to her head, but she shoved her fears aside. If nothing else, Darcy taught her to listen to all the facts. "

"Does not a hope exist that the magistrates will bring no indictment?"

"I would like to think so, but my doubts rule," her husband admitted. "Darcy and Cowan assure me there is enough evidence to tend me over for trial. It will be another black moment."

If her husband had his way, Edward would be marked forever as a *murderer*. Of late, she wondered if the major general accepted the idea of being labeled as a killer of the innocent as punishment for the number of lives he claimed in the name of war.

"Will you not fight for Colleen and me? For our life together?"

"Certainly, I intend to perform as Darcy advises, but we must be realistic, Georgie. It would be a sound slap in the face of the aristocracy if I am named guilty of these crimes."

He brought the back of her gloved hand to rest against his chest.

"Men have died for less than what is charged against me."

"And without you, what is to become of Colleen's future?" she demanded.

"My beautiful wife," her husband whispered as he caressed Georgiana's cheek. An odd sort of shadow flickered in the depths of his eyes. "It is so like you not to ask of your future."

Georgiana's chin rose in defiance.

"When I gaze upon your countenance, I behold my future. I shall serve our daughter well, but without you, my stars will grow dim."

Edward shook his head in denial.

"I wish you a long and fulfilling life, Georgiana."

Everything within her broke, but Georgiana fought for her composure: the major general meant to set her free.

"I spoke to the earl, and Matlock agreed to make arrangements for you and Colleen to live abroad. I know Darcy will wish for you to return to Pemberley, but the stigma of my trial will haunt Colleen's future. You must promise me, Georgie, you will take her away from England."

Georgiana wished to curse the injustice: Her husband not only meant to abandon her without a fight, but Fitzwilliam meant to banish her and their daughter to a life without family to support them. She wanted to lash out at Edward and his pompous all-knowing attitude.

"I shall only promise to listen to Uncle Matlock's arguments," she hissed. "But the decision will be mine alone, especially as my husband appears determined to punish his family."

"I apologize, Georgiana," Edward said in that somewhat condescending tone she had grown to despise.

"If you offer me another apology, Edward Fitzwilliam, I swear I shall strike you." She was on her feet and pacing. "I despise this woebegone mantra you assumed. Where is the man I knew all my life? The man who claimed the trust of each man who served under him…"

Georgiana halted her progress: Edward treated her with the same type of care he displayed with each of the raw recruits the major general turned into seasoned soldiers. With the same loving nature, her husband always displayed with her. With the same conscious deliberation Georgiana's late father recognized in his nephew.

"I promise," she said through trembling lips. "I promise to oversee Colleen's future with the same enthusiasm as you did mine, and if leaving England will best serve our daughter, then I shall welcome the opportunity to explore the world. Colleen will enjoy each minute of every day. I warrant my loyalty to you and our daughter."

Edward stood to wrap Georgiana in his embrace. His kiss spoke of tenderness.

"Georgie," he whispered close to her ear. "I have one last request."

He paused to place a stray curl behind her ear.

"It is not something of which you will readily agree."

Without his pronouncing the words, Georgiana knew what her husband would say. She attempted to pull from his grasp, but Edward tightened his hold.

"Please do not ask it of me!"

She succumbed to a strangling sob. The tears she withheld since walking into the room streamed down her cheeks.

"Georgie, you must see what my situation does to my mother and father," he whispered on a dry rasp. "The earl aged a decade in the last month, and my mother...I cannot bear to think what my public hanging..."

She heard the terror in his breathy inhalation.

"It will kill her, Georgie. You will suffer, but you will survive because of Colleen."

Edward pulled her to him.

"I promise I will do nothing until the last moment. Permit me to name my death on my terms. If you truly love me, you will allow me my last prideful action."

Georgiana's shoulders shook from the sobs she wished to hide. Her fingers clawed at the line of his coat.

"Tell me what you wish of me," she pronounced in defeat.

"When next we are together, bring me the Queen Anne pistol—the one the earl presented me with my first commission. Be certain it is loaded. It is all of which I can think to do if this matter plays to script."

Chapter Thirteen

"Did the major general say something to upset you? You appear quite distracted."

Darcy watched his sister lace the ribbon holding her reticule closed through the fingers of her gloved hand for nearly a quarter hour. In complete silence, Georgiana permitted Darcy to escort her from the private room provided for their visit with Edward and into his waiting carriage. She had yet to speak of her conversation with her husband, and that particular fact worried Darcy more than her quiet tears.

"No," Georgiana said in too much haste for Darcy's sensibilities. "My husband expressed concern for the effect his incarceration had upon his parents."

Darcy could not keep the scowl from his lips.

"And what of the effect upon you and Colleen? Has the major general no regard for the pain he brought you?"

Georgiana's gaze left Darcy's and sought the passing scenery.

"As long as I have Colleen as my impetus, my husband considers me capable of surviving the worst God can deliver. Do you judge me otherwise, Brother?"

Her eyes returned to his in a challenge. Darcy's frown deepened, and a feeling of things beyond his control pierced his awareness.

"I admit to knowing difficulty in thinking of you as a wife and a mother—of your being more than my beguiling little sister. Even so, I never thought of you as unqualified. The only attribute you ever required was a bit of self-confidence. I like to flatter myself in thinking my choosing Elizabeth as your sister provided you the opportunity to accept your mettle."

"Then when I make the decision to follow my husband's lead, you must trust my judgment," she said in cold tones, but Darcy recognized the hidden double *entendre* in his sister's meaning.

꙳ ꙳ ꙳

Nothing much occurred over the following two days, and Darcy knew he should celebrate the silence and use the lull to concentrate on his estate business, but instead the silence drove him nearly mad. More of the nature of a caged animal, even Elizabeth and his children gave Darcy a wide berth.

"Tell me something worth knowing," he demanded of Thomas Cowan when the investigator appeared at Darcy House in midday.

Cowan collapsed into a chair. With regret, Darcy noted his friend's countenance spoke of Cowan's complete exhaustion. As well as maintaining his full schedule of appointments for his firm, the man devoted countless hours to Edward's investigation.

"I fear you will not be pleased with much of my news."

"Do you have anything *positive* to report?" Darcy felt as fatigued as Cowan appeared. He leaned a hip on the corner of his desk.

Cowan scrubbed his cheeks with his dry palms.

"Spoke to Rumbradge earlier today. The officer alerted the local watchmen regarding the possibility of another attack. He asked the watchmen to warn the households under their jurisdictions, which include multiple women occupants."

"Is there a probability we are correct on this crazy scheme?" Darcy asked with renewed doubt.

"I witnessed stranger happenings." Cowan leaned into the chair's cushions. "Bloody hell, we both conquered insanity in your Cousin Samuel's death, why should we not prevail again?"

Darcy scowled, the lines of his forehead deepening.

"There are several hundred thousand people in London," he protested.

"One thing I know about criminals: They follow patterns. Certainly London's populace is large, but only a few can take down the King's piece in the game of strategy. We will saturate the streets with men on the eve of the first and pray to know success. Sometimes we must place our trust in God to aid our efforts."

"Even though more deaths will prove Edward's innocence, I want no one else to know such devastation."

Cowan sat straighter.

"Your comment brings me to the ill part of my news. Rumbradge sent word the grand jury will convene on Monday."

"So soon?"

The information stunned Darcy.

"I hoped a true bill would not be delivered until closer to the first of the month. What if my cousin is tried prior to the next attack?"

"As Monday is the twenty-eighth, it is probable the major general will be brought to trial before month's end."

Cowan appeared most anxious.

"We are aware of the prospect Fitzwilliam will be found guilty," Darcy nodded his agreement. "All the same, it will be several days following the trial before he is brought to hanging."

"We can only hope, but what if the authorities mean to be rid of the case before the rabble rise up to claim my cousin's body?"

Darcy experienced a flare of panic in his stomach.

"What if the real criminal does not act again until after Edward's execution?"

Cowan shook off the possibility.

"We must depend upon the attacker's arrogance. At the moment, he thinks himself supreme and the authorities lacking forethought. Even if Fitzwilliam is found guilty, our assailant will make his appearance. He will assume no one will think to expect another attack—will realize even if the crime is discovered prior to the major general's execution, the authorities will believe the deaths the work of a poor imitator. The law will be slow to reverse its opinion of Fitzwilliam's guilt."

❧ ❧ ❧

Georgiana found her husband's pistol among the major general's belongings retrieved by Darcy's servants when they tended Edward after his removal from The Sephora, but she left the weapon at the bottom of the bag the major general carried to London.

"How can I participate in my husband's death?" Georgiana asked multiple times over the three nights and two days since she saw Edward.

"The major general demanded your promise," Georgiana argued with her reflection in the dressing room mirror. "And you made the pledge rather than to disappoint your husband."

"I could not deny Fitzwilliam's plea," she countered. "Aunt Nora's lamentations played heavy upon Edward's conscience. I never witnessed him so distraught. Yet, even with my husband's pain, I am not brave enough to permit him to claim his life. Such an act is against God's teachings.

"But to think of Edward hanging at the end of a rope—of witnessing the life being ripped from his body—suffering so."

Georgiana shivered with dread.

"I cannot permit such degradation to claim him. My husband was a war hero—a great leader of men. The major general merits his dignity, and Edward did promise not to use his weapon unless he possessed no other alternatives."

A soft knock accompanied her brother's entreaty.

"Georgiana? Are you within? It is William."

"Yes," she called as she dabbed at her eyes with a damp handkerchief and pinched the skin at her cheekbone for a bit of color. "Come in, William."

The door opened to display the familiar worried countenance of her brother.

"Are you well? Elizabeth says you missed your midday meal. Mrs. Darcy feared your visit with the major general left you distraught."

Georgiana stood, but she did not meet his eyes. William often had that effect on her. Self-consciously, she smoothed the wrinkles from her gown.

"I forgot the time, but Sarrie brought me some bread and butter and fresh tea upon a tray. I apologize if I worried Elizabeth."

"Your sister wishes only what is best for you, as do I," William assured.

Georgiana glanced up to note the look in her dear brother's eyes—the unspoken questions of honest concern.

"You and Elizabeth are very patient with me. No one could ask for a better brother and sister."

William did not speak for several minutes; they stood in silence, each deep in his personal misery. At length, William sighed.

"I thought you should know, Mr. Cowan brings the news the major general will be brought before a grand jury on Monday. I mean to call upon our cousin to determine what he knows of the proceedings. If you insist upon attending the magistrates' call, Elizabeth and I will escort you. In truth, I would prefer you would permit me to act upon the family's behalf in this matter."

"Would you remain at Darcy House if Elizabeth were the accused?" Georgiana challenged.

William shook off the suggestion.

"You know I would not."

"I love Edward equal to your affections for Elizabeth. I shall see this through to its bitter end."

Her bottom lip trembled, and William reached for her; yet, Georgiana took a step backwards. It would be too easy to accept her brother's comfort. In William's embrace, her weaknesses and her insecurities would reign, but there was no time for such girlish foibles: Edward expected her to be strong, and Georgiana meant to see him proud in his choice of her as his wife.

"I would appreciate being made aware of the specifics of the major general's call to the grand jury."

"As you wish," William said, any irritation he felt for her stubbornness concealed. "I should go. The day is fast falling into evening."

Georgiana swallowed hard the guilt choking her breathing.

"Be safe, William, and if the opportunity arrives, express my devotion to the major general. Tell Edward all he requires of me, as his wife, will be done. Assure him I shall keep all my promises to him."

༃ ༃ ༃

"What do you make of Georgiana's worried resolve since her visit with the major general?"

Darcy and Elizabeth snuggled together upon a chaise in the sitting room after Georgiana excused herself following supper. Captain Southland agreed to dine with the Matlocks, and so the Darcys had the room to themselves. In distraction, Darcy stroked his wife's back as she rested her head against his chest.

"It is all so very odd. For weeks our sister was a watering pot, but now her grief turns in upon itself. Georgiana does not speak of what occurred, and that fact brings me the most worry."

Elizabeth's finger traced the rounded edge of the ruby in Darcy's stickpin.

Darcy bent to kiss the top of his wife's head.

"Edward appeared quite satisfied when I delivered Mrs. Fitzwilliam's message. It was the first time I observed the major general's calm, and I find his reaction disconcerting. It provides me pause to wonder what promises the major general exacted from my sister."

"It is obvious Edward and Georgiana came to a new understanding, but the basis of their compromise remains unknown to the likes of me. It is perplexing."

Darcy lifted Elizabeth's chin where he might look upon his wife's handsome features.

"Elizabeth, I am conflicted," he said with a heavy sigh. "I told myself it is best…that I must protect you from this insanity, but…"

"Mr. Darcy," his wife's familiar scolding tone gave him comfort. "I am not made of fine porcelain."

Darcy smiled: Elizabeth never disappointed.

"What I would divulge is not easy for a man to stomach; yet…"

"Yet, you require a different perspective," she said with smugness. "I suppose both Mr. Cowan and Captain Southland are aware of what you mean to speak."

"I will not apologize for seeking the advice of two intelligent men," Darcy teased.

Elizabeth's eyebrow rose in a customary challenge.

"However, the insights of an intelligent woman are not beyond your needs."

Darcy kissed her upturned nose.

"A woman who improves her mind by extensive reading is exactly what I require every moment of every day for the rest of my life."

≈≈≈

Before they broke their fast, word arrived early Monday morning from the earl stating he received a two-line message from Edward. The major general informed his family he would not be transported to the magistrate's hall. Darcy thought it odd, but he passed the message to Georgiana, who announced she would not accompany Darcy to the proceedings and planned to return to her quarters.

Darcy was not certain whether his sister knew relief or frustration at not being required to view the grand jury's evidence. Cowan also thought the situation did not play to form.

"In such a case, I would think the few possible witnesses would be particularly questioned as to whether they recognized the accused."

As she placed jam on her toast, Elizabeth spoke absent-mindedly.

"Perhaps the magistrates questioned the major general last evening."

Darcy shot a glance to Cowan, who nodded his agreement.

"After the proceedings, I think it best if the earl and I call in at New Prison," Darcy announced.

Elizabeth's forehead crunched up in disapproval.

"I assume you mean to inform your cousin of what you learned."

"Certainly," Darcy said in too much haste, and his wife's frown lines deepened.

Elizabeth placed her knife down with a heavy hand.

"And your true reason for calling upon the major general? It will be quite late."

Darcy rolled his eyes heavenward.

"It is quite bewildering to have you know me so well, Mrs. Darcy."

"I am waiting for a response to my question, Mr. Darcy. You shan't divert my curiosity with your flattery."

Cowan's grin widened.

"I will save you, Darcy. It is a sad fact, Ma'am, that some magistrates use force upon a prisoner in order to elicit a confession."

Elizabeth paled, but his wife maintained her composure.

"If such a fate befell the major general, I expect you and the earl to bring down the family's wrath upon Middlesex. Do you understand me, Mr. Darcy? Although I know this trial is a dire situation, there is always the hope reason will rule, but I will not tolerate those who manipulate the justice we English claim most dear!"

"Yes," Darcy said without artifice.

In the four years of their marriage, he knew never to cross his wife when she spoke in that precise tone.

"I will act to right the family's reputation."

Elizabeth placed her serviette upon the table.

"I plan to attend this proceeding today. If you will excuse me…"

"Do you think that wise, Mrs. Darcy?" Captain Southland asked.

Elizabeth leveled a steady gaze upon the man, and Darcy knew Southland still had much to learn regarding stifling his opinions in the presence of a decisive woman.

"Captain, I supposed your residing with Lady Catherine De Bourgh would assist you in the knowledge that some women should not be questioned when their minds are set on a task. However, it appears you require a reminder. I mean to accompany my husband in this matter. Only he has the right to object, and I believe my husband possesses too much intelligence to do so. Mr. Darcy described the murder scenes, and I will hear the worst the Middlesex Sessions House can provide. Now, please excuse me while I give the household instructions for the day."

♁ ♁ ♁

"What brought your notice to Major General Fitzwilliam?" the magistrate asked the night watchman whose jurisdiction included The Sephora.

"I's stopped to check upon the establishment, and Mr. Martindale, the innkeeper, mentioned the sorry state of the officer's clothing. I knows me duty so I spoke to the Thames police."

Darcy suspected the man had stopped for a drink or two rather than doing his actual duty, but no one in the audience would give a care for that fact.

"Did you view the major general's uniform?"

The watchman, a Mr. Bernard, shook his head in the negative.

"No, but Mabs described it as covered across the chest and over the left shoulder with dark stains."

Next up was Mr. Richards, one of the Bow Street Runners who called upon Darcy House to question Edward.

"Were you able to retrieve the major general's uniform when you took the officer in for his initial questioning?"

"No, Sir. The major general's cousin, Mr. Darcy, said he burned the uniform to protect his household from the fleas and lice the major general carried home from Wapping to Mayfair."

A scoff of condemnation crossed the countenances of the other members of the audience.

Darcy stiffened, but he did not turn his head to look upon their disapproving expressions. Mr. Richards would be sorry to learn his words elicited no response from Darcy. When Richards shot a glance to Cowan, whose glare hardened into something lethal, Richards softened his remarks.

"To his credit, Mr. Darcy does have several small children in his household, and I am certain the gentleman meant only to protect his family. Moreover, Mr. Darcy's actions were before suspicion rested upon the major general's shoulders, so I doubt anyone would think Mr. Darcy manipulated the evidence. Mr. Darcy explained the stains quite thoroughly: Major General Fitzwilliam was in an altercation with several men who meant to impress Fitzwilliam upon an outgoing ship."

Elizabeth slipped her hand into Darcy's, but he looked straight ahead, as did his wife, Lindale, the earl, Southland, and Cowan. They each learned long ago when to harden their countenances. No shouts of dismay or denial would fuel the magistrate's taunt for they came to Middlesex to learn more of the prosecutor's case against Edward.

"And what of the major general's sword?" the magistrate prompted.

"Shadwell found a sword with a broken tip at the first murder," Richards continued. "When we questioned the major general regarding his sword, Fitzwilliam explained he could not recall the last time he saw the weapon. Without doubt, the major general spent many hours drowning his sorrows in spirits, but Fitzwilliam admitted wearing the sword when he departed Oxfordshire for London."

"Who is to say there are not more than one sword?" Elizabeth hissed from her mouth's corner.

"Shush," Darcy warned, but he squeezed her fingers to say he understood her indignation.

At length, the court called Rumbradge to testify. The officer described the murders in great detail, including the condition of the bodies, the weapons, the bloody footprints, and the conjectures made based upon the evidence. Unfortunately, nothing new came to light from the officer's testimony. The man kept his own counsel regarding the possibility of a repeat performance by the attacker.

Darcy found the workings of the magistrates' court interesting. The prosecutor did not bring forth any contradictory evidence: Nothing from the harbormaster, Mr. Belker, the medical attendants to the sailors with whom Edward fought, nor the woman from the tenements behind the third scene.

Had the authorities kept the major general from today's proceedings to silence any objections Edward might lodge to the case against him? It appeared probable that the authorities wished to rid themselves of the case, and arranging for the major general's speedy trial would resolve the issue of their incompetence.

Although Darcy expected a grand jury would hear the evidence, he was quick to learn in charges of murder formed by coroner's juries, the grand jury did not need to approve the case for it to be sent to trial. The magistrates held Edward's case over based on evidence: The date set for the trial was 31 October, the day before the next attack would supposedly occur.

Chapter Fourteen

"Lindale, would you escort Mrs. Darcy home? Lord Matlock and I should call upon your brother," Darcy instructed.

The viscount nodded his agreement.

"Inform your mother I shan't be long," the earl instructed.

Darcy squeezed Elizabeth's hand in parting.

"We will discuss this when I return to Darcy House," he whispered for her ears only. "I mean to ask Cowan and Southland to join us."

"Be safe, my husband," she said before departing on Lindale's arm.

The room cleared. The poor of Middlesex filed out, each discussing the merits of the evidence. Darcy and Matlock waited until they were alone in the earl's carriage before either spoke of what they observed.

"Have you employed a competent barrister to assist Edward?" Darcy stared out the window at the approaching dusk.

"You know I would not hesitate to secure legal counsel for my son." Weariness colored the earl's words.

"We should meet with the man tomorrow," Darcy suggested in equal tones of exhaustion. "In my estimation, Edward will require several legal minds to address his case. I did not like how today's proceedings performed. Edward should have a say in the evidence. This was nothing more than a magistrate's hearing with an absent defendant. Shadwell is assuming too much latitude in this matter."

"I will ask Mr. Hutchison to call upon me tomorrow." The earl pushed his fingers through his thinning hair. "If my son walks away from this unscathed, it will be a miracle."

"None of us will invite a new day unscathed," Darcy predicted.

A half hour later, they waited for Edward's gaolers to escort him into the private room they employed previously. As Darcy feared, it took two men to *walk* the major general into the room, each man supporting Edward under his cousin's arm. Without ceremony, they dropped Fitzwilliam into the room's only chair.

"I will see to this offense," Matlock growled.

"Southland, assist the earl," Darcy instructed.

He signaled to the captain to prevent Matlock from committing an act, which would bring further abuse to Edward's cell door. If the earl employed his status in Society in his threats, it would prove rough for his son.

Meanwhile, Cowan braced Edward against the back of the chair.

"Where are your injuries, Sir?"

Edward attempted to suck in a deep breath.

"My ribs," he murmured.

Cowan's fierceness showed upon his lips and rang in his tone.

"I will fetch the necessary bandages and ointment."

Darcy felt a bit sorry for whoever committed this offense. Cowan remained a loyal friend to his former commanding officer, and he held no doubt the investigator would "express" his displeasure, in all probability, more effectively than would Matlock.

Darcy replaced Cowan at Edward's side. He placed a steadying hand upon his cousin's shoulder.

"I realize you are in pain, but time is short and we must speak regarding today's hearing. I suspect once Matlock addresses your condition with the higher ups, the authorities will push back by denying us full access to you."

A faint consternation crossed Edward's expression, but he did not respond. "The magistrates presented a compelling case against you. You were held over for trial in three days—31 October."

"All Hallows Eve. How appropriate for a murder trial," Edward murmured.

Darcy took no note of the date's significance until his cousin's remark.

"A night to remember the dead," Darcy said in quiet response. "I pray it does not become a day beyond our control."

In obvious discomfort, Edward shifted in the chair.

"Tell me quick what I must know. I would prefer your calculated intelligence to the earl's passionate response."

Darcy did not approve of his cousin's evaluation of Darcy's personality, but he did not argue.

"The magistrates called upon the night watchman from the Sephora, Mr. Richards, the Bow Street Runner who questioned you regarding your sword and your bloody uniform, and Mr. Rumbradge.

Nothing new came from the proceedings, but I fear the prosecutor only disclosed enough to bring about the true bill, but, more damaging evidence will be forthcoming."

Edward's fingers tightened against his side, and his cousin exhaled in pain.

"What should I do?"

Darcy examined his cousin's countenance: Edward survived the worst of history's ill abuse; yet, the major general possessed few life skills.

"Matlock and I will meet with Hutchison tomorrow, but you must be prepared to counter the prosecutor's efforts." Darcy's fingers tightened against his cousin's arm. "It is possible, with their *interrogation*, the authorities intended to dull your effective response to the evidence. To make you appear as a weak, sniveling villain."

Edward paused as if considering Darcy's words.

"I understand. I will not fail you."

Darcy's approval preceded a rush of silence.

"Most certainly I will be called to testify upon the condition of your uniform," Darcy explained. "Mr. Richards included my name in his remarks."

"I regret involving you in this folly," Edward said in contrition.

Darcy could feel the weight of his cousin's gaze.

"It is of no consequence."

A tentative truce was necessary to protect Georgiana's interests. Upon another day, he and Edward would have a difficult conversation on what Darcy would expect of his cousin in the future.

"You must ask Mr. Hutchison for assistance in presenting a balanced defense. The authorities made no mention of Mr. Belker and only a brief acknowledgement of the fight with the men aboard the *Towson*. Cowan should be named to your defense, as he led Officer Rumbradge through Shadwell's investigation. And do not dismiss the likelihood of Mr. Martindale's appearance or that of the innkeeper's employees, who observed your comings and goings while you resided at the inn."

"What if those I seek to collaborate my story do not appear?"

Edward spoke a legitimate concern: Although the major general possessed the right to call witnesses, the law did not compel them to appear.

"Make a list of whom you wish to testify, and Matlock and I will make every effort to encourage them to appear. The issue may be to clear a person's calendar of previous engagements. Despite knowing the date of the trial, we possess no means to determine the time of day for the witness's presence at Old Bailey. It would be best to have too many possibilities rather than a select few. You should also consider someone such as Leigh-Hunt who could speak to your character, but not to your ruthlessness."

Edward winced, as he pressed harder against his ribs.

"I will take your suggestions in careful consideration."

He pinned Darcy with his eyes.

"How has Mrs. Fitzwilliam fared? Did she attend today's testimony?"

Darcy shook off the question.

"When Georgiana discovered your presence would not be required, my sister did not attend." Edward's expression displayed his cousin's approval. "In truth, I am gladdened by Georgiana's decision. I would not permit Mrs. Darcy's presence if I did not prepare her sensibilities with a previous explanation of what to expect."

A frown marred Edward's brow.

"I assure you, Darcy, Mrs. Fitzwilliam possesses a similar inner strength. Georgiana should be made aware of the brutal details before the trial. My wife is a very sensible woman."

"Then why did you never take Georgiana into your confidence?"

Darcy knew this was not the time or place for this particular discussion, but he could not stifle the words upon his lips.

"Why did you keep Mrs. Fitzwilliam at arm's length? If you believe Georgiana should be made privy to these horrendous crimes, my sister should be judged qualified to understand the devastation you witnessed in service to your country."

The gaze Edward fixed upon Darcy was not one of anger—was not the one Darcy anticipated. Instead, the major general's expression showed thoughtfulness.

"I wish I could pronounce an excuse, which would drive away your censure." Fitzwilliam's lips compressed in obvious frustration. "I made a cake of this situation, have I not, Darcy?"

Darcy took a sharp, agonizing breath. No criticism on his part would solve his sister's dilemma. What occurred between a man and a woman was not easy to define.

"All I can say for certain is if Mrs. Fitzwilliam is truly of the same nature as Mrs. Darcy, then it is unwise to deny your wife the secrets of your soul. Doing so will only widen the chasm looming between you and my sister. Despite it being from vogue for a man to look upon his wife as more than chattel, anything less upon my part would destroy the marriage I achieved with Mrs. Darcy. Perhaps it is time to open your life."

"I fear these charges against me mean any effort on my part would be too little and too late."

"It is never too late for a man to claim the sincere love of either his God or of the woman who completes him."

❧ ❧ ❧

"What have you there, Southland?" Darcy, Cowan, and the captain arrived at Darcy House to find Elizabeth and Georgiana waiting for them.

"A message from Maxen Rhys," Southland said "The man returned from Liverpool and requested I call upon him tomorrow."

When Southland called upon his fellow soldier previously, Mrs. Rhys explained her husband's mother took ill and summoned Rhys to her side.

"It will be good to know closure on that particular front," Cowan observed. "Each of Leigh-Hunt's men returned to London with news that the others in the major general's former squad were in London for many months—some never. Only Rhys could shed new light upon what occurred in Upper Canada. If the soldier had nothing to share, their assumption of a new attack would lose credibility.

"Was the major general well?" Elizabeth asked as she slid her arm through Darcy's.

Darcy shot a wary glance in his sister's direction.

"Perhaps we should retire to the sitting room," he suggested as he ushered his wife forward.

Georgiana caught Darcy's other arm.

"My husband is ill?"

"In a moment," Darcy spoke in firm tones. "Mr. Thacker, we will require tea for the ladies and claret for the gentlemen."

"Immediately, Mr. Darcy."

When the door closed behind them, Georgiana renewed her plea. "Tell me quick, William."

Darcy paused to seat Elizabeth.

"As Mrs. Darcy predicted, the magistrates questioned the major general, hoping to secure a confession."

Georgiana wrung her hands.

"Tell me my husband did not succumb to their manipulations."

Darcy nudged her into a chair.

"The major general did not confess to a crime he did not commit."

Darcy gathered his sister's hands in his and knelt before her.

"When we arrived at New Prison, Fitzwilliam was in poor condition."

From behind Darcy, Elizabeth hissed her vehemence.

"They *beat* him?"

"How bad?"

Tears pooled in Georgiana's eyes.

"Mostly bruises." Darcy explained. "Our cousin's ribs are quite sore, but he will recover. There are several marks on his cheek, and he possesses a cut upon his lip; yet, the major general has known worse."

"Did you keep your promise, Mr. Darcy?" Elizabeth asked with a sob of despair. "Did you and Lord Matlock bring the wrath of the earldom upon Middlesex?"

Darcy presented his wife an all-knowing smile.

"I assure you, Mrs. Darcy, Matlock was most articulate. Upon his return home, the earl meant to call upon Secretary Ryder. No one will dare to touch Edward again."

"Are you certain?" Georgiana whispered.

"Edward has all he requires to recover." He said over his shoulder to his wife. "I suggested to the major general that the authorities likely acted against Fitzwilliam in order to distract him from his defense."

Elizabeth's frown lines met.

"You jest, Mr. Darcy."

"I have witnessed worse policing," Cowan clarified.

Elizabeth shook her head in disbelief. "And England claims itself the jewel of the world."

"I am assuming, Mrs. Darcy, you explained to our sister what occurred today," Darcy asked as he stood.

Georgiana dashed away her tears.

"Even so, I would appreciate hearing your evaluation of the proceedings. I do not doubt Mrs. Darcy's observations, but we women hold a different perspective on such matters."

For the next hour, Darcy, Cowan, Southland, and Elizabeth explained the type of evidence brought against Edward. Darcy noted how Cowan and Southland, as well as Elizabeth, sidestepped the more horrific details of the crimes. Darcy found that fact ironic, especially in light of Edward's earlier claim that Georgiana was as resolute as Elizabeth.

"I assume, Georgiana, you plan to attend Edward's trial," Darcy cautioned.

"You know I shall."

"Then I suggest you prepare yourself for the spectacle. We tended to your sensibilities this evening, but the investigating officers and the coroner will not give a care to your resolve or your feminine response. In fact, I imagine the masses will take delight in your lack of composure. If you have not done so, I suggest you familiarize yourself with the specifics of the crimes; otherwise, you will make a perfect caricature of the grieving wife for the newsprints."

᪬ ᪬ ᪬

When the notice came of being petitioned to testify for the prosecution, Darcy accepted the message with resigned endurance.

"Thank you, Mr. Thacker." Without breaking the seal, Darcy placed the official looking note upon his desk.

"Should I... should I leave the one for Mrs. Fitzwilliam with you or deliver it to your sister?"

Darcy looked up into assessing silver-brown eyes.

"Are you certain, Mr. Thacker?" One brow lifted in mistrust.

Thacker extended a second silver salver in Darcy's direction. His butler responded in dry tones. "As you may note, Sir."

Darcy removed the folded-over paper from the tray.

"Perhaps it would be best if you ask Mrs. Fitzwilliam to join me here." Darcy concentrated upon tamping down his growing ire.

"Immediately, Sir."

Thacker disappeared to do Darcy's biding. Meanwhile, Darcy turned the message over within his fingers. His brows slanted downward in a ferocious frown.

"I suspect the secret Georgiana quashed for weeks is about to become public knowledge."

When his sister appeared at his door some ten minutes later, Darcy still studied the paper.

"You wished to speak to me, William?"

He extended the message in her direction.

"It appears the authorities summoned you to speak against your husband in this matter in Middlesex."

Georgiana paled, but she rushed forward to snatch the paper from Darcy's fingertips.

"There must be a mistake."

She ripped at the wax seal.

"No one can believe I would condemn my husband."

Her hands trembled as she searched the paper Darcy suspected read the same as his. Georgiana leaned a hand against the corner of Darcy's desk. "What am I to do?"

As he did since she was no more than a babe in her crib, Darcy thought to promise to right all her wrongs. However, for weeks his sister pronounced herself as equal in her determination as Elizabeth Darcy: It was time Georgiana substantiated the major general's approval.

"You will send word to both Uncle Matlock and your husband. It is essential they know what the prosecutor plans. Your presence will rattle Edward's thinking; it will be your domain, Georgiana, to ease your husband's mind and to prove yourself worthy of the major general's continued regard."

๛ ๛ ๛

It was late afternoon when Captain Southland returned from Southwark.

"How went the discussion with Rhys?" Darcy asked when the captain collapsed in his chair. "You appear frustrated."

Southland sucked in an audible breath, attempting to organize his thoughts. His voice sounded grim.

"It was all so odd. I mean I spoke to Rhys in length, but I cannot say I came away feeling the man innocent."

"I am intrigued," Darcy admitted.

Southland ran his fingers through his hair in what appeared to be a gesture of annoyance.

"Mrs. Rhys warned me her husband suffered an injury in one of the war's later theatres, and so I expected something similar to my *souvenir* from Napoleon."

The captain gestured with the stump of his arm.

"Yet, it was not so?"

Puzzlement crossed Darcy's expression.

"Rhys is as able bodied as any man I ever encountered," Southland explained as he stared off in disquiet. "Yet burn scars cover the man: his face and neck and across Rhys' upper back and chest."

Southland's expression appeared grim.

"I saw others with burns from exploding cannons and the burning of the enemy's shelters, but nothing like those scars Rhys sports. It surprises me Rhys survived."

"Tell me what bothers you about the encounter," Darcy insisted.

Southland's brows drew together in fierceness.

"Rhys and I spoke of the time upon the American continent and of the murders."

As if strangely reluctant, the captain continued.

"With my prompting, Rhys recognized the similarities of the East Side Slayer, but he appeared not to possess any original thoughts upon the matter. I found that peculiar. He was even less forthcoming regarding those with whom he served in Upper Canada, going so far as to say he could not recall the names of those among our company."

"Mayhap the man saw so much war it dimmed his memory or Rhys chose to place all the memories behind him. Needless to say, an injury of the magnitude you describe must wreak havoc with the man's confidence," Darcy suggested.

"Mayhap," Southland said with distracted emotions. "However, if Pugh recognized the similarities between the Youngblood murders and the Wapping attacks, why did not a man residing across the Thames do likewise?"

"Did you pose a similar question to Rhys?"

"Aye."

"And his response?"

"The former private claims he was in Liverpool for the prior month and held only a vague awareness of the crimes."

"Do you believe him?" Darcy asked with a hint of exasperation.

Fire flashed in Southland's eyes.

"Not bloody likely."

Chapter Fifteen

"How shall this end?" Elizabeth slipped into Darcy's sitting room without his notice.

Darcy dressed for the night, but he did not possess the energy to cross through his and Elizabeth's adjoining dressing rooms to crawl into his wife's bed. Instead, Darcy collapsed into a winged chair to sit alone in the dark and stare into an empty hearth.

It was years since Darcy felt so despondent: There were his mother's and later, his father's passing, as well as that maddening incident between Georgiana and Mr. Wickham, and most recently, Darcy thought never to claim Elizabeth Bennet as his wife; yet with each of these, Darcy clung to a flicker of hope for better days, but not in this instance.

"My cousin will be found guilty and sentenced to death, and there is nothing I can do to change the outcome," he spoke in grave acceptance.

Elizabeth remained by the still open door.

"No one will ever criticize your devotion."

Darcy closed his eyes and rested his head against the high-backed cushion.

"No one will pronounce blame, except me. I failed Georgiana. I broke my solemn promise to my father."

Elizabeth tutted her disapproval, and under different circumstances his wife's defiance would bring a smile to Darcy's lips.

"Even George Darcy could not mold you into God, Mr. Darcy. I would say Georgiana and the major general failed you rather than the contrary. Our sister and her husband made promises to each other and to their dear family. They acted selfishly—abandoning the trust required by a forgiving God and doubting each other's love."

"Yet, still I cannot bear the idea of Georgiana witnessing Edward taunted and defiled as a monster." He shook his head in denial of the obvious.

Elizabeth had yet to approach, a frustrating fact, which increased Darcy's self-loathing. He imagined his wife withholding her touch in disgust.

"Did you learn nothing new of a different attacker?" she asked at length.

Darcy sighed in exasperation, but he did not open his eyes.

"Despite Mr. Cowan's assurance otherwise, if you were the perpetrator would you risk everything? The true villain in this insanity could wait a week to resume his attacks, and Edward would be dead, the family name ruined, and all for naught."

A long silence followed.

"We must pursue every opportunity, nonetheless, Mr. Darcy. I will not have you spend a lifetime questioning your actions in this matter. Your devotion to others is unfathomable, but my devotion is directed solely at you and the children. Provide me with a task to aid your efforts. I am not a fainting flower; you may depend upon me."

Darcy opened his eyes to look upon his wife. He knew she spoke foolishness: Elizabeth Darcy was the most warmhearted woman of his acquaintance. It was one of the reasons Darcy fell in love with her, but it was soothing to his soul to hear her words.

"I hold no doubt of your loyalty, Mrs. Darcy, but, in truth, I am at a loss as to how to proceed. Every hope knows extinction."

His wife crossed to where Darcy sat.

"Come, Mr. Darcy. We will discuss what has been done and determine what must yet be completed. We always were of a like mind, and when we are together, we are quite invincible."

Darcy accepted the hand Elizabeth extended, lacing their fingers before he stood to gather his wife into his embrace.

"You are without comparison, Mrs. Darcy. If there is a means from this folly, it will be you who leads us into God's grace."

❧ ❧ ❧

From a respectful distance, Darcy watched the interactions between Georgiana and Edward. His sister addressed Edward's bruised cheek and the crusted over cut upon their cousin's lip. He objected to the idea of escorting Georgiana to New Prison again, but his sister pleaded, and when Elizabeth vocalized her support, Darcy relented. Georgiana claimed the need to discuss her being petitioned to speak against Edward as her purpose, but Darcy held his doubts. He suspected his sister's doggedness had something to do with what occurred between his cousin and Georgiana prior to Edward's exit from Yadkin Hall or something to do with the promise the major general recently exacted from Mrs. Fitzwilliam.

To give rise to Darcy's misgivings, the officers insisted upon Georgiana leaving her cloak, bonnet, and reticule at the door, a request, which brought forth his sister's indignation. Initially, Darcy agreed with Georgiana's objections; on balance, the authorities never asked him or Cowan or Matlock to leave their beavers or other belongings behind. However, Darcy's protestations disappeared when, in anticipation of their departure, he retrieved his sister's belongings from the table upon which they rested.

Why is Georgiana's reticule so heavy? Darcy wondered as his fingers worked against the soft muslin to identify what the ribbon-tied pouch held. He knew Georgiana carried a lace handkerchief, which belonged to their late mother, a few coins, and a lady's vinaigrette, but today something else remained within.

As casual as possible, with two officers looking on, Darcy's fingers traced the shape. He masked his movements by placing his sister's cloak across his lap and by balancing her bonnet upon his knee. The wide brim hid Darcy's movement as the shape took form.

A gun. A very small one, but a gun nonetheless.

His heart sank.

Why would Georgiana feel it necessary to carry a gun?

Shortly after marrying Elizabeth, Darcy taught his wife and Georgiana how to use a weapon. Elizabeth unexpectedly asked for a gun, a Queen Anne pistol, in truth, in their early days of marriage. Darcy smiled with the remembrance. A gun, a horse, and an English Springer spaniel, which was forever underfoot at Pemberley, but an animal his wife loved without reserve, as did he, for the dog, early on, saved Elizabeth's life. She once used the gun against Mr. Wickham, when the rascal made an unexpected call upon Pemberley and refused to leave, and Elizabeth often carried the small pistol with her when they traveled.

The roads proved quite dangerous with so many unattached soldiers and scoundrels turning to thievery, but this situation was different. Although Darcy supposed it possible for his sister to feel a need of protection, he possessed no knowledge of Georgiana following Elizabeth's example. Generally, Darcy thought his sister learned to use the gun he purchased for her to please him and Elizabeth.

Darcy fought the urge to rip the ribboned knot open to confirm his suspicions, but he managed to keep the slant of his shoulders casual.

Was Georgiana frightened by the severe nature of the crimes of which Edward stood accused? Did she think someone would do her harm in retaliation? Or worse, did Georgiana plan to do herself harm if Edward was not successful in his release?

Darcy glanced again to where his sister kissed Edward's swollen mouth. The fact Georgiana displayed no discretion in her open affection for the major general spoke of the changes in his once soft-spoken, dependent sister. A second kiss lingered, and the obvious dawned: *Edward asked his wife to bring him the gun. The major general held a plan, and it would bring more shame to Georgiana.* Swallowing the curse screaming to be free, Darcy stifled the bile rushing to his throat.

꽁 꽁 꽁

"Forgive me," Georgiana whispered as she dabbed a foul smelling ointment upon a gash along Edward's brow line.

Her husband smiled through a wince of discomfort.

"There is nothing to forgive, Georgie. It was a plan of desperation: I should never have asked it. I will find another means. If I feel compelled to act upon my beliefs, Lindale or the earl will oblige me."

"Perhaps a guilty verdict will not be found." Even as Georgiana said the words, she recognized the futility of such hopes.

"We will do our best and place the outcome in God's hands." The major general interlaced their fingers, and Georgiana knew the regret of opportunities lost. It took a prison and a threat of hanging to bring them to this moment. "Instead of dire consequences, I must speak of my love for you. To declare what joy you bring to my life. A man should never squander his blessings, but I did so."

"As long as we may know each other again, I would suffer far worse," she whispered as she kissed the corner of Edward's mouth.

"Upon thy lips I lay this zealous kiss, as seal to the indenture of my love." Her husband kissed Georgiana more fully.

When Edward withdrew, Georgiana opened her eyes to stare into his. There was such goodness there. Character. Moral courage. Integrity. Honesty. All in one man—in her husband.

"You realize you misquoted Shakespeare," Georgiana teased.

Edward's customary easiness won out, and for that fact, she knew thanks for her husband had not smiled in what seemed forever.

"If Shakespeare believes I would claim your cheek, as the quote suggests, rather than your so tempting lips, the Bard is sadly mistaken," Fitzwilliam declared.

Georgiana sighed. If only she could stop time with this moment— not permit the future to unfold. At least, her husband did not quote Act Five of *Romeo and Juliet*: "With this kiss I die."

❧ ❧ ❧

There was nothing to be done but to wait, and Darcy never was a patient man. They investigated every possibility and was found wanting. Not one lead proved the major general guilty nor did any prove him innocent. The trial would be the defining moment in his family's future, and Darcy had no control over its outcome, a fact he found deuced frustrating.

When he and his sister returned to Darcy House after visiting with Edward, Georgiana announced her intention of spending the time leading to the trial with Uncle Martin and Aunt Nora.

"My aunt may take comfort in spending time with Edward's daughter." Captain Southland volunteered to escort Georgiana to Lockland Hall, and so Darcy House became quieter: The silence, a solemn knell.

"Mr. Darcy, we are going out."

Elizabeth appeared at his study's door, wearing her cloak and bonnet.

"Enjoy your outing," he said in a lackluster manner.

"I said *we*, Mr. Darcy," his wife corrected.

Darcy responded with a heavy sigh.

"I possess work to complete, Elizabeth." His wife meant the best, but Darcy did not think he could muster the effort for joviality.

"The work shall be upon your desk when you return to Darcy House, but the smile upon your son's lips at the prospects of spending part of his day with his esteemed father will not. *We* are taking the children to the park. Afterwards, you will escort your most loving wife to Bond Street for your lady requires a new bonnet, and you, Mr. Darcy, have of late, sadly neglected Pemberley's library. *We* will tend to both tasks today."

Despite his earlier dudgeon, Elizabeth broke through Darcy's armor.

"A new bonnet is it?" he asked through an easy smile. "Where has my most frugal wife gone?"

Elizabeth's chin rose in mocked defiance.

"I banished my ego to its private quarters so it might consider the error of its ways. Today, your lady donned the mantra of her youngest sister, who believes nothing can heal a weary heart as easily as a fancy ribbon upon a new lace bonnet."

The sparkle in his wife's eyes spoke of the enjoyment Elizabeth experienced in teasing him.

"And of the books, Mrs. Darcy?"

"Very much as a bonnet in Lydia's hands improves Mrs. Wickham's spirits, rare books bring life to you, Sir." Darcy liked his wife's logic: Elizabeth knew him better than anyone, and sharing his life with her was the most comforting thing in his existence. She stepped closer to assure privacy. Pursing her lips, she whispered, "If you are persuasive, Mr. Darcy, your lady would find it agreeable to secure quarters at Mivart's for private time."

Darcy's eyebrow rose in curious approval.

"Mivart's?" Had his ears failed him? Had his wife suggested an assignation at one of London's newest hotels? The idea took Darcy's breath away. Would he ever truly know what to expect from Elizabeth Darcy? Somehow, he did not think so. "We possess acceptable quarters at Darcy House."

His wife shook her head in denial.

"No, at Darcy House, you are Fitzwilliam Darcy, Master of Pemberley. I wish to spend the afternoon and evening with my *William*. With the man who calls me *Lizzie*. I wish to hold the world at bay for a few precious hours. I instructed the staff we will be dining with old friends this evening."

"Mr. and Mrs. Darcy are not at home for the evening," Darcy spoke in a seductive rasp. "I like the idea. Come along, Mrs. Darcy. Our children require a warm embrace from their parents, and I crave a few private moments with the woman who holds my heart in her dainty hands."

࿔ ࿔ ࿔

Yesterday was a superb day of loving his wife and family, but today was everything but glorious. They arrived at Old Bailey early for the proceedings. Georgiana traveled with Edward's parents, but his sister assumed one of the few available seats beside Elizabeth in the gallery.

When instructed to report to the room set aside for witnesses for all the proceedings, Darcy refused and kept Georgiana with him. He would never permit his sister to sit in a room and fret over what was going on within the courtroom; she meant to support Edward in this matter, and Darcy meant for Georgiana to see it through to the end.

Moreover, in the gallery, Georgiana would be surrounded by family and friends rather than by strangers, and it was not as if either he or his sister would speak out against the major general. The proceedings would not sway their allegiances.

All matter of humanity packed the viewing area, and dread found a home in Darcy's stomach.

"Fitzwilliam will be brought in with the other cases on the docket," Darcy explained in soft whispers. "All the cases are heard before the jury and judges announce the verdicts. You will be exposed to more than Edward's case today."

Elizabeth squeezed the back of Georgiana's hand.

"We shall be well, Mr. Darcy," his wife assured as Georgiana nodded her understanding. "Mrs. Fitzwilliam and I discussed the possibilities."

After an hour of waiting, the guards brought in the prisoners. In addition to Edward, there were two thieves—one accused of stealing from his master and the other of being a pickpocket, a third man charged with intent of rape, and a fourth accused of threatening behavior. Each prisoner was in chains. From where Darcy stood along the wall, he heard the countess gasp and Elizabeth sob.

Needless to say, the authorities anticipated the sensationalism of Edward's case and kept the other proceedings short, while providing the public a taste of normalcy. Despite his disheveled appearance, the major general stood tall and proud and stone-faced. It pleased Darcy to observe how his cousin prepared mentally for the battle ahead: Darcy never knew more pride in the man's connection; however, from the buzz of excitement, which brought a collective gasp from those in attendance, Darcy feared the worse could not be averted. Even the judges appeared apprehensive.

In a break with the customary order, the judges dispensed with the other four cases quickly, even meting out the punishments before opening the proceedings against the major general. The disruption from the normal added to the spleen gathering in Darcy's throat. He glanced to his sister, who paled, but who appeared as stone-faced as her husband. Darcy's heart went out to her; Georgiana entered her marriage with great hopes only to be brought low.

At length, only Edward remained from those accused of crimes. Darcy thought some in the crowd would depart after the judges excused the other cases, but it appeared more interested parties pressed into the space. However, when Mr. Jenkins, the prosecutor assumed his place before the room, silence reigned.

"Major General Edward Fitzwilliam was indicted by the magistrates' court of Middlesex for the willful murder of Isles Vaughn, Sarah Vaughn and infant Drey on 5 October; the willful murders of Louis Thorne, Willow Thorne, and Mildred Winthrop on 9 October; and the willful murders of Theodore Weldon, Samuel Urick, and Fanny Urick on 17 October. At the time of the Coroner's Inquisitions, Edward Fitzwilliam was not a suspect in the Vaughn or the Thorne case, no suspect being named; he was, however, a suspect in the cases after the Inquisition based on evidence from London's citizenry.

"It is my duty as Counsel for the prosecution to lay before the court evidence to support the indictment against the prisoner at the bar."

All eyes in the audience followed Darcy's to where Edward stood erect and solemn countenanced.

"The crime of murder," Jenkins continued, "is a crime against the laws of God and of men. England, as a God-fearing country abhors the deliberate taking of life and has decreed a punishment of death for those proved to have exacted harm upon another.

"The crime of murder rarely lends itself to witnesses; therefore, the prosecution will offer testimony of a more plausible nature: a series of circumstances, which lead clearly to the guilt of the prisoner at the bar."

Jenkins paused to sip upon a glass of water before continuing. Meanwhile, Darcy shot a quick glance to his Uncle Matlock; the earl went as colorless as the white paint upon the walls.

"Edward and Hutchison are prepared," Darcy hissed from his mouth's corner.

Matlock nodded curtly before resting his hand upon his countess's shoulder. Elizabeth and Georgiana huddled closer together, their heads touching. From across the gallery, Darcy noted how Cowan and Southland stood alert, as if preparing for battle.

"Gentlemen," Jenkins said with a command of his surroundings. "Both the Indictment and the Coroner's Inquisition describe the victims of these aforementioned crimes. The deceased Isles Vaughn once was a mate upon a German sloop before returning to his homeland, marrying, and opening a bakery some three years previous. Vaughn and his wife Sarah welcomed a son to the family six months prior to meeting their demise at the hands of a violent and Bedlam-induced perpetrator.

"As was his custom, a provisioning merchant called upon the Vaughns in the wee hours of the morning. When he could rouse no one, the supplier, a Mr. Sambert, summoned a night watchman, Mr. Lester, who entered the shop to discover the bodies. Vaughn was outside a storage room door. Mrs. Vaughn and Baby Drey were found in the smaller of the two sleeping quarters.

"All three had their throats slit; investigators found a broken military sword located among the artifacts at the scene. Major General Fitzwilliam admits to owning such a sword, but it went missing since his coming to London."

Again, Jenkins paused for emphasis.

"Bloody footprints also suggest a man wearing boots."

Darcy thought of those squeezed into the courtroom. Likely more than ninety percent of the men in attendance wore boots, but the inference did its damage. Including Darcy's, every eye in the room fell upon the major general's footwear.

"Mrs. Vaughn," Jenkins took up the charges again, "fought her attacker violently, her hands and shoulders displaying the marks of the sword coming down upon her. Although the attacker's invasion cannot be proved, Mrs. Vaughn was raped, likely after she was stabbed; therefore, the prosecution, in this instance, can only ask for an intent of rape."

Darcy cringed; Jenkins was a well-trained counsel. The man knew how to speak the truth, while twisting it at the same time.

"The woman's body displayed the voluntary violation upon the perpetrator's part. In addition, her attacker carved Mrs. Vaughn's left breast from her body."

A gasp spread across the gallery.

"The breast was not found at the scene. It is assumed the woman's attacker took it with him. The perpetrator left Baby Vaughn to die in a cradle filled with the child's blood."

Darcy studied his cousin. Only those who knew him well would recognize how such charges would affect the major general, a man who spent a lifetime defending women, children, and his country. Edward's gaze rested upon Georgiana: Darcy remained certain the major general considered what he would do to a man who perpetrated such evil on Georgiana and Colleen. Edward's fists clenched at his side, but he did not turn his head toward where Jenkins stood before the bench.

"Louis and Willow Thorne were the owners of a public house less than a half mile from the Vaughns' bakery. Married for some thirty years, the Thornes owned The Willow Branch for only five years.

Thorne sold his business as a meat dresser as his hands knew stiffness in the joints. Mrs. Mildred Winthrop was a war widow, forced into employment after the demise of her husband. The Thornes and Mrs. Winthrop knew a similar fate as did the Vaughns: throats slit."

Darcy noted how Jenkins avoided any reference to the weapon used against the Thornes' household, and he prayed Edward meant to make the best of Jenkins' earlier assumption of a military sword being the attacker's weapon of choice.

"Their attacker sexually violated both Mrs. Thorne and Mrs. Winthrop. Both women had their left breasts removed."

Jenkins lifted his hands in a gesture of supplication.

"In addition, Louis Thorne's left eye was crudely cut from his head, as if the man's attacker wished to execute some sort of medieval punishment on Thorne."

Darcy heard Rumbradge suggest the culprit did not wish Thorne to identify him. Darcy wondered why at the time he did not find the statement an odd one. Surely, the attacker removed Thorne's eye *after* the tavern owner's death.

"At length, London's most conniving attacker came upon the home of Mr. Theodore Weldon, a man who dealt with candles and candlesticks. Weldon apprenticed to a candle maker when he was but twelve. He remained in the profession when he reached his majority. Weldon was killed within the shop he saved all his pennies to purchase, while his two servants and shop employees, Samuel and Fanny Urick, were overpowered in the first storey kitchen. Samuel Urick sustained a blow to his head, hard enough to crack his skull. Mrs. Urick knew the horrors of the previous female victims. Weldon's throat was slit and his left ear removed from his head.

"The deaths of these nine citizens of London were violent, coming at the hands of a hardened murderer, a man who tasted the thrill of death for more than a decade and was starved to know it again. Each victim suffered a slow, painful death—deaths at the hands of someone accustomed to killing—from someone accustomed to wielding a slicing instrument, such as a sword or a dagger."

Darcy grimaced. The counsel for the prosecution replaced the idea of a heavy sword with that of a dagger. Both were weapons common to a soldier. Edward's defense became more problematic.

"The prisoner at the bar is such a man. Although Edward Fitzwilliam is the son of the Earl of Matlock, the major general knows more than his share of the devastation of war. Some will argue of the major general's honor and his dedication to King and Country, while I will argue of Edward's Fitzwilliam's personal Bedlam, the nightmares, which drove him to act from character."

Darcy wondered if the gaolers observed Edward's nightmares and reported them to the prosecution.

"As such, I beg your attention, Gentlemen, for I will ask you to do the unthinkable: to consign a fellow of God's creations to a quick and discreditable death. Your oath to God and Country will require you to name Major General Fitzwilliam as guilty of these horrendous crimes and to name the day of his death and the means by which he will meet it."

Chapter Sixteen

Having studied the major general as Mr. Jenkins described the crimes, Darcy recognized the exact moment Edward made the connection to the Youngblood murders. His cousin's frown lines deepened before a look of despondency escaped. Most in the audience would believe the major general reacted to charges being pronounced against him, but Darcy knew Edward Fitzwilliam's mind.

Edward shot a questioning glance to Captain Southland, and a barely visible nod on the captain's part confirmed the major general's unspoken assumptions. Darcy watched as his cousin analyzed the possibilities of Bleddyn Youngblood's ghost returning to his wicked ways.

He knew when Fitzwilliam thought to bring the information to the court's attention and when the major general discarded the idea. If Edward brought the news forward, it would appear he reconstructed the crimes of another. His cousin's eyes scanned the courtroom as if he searched for a familiar countenance among the gallery.

Darcy's eyes followed his cousin's lead. He had no idea for whom Edward searched—whether his cousin expected Youngblood among the attendees—but Darcy searched for anything from the ordinary. He wished he were close enough to Southland to instruct the captain to conduct his own search of the courtroom for someone he and the major general encountered in Upper Canada. To Darcy, nothing appeared from the ordinary, but Edward's gaze rested upon a space where spectators elbowed one another for a better view.

Had his cousin seen someone of note?

"How plead you, Major General Fitzwilliam?" The judge's gravel-laced voice brought both Darcy and Edward from their musings.

With reluctance, his cousin withdrew his gaze from the audience.

"Not guilty." The major general's voice spoke with renewed confidence. It was the first glimpse Darcy had of the man he admired all his life.

"Very well. Proceed, Mr. Jenkins."

With those five words, a sense of anticipation ran through the courtroom. Many within came to Old Bailey to know an end to the Bedlam, which afflicted London for a month. Only a handful in attendance wished for Edward Fitzwilliam's release, and that thought frightened Darcy to his core. This was one situation where wealth and family influence would prove a disadvantage.

The early testimony went very much as Darcy expected: the coroner detailed all the repulsive facts the gathered audience came to learn. The most telling question from the prosecution came as the coroner finished his report of the crimes. "Did you examine each of the three scenes in question?"

The coroner, a man of some fifty years and a weary expression, cleared his throat.

"There not be many who would wish to look upon such carnage unless his duty to his employment required it."

Darcy thought the official in error: According to Mr. Rumbradge. hundreds streamed through the Vaughns' house to look at blood stained walls and floors.

Jenkins smiled with intent.

"As such, you have a better than average grasp of the type of man who would create such destruction. Is that not correct, Sir?"

"I imagine you have the right of it, Mr. Jenkins."

"Then please tell the jury what assumptions you made of the man who committed these crimes."

"The attacker is one man. A man of great intelligence and stratagems. A man who is not frightened by the possibility of meeting several foes at the same time. A man familiar with weaponry and fighting."

"And, in your opinion, is Major General Fitzwilliam such a man?"

The coroner cleared his throat several times.

"The major general would possess the physical ability to overcome those within each of the households. However, I cannot speak of the gentleman's mental state: I have had no personal contact with the man. All I can add is, within my experience, those who act with violence do not take benignly to gestures of kindness offered by his fellow man."

Next, the Sephora's innkeeper, Mr. Martindale, spoke of the major general's drunken state.

"What would make a man drink so deep into his cups?" Jenkins asked.

"Seen many a man kissing the stone," Martindale responded in all seriousness. "Some kint leave the d'ink behind, while others hide from the world in the ale. The 'ajor general be of the second nature. His demons 'ollowed the 'ajor general to London.'"

Mabs, Martindale's tavern maid, testified to the condition of Edward's uniform.

"All 'overed in blood, it was," she said in importance.

Fortunately, with Hutchison's assistance, Edward solicited an admission from both the innkeeper and the maid that they never witnessed the major general acting aggressively.

"The 'ajor general 'ppeared sad—be all," the maid conceded. "As if'n he be losing his best chum."

The Runners, Mr. Richards and Mr. Parker, spoke of how they heard of the fight on the docks and traced the report to the Sephora. A sharp-eyed resident of the area spotted the hack Mr. Cowan hired to remove Edward from the inn. It did not take long to locate the driver and learn the address to which the passengers were delivered. Richards described in some detail the questions they asked of Edward's missing sword and the possible connection to the broken-tipped one found upon the Vaughns' bloody floor.

"Could the sword belong to another officer?" Edward asked Mr. Richards. "Were there any markings, which would prove the weapon used against the Vaughns my missing sword?"

"No, Sir," the Runner admitted. "But it be a huge coincidence."

"Yet, a coincidence, nonetheless," Edward countered with the authority of one accustomed to his word being final. Edward was a man in control of his destiny, while expressing no haughtiness in his tone or stance.

Neither the night watchman, who entered the Vaughns' residence after being summoned by a provisions merchant, nor the two tenants of the neighboring boarding house, who claimed hearing the clamor of the attack, added to the prosecution's case.

Mr. Jenkins called Darcy to speak to the burning of the major general's uniform, and so Darcy reiterated his concern for the health of his household.

"My family has three children under age three in the nursery. I could not assume accountability for bringing disease into my home. Neither my family nor my staff merit irresponsibility on my part."

Edward's questions of Darcy were more personal.

"Please explain for those who do not know our relationship, Mr. Darcy."

"We are first cousins—my mother and your father are siblings."

Darcy understood the necessity of speaking of Edward's character.

"However, we are more than that. My esteemed father named you to serve with me as guardian to my sister. George Darcy would never do so if he considered you less than the most honorable of men."

Edward smiled with that secretive turn of his lips, so familiar to Darcy.

"Was there ever a time you considered me lacking in honor?"

Darcy hoped he understood his cousin's purpose in the question.

"I was most ungrateful for your interference when I thought you a candidate for Mrs. Darcy's hand; however, in the end, you proved yourself useful in my suit."

"Any other time, Darcy?" Amusement warmed his cousin's eyes. "What of when I asked your permission to marry your sister? Many would consider such actions a break in my bond of guardianship."

A buzz of interest spread across the room at the major general's bald statement, and Darcy eyed his cousin with some misgivings.

"Although Mrs. Darcy assured me my sister's maturity, I tend to be quite protective of my family. I always was of the persuasion that guardianship ought to be directed to the good of those who confer it, not of those who receive the trust."

"You quote Cicero well, Cousin, but I wish to know if you thought me without honor for applying for my cousin's hand."

"I was not best pleased," Darcy admitted. "But my objections fell not on your shoulders. Until I married, my sister was my only family. I feared Mrs. Fitzwilliam did not know her heart. I was soon to learn otherwise." Darcy waved his hand in an impatient gesture. "You never acted against your honor. My father named you as the former Miss Darcy's guardian for he recognized your character as equal to your blessedness. Unlike many who enter matrimony without knowledge of their future mate, you and Mrs. Fitzwilliam were joined by shared memories. Pleasant memories to pave your way. One must recall Cicero also said, 'Memory is the treasury and guardianship of all things.'"

Private Walters followed Darcy's testimony with his own. It made no sense to Darcy as to the order of those who spoke for the opposing sides, and the lack of structure rang with doom in Darcy's estimation. Some were for the prosecution and others for the defense. That being said, Darcy was glad to note Walters took Cowan's advice and cleaned up his appearance.

"You have known Major General Fitzwilliam long?" Jenkins asked as he came around the curve of the table.

"Served under the 'ajor general through 'everal campaigns."

"Was the major general a good officer?"

Walters shrugged.

"Kint say I enjoyed the 'ajor general's need to be the first 'nto the fray, but he be good to 'is men. Better than most."

Jenkins nodded his encouragement.

"When was the last time you saw Major General Fitzwilliam?"

"Ye mean since the war?"

"Yes. Yes. Have you seen your former commanding officer since you departed the service?"

Walters shot a glance to Cowan.

"Told me former sergeant when he'd asked, I sees Old Fitz, I mean 'ajor General Fitzwilliam, down by the docks. Told Sergeant Cowan how Fitzwilliam be stumbling drunk—didn't recognize me when he passes. I saluted jist the same."

"Did Mr. Cowan recently provide you employment, Mr. Walters?"

Walters' ire rose quickly.

"I believe yer insinuatin Sergeant Cowan paid me to speak well of the 'ajor General."

Jenkins answered with a simple lift of his eyebrow.

Darcy enjoyed how Walters glared at the barrister with a look only those who witnessed history could.

"Sergeant Cowan offered me a position when no one else would! But not jist me. There be Brammwell, Logan, Pinter, Jamison, and Tutelage that I knows of, but I hears of more. Sergeant Cowan treat me and the others with respect. Permit us to earn our keep. Kint say I knows much of 'Ajor General Fitzwilliam. We's don't travel in the same company." A collective chuckle filled the courtroom. "But I's saluted Fitzwilliam becuz he be a good man. Like Sergeant Cowan, the 'ajor general always acknowledged the importance of the man, not the uniform. Fitzwilliam personally carried Cowan from the field in '09. Sewed 'im up hisself. I seen it all. Say what ye will of the 'ajor general, but I'll not be among those callin' foul."

Following Walters's dismissal from the box, the judges again responded in an unprecedented manner. They adjourned the proceedings for the midday meal. A quick glance at his watch told Darcy it was three of the clock, but he was not aware of another instance where the customary midday meal interrupted the proceedings.

All the judges and barristers and clerks were gentlemen's sons, and such a meal would be the norm; in fact, Darcy was aware there was a kitchen below stairs for that purpose. Yet, what Darcy did not understand was why the judges did not break after the other four cases and before Jenkins's opening statements and the early testimony. Court officials hustled the jury from the room.

"How do they keep people from discussing the testimony?" Darcy whispered as his family joined him along the wall.

"Will it matter?" Elizabeth mumbled in what sounded of disgust. "The gathered jurors talk throughout the proceedings. Who is the man with the dark green coat in the chair on the far right?"

"Jurors are chosen from a pool of men, usually of the middling classes—those with some education," Cowan explained. "There are juries that hear cases from London with different juries for cases from Middlesex. The crimes being adjudicated today are all from Middlesex, and this is Middlesex jury number two. The men who regularly sit upon juries hold some knowledge of the law simply from their multiple appearances in the courtroom. The gentleman you describe has much experience and is advising others of the legalities of which he is aware."

Elizabeth's frown lines met.

"How convoluted! I must say I am highly disappointed in the English court system."

Matlock caught the countess's arm.

"Come. I am aware of a decent public house where the ladies might know a cup of tea. It is but a few streets over."

"Excuse me, Mr. Darcy."

Darcy looked up to see one of the guards assigned to Edward.

"The major general requests a word with you."

It was another break from the customary, and the idea shook Darcy to his core.

"Permit Captain Southland to escort you," Darcy whispered to his wife. "Someone should remain to assure you have a seat upon your return."

Elizabeth squeezed his hand. "Give the major general our regard."

She walked away to claim the captain's arm. As always, Darcy watched Elizabeth go before returning to the issue at hand. Only he and Cowan remained in the area.

"Fitzwilliam requires our advice," he explained, and Cowan followed him and the officer to a small room at the back of the courthouse.

Darcy knew there was a holding cell for prisoners, but the guard surprised him by conducting Darcy and Cowan to a room used for storage. The space sported only two small windows for light, both high and from reach unless one stood upon a chair or table. Darcy suspected the two chairs in the room's middle were not part of the décor. To accommodate Cowan's presence, the guards fetched a third chair from a nearby room.

When the officers stepped outside, Edward turned upon them.

"Why did you not speak to me of the similarities between these crimes and what happened upon the American continent? This is unconscionable, Darcy!"

Exasperation claimed Darcy's tone. "Why did you not note the parallels upon your own? You lived the events in Upper Canada."

"You think me guilty!" Edward accused. "You think I stepped into the abyss! That I perpetrated these crimes upon those in London!"

"Most certainly we think no such thing," Cowan mediated.

Edward spoke through tight lips. "I wish to hear my cousin say the words, Cowan."

Darcy employed his customary calm, the one that served him well in difficult business dealings.

"In truth, I do not understand a man who walks away from his family. I do not understand how you could deny Mrs. Fitzwilliam your heart," he confirmed in indignation. "When this is over we will hold a serious discussion regarding your role in Georgiana's life. That being said, I do not think you guilty of such evil."

"Then why did you not mention the American crimes? In all our discussions regarding my defense, why were those particular facts omitted?"

"For the same reasons you rejected Youngblood's legacy as part of your defense!" Darcy snapped. "Do not deny it. When the details of the three crimes were read together, you recognized the connections; yet, you could think of no reason why someone would commit such crimes and blame them on you. Admit it. I observed your countenance. You know the coincidence would do nothing to prove your innocence."

Edward expelled a huff of grim laughter.

"Yes. Damn it. I realized the ramifications. But bloody hell, Darcy, you cannot expect me to overlook the possibilities. What has been done to find the culprit?"

Cowan checked the door for privacy.

"Southland was the first to recognize the irregularities. The captain made a list of those who served under your command. Of those who did not succumb to battle wounds, all were questioned. Leigh-Hunt aided in locating the former soldiers. One is employed in Cheapside. A second at the Greenland Docks. None of the others were near London for well over a year."

"Then these two?" Hope filled Edward's voice.

"Cannot be named as suspects," Darcy assured. His mouth twisted in a humorless smile. "Our only hope is to catch the offender in the act. If Captain Southland is correct, the real murderer will strike again after midnight tonight. We devised a plan of sort to apprehend Youngblood's imitator."

"The pattern." Ominous silence filled the space between them. "Three women will be next." The major general closed his eyes as if in pain. "We tracked Youngblood for weeks on end, but I witnessed the bastard's hanging—watched his legs dangle and twist until the life drifted from his body." Fitzwilliam's eyes opened to meet Darcy's. "Very much as my life will leave me when the rope is placed about my neck." Realization arrived. "What if our imitator does not strike again until after my execution?"

Darcy responded in bitterness.

"We have no answer, so I suspect you must fight to prove your innocence."

❧❧❧

"Did you observe anyone of note—anyone familiar when you searched the gallery during the prosecution's opening statements?" Darcy asked his cousin before the officers ushered Darcy from the room.

Edward shook his head in the negative.

"No one, but I could not shake the idea someone watched me with more interest than the others in the gallery. The same cold shiver down my spine haunted me for months upon the American front."

Disappointment tagged Darcy's heart.

"I will ask Captain Southland to survey the audience when the session recommences."

When Darcy returned to the courtroom, more than a third of the audience reclaimed their positions in the gallery. He and Cowan blocked off the necessary seats for Matlock, the countess, Georgiana, and Elizabeth. Within a quarter hour, his family reappeared.

"I brought you some bread," Elizabeth whispered as she placed a wrapped package in his open palm. "I wish I could bring you more or add a bit of butter, but my handkerchief is not so large." She whispered, "You must have a bite or two. According to Lord Matlock, the day appears to be a long one."

Darcy smiled at his wife, enjoying her guileless innocence.

"I will share it with Mr. Cowan."

"No need, William. Georgiana and I practiced great stealth. I do not think the owner of the public house noticed. Your sister holds a like 'gift' for Thomas."

"You are too clever, Mrs. Darcy." He peeled back the lace-trimmed cloth to look inside. "Perhaps you possess a bit of larceny in you. I must be more careful of my purse," he teased.

A mocking smile curved Elizabeth's lips.

"I have no need of larceny where you are concerned, Mr. Darcy. I quite own your heart. You would gladly purchase whatever I desired."

Darcy leaned closer to whisper into the hair close to her ear. "That truth is evident for the world to see, my dear."

A noise behind him announced the return of Edward and the court officers.

"Guard my sister. This afternoon will be difficult for her."

"You still believe the major general will not know success?" Elizabeth asked in anxiousness.

"I think the world is turned upon its head, and Georgiana's heart will learn how hard is it to beat when one's heels remains above one's head."

෧෧෧

General Leigh-Hunt was the first of those Edward requested to speak to the court. The general spoke of the valor displayed by the major general upon the battlefield, of Fitzwilliam's glowing evaluations by his superiors, and of the major general's extensive military history.

"In your opinion, could a man who knew so much devastation turn upon the innocents he swore to protect?" Mr. Jenkins asked in counterpoint.

The insinuation brought forth the general's pompous authority.

"I have known the major general since before his enlistment as a mere lieutenant some twelve years prior. Edward Fitzwilliam is a superb officer, as is witnessed by the men who previously spoke in his defense and who rally behind him now."

When Jenkins meant to repeat his question, Leigh-Hunt ignored the gesture with a flick of his wrist.

"Any man, from the lowest peasant to those of royal birth, is capable of great ambitions and great evil. We have only to look upon the French commander whom the Duke of Wellington gloriously defeated at Waterloo to recognize that particular truth; yet, it is my opinion, as well as the opinion of Prince George, that Edward Fitzwilliam is not of such a nature."

"Prince George?" Jenkins asked with a raised eyebrow, and Darcy smirked at the prosecutor's obvious surprise. "Did not the major general receive his current rank for his exemplary service at Waterloo?"

"No, Sir." Leigh-Hunt retorted. "At Waterloo, Edward Fitzwilliam entered the dispute as a major general. Fitzwilliam received a promotion from colonel in reward for his personal service to our future king."

"Can you elaborate on the then colonel's actions?" The humor disappeared from Jenkins's countenance, his expression hardening. Evidently, the prosecutor held no knowledge of Fitzwilliam's service.

Leigh-Hunt responded in a dark, roughened warning.

"I can, but I will not."

The general's lips thinned.

"The business of the Royal family is not meant for idle gossip. All I can say is the colonel placed himself in a position to save our Prince and received his promotion as a result."

Next, Mr. Belker knew the witness box. Recognizing the harbormaster's testimony would be vital in explaining the blood upon Edward's uniform, the earl guaranteed Belker a healthy allowance for his appearance at court.

"Pardon my saying so, Sir, but you were well in your cups," Belker responded to Edward's question regarding the major general's condition upon the docks.

"I do not doubt it," Edward said in contrition. "Was I conscious of the attack by the crew of the *Towson*?"

A man accustomed to the drama associated with his position, Belker sent the anxious countenances of those in the audience a flashing look of contempt.

"It is my responsibility, Major General, to know everything which occurs upon my docks. The mates from the *Towson* thought you incapacitated by drink. From their testimony, you were unresponsive when they approached. Alas, for the *Towson's* crew, when they pulled you to your feet, you reacted. They admitted to being no match for you. As to how lucid you were, despite your heavy drinking, you responded to my questions with reason."

"Did I possess a sword at the time?"

Edward asked the question he knew Jenkins would offer.

A slight frown line indented Belker's brow.

"Not that I recall. Nor did any of my men report it."

"Pardon what may ring of censure, Mr. Belker," Edward masterfully led the harbormaster's testimony, "but, assuming I wore my sword, a fact none of us can prove, could someone have found it after the confrontation and sold it or, even worse, used it against the Vaughns?"

Belker viewed the crowded gallery.

"Anything is possible, Major General. The docks are a busy place. Ships arrive and depart constantly. The world brings it wares, much of which is under my supervision, to London's doors."

From the beginning, Darcy did not appreciate Belker's pompous attitude, nor the rumors of the man's involvement in smuggling, but Lord Matlock's money was not wasted on the harbormaster. Belker controlled his environment.

"And what of the crew from the *Towson*?" Edward asked.

Belker presented Edward with what appeared to be an irritated frown.

"As you chose not to press charges against your attackers, the *Towson* sailed the following day. I am certain the *Towson's* captain wanted nothing to do with an attack upon an earl's son. A local surgeon treated the two most injured by your fists. My men report your attackers departed on a ship set for Dover."

Edward asked one final question.

"As this attack upon the docks occurred upon the same night as the invasion of the Vaughns' home, is it possible for my being in two places at the same time?"

"You were late with us while we sought the truth of the incident," Belker responded in earnestness. "And although you managed to place part of your stupor behind, when you left us, you were not well. I assumed you returned to your lodgings, but I cannot say for certain. However, it is not in my providence to imagine a man, who consumed so much drink, capable of overpowering both Mr. and Mrs. Vaughn without suffering his own injuries."

Chapter Seventeen

As Belker exited the courtroom, Elizabeth shot Darcy a look of triumph, but Darcy shook off the gesture. Although the harbormaster advanced Edward's cause, Belker held the reputation of a man who would sell his brother for a profit. Mr. Belker's word would not hold the weight of Simon Rumbradge, who was summoned from the witnesses' waiting room to the box.

Darcy learned from his private inquires that although the officer held a reputation for a no nonsense response, the citizens he served viewed Rumbradge as a man of his word. Those inquiries were the reason Darcy agreed with Cowan to place their trust in the officer; however, Rumbradge left no doubts he thought Fitzwilliam guilty, and Darcy knew the man would do all he could to prove it in court.

"Must admire a man who sets his eyes upon the truth," Cowan whispered.

"I would admire the man more if he believed in the same truth as you and I," Darcy grumbled.

Silence formed between them. For several elongated moments Cowan said nothing. Their gazes locked and held in assessment. "

"Even if the major general is excused," Cowan asked, "we will still execute our plan, will we not, Darcy? Tell me we will not abandon our quest simply because the victims are of a different social class."

The challenge hung between them.

"We will see it through, Cowan," Darcy promised. "In that aspect, we are of similar minds."

As expected, Mr. Rumbradge addressed the minute details of each of the crimes. Rumbradge completed a thorough study of each of the victims. For a moment, Darcy wondered if standard procedure asked the investigating officer to avail himself of such details or whether

Rumbradge was an aberration. And was the man's natural curiosity an asset or a fault?

The officer spoke with feeling of Vaughn's time at sea and the man's dream of family and home, as well as Weldon's saving to send his elderly mother to the country for her health. The court's audience could not help but to experience sympathy for the lives cut short. For the first time that day, Darcy wondered if some of those sharing the gallery were family members of the deceased. He had not given the possibility much thought, and his lack of humanity brought shame.

"Speak to us of the evidence you uncovered at the scenes," Jenkins encouraged.

Rumbradge shot a glance to Darcy, and Darcy knew, without a doubt, Rumbradge's testimony would bring Edward's case to its knees. Dread claimed Darcy's chest, and he felt oddly vulnerable.

"Until of late, we thought the weapon in question for the Vaughns was the broken sword discovered upon the scene. The sword displayed blood upon it, but it was not the weapon used by the assailant. We since determined the perpetrator left the broken sword behind by accident or even perhaps on purpose to sway our investigation. The murderer of the Vaughn family used a knife rather than a sword."

A gasp spread across the open space.

"How can you be so certain, Mr. Rumbradge?"

"I called in an American-trained surgeon, of late settling his practice in our area. The man, a Mr. Granvall, served with the City of Glasgow's coroner's office for the past five years. With Granvall's assistance, we discovered the bruising on each of the victims fooled us."

The officer demonstrated his point by cupping his hands together to form an imaginary guard, grip, and pommel.

"The sword had a hilt, so we thought the bruises at the end of the wound came from the impact of the hilt with the skin. We were to learn later the bruises were the result of the assailant's fist against the victim's skin, rather than the metal base of the sword striking the flesh."

A buzz drowned out the next of Rumbradge's declarations, but Darcy heard them nonetheless.

"We believe the knife used against the Vaughns was either procured at the scene or carried specifically to the scene for the purpose of the attack."

Jenkins frowned, as did Darcy.

"Perhaps you should explain, Mr. Rumbradge."

The officer sighed, as if Rumbradge blamed Jenkins for not recognizing the obvious. Darcy imagined the officer explaining his theories to his supervisors with little success: Rumbradge's testimony would contradict some of what the coroner shared.

"We discovered several knives upon the floor of the Vaughns' home, but we assumed the culprit and Vaughn knocked them about during their struggle. However, after we took a closer look at Mrs. Vaughn's defensive marks upon her hands and shoulders, we discovered they were more of a stabbing nature than of a slicing one, which brought into question the use of the heavy sword. During a separate autopsy, we took the time to match the broken sword and several of the knives gathered from the scene against Mrs. Vaughn's wounds. One particular knife fit perfectly."

The man they trusted withheld essential information from them!

Despite feeling the earth giving way beneath his feet, Darcy found Rumbradge's explanation fascinating. He never considered that medical science could be so exact. He glanced to his cousin to find the major general's expression hard and unrelenting. Needless to say, Edward thought Rumbradge set them up: Nothing of this "change" in weapons became public knowledge at the magistrates' hearing. The major general and Hutchison planned a defense against the sword not being Edward's; now they possessed no time to prepare counter testimony for the knife.

"The broken sword in question displays double cutting edges," Rumbradge continued. "The wounds upon Mrs. Vaughn's body—most prominently the removal of her breast—were executed by a weapon with a single cutting edge. With an expert's eye, one can take note how the wound on Mrs. Vaughn's body displayed a starting point where the weapon entered her skin. A jagged depth one can feel with his fingertips is evident. It is as if someone carved the breast from her chest as one might carve slices from a ham. At the end of the circle, there is a blunt or 'T'-shaped cut. Such a cut, where the ending point meets the initial entry is indicative of a single blade knife rather than a double edged sword."

"Then the idea of whether the major general lost his sword has no bearing on this case," Jenkins said with a satisfied smirk.

Providential to Fitzwilliam's cause, Rumbradge spoke with complete professionalism rather than from a vindictive attack.

"I would never declare the broken sword as insignificant," Rumbradge corrected. "The sword is from the ordinary within the Vaughns' household. It is possible Isles Vaughn acquired the sword as a souvenir of the recent war, but from all who knew him, we learned nothing of the blade. I would think if Vaughn purchased it or found it, the baker would share his possession with his close acquaintances. That being said, the broken sword is not the weapon used by the assailant."

"Does any part of your investigation name me as that assailant, Mr. Rumbradge?" Edward asked in doubtful tones.

"No, Major General. But neither does it exclude you."

Rumbradge turned to address the court.

"What I have yet to disclose is the knife we believe used by the Vaughns' attacker is one a person might find in a butcher shop."

The officer's eyes met Darcy's, and Darcy recognized Rumbradge used the information they shared regarding the nursery rhyme to solve part of the investigation. Darcy cursed himself for trusting the man: He and Cowan had, in essence, delivered Edward to the gallows.

"Mr. Thorne was formerly a butcher."

Edward's demeanor said the major general made the natural leap in solving the puzzle.

"Are you suggesting, Mr. Rumbradge, that the knife used against the Vaughns belonged to Mr. Thorne?"

"I am making that assumption," Rumbradge confirmed.

Darcy noted Edward's knuckles whiten as his cousin gripped the banister marking the bar behind which he stood.

"Then you are also suggesting whoever killed Vaughn and then Thorne 'chose' them as his targets—that these were not crimes of passion: They were deliberate murder."

"If I had more time to dedicate to the investigation, I am certain the evidence would lead to that conclusion; however, at this time, only a postulation can be made."

A supposition, which would remain in the memory of those determining Edward's guilt or innocence.

Darcy glanced to Georgiana, who paled. His sister would soon know heartbreak. Darcy turned his head in time to note the expression of regret, which crossed the major general's countenance when Edward's eyes met Georgiana's.

Rumbradge's testimony continued for another hour, and not one among the gallery departed the crowded space. The officer discussed in detail the deaths of the Thornes and their employee, Mrs. Winthrop.

"The perpetrator attacked the Thornes sometime after closing. As was his custom to escort the widowed tavern maid Mrs. Winthrop home, Mr. Bernard, the night watchman, called at three. In the early morning hours of 9 October, Bernard discovered the crimes and then summoned the authorities."

"How did the Thornes die?" Jenkins asked.

"From what we could decipher from the scene, the attacker overpowered Mr. Thorne near the kitchen's entrance. We assume from some of the marks upon the doorframe, Thorne attempted to escape through the door. His body rested half in and half out. The villain struck Thorne in the forehead—between the eyes—with an odd-shaped object, which cut a chuck of skin from his head. Our attacker slit Mr. Thorne's throat, but prior to that wound, the assailant wrestled with Thorne, a beefy man, who once was employed as a butcher. The man broke Thorne's neck in two places. More significantly, the attacker cut Thorne's left eye from his head, but we think this occurred as the murderer escaped rather than being part of the initial attack upon the tavern owner."

"How was this determined?"

A cold sweat broke over Darcy's brow: Rumbradge withheld information, which could prove beneficial to Edward's defense. Darcy could not believe the authorities discovered all the facts the officer disclosed after Darcy's and Cowan's discussion with Rumbradge. Some part of Darcy's logic said such was not possible.

"There were two roughly circular bloody stains on Thorne's shirt front," the officer explained. "We realized they were the outlines of the women's breasts, and the murderer placed them upon Thorne's chest while he used a knife to cut Thorne's eye from its socket."

A few of those within the gallery gagged, while others stifled sobs. Many of the onlookers said a prayer to God not to know the evils perpetrated upon both the Thornes and the Vaughns.

"We found Mrs. Thorne in the hall leading to the cold cellar. Mrs. Winthrop in the tavern area. Both were stabbed several times prior their throats being slit."

"Do you hold a guess, Mr. Rumbradge, as to the nature of the weapon used to stun Mr. Thorne?" Edward inquired.

Darcy knew his cousin thought of the Youngblood case, but Edward should be looking for weaknesses in the officer's tale instead. On purpose, Darcy cleared his throat in warning, but his cousin's countenance announced the major general's distraction.

"An object of some weight with a square-shaped base."

Neither Rumbradge nor Edward gave voice to the conclusion they recognized, but Cowan turned to whisper, "A candlestick from Weldon's shop."

Darcy nodded his agreement. They missed those particular details. He shot a quick glance to Southland on the other side of the gallery, but the captain shook off Darcy's unspoken question. The use of an item from the second victims to kill the first and the third to kill the second was a new aspect to these murders—one that had Darcy scrambling to make adjustments in his previous suppositions.

"Speak to us of the third incident," Jenkins suggested.

Rumbradge shot a glance to Cowan before continuing his testimony. "The attacker killed Mr. and Mrs. Urick in the kitchen. I interviewed a woman in a nearby tenement, who told us of seeing a man outside the Weldon's kitchen window, but she thought it Mr. Tern, the gentleman who owns the adjoining shop, returning from spending time with his lady."

"Did the woman's description provide information as to the attacker's size?" Jenkins asked as he looked to where Edward maintained a military bearing.

"The woman only observed the figure for a few seconds. She was tending a sick infant and glanced out the one time. The witness did say she thought the figure Mr. Tern, who is several inches shorter than the major general."

Darcy silently thanked the investigator for that simple statement.

Jenkins scowled.

"Yet, the woman cannot be certain at a distance," the prosecutor encouraged.

"No, Sir," Rumbradge agreed: The officer would not challenge the court. When Jenkins remained in smug silence, Rumbradge continued. "Urick, like Thorne, was struck with a heavy object. The blow broke through a section of the man's skull. Although Urick was a fair-sized man, I am certain he could not save his wife from the attacker. We are still uncertain how Weldon did not hear the commotion below. Despite the attack occurring in the night's middle, Weldon remained dressed in his work clothes and apron above stairs. Perhaps the man fell asleep at his desk. A ledger book remained open upon a table beside the even smaller desk. The ink well was upset during the struggle so we do not know if it was corked or not.

"Alternating steps ascending to the level where Weldon's body was located displayed boot prints. The steps were narrow, and the only full print was outside between the buildings. We made sketches of the prints to determine boot size, and before you ask, Mr. Jenkins, the major general wears a comparable-sized boot, although the same could be said of half the men in this room."

"Anything else of import, Mr. Rumbradge?"

"The attacks against the Weldon household were very much of the nature of the previous crimes, except Weldon suffered a different mutilation than did Thorne. The culprit removed Weldon's left ear."

"I will discover if Rumbradge holds knowledge of the weapon used against Urick," Cowan turned to whisper. "That information may assist us in locating the females chosen for this evening's attack."

Darcy lowered his voice for privacy.

"I fear this is not going well for the major general. Our only hope to save my cousin could be to capture the real villain in this madness. You remain certain the man will strike again?"

Cowan's brows drew together in fierceness.

"Absolutely. The man's pride will demand it."

Darcy checked his watch when the prosecution excused Rumbradge. It was well past the supper hour when the court summoned Georgiana to the witness box. His sister rose regally from her seat, and he noted Georgiana handed her reticule to Elizabeth. Earlier, Darcy wondered if she planned to deliver the pistol from the previous day to Edward, but it would seem Darcy misjudged her.

She carried the weapon for peace of mind or perhaps as a memento of Edward.

After all, Darcy had no idea whether the Queen Anne pistol was loaded or not. Yet, even as he thought he erred, Darcy could not shake the idea, if he were in his cousin's position, he would ask Elizabeth to assist him in choosing his death rather than to permit his family to know the degradation of a public hanging. *Was Edward a lesser man?* Darcy knew better.

When Georgiana settled, Jenkins emerged from behind the semi-curved prosecution table to approach.

"Mrs. Fitzwilliam, I wish to apologize for the necessity of bringing you before this court."

If the prosecutor expected Georgiana to act the role of watering pot, the counsel erred. Darcy's sister responded by inclining her head in an aristocratic manner. It was a gesture Darcy observed used often by both their mother and their aunt, Lady Catherine de Bourgh. As their mother passed after giving birth to Georgiana, his sister learned it, by instinct, from their boorish aunt. Georgiana would be aghast to hear Darcy say so.

A long awkward pause followed

"Very well. Perhaps, Mrs. Fitzwilliam, you might tell us how long you and the major general have been married."

Georgiana licked her lips in a nervous gesture, but her voice sounded calm when she responded, "Major General Fitzwilliam and I spoke our vows when word arrived of Napoleon's escape from Elba. I refused to permit the major general to return to the Duke of Wellington's side without first recognizing our joining before our dear family and friends. There was too much danger in the confrontation."

"But you planned a longer engagement?" Jenkins self-satisfying amusement returned.

"My brother preferred for me to choose a Season, but my mind was set several years prior in the major general's favor."

"And when a woman sets her mind, few men can refuse, Jenkins said with a condescending tone.

Georgiana presented the prosecutor another of Lady Catherine's favorite gestures: His sister looked down her nose at the man.

"A young woman's heart is more easily turned to affection when a man of honor presents himself if that is your insinuation, Mr. Jenkins. It is well documented that men consider themselves the masters of the world, but a happy home is only achieved if a woman is convinced it is possible. Otherwise, master or not, a man's life is a miserable existence."

A snicker followed Georgiana's set down.

The prosecutor turned his face away, but not before Darcy noted a blush crossing the man's countenance.

"And this heart of yours, Mrs. Fitzwilliam? What characteristics did it admire in the major general?"

Georgiana's eyes met Edward's.

"Caring. Honesty. Principles. Empathy."

"I noticed you did not speak of love, Mrs. Fitzwilliam," Jenkins accused. His sister's lips did not speak of love, but her gaze did, the strength of Georgiana's resolve remained etched upon her countenance. "Do you love your husband, Ma'am?"

"With every chord of my heart's song," Georgiana rasped.

"And does the major general return your affection?"

Jenkins' question came too quickly upon Georgiana's response. With skill, the man maneuvered Darcy's sister into an incriminating confession, and Georgiana did not recognize the ploy. Darcy heard the anticipation in the prosecutor's tone, but there was no means to warn his sister. He shot a glance to Elizabeth: His wife sat on the end of her seat, as if calculating when disaster would occur.

Georgiana's eyebrow rose in question.

"My husband speaks of his satisfaction with our joining."

"Does he?" Jenkins said in a taunt.

"Yes."

The counsel eyed Georgiana in anticipation.

"Was the major general satisfied to return to England to discover you missing from the family home?"

Darcy's ire grew. He would sack whoever carried such tales from his sister's household to London.

"I wandered into the Scottish moors and my horse threw me. I was injured and sought out a place to recover before returning to the Fitzwilliam property. It was an honest mistake," Georgiana explained.

Jenkins' tone turned caustic.

"Do you think, Mrs. Fitzwilliam, that your 'honest mistake' exasperated your husband's apprehension after the great Battle of Waterloo? It is my understanding the major general raced across England to his family's Scottish property because he feared you dead."

Georgiana shot a pleading glance to Darcy; it was the same look she always presented him when his sister wished Darcy to solve her problems. However, this situation was beyond his control. Darcy gestured for her to take a deep breath before answering. He slowly sucked in a steadying breath to demonstrate. His sister mimicked his actions—twice.

"I am certain the major general knew great anxiety, but my brother's wife resolved the issue. Mrs. Darcy determined my whereabouts, and the day was saved."

Jenkins ignored Georgiana's smoothing over the details of the incident.

"How did the abominable spring through which England suffered affect the major general's disposition of late?"

Georgiana flinched. Without question, his sister had not considered anyone else would know of Edward's turmoil. A look to his cousin's countenance said the major general thought to break the prosecutor into two.

"All of England suffered from the weather's frailties, and if the newsprints are to be believed, England is not alone in this test of God's will."

"I understand your brother is the Master of Pemberley. Is that correct, Mrs. Fitzwilliam?"

Georgiana looked beseechingly to Darcy. His sister recognized the prosecution's objective, but she held no means to prevent what was to come.

"Yes," she guarded her response—her earlier bravado gone.

"Did the great estate of Pemberley suffer as deeply as did Yadkin Hall?"

Georgiana looked between Darcy and Edward.

At last, the major general interrupted Jenkins' questioning.

"If you wish to question me on the success or failure of my estate," Fitzwilliam gritted out in bitter tones, "please direct your inquiries to me, Mr. Jenkins. Mrs. Fitzwilliam is my wife, but she is not accountable to my tenants or my servants. That responsibility rests upon my shoulders."

Jenkins shrugged off the major general's intrusion as if the two conversed in a Mayfair drawing room.

"What I wish to ascertain, Major General, is whether you achieved your expectations for Yadkin Hall?"

Edward's shoulders stiffened: If the Fitzwilliam family survived this disaster, the major general would be making a private call upon Mr. Jenkins.

"I imagine what you wish to determine, Jenkins, is whether my supposed failure at Yadkin Hall led me to London's taverns."

"Did it?" Jenkins asked in triumph.

Edward's stare hardened upon the counsel for the prosecution.

"Yes."

"A man's choice to seek a few hours of drink does not make the man a murderer," Georgiana added in haste. "If it did, the court would need to gaol every man in this room as well as many of the women."

A chuckle spread across the room.

"True, Mrs. Fitzwilliam," Jenkins spoke in disdain. "But a man who finds failure after years of accolades—a man who would raise his hand to his wife—such a man might carry his sense of failure to London's streets. Such a man might easily dispel four attackers who meant to impress him upon a foreign ship."

Tears coursed down Georgiana's cheeks.

"You do not understand. It was my fault—never the major general's. I spoke with a shrewish tongue."

Jenkins verbally pounced.

"When your husband struck you? Is that what you mean, Mrs. Fitzwilliam? You spoke in a waspish manner, and the major general raised his hand to you?"

"I never," Edward growled, but the major general's self-control slipped.

Darcy found his own restraint in danger. He imagined many schemes, but he never considered the idea Edward would physically harm Georgiana. Darcy found his fists clenching and unclenching.

"My husband did not strike me!" Georgiana shouted above the growing hubbub. "I tripped on the carpet and stumbled into the hearth.

I swear it, as God is my witness! The major general and I argued, and I stumbled in my retreat from the room."

Jenkins played to the gallery, turning his back upon both Georgiana and Edward.

"As you say, Mrs. Fitzwilliam."

The counsel for the prosecution was an experienced man of the law, as well as a bit of an actor. He performed for his audience.

"It is most unfortunate the four women of whom we speak today could not simply trip upon a Persian carpet and know your fate instead of the one they suffered."

"No!" Georgiana screeched. "No! It is not possible! My husband would never commit these travesties!" Georgiana sank to her knees in sobs.

"Georgie!" Edward called. The major general turned to the judge. "Please, Sir. Permit me to go to her. I mean only to comfort my wife— an innocent in this madness."

A simple nod of approval sent Fitzwilliam half crawling and half stumbling, thanks to the chains about his feet and wrists, to where Georgiana's shoulders rose and fell in anguish. Ignoring all the commotion of the room, the major general pulled his wife into his embrace to rock her against him. The crowd went silent.

Darcy's fingers opened to reach for Georgiana: It was always Darcy's domain to comfort and protect Georgiana, but with her marriage, his sister placed her trust in their cousin. Fitzwilliam caressed Georgiana's cheek and whispered private encouragements in her ear. As they all watched in horror and fascination, Georgiana nodded her head and straightened her shoulders as Edward whisked away Georgina's tears with the pads of his thumbs.

At length, the major general assisted his wife to her feet, kissing Georgiana's fingertips before she walked toward the door leading to the gallery. Jenkins had not excused her, but the major general placed himself between the prosecution and his wife. Anyone who looked into the eyes of Edward Fitzwilliam would not dare complain of Georgiana's exit.

Darcy's sister did not turn to look at her husband, or at anyone else in the room: instead Georgiana accepted Elizabeth's comfort and returned to the chair she occupied throughout the day. Never once did she look to Darcy for reassurance for she belonged to Edward Fitzwilliam. Darcy could no longer think of the woman before him as Miss Georgiana Darcy.

Edward watched her go before turning to Mr. Jenkins.

"You will address your questions to me, Jenkins."

Fitzwilliam adopted the same authoritative tone the major general used to leave new recruits quaking in their boots. The counsel for the prosecution nodded in curtness. The major general spoke in a clear voice so all could hear.

"I am a second son and know little of estate management, and my pride prevented me from seeking the advice of my cousin or of my revered father. I felt the hand of disappointment pressing hard upon my shoulders. I acted foolishly, thinking my wife and daughter deserved a better husband and father than I could ever be. That being said, I never raised my hand to my wife nor did I take a life other than those considered enemies of our King. I would not. I could not."

In dejection, Fitzwilliam turned and walked toward where his fate awaited him.

Chapter Eighteen

With no one remaining to speak on either side, Mr. Jenkins summed up the many coincidences, which could connect the major general to the crimes. Darcy remained thankful they did not bring the Youngblood crimes to the notice of the authorities. If so, Jenkins' case would hold more substance.

As it was, rumors of Edward's fighting ability, his cousin's extensive experience with a sword and other weapons, reports of the major general's bloody uniform, and the opportunity to commit the crimes served as the basis of the prosecution's assumptions. Although Jenkins skillfully applied each concurrence to the case against the major general, Darcy was certain no one could declare Edward guilty of the crimes. The shadow of the indictment might follow his cousin for many years, but that fact would be preferable to the alternative.

The court permitted Edward the occasion to speak a final time in his own defense, and the major general rallied to the occasion.

"In my service to the British Army, it is true I dispatched more than one man to his God, but I also stood between the evils mankind perpetrates upon one another. At my venerated father's knee, I learned honor, as well as a charge to protect women and children. My crime is a severe one, but not a dangerous one.

"I nourished my pride and my vanity, but I did not commit deliberate murder. My bruised conceit led me to seek comfort in the bottom of an ale-filled cup rather than the company of my most loyal wife. My folly will haunt my family's name, and for that fact, I plead with my dearest loved ones to forgive my lack of forethought. I also beg this Court to permit such public censure to be the extent of the punishment my family knows: I plead with you to spare my life."

For the first time since receiving Georgiana's plea for Darcy's presence in Oxfordshire, he experienced the flicker of hope. Their family weathered the worst of the public's disdain, but Darcy's hopes were short lived when the jury accepted the case. Fitzwilliam had no more finished his plea for mercy when the first of many voices called out: "Guilty!"

A masculine voice from somewhere behind Darcy began the verbal assault. Darcy and others whirled around to face the accuser, but before anyone could act or identify the protestor, a second call—this one closer to where Southland maintained his watch—took up the word, "Guilty!"

The judge demanded silence, but the gallery did not relent. One after another the words "Death" and "Guilty" could be heard above the hubbub. As Darcy searched the angry and bewildered countenances of the audience, his eyes fell upon his sister, whose thin composure from a few minutes earlier dissipated. His sister buried her face in Elizabeth's shoulder. Darcy shot a quick glance to the major general, who remained perfectly still, as if Fitzwilliam transformed into some sort of warrior god.

The judge ordered officers to clear the rabble from the gallery, but their efforts were met with fists and jeers. Darcy and Cowan shoved several onlookers from their way as they moved to protect Darcy's family. Lindale received a solid jab to his jaw for his aristocratic objections to the row, while Matlock sheltered his countess with his body.

Within minutes, additional officers streamed in through the one door to the gallery to toss people into the hall where fellow representatives of the court drove the dissenters from the building. Before Darcy could determine what would come next, the guards removed more than half of the spectators from the gallery.

Tentatively, Darcy lowered his arms as quiet reclaimed the audience. Loud shouts could be heard from below, and he suspected the officers ordered those dispelled from the gallery driven through the narrow gates to wait outside Old Bailey's walls for news of the verdict.

"Are you injured?" Darcy pleaded as Elizabeth and Georgiana clung to him. Below, Fitzwilliam maintained his statue-like stance. It was all quite surreal.

"We are well," Elizabeth assured as she turned to look upon the major general's hard stare. "What is amiss with the major general?" she hissed in urgency.

Georgiana turned quickly in Darcy's embrace.

"Oh, my Heavens," she gasped. "I observed the major general in such a state before. My husband sees only the war."

Georgiana caught Darcy's lapels.

"*Do* something, William, before Edward acts in a manner, which will add to the prosecution's case against him."

Darcy looked about in fear. There was nothing he could do: He could not reach Edward in time.

"Sing." Cowan hissed.

Darcy did not realize the former Runner remained beside him. "Sing a lullaby. Anything. Remember Mrs. Darcy's voice in Somerset. It kept you alive, Darcy."

"Sing, Elizabeth," Darcy ordered.

His wife opened her mouth, but before Elizabeth could utter the first note, Georgiana snatched the main melody. His sister sang the lullaby Darcy often heard Georgiana use to comfort Colleen. Within seconds, Elizabeth's and Georgiana's voices filled the high-ceiling room.

His wife and sister looked only to each other for support, but Darcy watched Edward to gage whether the tune had any effects upon the major general. It took several strands of the song before Darcy noted the slight shake of Fitzwilliam's head, indicating his cousin left behind the image of destruction and instead sought his wife's countenance.

Darcy breathed easier.

"It is enough," he whispered as he noted the frowns upon the lips of both the jury and the judges.

"Thank you, Ladies." The lead judge said in awkward bemusement. "Needless to say, pleasant tunes can sooth the savage beast." The judge meant his remark in mild chastisement, but his words were very near the truth. Without incident, the song settled the major general's angst. Both Elizabeth and Georgiana blushed, but order prevailed.

Before another interruption, the jury gathered for their consultation. With those who remained in the gallery, Darcy attempted to gage the reaction of the men who would decide Edward's fate.

Many appeared affected by the ruckus: fearful, sending furtive glances to the gallery. Had the noisy removal of the spectators swayed the jury's decision? Darcy found himself studying each man—attempting to judge how the juror would vote, and the more he watched them, the more Darcy became certain his family's efforts knew failure: Edward would be convicted.

He motioned Cowan away from the others.

"What occurs next if my cousin is found guilty?"

Cowan did not appear best pleased with the question, but the investigator responded in his customary professional manner.

"A guilty verdict could result in a public whipping, hanging, or a branding of the major general's cheek with an 'M.' Of course, branding is only used in accidental deaths, not deliberate ones. Dissection and hanging in chains is more likely. There is also the possibility of transportation or imprisonment. Imprisonment could include being held at Newgate, or it could take the form of hard labor. On the lesser end, there are fines, the forfeiture of lands and goods to the Crown, or even military duty." A bit of irony crept into Cowan's tone. "Odd that is what the major general sought in traveling to London: a return to his military service."

"Is there room for an appeal?" Darcy spoke with urgency. "I fear the earlier row will convince the jurors to deliver a guilty plea. Gaze upon their countenances as they debate whether Fitzwilliam is innocent."

Cowan's eyes followed Darcy's, and the investigator's scowl deepened.

"Tell the earl to file a writ of error."

"Because the prosecution failed to offer specific evidence against the major general?"

"Yes," Cowan confirmed as he looked about him for privacy. "But also for fault in the indictment. When I sought Rumbradge, after the officer's testimony, regarding the weapon used against the Uricks, another of the court officers said something odd. The magistrate's hearing was to be a grand jury. The Middlesex grand jury, in their deliberations for court proceedings, accepted the hearing as an indictment. According to the court clerk, he never heard of such a thing."

Darcy mentally arranged the writ's many issues.

"And the afternoon break coming after Edward's trial began."

"Include all the irregularities of the hearing in the document."

"How might that save Edward?"

"The writ would force the verdict into the hands of the senior judges at Westminster or turn the verdict over to the King and His Majesty's ministers, where Matlock's and Leigh-Hunt's influences would hold more sway," Cowan explained.

A noise below brought Darcy and Cowan's attentions to the courtroom. One of the jurors approached the judges, and the central judge listened with care as the juror whispered into his ear. "And this is your verdict?"

"Aye, my lord."

The judge turned his regard upon Edward.

"Major General Edward Fitzwilliam," he said in a sad tone, and Darcy's heart sank. "Deliberate murder is most justly ranked among the highest crimes known to mankind. You have been found guilty of such crimes—of exercising the circumstances of uncommon aggravation upon the household of Isles Vaughn, Louis Thorne, and Theodore Weldon."

Georgiana cried out "No!" while the countess collapsed into Matlock's protective arms. Darcy found his fist curling into tight knots, but he could say nothing in objection. The jurors succumbed to the intimidation of the populace; he could understand their need to protect themselves and their families, but Darcy's honor could never approve of such cowardice. Edward stood as rigid as before, but this time his cousin's cheeks were damp with tears.

"Those who stood as objects of your fury," the judge continued, "had no time to beg God for mercy. I hope your heart can know contrition, and you prepared yourself for the sentence I am now to pass upon you. Pray lose not one moment more in seeking God's forgiveness for Christian charity requires me to inform you that your time in this world is short. The law of your Country, in conformity with the law of God, has pronounced death as the punishment for the crimes of which you were found guilty. Therefore, at noon tomorrow, you shall be conveyed from the prison in which you have been held to the place of execution, where you shall be hanged by the neck, until you shall be dead, and the Lord have mercy upon your soul."

Pure chaos erupted. Some of the onlookers cheered, while others broke into prayer.

"It be over!"

"God save his soul."

"The end of the world draws near!"

Elizabeth struggled to hold Georgiana upright until Lindale stepped in to catch Georgiana to him. Free of Georgiana's weight, Elizabeth rushed into Darcy's open embrace.

"How?" she sobbed. "It cannot be, Mr. Darcy"

He bent to whisper in her ear.

"The jurors were cognizant of the gathered crowd. But Cowan led me to a plan. I will explain when I return to Darcy House. For now, I must ask you to return to overseeing Georgiana's care while I speak to the earl. Just know the skirmish is lost, but the battle is not."

"Are you certain, William?" she asked through tear-filled words.

He kissed her forehead.

"I promised I would see this through to the end, and today is not the end. Now permit me to gather the earl and Mr. Hutchison."

Darcy released his wife to join Matlock.

"You and I, Sir, must speak to Hutchison at once," he whispered in urgency.

Matlock braced his countess who sobbed in frenzied hysterics. Below them, the court's officers ushered Fitzwilliam toward a door at the rear of the courtroom, the same one Darcy and Cowan used only hours prior.

"I will see my son," Aunt Nora demanded. "Now, Martin, before the authorities snatch him away from me forever."

Matlock appeared near crumpling from his wife's weight mixed with the implications of the verdict.

"Cowan," Darcy summoned the man. "You and Lindale will escort the countess and Georgiana below. Demand the court permit my aunt and Mrs. Fitzwilliam a brief word with the major general."

The investigator accepted Darcy's aunt from the earl's embrace. Cowan looked quite awkward, but he treated the countess with unmeasured tenderness.

"Come, Lady Matlock," Cowan encouraged as he directed the countess's steps toward the still open door. "We must hurry before the officers return the major general to New Prison."

Cowan's words heartened Lady Matlock's composure: Darcy's aunt straightened her shoulders as if going into battle. She permitted Cowan to lead her onward, while Lindale followed with Georgiana, who wiped at the tears streaming from her eyes.

"I will remain with Mrs. Darcy," Southland assured.

"Thank you, Roman." Darcy caught his uncle's arm. "We must hurry also, Sir. Your position as Matlock is required."

The man Darcy always admired and sometimes feared took several weak, stumbling steps forward.

"How am I to go on, Darcy?" the earl said through trembling lips.

"Hope does not abandon our endeavor, Sir, but for us to know success, you must be the imperious Earl of Matlock, not Martin Fitzwilliam, father. For now, sentiment is not a luxury we can embrace."

❧❧❧

Within minutes, Cowan interrupted Darcy's meeting with Hutchison to announce he meant to seek out Rumbradge to learn more of the officer's thoughts upon the verdict and to discover something of the weapon used against Weldon.

"I could not find Rumbradge after his testimony; he escaped before I could follow."

Darcy nodded his agreement.

"Lord Matlock and I will be joining Mr. Hutchison at the gentleman's quarters. On your way out, would you please instruct Mrs. Darcy I will be quite late in returning to Darcy House? If you learn anything of significance call on us at Hutchison's residence."

Cowan glanced off to his right.

"I left the countess and Mrs. Fitzwilliam in the same room we used earlier. The authorities gave them ten minutes. Viscount Lindale awaits them outside the door." Cowan opened his coat to display a hidden pistol. "I was not permitted in the room this time," he said with a smirk.

"Another inconsistency," Darcy remarked.

Cowan's eyebrow rose half in amusement and half in curiosity.

"If it is no great imposition, I would take Southland with me. Rumbradge's disclosures must be reevaluated in relation to the Youngblood case."

"Youngblood?" Matlock asked. "I recall that particular name from Edward's time upon the American continent. The events took a dark toll upon my son's equanimity."

"I will explain in more detail later, Sir," Darcy assured his uncle. To Cowan he said, "Ask the captain to escort Mrs. Darcy to Lindale's side. I will instruct the viscount to see the ladies home after they speak to the major general."

Cowan bowed his exit. "I will call with whatever news I discover. I am certain Mr. Hutchison knows how best to proceed in this matter."

Darcy was not so convinced; Jenkins out maneuvered the young barrister, who held the reputation as a skilled counsel, but they held few choices in the matter. They placed Fitzwilliam's life in the barrister's hands.

ॐ ॐ ॐ

Darcy's eyes burned from reading numerous passages from Hutchison's law study books. He and Matlock made quick farewells to Lindale and Elizabeth, assuring the viscount and Darcy's wife he and the earl meant to petition first the judges at Westminster and, if necessary, the king's ministers upon Edward's behalf. However, with less than a day before the major general's execution, they had no time to sleep upon the possibilities."

Before they departed his family at Old Bailey, Elizabeth slipped her hand into Matlock's right one as she smoothed the earl's frown lines with her fingertips.

"Lord Lindale and I will tend your countess and Mrs. Fitzwilliam. Leave those worries in our capable hands," she coaxed. "You and Mr. Darcy must concentrate on freeing the major general. Our confidence rides with you."

The earl kissed Elizabeth's temple. "You are an exemplary Mistress of Pemberley. Lady Anne Darcy would be prodigiously fond of you."

Matlock's words brought a *controlled* smile to Elizabeth's lips. Darcy knew his uncle's praise pleased her, but because of the situation, his wife stifled the self-satisfied smile, which tugged at her lips.

"I shall prove myself worthy," she whispered to Darcy.

He leaned closer to speak to his wife's ear.

"It is only I that you must please, Mrs. Darcy."

Her eyebrow rose in a familiar challenge, and the gesture tilted his chaotic world closer to normalcy. The woman always had that particular effect on him.

"Solve the major general's dilemma, my husband, and then return to your sons and to me in your triumph."

"I pray my best will prove enough, Mrs. Darcy." He kissed the back of the hand he held. "Guard my sister and the countess, and present my sons a kiss from their father. I will be sorry to miss time in the nursery."

That was three hours prior. The ormolu clock on Mr. Hutchison's mantel announced it was near midnight. Darcy rubbed his eyes again to clear his vision. Matlock succumbed to both exhaustion and several stiff drinks on an empty stomach.

With his uncle's head drooping upon the earl's chest, Darcy made a silent promise to stay awake and wait for Hutchison to draft the required writ. The earl required his rest before rushing the writ to the offices of the judges who might change the outcome of this day's verdict.

Darcy watched the barrister as Hutchison scratched out the necessary wording for the legal document. He attempted not to distract the young man, who was less than five years Darcy's junior.

When had he become so ancient?

Darcy wondered in diverted amusement. He saw the arrival of his three and thirtieth birthday; his lovely Elizabeth neared five and twenty. Georgiana two and twenty and Edward five and thirty. Where had the years gone? Darcy could easily summon forth the emotions of those agonizing months when he thought he would never claim the former Elizabeth Bennet, and now they knew marital bliss for some five years.

Five years this month, he recalled when his mind registered November arrived on silent feet. Would they possess anything to celebrate? Or would the happiest day of Darcy's life go unrecognized because of the misery of his sister's marriage?

"I must speak to Mr. Hutchison!"

Cowan's familiar voice filled the hallway of the let rooms Hutchison kept.

"But Sir!" Hutchison's landlady protested as Darcy crossed the room to jerk open the door.

"Admit him!" Darcy called from the third storey.

"Darcy! Thank God you are here!" Cowan bolted up the stairs, with Southland following on the investigator's heels.

Darcy's heart jumped in fear. It was not of Cowan's nature to create a scene nor to speak with such urgency.

"What is amiss?"

Cowan caught Darcy's arm and dragged him into Hutchison's quarters while Southland closed the door to assure privacy.

"Someone attacked Viscount Lindale outside Old Bailey!"

Matlock staggered to his feet, still a bit incoherent.

"What means this, Southland?"

"Mr. Cowan and I returned to Old Bailey after speaking with Mr. Rumbradge and then with several of those who viewed the proceedings," the captain explained. "We hoped to learn something that would prove of assistance to the major general. We were perhaps an hour in our pursuits, but we left our mounts near the court. Upon returning to the area, we discovered several in attendance upon Lord Lindale's behalf."

"Was my son attacked by those driven from the gallery?" Matlock demanded.

"No, my lord." Cowan took up the tale. "As Lindale saw the ladies to your carriage, someone struck the viscount from behind."

A shiver of dread shook Darcy's shoulders.

"My wife?" He reached for the mantle to brace his stance for Cowan's explanation.

Cowan closed his eyes as if shutting out the truth.

"From all reports, Lord Matlock's carriage sped away with the ladies inside. Captain Southland and I left the viscount in the care of the surgeon the authorities summoned to attend him. Lindale has a knot on the back of his head and his shoulder is displaced, but the surgeon saw to both before we arrived. I left instructions to move Lindale to Lockland Hall and to summon the viscountess. Then the captain and I went in search of the carriage containing the countess, Mrs. Fitzwilliam, and Mrs. Darcy."

"And?" Darcy demanded.

"Neither the carriage nor the ladies are at Lord Matlock's residence or at Darcy House. While I spoke to Mr. Thacker, word arrived from one of the Old Bailey officers that the earl's coach driver was found dead behind the nearby mews." Cowan swallowed hard, forcing the words to reality. "I fear our Youngblood pretender claimed three female victims. Those we never expected. Your family, Sir."

Chapter Nineteen

Within seconds of Lindale's handing them into the coach, Matlock's driver mounted the box and set the horses to their paces. The coachman encouraged so much speed, that Elizabeth, the countess, and Georgiana were thrown hard against the squabs.

"What can John Coachman mean by the urgency?' the countess shrieked as she adjusted her turban. "Do the hordes give chase?"

Darcy's aunt used her cane to rap upon the coach's roof, but the driver ignored the unspoken order to slow the carriage.

Meanwhile, Elizabeth clawed her way to the side window. Pulling the drape away, she stared out into the darkness. Only the occasional light flickered as the carriage rocked and swayed upon the uneven stones.

"We are leaving the City," she observed.

"We cannot be!"

Georgiana squeezed in beside her.

"What is happening, Elizabeth?"

Darcy's sister craned her neck to look behind them.

"I do not see Lord Lindale anywhere. Could Uncle Matlock remove us from London so Aunt Nora and I cannot view the major general's execution?"

Elizabeth thought if that were so Darcy would inform her. William was not the type to make unilateral decisions; her husband would consult her before sending Elizabeth away. She bit her bottom lip to stifle the rising cry of panic.

"It is too dark to observe anyone." She caught at the overhead strap to keep from being pitched upon the coach's floor. Elizabeth glanced to the frightened countenances of her sister in marriage and of her husband's aunt. Darcy would expect her to protect his family. As she changed her seat to squeeze between them, Elizabeth caught the hand of each. The carriage shifted to the left, and Elizabeth thought they might be pitched upon their side.

"Someone abducts us," she announced when they again fought their way to a seated position. "I am certain what is happening has something to do with Fitzwilliam's trial. For now, we are on our own. No one, other than Lord Lindale, knows we are missing."

"And what of my eldest son?" the countess's voice rose in distress.

Elizabeth squeezed the woman's hand tighter.

"We are all mothers," she declared. "And we will fight to return to our children."

Elizabeth felt the pace slacken and heard the carriage creak from the abuse. "Assist me in discovering a means from this madness."

৵৵৵

For several elongated seconds, everything went black. *Elizabeth.* His wife's name beat a tattoo in his head. *Elizabeth.* He could not lose her: She was Darcy's complete world.

Matlock straightened his waistcoat.

"Come, Darcy."

He started toward the door.

"We must find the countess."

Yet, when the earl reached the opening, he paused, his hand gripping the latch.

"Where do we begin to look?" he said in perfect bitterness. Matlock rested his forehead against the door. "I cannot lose both my wife and my youngest son in one night."

A moment of shocked silence rocked Darcy's composure. He never thought to observe the Earl of Matlock so broken.

"Sit, Sir."

Darcy crossed the room to direct his uncle's steps to a nearby chair.

"Let us learn what Mr. Cowan and the captain discovered before we rush out into the night."

Although he spoke with complete reason, Darcy wished to abandon his logical mind and to dismantle ever house in London until he found his wife.

"Tell me you have something which will aid in our search," he pleaded.

Darcy cursed himself for playing the fool. He thought his wealth and his social position would protect his family, but even now his wife could be lying dead on some filthy floor—her body mutilated in the same manner as Youngblood's victims.

Edward's past life invaded every facet of Darcy's faultless world. At this moment, he wished he kept the Fitzwilliam family at arm's length rather than to foster a close relationship with his mother's family—a relationship that could rob Darcy of his sister, as well as the mother of his children. Every muscle in his body strained to remain immobile.

"We know the earl's carriage raced from the scene of Lindale's attack," Cowan explained. "From what the viscount disclosed, no one emerged when he approached the covered colonnades outside Old Bailey except the earl's driver, who stood at the horses' heads. Lindale said he thought it odd no footman appeared, but Lindale assumed Lord Matlock commandeered his servant for Darcy's coach."

"Was my coach still in one of the coach stands?" Darcy asked.

"No, Sir." Cowan confirmed. "I expected it to be at Darcy House when I called to verify Mrs. Darcy's arrival. I set Mr. Thacker the task of locating the carriage and your driver."

Darcy did not like the prospect of his driver having met the same fate as Matlock's, but he did not voice his concerns. He would face the possibility of losing a devoted servant when the need arrived.

"Was Lindale of any assistance as to who committed this crime?"

Southland took up the tale.

"The viscount's attacker wrestled Lord Lindale to the ground. Lindale struck his head against the brick pavers, which stunned him for a few seconds. The viscount claims he placed the ladies within the carriage and walked to where his horse waited; yet, before he could mount, someone struck him from behind."

"Did not the driver come to the viscount's assistance?" Darcy asked through a scowl.

Cowan returned Darcy's frown.

"Lindale claims the driver was his attacker."

"That is impossible," Matlock grumbled. "Mr. Lacey must be fifty if he is a day and is several inches shorter than Lindale. He could never subdue my son."

Cowan's mind made the logical jump only seconds before Darcy's.

"The attacker killed Mr. Lacey first and stole your driver's livery."

Darcy's frustration rose. "None of this tells me the whereabouts of my wife."

"We must return to Old Bailey and begin anew," Cowan suggested. "Someone surely noted the earl's carriage. We must trace it street by street."

Darcy jammed his fingers into his hair.

"That could take all night. What if…"

"Nothing will happen to Mrs. Darcy or the other ladies," Cowan assured. "Our pretender is playing a dangerous game. He means to torment the major general, not you."

"Then why is it I feel such despair?"

❧ ❧ ❧

"We are slowing down." Georgiana peered out the window of the coach again.

The trio discussed many possibilities after Elizabeth's declaration and decided to fight whomever thought them easy victims. To Elizabeth's amazement, Darcy's aunt rose to the challenge.

"Our abductor will know the wrath of the Matlocks for this offense."

"I can smell the river," Elizabeth observed.

"That means we are still close to London." Georgiana's voice held a flicker of hope.

"For as long as we were jostled about in this coach, we could be some twenty miles from the Capital," the countess observed.

Before they could give voice to their opinions, the coach's door swung wide, and a strangely familiar figure stood in the opening, pointing a gun at them. Although their abductor wore a scarf across his face, Elizabeth had the feeling she should recognize the slant of the man's shoulders and the forbidding stance.

"My God!" Georgiana gasped, her hopes dissipated by their captor's aggressiveness.

The man reached for the coach's steps and set them down, but the tension in his arms caused his jacket to pull tighter.

"Come with me," he ordered.

Elizabeth shot an anxious glance to the countess, who nodded her agreement to Elizabeth's unspoken question.

"You have no need for the gun," Elizabeth assured. "We are but women."

Surprisingly, the man flinched, tightening his grip on the gun. Elizabeth's words caught the stranger off guard, making him appear wary.

"The countess will leave her cane behind," he instructed in a less than steady voice. "We have not far to walk."

A gesture with his gun brought Elizabeth's attention to a row of wooden buildings outlined against the night sky.

"And Mrs. Fitzwilliam will leave her reticule in the carriage."

Elizabeth took note of how the man eliminated any possible weapons. What was more telling was the fact their captor knew Georgiana took to carrying Edward's Queen Anne pistol upon her person. Their captor knew the family's recent history. All Elizabeth had to do was to figure out who he might be and why the man wanted to take them prisoners.

"But…" Georgiana began a protest; however, Elizabeth's calming hand upon her sister's sleeve quieted the girl.

"Simply do as you are told, Georgiana."

Elizabeth's tone spoke of composure, but she felt anything but. It would be her responsibility to lead the countess and Darcy's sister to safety, and Elizabeth was not certain she was up to the task.

"Permit me to exit first, Countess, so I may assist you down."

Darcy's aunt nodded her agreement. "As you wish, Mrs. Darcy."

Elizabeth worked her way to the door; her body held the tension of the never-ending drama associated with the major general's trial, as well as the bruising along the side of her leg from being slammed into the coach's side. Their captor took a half step back and permitted Elizabeth to inch her way to the ground. She turned to extend her hand to Darcy's aunt.

"Come, Countess."

Elizabeth acted the role of footman, steadying the countess's stance on the narrow steps. Nora Fitzwilliam suffered from a bit of gout, and the two hours they spent cramped into the earl's carriage weakened the woman's legs; yet, when the countess reached the ground, she turned to Georgiana with a gesture mimicking Elizabeth's.

"Your turn, my dear," Lady Matlock announced patricianly.

"What have we executed to deserve such treatment?" Georgiana's mouth twisted in confusion. Despite her trepidation, Darcy's sister did as her aunt suggested.

The countess laced her arm through Georgiana's, and Elizabeth recognized the gesture for what it was: The countess would keep Georgiana from acting without reason. Elizabeth was thankful to possess such an intelligent ally in this endeavor.

"I am certain Darcy and Matlock still search for us. For the moment, we are *guests* of this gentleman." Lady Matlock gestured toward the man with the gun.

"But Colleen…" Georgiana dissented.

"Is safe in her nurse's arms," Elizabeth insisted.

Their kidnapper motioned toward a building standing in the shadows.

"You will lead the way, Mrs. Darcy. I will follow Lady Matlock and Mrs. Fitzwilliam. Do not choose an action that will put them in danger."

Elizabeth glanced to the self-assured countess before proclaiming, "I would never think of deserting my husband's family."

≈ ≈ ≈

They left Mr. Hutchison with the task of completing the writ without their oversight while they set about the search for the ladies. Although Darcy considered his uncle too exhausted for another night without sleep, Matlock insisted upon accompanying them. "If you think I mean to find rest while Nora is suffering at the hands of a madman, you have lost all reason, Darcy."

"Yet, should you not tend to Lindale? Rowland is the heir to the earldom." Darcy thought to appeal to Matlock's need to protect the family's heritage.

Matlock's tone spoke of his disdain. "Tell me, Darcy, would you abandon Pemberley if doing so was the only means to bring Mrs. Darcy home?"

Darcy found his throat thicken with dread when he thought of his wife.

"Within a heartbeat, Sir."

"Then why think you I would do less for Nora? The countess is the earldom; neither Edward nor Rowland nor I would be worth a fig without her."

Despite the chaos surrounding them, Darcy smiled.

"I apologize, Sir. As always, you are correct, Your Lordship."

Cowan led them through London's streets to the wall surrounding Old Bailey. Hutchison's let rooms were within a half-mile of the courthouse.

"Search each section. Look for anything unusual. A button torn from a jacket. A scuff mark on the pavers," Cowan instructed.

The life upon London's streets, even at such a late hour, never ceased to amaze Darcy. Living in the country, he retired early and enjoyed the silence of the night. He was never one to frequent the gambling hells or to drink the night away at his clubs. Even so, his party arrived to find several people still milling about the walled yard.

"Fer what duh ye search, Guv'nor?" One of the men, well into the midst of his revelry, called.

Cowan nudged the man from his way.

"Just looking for something we lost earlier," Darcy's friend explained. Cowan lit one of the lanterns he borrowed from Hutchison's landlady before they left the let rooms.

"Nuthin' of 'orth," the drunk assured. "If'n it were, it be long gone."

Cowan ignored the interruption, lifting the lantern high to illuminate a larger area. He bent to study the five coach stands along the wall. Darcy knelt beside his friend. He whispered the question pounding a steady rhythm in his brain.

"Does my family have a chance of surviving this?"

Cowan wiped his handkerchief across his brow.

"Tell me, Darcy. Would you know if Mrs. Darcy left this world? Would you feel the void as if someone ripped your soul from your body?"

Darcy searched Cowan's countenance, but the man's eyes remained shuttered, as if seeking a confirmation of an undefined truth.

"I would like to think so. I often say Elizabeth breathes out, and I breathe in."

Cowan's stone-faced expression faded, and a slight grin tugged at his lips.

"I thought as much. If I know Mrs. Darcy, whoever took her will be most assuredly sorry he sought the acquaintance of Mr. Bennet's second daughter. From what I heard, the lady led you upon a merry chase before she brought the Master of Pemberley to his knees. Imagine what your lady could do to a mere mortal. My God, Darcy! Back in Dorset, I witnessed Mrs. Darcy literally digging you from an early grave. Do not permit your self-absorption to cloud your thinking. Mrs. Darcy will prevail. Upon that, you may place your confidence."

"Cowan, over here," Southland called.

Darcy had little time to consider Cowan's declaration, but the man's confidence in Elizabeth provided a layer of assurance. He trailed behind the former Runner to examine the area to which Southland pointed.

"This is the colonnade that covered the earl's coach," Southland explained. "Signs of a struggle—gouge marks in the dirt and boot black on the pavers."

Cowan ran a finger over the boot mark in the soft earth.

"Lindale's horse would have been tied nearby. I imagine the viscount assisted the ladies into the carriage and pulled the curtain to protect them from the possible jeers of by-passers. These marks are more likely from the attack upon Lord Matlock's coachman than from the one upon the viscount."

Matlock looked off along the line of Old Bailey toward where St. Paul's could be viewed against the night sky.

"I wish we had more information on which to base our search. Lindale will be distracted regarding failing his mother."

Darcy never observed his uncle in such a state of melancholy. "If it will ease your mind," he said, "let us find a messenger to carry your pledges and orders to your butler and your assurances to the viscount."

Darcy considered whether to send a like message to Darcy House, but he rejected the idea: His servants would perform their duties without Darcy's oversight. His children were safely in their beds, but his wife was not present under his roof. It was a dismal thought.

"Should we send word to Fitzwilliam also?" Southland suggested.

Matlock shook off the suggestion.

"The major general can offer nothing to save his wife, and my son has more pressing thoughts. There is no reason to bring more pain and shame to Edward's soul. It is best, for now, if my son is kept unawares. Moreover, in light of his incarceration, our task will prove the major general's innocence."

While Hutchison wrote the introduction to the writ, Darcy explained to Matlock the suspicions Darcy, Southland, and Cowan shared regarding a connection to the Youngblood incident on the American continent.

"We must pray," Darcy instructed, "that the real murderer does not act until we discover our family. Cowan believes the man's pride will cause him to follow the pattern of the original crimes."

A fretful frown marred Matlock's forehead. "It would be a crime against all that is holy if the writ releases Edward to Society, only for him to discover his life as a soldier robbed him of the two women he adores."

Cowan rejoined them.

"Come along. We will attempt to follow Lord Matlock's coach."

He motioned to where Southland held the reins of several questionable looking horses.

"It will take time," the investigator warned. "We will need to backtrack often."

Both Darcy and the earl nodded their understandings. They had little choice but to permit Cowan his lead. Neither Darcy nor Matlock held expertise in this matter.

"We will begin with what we know," Cowan instructed. "From those gathered along Old Bailey Road, we know the earl's carriage turned onto Fleet Land. With no other leads as to the coach's destination, we will follow Fleet. Perhaps we will discover another lead before too long."

They did as Cowan suggested and at Seacoal Lane, the investigator dismounted to speak to several men outside a boarding house. The chase was slower than Darcy wished, but he had little choice in the matter.

"The coach displays an insignia in yellow and blue upon its side," Cowan explained to the men.

"Aye," the youngest of the three declared. "Nearly ran o'er Nell Watson as she crossed to fetch her man 'is nightly ale."

"Did you observe which way the coach traveled?"

"Wat be it to ye?" the shortest of the three asked.

Cowan extended his open palm. "Two coins to know the coach's destination."

The largest of the informants snatched the coins from Cowan's grasp.

"Seacoal. They'd turned on Seacoal. Thought the driver mit flip the coach on its side, so sharp be the 'urn."

Darcy wondered of the man's oddly accented English. Sounded to be Italian. He often forgot how diverse London's population had become. The man's accent reminded Darcy of a broken promise he made to Elizabeth.

In the throes of passion, he promised to show his lovely new wife the world beyond Derbyshire's border; yet, even after five years of marriage, Darcy never escorted Elizabeth further than London and Edinburgh. If he found Elizabeth safe, Darcy would remedy the deficit. His wife's innate intelligence deserved to know a world of beauty and art and books.

Their search continued. Stopping often. Speaking to many who noted the coach's passage. Darcy began to wonder if they would ever find the interloper. At length, they turned north toward St Martin-in-the-Fields, past the King's Mews, where the Strand from the City met Whitehall.

"Are we traveling in circles?" Matlock grumbled.

"Do you not think it peculiar that at each stop, we discover someone who observed Lord Matlock's coach?" Cowan asserted. "It is as if the driver wished to be seen. We found numerous observers who noted the speed of the carriage or the reckless manner in which the driver handled it."

"I am not certain I understand your question, Cowan."

The investigator's customary grim expression deepened.

"I have the distinct feeling whoever absconded with the earl's carriage knew we would follow, and he set a course to distract us from his true destination."

A cold chill ran down Darcy's spine. "What is the alternative?"

Before Cowan could respond, Southland added his opinion.

"If our wits are to run a wild-goose chase, might I suggest a twist to the trail we follow? This is in principle All Saints Day or as some call it, All Hallows or Hallowmas. We are not far from All Hallows Barking, near Tower Hamlets."

Darcy pounced on the captain's suggestion.

"Great Tower Hill: The site of countless public executions. Is this a prediction of Edward's shameful end?"

"Where better to taunt my son with the site's evil roots?" Matlock mused.

"Toward the Thames and the docks," Southland thought aloud.

"Are you thinking of Rhys again?" Darcy inquired.

Southland brows twitched together, deepening the unsmiling line crossing the captain's expression.

"I cannot explain the lack of confidence I held in Rhys' tale, and today at the hearing I felt as if someone watched me, and my first thought was it had to be Rhys."

"Would not the man's extensive scarring draw attention if he were in the gallery?" Darcy reasoned.

"I suppose...But, during the war, I became accustomed to following my instincts when making difficult decisions."

"A man who walks Society's line does likewise," Matlock insisted.

"What will it be, Darcy?" The quietness of Cowan's words drove the cold deeper into Darcy's soul. "Do we continue the trail, which appears a diversion, although we do not know this fact for certain, or do we listen to our innards and seek out ambiguity?"

"Both are a gamble," Darcy observed. "What if I choose the wrong objective? I could lose Mrs. Darcy forever."

Silence stretched among them, each comprehending the possible violent deaths awaiting Darcy's family. Terrible as it was to acknowledge his thoughts, Darcy wondered who would be the attacker's first victim? Would it be best to die first and not know the pain of the others? Or would it be best to fight against the cruelty? To attempt to defeat the evil brought to one's door?

"It must be your choice, Darcy, and whatever the outcome, you must come to know you acted your part with honor."

Darcy swallowed hard and closed his eyes to the world. An empty future laughed at him from the distance. How could he continue breathing if Elizabeth met her Maker? Despair filled him. How was he to choose?

"Mr. Cowan!" an uncultured, accented voice called from an approaching donkey cart.

Darcy opened his eyes to discover the young mother to whom they spoke after Weldon's death.

"Thank our Lord we found ye, Sir," the woman declared as the driver brought the cart to a standstill beside their horses.

Cowan dismounted and started for the cart. "Mrs. Dempsey? What is amiss? Why are you not at home with young Wimby?"

"I 'ad to warn ye, Sir," she declared.

"Warn me? Did you remember something of import, Ma'am?"

"Aye."

The woman wrung her hands.

"I goes to the court terday, Sir. To learn of Mr. Weldon and the Uricks." Darcy stepped down from his horse to stand beside Cowan. "They be good people. I stands in the back and listens."

"You should have spoken to me," Cowan assured.

"I's could not, Sir," Mrs. Dempsey insisted with a firm shake of her head. "Nots in a public place. It not be right. Ye be a fine gent'eman."

Cowan smiled easily. "I do not claim the gentry, Mrs. Dempsey, but I appreciate your kindness."

He patted the back of the woman's dirty hand.

"Now, tell me why you felt the need to seek me out. Mr. Darcy and I are most interested in your tale."

The woman turned to look upon the former Runner with admiration: Cowan made a conquest.

"As I says, I come to hears of Mr. Weldon, but I hears other things I never thought to know."

"What sort of things?" Cowan prompted.

"Others in the stands. They whisper of the lies the hangman speaks."

Mrs. Dempsey gestured to the man beside her on the bench seat. "This be me brother Tark. He hears it also."

Cowan attempted to soothe the woman's nerves.

"I understand the testimony was upsetting, but if you could share with us your concerns, we would be truly in your debt. What were the lies? And who is the hangman?"

"You's know him, Sir," the woman declared. "The one who speaks of the crimes. The one who asts me who I sees when Weldon dies?"

"Mr. Rumbradge?"

"That be the name he uses now, but 'veryone call him 'The Hangman.'" Tark spoke for the first time.

"Is Rumbradge that violent?" Darcy looked in question to Cowan. "Has the man a reputation for sending many to the gallows?"

Cowan shrugged.

"Not of which I am aware."

"This fella was once an 'angman before he'd come to London," Tark explained. "From wats I hears, he likes the role of executioner; he 'as 'is sights on a 'igher position though."

"Were you aware of this when we spoke to you after Mr. Weldon's death?" Cowan asked the woman.

"No, Sir. Only 'fterwards. When we sees the gent 'ater on the street, Tark tells me. Then I be's afeared he mite not like it if'n I's come too friendly with yous. You make him 'ppear bungling."

"Should Rumbradge's previous occupation matter?" Matlock reasoned. "He is still protecting the law."

Tark responded with a bit of a snarl.

"Not matter much if'n ye wish tu see yer boy hung, me lord."

Cowan's impatience showed.

"One of you please tell me what brought you after me. I promise none of us will interrupt again."

He shot a warning glare to his riding partners. Tark cleared his throat to take up the tale.

"Masie and me overhears the 'angman tellin another to stir up the crowd, but not 'til the 'angman makes his exit."

Cowan nudged Darcy with a sharp elbow to prevent Darcy from asking the question springing to his lips.

"Masie say she shuld wern ye, but the officers burst in, and we gets driven from the room; but we waits outside to hears the verdict. When ye leaves, Sir, Masie and me follow, but ye be talkin tu the 'angman, and we's be afeared to be seen seekin ye out. The 'angman 'as a reputation for evil. No one crosses him."

"Then what followed?" Darcy knew Cowan wished to ask more, but the investigator kept his word to Tark.

"We's didnae know wat tu do, so we walks back to Old Bailey, but a carriage came speedin by. His Lordship's carriage," Mrs. Dempsey declared. "Seen the earl's mark on the side."

She paused to glance to her brother, who nodded his encouragement.

"Mr. Rumbradge be drivin' and I hears a woman scream."

Darcy's heart stuttered to a halt.

"Rumbradge is the kidnapper we seek?"

Darcy mistakenly interpreted the fear the residents of Wapping presented the officer as respect.

"Are you certain, Mrs. Dempsey?" Cowan asked in equal amounts of disbelief.

"Saw 'im with arn own eyes," Tark insisted. "The 'angman be tu big fer the coachman's livery."

"We didnae know of the viscounty 'til later," Mrs. Dempsey added. "We thinks ye sent yer ladies with the officer to get them away frum the crowds, but whens we gits home neither Tark nor I culd shake the bad feeling so we's borrow the 'art and comes lookin' fer ye. When we's return to Old Bailey, one of those outside say you rode off tu find the earl's carriage. So we's follow."

Despite his best efforts, Darcy's voice shook with apprehension. "If Rumbradge is truly our kidnapper, is he the killer or is he assisting the murderer?"

"Ye think the 'angman kilt Weldon and the others?" Tark asked.

"More likely his cousin," Mrs. Dempsey reasoned. "The one who calls the 'ajor general guilty."

Southland edged closer. "Does the cousin have scars upon his face and arms?"

The lady shook off the suggestion.

"That one not be the cousin. I hears others say Rumbradge be the cause of the scars, but I don't know the truth of it. The man who calls out is the one with the coins."

"Coins?" Panic filled Darcy's chest.

"Pugh!" Southland deduced. "It was not Rhys I saw, but the banker. I saw him in the gallery. From the corner of my eye, but not clearly enough to register his identity at the time."

Chapter Twenty

"How long do you suppose we must wait before someone discovers us?" Georgiana whispered.

Elizabeth thought her sister in marriage should count her blessings, rather than to dwell upon what could not be changed. Several hours passed since their kidnapper deposited them in a storage room of a large warehouse, one that held the odors of heavy oil and fresh cut wood. Originally, she and the countess thought their abductor removed them from the City, but now Elizabeth suspected he led them on a less than direct route, one meant to disorient them and to confuse those who might follow.

"I hold no doubt William and Lord Matlock search for us. We must remain strong. We cannot lose hope."

"Mrs. Darcy is correct," the countess reasoned. "We must stall as long as possible to provide Matlock and Darcy to follow the trail our malefactor provided. The man was quite ingenious, and it may take our husbands a bit to unravel the pieces of the puzzle."

Bitterness laced Georgiana's tones.

"*Your* husbands. But not mine. Edward awaits a fate equal to ours."

"If what you say is true," Elizabeth warned, "we will join Edward Fitzwilliam in the Lord's grace."

"Edward is in a safer place than are we," the countess reprimanded, "and it is tantamount you maintain your sensibilities. My son would expect his wife to act with honor. Follow Mrs. Darcy's lead. We possess a plan, and your lack of resolve will doom us to failure. We are in this together."

Their kidnapper chained them to a support post in the center of the room. They were all chained to one post, their hands bound in the same manner, as was Edward's during the trial. A chain wrapped and locked about the post, tightly bound their wrists. As the shortest of their trio, Elizabeth's arms were above her head, and they long knew a tingling numbness.

Prior to chaining her and her companions to the post, their captor permitted them each a moment to meet her personal needs behind a makeshift screen made from empty wooden boxes; however, that act of kindness occurred hours earlier. Their kidnapper disappeared into the night and did not return. Elizabeth prayed, if nothing less, workers would fill the space with the new day, and she and the others would be released.

In the dim moonlight streaming through the high windows, Elizabeth watched Georgiana's profile. An array of emotions caused Georgiana's features to contract into hard lines. Elizabeth last witnessed those lines when Georgiana confided her part in Mr. Wickham's seduction.

"I brought such pain to William," the girl admitted.

Mr. Darcy saved his sister's reputation, but not before William suffered with what appeared a betrayal on his innocent sister's part. Later, Darcy and Georgiana came to a better understanding, but not before each wallowed in the grief of losing the other's respect. Now, the lines upon Georgiana's countenance spoke of fear and shame and devastation. If they were at Darcy House, Elizabeth would offer her sister in marriage the comfort of reasoning words, but in Elizabeth's opinion, self-pity remained a wasted emotion.

"Georgiana," Elizabeth said with encouragement, "before William left us this evening he expressed hopes of a means to save Edward."

Georgiana's lips trembled.

"I cannot bear another disappointment."

"You can," Elizabeth insisted. "You can prevail because your brother would know devastation if you did not, and you will remain strong for your daughter because Colleen requires at least one of her parents in her life. Think, Georgiana. As much as your life was not complete without Lady Anne Darcy, what would it be if you lost both parents at the same time? George Darcy did everything within his power to protect you. Do the same for Colleen Fitzwilliam."

A long silence filled the room.

"I shall ask God for his assistance."

Elizabeth was not completely satisfied with Mrs. Fitzwilliam's response, but she permitted a quarter hour to pass before she spoke again: This time to the countess.

"We are fortunate our captor did not discover the weapons upon ourselves," Elizabeth whispered. "They will provide us a bit of promise."

Georgiana scowled. "He took my reticule and Edward's favorite coat pistol."

"What is more important is the man did not discover the others," the countess corrected. "Moreover, Edward would hold no qualms at losing the gun; it is replaceable: We are not."

Before Georgiana could give voice to yet another protest, Elizabeth added, "When our interloper returns, we must insist upon his providing us another moment of privacy."

Their abductor searched their persons once they were in the warehouse. He even ran his hands along their calves in case they had weapons beyond the one in Georgiana's reticule, but the man did not find what Elizabeth and the others concealed.

After Elizabeth calmed the countess in the carriage, Darcy's aunt proved herself an excellent collaborator in planning their escape.

"If we were in Mr. Darcy's coach, there would be a few guns and a knife or two under the bench," Elizabeth mused aloud as the coach barreled through another sharp corner, slamming them hard against the side of the carriage.

The countess removed her stylish turban.

"Where do you think Darcy came by such notions?" Lady Matlock knelt on the floor of the swaying coach. "Assist me with the seat."

Elizabeth scrambled to Nora Fitzwilliam's side. Within the compartment under the rear-facing seat were two short antique rondel daggers and three guns.

"The earl prepares for the prospect of highwaymen," the countess explained.

Elizabeth suggested that they tie the pistols to their thighs, using the ribbons from their bonnets. While the countess thought they might lace the daggers about their waists, using the ribbons of their petticoats and drawers to secure them to their sides. Completing the task was a rough go in the carriage, for the uneven roads bounced them about, but with a bit of embarrassment and a great deal of determination, Elizabeth and the others armed themselves against whatever Fate held in store.

While plotting a means of fighting off their kidnapper, Elizabeth provided the countess and Georgiana with an abbreviated version of the incidents upon the American continent.

"Are you thinking the Youngblood imitator means to make us his next victims?" the countess asked as Elizabeth assisted Darcy's aunt with securing the gun to Lady Matlock's upper leg.

"I am not certain whether we are 'the three maids in a tub' or whether we are the distraction to pull Mr. Darcy and Mr. Cowan away from the real victims; however, either way, we must be prepared to fight for our freedom."

❧ ❧ ❧

Darcy shook his head in denial, "Pugh cannot be our murderer. He is too slight in his physical presence to overcome three victims each time. Even if he were the one in the crowd today and called out for Fitzwilliam's guilt, there must be more to the story. What are we missing?"

Cowan summarized what they knew.

"If the rumors Tark and Mrs. Dempsey bring us are true..."

"They be so," Tark insisted.

Cowan continued as if the man did not speak. "Then we erred in our judgment of Rumbradge. The officer holds ties to both Pugh and Rhys. Southland, could Rumbradge have earned his reputation in Upper Canada? Did Rhys or Pugh hold connections to Youngblood?"

The captain pulled at his pinned sleeve, an obvious nervous habit, and Darcy assumed Southland often forgot he no longer had both arms.

"Not of which I recall, but it is possible. Youngblood held Welsh relatives, and both Pugh and Rhys possess ties to Wales."

Darcy closed his eyes so he could concentrate. There were so many loose ends and so little time to bring them together. Would he find Elizabeth in time? It struck him that he did not once think of the possibility of losing his sister, who for many years was the center of Darcy's life.

As sad as it was to consider, although Darcy would grieve for Georgiana's loss, the fact remained, the local sexton would need to dig a second grave if something dire happened to Elizabeth. Darcy did not think he could live without his wife.

Speak to me, he prayed. *Tell me what to do, Lizzie.*

As the conversation swirled about him, Darcy listened for her voice. She was his everything, and Darcy needed to know in his heart that his wife was still alive.

I am not certain whether we are the three maids in the tub or whether we are the distraction to pull Mr. Darcy and Mr. Cowan away from the real victims.

It was as if his wife whispered in his ear. Darcy squeezed his eyes tighter and attempted to hold his wife's closeness near him.

In regret, he realized Elizabeth left him as quickly as she came; therefore, Darcy swallowed hard and returned his consideration to the group gathered in the street's middle.

"What if their abductor took Mrs. Darcy, the countess, and Georgiana to divert our attentions from the real crime planned for this evening?"

Cowan's features screwed up in disbelief.

"A decoy?"

"We provided Mr. Rumbradge with all the details of our investigation," Darcy reasoned aloud. "Rumbradge knows where we meant to be this night."

"And he drew us away from the task on purpose," Cowan concluded.

Matlock attempted to understand. "Why? What does the man gain with the diversion?"

"If Elizabeth and the others could not recognize him as their abductor, could Rumbradge sweep in and pretend to save my family–to earn favorable recognition? Tark, did you not say the hangman desired a higher position?"

Tark nodded his agreement.

"Are you suggesting we abandon our search for Mrs. Darcy and your family and return to our former plans?" Cowan questioned.

Darcy's heart lurched to a standstill: He could not, of his own accord, turn from his pursuit to save Elizabeth, but neither could he accept the fact the murderer they sought would succeed in claiming more victims. Thankfully, his uncle stole the decision from him.

"There is no time for you to apprise us of all the details of which you are privy, Mr. Cowan. Therefore, Captain Southland will accompany me in the search for the countess and your ladies, Darcy. If necessary, we will seek the assistance of the Thames Police, as we mean to examine the areas along the banks. Southland knows enough of this man called 'Rhys' to guide the search. You and Cowan should stop whatever menace is stalking London's streets. Take Mrs. Dempsey and her brother with you. They may be of use in identifying potential victims."

Darcy knew relief at having the decision removed from his hands; yet, a nagging sense of failure filled him. A man's duty was always first to his wife and children.

"I suspect," Cowan mulled over what they knew and what they had yet to discover, "if Rumbradge has a part in this insanity, he did not give us an accurate list of names of those who fit the killer's pattern."

"You think Rumbradge meant to find glory by proving an earl's son a madman?" Darcy asked in trepidation.

"He would not be the first to manipulate England's justice system for personal glory."

Acrimony filled Cowan's tones.

"It grieves me that Rumbradge's supposed sincerity fooled me."

"If this ruse proves true, where do we begin?" Darcy said, his anxiety hitching higher. "Those we assumed to be possible targets for this night's attack are likely more deception. We have no possible means of knowing where to look for the real killer!"

"Yet, we do," Cowan declared. "Rumbradge provided Southland and me a bit of information when we tracked him down at the public house."

"And?" Matlock demanded.

"Although I was a bit surprised at his being so forthcoming, Rumbradge shared the type of weapons used against Weldon. His disclosure made little sense at the time, but..."

Curiosity held them each in suspense.

"Of what insensibility do we speak?" Darcy's mind searched for reason.

"Rumbradge claimed the Slayer killed Weldon and the Uricks with a farrier's hammer and knife," Southland supplied the necessary information. "Cowan and I assumed the murderer abandoned the idea of using a weapon from victim number four to kill victim number three, for if we truly assume the man for whom we search will follow the rhyme and kill three women, then he chose his weapons to kill Weldon differently. What woman owns such tools?"

"A woman whose 'usband tended the 'orses 'til his passing," Tark suggested.

Cowan's eyebrow rose in curiosity. "Do you know of such a woman living near your sister?"

"Aye."

"Does she reside with two other women?"

"Her spinster sisters," the man confided.

Darcy pushed regret away as a new reality took hold. "Can you provide us directions?"

"Aye, Sir."

While Cowan secured the address, Matlock caught Darcy's arm. "The captain and I will find Mrs. Darcy. Do what you must to put an end to the chaos surrounding us."

"I will follow as quickly as Cowan and I can secure the women's safety. If you reach Mrs. Darcy before I return..."

"Your wife will understand," Matlock assured. "Mrs. Darcy is as courageous as my Nora and as was your mother. Neither Elizabeth nor Lady Anne Darcy would wish an innocent to die if you held the means to prevent the death. Now hurry, Darcy. The hour is late."

"Go with God, Sir," Darcy whispered.

"You, too, my boy."

❧ ❧ ❧

Darcy's heart and mind were certainly not in agreement, but he followed Cowan through London's streets. He knew his uncle spoke the truth of Mrs. Darcy's benevolence, but Darcy privately acknowledged if he chose incorrectly, he would never forgive himself. *Protect Elizabeth*, he prayed. Without realizing his friend did so, Darcy discovered Cowan caught the reins of Darcy's horse to bring it to a halt.

"We will leave the horses here and approach the shop on foot," Cowan instructed. "I know a couple of lads who work in the kitchen of yonder house. For an extra coin, they will keep a close eye on our horses."

Darcy dismounted, ordering the thoughts tugging at his conscious in a demand for dominance. He glanced up at the building to which Cowan gestured. It was a house of ill repute. It never ceased to amaze Darcy the variety of people the investigator could call by name and the places with which Cowan was familiar.

"Tell me what I must do. I will follow your directions."

Cowan greeted the two youths, both younger than twelve, before returning to Darcy's side.

"Mrs. Dempsey's brother provided detailed directions. You should know the household we seek is *not* one identified by Rumbradge. We will have no one to assist us if we encounter the perpetrator. The men we hired are standing guard at the other addresses."

"At least if we made an error in judgment, someone will be available to prevent another travesty," Darcy reasoned.

Cowan shook off the suggestion. "We did not err—not this time. I feel it in my bones. Even so, we should hurry. It is nearly two of the clock–the bewitching hour."

Darcy shoved away the feeling of dread building in his stomach. "Which way?"

"Two streets to the south. Stay close. We do not want a stray dog or a street gang to signal our arrival."

Darcy did as Cowan asked. He moved when his friend did and remained still, holding his breath to disguise his anticipation, when Cowan motioned for Darcy to wait. It was quite ironic that Darcy no longer felt so from place in London's east side slews. True, his clothes were finer and his accent more acceptable, but he long since abandoned turning up his nose at the filthy stench filling each breath he took.

At length, Cowan pulled up to peer around the edge of the building.

"It is the one across the street. The seamstress shop. According to Tark, the sisters in question buy old rags, as well as perform a variety of sewing needs for the locals," Cowan grinned. "Tark has a special relationship with one of the sisters."

Darcy shook his head in disbelief at the luck they encountered in making the acquaintance of Mrs. Dempsey. God favored them in that matter. The lady brought them information they would never discover until time robbed them of the opportunity. He prayed Luck would continue to follow them—that they, as well as Lord Matlock, would know success.

"How do we proceed?" Darcy's breathing tightened in his chest, and he concentrated on any signs of life in the house.

"Give me five minutes to make my way to the back of the building and to beg admittance. Tark shared with me a secret, which will have the ladies trusting me. Our killer shows a preference for entering the premises by way of the kitchen. Tark says the women keep no servants. They will all be asleep in the upper storey."

"What should I do while you determine if the man we seek is about?"

Darcy was more than glad Cowan did not ask him to search the dark alley running along the side of the seamstress shop. Darcy was not certain he knew such bravery.

"Just keep a close watch and come running if you hear anything unusual."

☙☙☙

Elizabeth's arms ached so badly she concentrated hard to keep the tears from her eyes. The countess sagged against the support beam, asleep on her feet. From Elizabeth's calculations and from a distant bell, she estimated it to be near two of the clock. They were chained to the post for nigh onto three hours.

Elizabeth rested her forehead against the back of her raised arms before closing her eyes to bring forth an image of her husband. Oh, how she fought her initial reaction to the man—her dear William appeared so priggish, when he was simply uncomfortable with the excessive attention his position brought to Darcy's threshold.

In vain I struggled. It will not do. My feelings will not be repressed. You must allow me to tell you how ardently I admire and love you.

Foolish girl that she once was, Elizabeth sent Mr. Darcy packing, after attacking the man's backbone: Darcy's pride; yet, her dear husband rose above Elizabeth's admonishments—teaching her how a truly honorable man responds to adversity. So while she cursed his abominable pride, Elizabeth secretly found it most gratifying to inspire, although unconsciously, so strong an affection.

And even with Elizabeth's rejections, William never abandoned her, proving himself by saving her reputation and that of her sisters from ruination after Lydia's elopement with Mr. Wickham. With each of Darcy's gestures of tenderness, Elizabeth's heart swelled with love for a man she thought never to know.

Yet, Darcy preserved, bringing Jane and Mr. Bingley together and providing Lydia and Mr. Wickham with a future. At length, Darcy spoke the words Elizabeth longed to hear.

You are too generous to trifle with me. If your feelings are still what they were last April, tell me so at once. My affections and wishes are unchanged; but one word from you will silence me on the subject forever.

With ease, Elizabeth could recall her blossoming feelings, as well as all the more than common awkwardness and anxiety for Mr. Darcy's situation, but she forced herself to speak, and immediately, though not very fluently, brought Mr. Darcy to a mutual understanding.

My sentiments, Mr. Darcy, have undergone so material a change since the period to which you allude, as to make me receive with gratitude and pleasure your present assurances.

"I love you, William," Elizabeth mouthed the words—a solemn vow to the image of the man she held before her.

The sound of a scrap of wood upon wood broke through her musings. Elizabeth's head snapped up to listen, every nerve upon alert.

"Countess."

She nudged Darcy's aunt. Nora Fitzwilliam became vigilant.

"What?"

The countess's lips formed the word, but no sound escaped. Elizabeth leaned closer.

"Someone has come."

The countess swallowed her fear. Squeezing her eyes shut for a brief moment, she nodded her understanding.

Elizabeth watched as Darcy's aunt tapped Georgiana's side with her elbow.

"It is time," she whispered.

Darcy's sister paled, but she, too, took a defensive stance.

"We each know what to do," Elizabeth instructed, but before she could say more the door to the small room where they were being held swung wide, banging against the wall.

Gasps and shrills filled the air around her, as a deep voice boomed.

"What have we here?"

Chapter Twenty-One

Darcy stared hard at the building where the women resided. In hindsight, he wondered if he should have accompanied Cowan. At the time, he thought his friend meant for Darcy to prevent an escape from the shop's front, but on second thought, that idea made little sense.

He doubted anyone with murder, as his intent, would risk meeting a locked shop door in his retreat. More likely, Cowan considered Darcy's divided allegiance a detriment. He could not blame his friend: All Darcy wanted was to hold Elizabeth in his embrace and never permit her from his sight again.

The "theatre" surrounding his extended family exhausted Darcy. As unreasonable as it was to think, he wished all involved to Hades, as he cursed the sense of duty instilled in him from the time he was a wee lad.

"I should be seeking my wife and sister rather than staring into the dark pit of London," he murmured in quelling accents.

He scowled with sudden keen-eyed interest when a noise from further up the street caught his attention. Shaken, Darcy slunk into the shadows, keeping his presence hidden. His heart lurched with anticipation—the noise was that of footsteps. Decisive, but muffled footsteps.

A night watchman, Darcy's mind announced, but there was something different about the man who strode along the wooden walkway. *Moving fluidly. Younger. And almost wary. Most who assumed the civic position were in their later years*, Darcy thought.

As the man drew nearer, Darcy pressed his back to the building's side. His heart stuttered to a halt when the cloaked figure paused before the small shop to survey the area. Where life teemed on the street upon which he and Cowan left their horses, Darcy realized how quiet this one appeared. Other than the man across from him, no one could be noted.

Without conscious thought, Darcy filled his lungs with the stagnant air as he studied the figure.

There was something very familiar about the man's stance: *commanding, in control, broad shoulders and a recognizable physical stature.* The stranger turned his head to scan the area a second time, as a hundred questions filled Darcy's mind: Was this their murderer? The East Side Slayer?

Had this enigma used the guise of a night watchman to gain entry into the other homes? Darcy wished he possessed a closer look at the stranger's countenance—to look upon evil, but the cloak served its purpose in disguising the man's features.

Why a cloak? True, it was a cool night as it was the first of November, but not so cold that a long cloak would be required.

The spider's web of deceit associated with Edward's arrest began to make the necessary connections. Threats they overlooked. The violence of the attacks. Darcy's mind spun with the possibilities. Nothing made sense; yet, his logical nature shunned the impracticality of not finding a solution.

Fitzwilliam's enemies followed his cousin to England's shores, and until this very moment, Darcy held no indication of who they might be. Yet, one thing was for certain, the major general's enemies did not deal in small deaths.

As if floating above the ground, the stranger swept his cloak about him and turned into the alleyway into which Cowan disappeared earlier. Even so, Darcy's feet would not respond to his mind's call for action, and so, Darcy asked his heart, "Should I follow? Is Cowan waiting in the narrow passage?"

However, Darcy heard no sounds of a struggle bursting forth from the noiseless street. Had the stranger subdued his friend? Should Darcy send up a warning? Could Cowan be lying in the alley's dregs, the former Runner's throat sliced from ear to ear? Or did the *night watchman* note Darcy's presence and now waited for Darcy to follow in order to quash his curiosity?

Darcy's fingertips dug into the building's soft wood, as he attempted to quiet the rising panic claiming his breathing. No one tutored him in such wickedness: He remained a novice in the stratagems Cowan embraced.

Fear rolled through Darcy's limbs, which hardened, inch-by-inch, securing his body to the wall. He could not move—could not make a sound. Could not swallow.

Even so, his eyes never left the place where the cloaked stranger entered the alley. He searched for any sign of activity. "Move!" his mind ordered, but Darcy's body would not respond. Dread held him impaled by its grasp. Yet, the sound of broken glass and a shriek of surprise freed his feet and set them into motion.

Plunging full speed into the alley's darkness, Darcy never paused to consider the danger. The sound of a scuffle drove him forward. Another shriek of female origin empowered him. The sound of broken glass and cracked furniture spoke of a confrontation. Reaching an open door, Darcy shoved it wider to dive into the melee sweeping the mutely lit room, only to barrel into the solid mass of the man he observed earlier.

"Humph!"

The air rushed from Darcy's lungs, but he managed to grasp the interloper's arm, as they tumbled to the floor. Darcy's backside slammed into the uneven wood planks only seconds before the stranger's weight banged into Darcy, sending another whoosh of air bursting from his throat.

Yet, there was no time to consider his injuries: Darcy found himself in a struggle for his life. His attacker rained down blows upon Darcy's head and shoulders. Pinned beneath the man, all Darcy could do was to protect his body with his arms.

At length, the onslaught slowed as the man's breathing turned shallow, and Darcy freed his legs long enough to buck his attacker's weight to the side. Rolling to his left, he heard the curse clearly as the man's fist struck the floor beside Darcy's ear rather than to strike Darcy's jaw.

Using the man's pain as a distraction, Darcy shoved hard against the solid mass, which held him in place. Scrambling to his feet, he kicked at the giant rising from the floor. From above, he heard Cowan ordering the women from his way. Darcy had no time to consider how this stranger escaped Cowan's attack for the interloper brought a fist up from the floor to land upon the point of Darcy's chin.

Darcy's head snapped back, but he stayed upon his feet. His only fighting experience came under the vigilant eye of Gentleman Jack, but this was no contest between men of aristocratic lines. This was a fight for dominance—a fight for life.

The man turned to escape, and so, Darcy dove at his attacker's legs, bringing the hulk of a man to a crashing jolt upon the threshold. He wrapped his arms about the stranger's knees and held on for all that was holy. Cowan's steps echoed upon the stairs as his friend rushed to Darcy's aid.

Voices of confusion filled the air, while Darcy squeezed his eyes shut and tightened his grip. His lone thought was he must prevent the man's escape: This intruder was Darcy's only clue to where Elizabeth could be found. At long last, Cowan stood beside where the culprit struggled to escape.

Darcy felt rather than saw his friend place a knee upon the intruder's back and heard a gun's hammer lock into place as Cowan growled.

"Move another muscle, and your brain will be staining Miss Spangler's polished floor."

Darcy knew the man went limp, but still he held on, unable to open his grip.

"Hand me something to bind him," Cowan ordered, and three distinct sets of footsteps scrambled to do the former Runner's biding.

"Do not release him, Darcy."

Darcy blew out his breath on an ironic chuckle.

"Incapable of doing so, Cowan," he groaned. "Perhaps never."

He heard an answering grin in Cowan's words.

"I would have been bloody proud to serve with you, Darcy. You are a remarkable fighter for a gentleman. Not like those namby-pamby officers who thought themselves heroes. You are made of uncompromising valor."

Darcy did not think of himself as a hero. Only moments earlier he clung to a wall, unable to move.

"I imagine you would find me wanting," he said in rough tones.

Cowan changed his position, straddling the man and wrenching the intruder's arms behind him. Darcy raised his head long enough to note Cowan handing his gun to a woman of some thirty years, who determinedly jammed it into the stranger's temple.

A string of curses announced the culprit's displeasure until the woman added a colorful warning to the mix.

"Ye stole me husband's tools, ye bastard. Ye turned me man's legacy fer his son into a weapon of death. Provide me a reason to ret this wrong."

At once, the suspect stilled; only a grunt of disapproval accompanied Cowan's securing of the man's arms. After what felt a lifetime, Cowan tapped Darcy's shoulder.

"You may release him."

Darcy sucked in a breath filled with the scent of soap, heavy dust, and stale water. As if a statue coming to life, he willed his fingers to open, before placing his palms flat on the floor on either side of his attacker's legs to lift his body from where he landed.

He straightened to look about him. Candles had been lighted, and the small kitchen filled with activity. Three women huddled together near the stairs, but Darcy noted the tallest female still held the gun Cowan provided her. Darcy heaved a deep sigh of approval.

"Even with a bloody bruise gracing your forehead, I was never so glad to look upon your countenance, Cowan."

He nodded toward the women.

"I see you were able to talk your way into the house."

His friend's grin widened.

"Miss Alice is a special friend of Tark Hardy. The man provided me with a special phrase to convince the Spangler sisters of my honesty. We were setting up a trap when our intruder made an early appearance."

Darcy only half listened to his friend's explanation. The blood pulsing through his veins only moments earlier rushed to his head, and he felt the room spin. To disguise his emotional turmoil, he suggested through a shaky voice, "Should we not have a look at our perpetrator?"

"Miss Alice," Cowan asked. "Would you wake your neighbor and ask him to send for the watch and other officers?"

"Aye, Sir."

Darcy bent over to catch the stranger's shoulder to assist Cowan in lifting the man to his feet. It was then he felt the bruises forming along his arms and chest. His attacker left his mark upon Darcy's body.

The man resisted their efforts, and before they could bring him about, the stranger gave Darcy a shove and attempted to run. With expertise, Cowan caught the man's shoulder, jerking him backwards.

"Miss Sessie, I will require additional rope for our *visitor's* legs."

"Yes, Sir."

The shortest of the three women scampered up the stairs to do Cowan's biding.

With his foot, Darcy dragged a straight-backed chair closer, but he never released his grip on their captive. Cowan shoved the man into the chair.

"Let us have a look at our East Side murderer."

"Murderer?" the man snapped. "I am the night watch, and you will pay for this indignity."

The female with the gun snarled.

"Ye no more be the watch than me dead husband."

Darcy was anxious to look upon the man, who wore a hooded cloak and who kept his gaze upon the floor.

Cowan moved with muscular grace. He lifted a lighted candle with one hand and swept the hood from the intruder's head with the other.

Darcy's heart faltered as a familiar countenance appeared from behind the fabric.

"Rumbradge?" he murmured.

If the officer was their murderer, what had the man done with Darcy's family?

"This is not Rumbradge," Cowan scowled.

Darcy glanced to his friend.

"What do you mean? It is Rumbradge's countenance before me."

He caught the man's lapels.

"Tell me why you targeted my family!" he growled. "You were seen driving the Matlock coach!"

The man's smile filled with contempt.

"I assure you, it was not I."

"You tell me or I will tear you apart, limb by limb!"

Cowan pried Darcy's fingers from one of the man's lapels.

"This man has the look of Rumbradge, but we are dealing with two different men. I should have recognized the duplicity for what it was."

Their captive continued to smile in mock innocence.

"Yes, you should have. I told Seimon you were not as astute as my twin thought."

"Twins?" Darcy murmured in disbelief.

"You are all so foolhardy. I tricked the then colonel on the American continent and now I manipulate his cousin in London. I must tell you, it was most satisfying to encounter upon London's streets the man who sentenced me to hanging. How convenient to place the blame for my masterful deeds upon the colonel's shoulders—to watch his loved ones suffer! It will be just as satisfying to know Fitzwilliam knows the end of a rope. Personally, I found the experience not to my taste, but perhaps, the major general holds more honor than I."

"The major general will be released when you are turned over to authorities," Cowan growled.

The man shook his head in the negative.

"You do not understand. If the authorities delay or halt the major general's execution for any reason, Seimon has orders to kill Fitzwilliam's family. My younger brother holds quite a fetish for the role of hangman. Even as a child, he strung up cats and squirrels and birds to watch them die. So, although you know my crimes, you will be forced to release me in order to save the man you admire. Three maids in a tub," he cackled with manic glee.

ॐॐॐ

"Martin!" the countess squealed. "You found us!"

In thankful weariness, the earl entered the room, followed closely by Captain Southland, who, in caution, surveyed the open area of the warehouse.

As glad as Elizabeth was to know freedom, a bit of disappointment at not seeing Darcy among her rescuers crossed her heart. She was certain Darcy would come for her.

"Naturally, I sought you out," Lord Matlock said as he placed a lantern upon the floor before crossing to his wife. "My home is empty without you."

When the earl embraced his wife, Elizabeth knew instant jealousy. She wanted to know her husband's comforting nearness.

Southland circled to where Georgiana shuffled her weight from one foot to another. The captain fingered the chain securing them to the support post.

"Do we know the location of the lock's key?"

"Our captor placed it in his pocket before he abandoned us," Elizabeth explained. Despite her best efforts, her eyes returned often to the still open door, seeking Darcy's countenance.

Southland nodded his understanding.

"I will look for a cutter or bar to wedge the lock open." Catching up one of the lanterns the men brought into the storage space, the captain disappeared into the warehouse.

Elizabeth could no longer avoid the question springing to her lips.

"Is Mr. Darcy outside?"

Matlock caressed the countess's cheek before he answered.

"I insisted Darcy accompany Mr. Cowan. We encountered a couple who knew much of this chaos."

"I see," Elizabeth said in regret. "Who were the couple?"

Her mind raced through the possible schemes. Had Darcy not thought of her safety? If the earl and Captain Southland followed the trail, Darcy realized they were in peril. Did she mean so little to her husband?

"The woman spoke to Cowan after one of the deaths and witnessed the trial," Matlock explained as he worked at his wife's bindings. "She and her brother observed my coach's speedy withdrawal from Old Bailey. Recognizing the driver, they sought Mr. Cowan."

While he spoke, the earl pulled upon the lock, attempting to release it.

"We followed your trail to the vicinity of King's Mews before Mrs. Dempsey and her brother overtook us."

Elizabeth guarded her tone.

"If you learned of our kidnapper from Mrs. Dempsey, why did Mr. Darcy and Cowan not accompany you?"

The earl looked up in disapproval.

"I assured Darcy you would wish him to stop the murderer from striking again. I pray I did not mislead my nephew."

Elizabeth felt the sting of Lord Matlock's rebuke.

"Certainly, I would wish my husband to protect an innocent, but I remain confused as to the sequence of the events you describe."

The captain returned with a bar used to open wooden crates. He took up the tale as he permitted Matlock the use of the tool.

"His Lordship noted the erratic course your kidnapper set for us to follow. When we neared Tower Hamlets, I assumed Mr. Rhys had a hand in your disappearance. As we debated on whether to continue following a deceptive trail, Mrs. Dempsey and her brother arrived. They recognized your abductor as Mr. Rumbradge."

"Rumbradge?" Georgiana gasped, as Elizabeth acknowledged, "I thought our captor appeared familiar. He wore a mask when he led us to this place."

The captain lent his one arm to Matlock's grasp upon the bar to bend the metal. When it sprung open, the chain's tautness slackened, and Elizabeth lowered her arms enough to drive the blood downward. It would take a few more minutes for the earl to work the chain free from their wrists.

As Lord Matlock untangled their constraints and the good captain resumed his sentry duties, Southland continued his explanation.

"Mrs. Dempsey's brother also knew something of the murder weapon used against the Weldon household. Cowan discovered the weapons were a farrier's knife and hammer, which would not indicate an all-female household. However, Tark Hardy knew of a woman whose late husband's tools were recently stolen. Darcy and Cowan meant to stop the murderer to prove the major general innocence."

During the captain's explanation, Elizabeth regretted her earlier disappointment; however, her very feminine need for Darcy raised its ugly head again. She spoke through tight lips.

"Then I must pray for my husband's success. Mayhap then, this madness will know an end."

Matlock worked the chain from Elizabeth's wrists while the countess freed Georgiana. The links left deep red marks, several of them rubbed raw.

"We should know speed before your kidnapper returns. My carriage is but a short distance away, but neither the captain nor I saw signs of your abductor. Rumbradge released the horses and cut the harness. Therefore we must walk out of here; we should put distance between this place and the culprit."

Matlock turned to his wife.

"Can you walk, Nora? It is not likely we will find a hackney at this hour and in this area of London."

"I shall persevere, my lord, if you will lend me an arm."

"We should step behind the boxes, Countess," Elizabeth suggested. "It is likely a bit dangerous to walk far without divesting ourselves of our accouterments."

The earl and Southland appeared confused.

"We removed the items from beneath the coach's bench," the countess explained. "We tied them under our skirts."

Matlock barked a laugh.

"You, Ladies, are quite ingenious. Mr. Rumbradge misjudged your tenacity."

Elizabeth herded Georgiana and the countess behind the boxes while Matlock and Southland stepped from the room.

"Be careful, Countess," Elizabeth warned as she assisted Darcy's aunt with her gown.

Lady Matlock tied the short dagger loosely about her waist, and Elizabeth moved quickly to release it. Meanwhile, Georgiana retrieved the Queen Anne pistol she tied just above her knee. As the countess recovered the gun attached to her outer thigh, Elizabeth sought the weapons she hid from the kidnapper.

"Mr. Rumbradge will return for us if Mr. Darcy is successful. We should be prepared to defend ourselves," Elizabeth insisted as she worked the knot from the ribbon, holding the gun.

The countess straightened her gown.

"Mrs. Darcy is correct. The earl provided us a reprieve, but we are not yet safe."

The noise of shuffling feet on the other side of the barrier froze them in place. Elizabeth knew neither Matlock nor the captain would offer the offense of entering the room with women being indisposed.

"I suggest you make your appearance known," a familiar voice called in menace. "Or your men folk will be on the receiving end of my ire," the captor said in amusement. "And leave the weapons upon the floor. It was kind of you to save me the work of another search of your bodies."

"You dared to touch my countess?" Matlock growled.

Their abductor answered the accusation with what sounded of a solid blow. A grunt of pain announced Elizabeth's hope of Matlock and the captain overtaking their captor knew failure.

"Do as the man says, Countess," Matlock spoke through a grunt of pain.

The countess led the way, holding her hands in supplication before her. Georgiana followed, mimicking her aunt.

Elizabeth's mind searched for a solution to their dilemma. With purpose, she permitted the dagger she freed to fall to the floor with a clanking sound. However, the pistol still hung from the ribbon about her waist. She loosened the knot but had not removed the item before Rumbradge interrupted them.

As Elizabeth stepped around the edge of the barrier, the gun banged against her upper thigh, and she prayed it did not drop at her feet until she could find a means to fetch it. Elizabeth showed their captor her hands as she exited the space.

"Move to the other side of the room and have a seat," the interloper instructed.

Elizabeth edged toward the back wall, constantly aware of where the gun barrel touched her skin. From her eye's corner, she noted Southland's body slumped against the wall: The captain was no match for their captor.

"We must wait for word as to whether I release you or see you to your Maker."

The man still wore his mask.

"How long must we wait?" Matlock demanded.

The earl again wrapped his arms about his countess, who brought Georgiana into her loose embrace. Darcy's aunt dabbed at a trickle of blood at the corner of Matlock's mouth.

"Until Major General Fitzwilliam dances at the end of a rope. If your son escapes punishment, it will be you who pays the price."

Chapter Twenty-Two

Darcy tied their captive's legs as Cowan stood guard.

"We must act with haste. I wish Mrs. Darcy safely under my roof."

Their attacker scowled with continued disdain.

"If you think to make me disclose where Seimon hid the ladies, you will find me most reticent."

Cowan shot a quick glance to where Darcy looked on before speaking. The former Runner assumed a nonchalance stance.

"We do not require your information. Your brother's efforts to hide his trail did not distract my men. We recovered the ladies, and the Earl of Matlock and the Thames River police tend their sensibilities."

Darcy turned so their prisoner could not observe the anxiety crossing his countenance: Cowan executed a guise, and he expected Darcy to participate. Pulling his expression under control, Darcy eyed their suspect with contempt.

Rumbradge's twin reacted with surprise to Cowan's assertion.

"You speak an untruth! My brother is more clever than that!"

He shot a glance to Darcy for confirmation.

"If you recovered the major general's family, Mr. Darcy would not be so incensed as to tear me apart 'limb by limb,'" he taunted.

Darcy pulled himself up to his full height before leaning over the man.

"Your brother placed his filthy hands upon my wife, my sister, and my aunt. If you think I will not enjoy seeing you brought to justice, you erred. I did not ask you *where* my family was held; I asked *why* you chose to make the women I most cherish a means of revenge on my cousin."

He pulled back slowly.

"However, I suppose a coward possesses no code of principles."

"We know how Morgan Pugh incited the audience at Old Bailey," Cowan added. "We know how you punished Rhys for his knowledge of your actions."

Darcy's friend paused for emphasis, and Darcy found even he believed Cowan's fabrications.

"Although a bit late, I see it was you who testified before court today. I would venture there is no physician from the Glasgow police. You were quite eloquent on Doctor Granvall's evaluation of the injuries, but I suspect the knowledge came firsthand, as it was you who inflicted each wound."

"You expect me to confirm your assertions?"

Their captive shot another glance to Darcy, who inclined his head in aristocratic corroboration.

"Impossible!"

Cowan chuckled.

"You think yourself so above those who sought to bring you to justice, but you make amateurish mistakes."

The man's eyes narrowed.

"Such as?"

Cowan's eyebrow rose in amusement, and Darcy knew his friend enjoyed the mental challenge of pulling all the puzzle pieces together.

"Such as your ring. I noted something was amiss the first time that you wore your ring upon a different finger. You almost convinced me I erred."

Rumbradge's twin said with disgust. "Seimon is left handed. One of our few differences."

Cowan caught their prisoner's collar and jerked it lower.

"I doubt if your brother wears the marks of a hangman's noose upon his skin. You are Bleddyn Youngblood, are you not?"

The man snorted his contempt.

"It took you long enough to discover the truth. I admit it brought relief to know the major general did not recognize me. A change of hair color and shaving my beard should not cloud his memory: On balance, I was a formidable adversary," Youngblood snarled. "Of course, to his credit, Fitzwilliam assumed I was dead, and I doubt the major general believes in ghosts. The then colonel thought he rid the Upper Canadian territory of my so-called *insanity*. He never bothered to know the man behind the hangman's hood was my twin. Needless to say, Seimon would never permit my death, especially at his hands.

"Seimon taught me how to support my weight as I grasped at the rope to prevent it from sapping the life from my lungs. I kicked and squirmed, as do all who know such punishments, and then I went limp—the reason for the marks. Within minutes, Seimon pronounced me dead and cut me down. He and two men who volunteered to assist the hangman carried me away for an unsanctioned burial. Colonel Fitzwilliam never bothered to confirm my death. Instead, he celebrated bringing me before the law."

"The other men were Rhys and Pugh," Cowan prompted.

A smile of satisfaction crossed their prisoner's lips.

"My cousin and another from my village. Seimon pleaded for their assistance when the colonel charged me with the crimes."

"But Rhys did not look the other way when you returned to your murderous ways?"

Darcy's mind raced to keep up with the burgeoning tale. It was sobering to look upon pure evil.

There was no shock–no empathy–no distress in the man's tone when he responded.

"Just a touch of mayhem in Liverpool and later in Edinburgh some years back, but Maxen Rhys refused to turn his vision from my actions. He meant to contact the authorities. So, I arranged a warning. A fire in Rhys' cottage, but the fool returned to save his babe and a stray dog."

Darcy felt Rhys' pain—raw and never ending—as if it were his own. The Welshman aided someone he thought he could trust and paid dearly for his allegiance to a madcap. Rhys would forever wear his shame.

From beside Darcy, Cowan summed up what was to occur next.

"The watch will arrive soon enough, as will Tark. The Misses Spangler and Mrs. Buckham will assist me. You should depart; Mrs. Darcy will require your company. The Thames force will need to know although Rhys played a role in the chaos, Rumbradge is the real culprit. They should be gathering the evidence at Rhys's place of employment." Darcy knew his friend hoped to learn the whereabouts of Darcy's family, but he feared Cowan went too far in his manipulation. He held his breath, praying their captive would disclose the information, which would deliver Elizabeth into Darcy's embrace.

For long, agonizing minutes, the man before them tightened his lips, but when he and Cowan set about righting the furniture as if in preparation for Darcy's departure, a string of curses announced the return of their captive's bragging.

"Surely you do not think my twin ill abused the women?"

Cowan shrugged.

"We will permit the authorities to sort it out. For now, Darcy, you should hurry your return to Tower Hamlets. Meanwhile, I will contact New Prison regarding the major general's reprieve."

"No! It cannot be! The major general cannot turn back the clock!"

Darcy smiled with a conniving slant to his lips.

"The High Judges permitted my cousin a writ of error. Fitzwilliam awaits our substantiation of your arrest before he knows freedom. It is difficult to deny the Earl of Matlock his will once my uncle sets his mind to an action."

"Provide Mrs. Darcy my regard," Cowan encouraged.

Darcy realized their interloper did not deny the fact his brother held Darcy's women in the warehouse associated with Rhys' employment. It was the only clue of any merit that Darcy possessed, and time was too short to bank on more from their deceitful prisoner. With a nod of gratitude to his friend, Darcy left Cowan to the official details of the crime. He raced the two streets to where he left his horse with the sporting house's kitchen lads.

He tossed the boy a coin.

"Deliver the other horse to the seamstress shop two streets south. Do you know the place?"

"Aye, Sir."

He mounted and set his feet to the stirrups and turned the horse in a tight circle.

"See it is done with haste."

Then he jammed his heels into the animal's sides and raced off into the night.

∽∽∽

"May I tend the captain's wounds?" Elizabeth implored.

Their captor sat in a chair before the still open door. As it was officially Friday, she assumed workers would fill the warehouse at dawn's light, and she feared their interloper would act before then.

The man she knew to be Officer Rumbradge shrugged his shoulders.

"As you wish, Mrs. Darcy."

As if by silent consent, no one spoke their kidnapper's name, although they each knew the man's identity. Like the others, Elizabeth presumed if she exposed his identity, their situation would escalate.

On hands and knees, Elizabeth crawled to where Captain Southland slouched against the wall. He pressed his hand to a wound in his side. Blood seeped from the slashed opening in the captain's shirt. His breathing shallowed, but Elizabeth thought the captain's reaction was due more to hurt pride than from the wound. From what she could observe the gash was long, but not deep. With gentle fingers, Elizabeth brushed Southland's hand aside.

"Permit me to examine your wound," she said with more calm than she felt.

While in the carriage, Elizabeth and the countess concocted a plan to retrieve the weapons they hid from their kidnapper, but those plans went awry. Now, the only useable weapons were the one in their captor's hand and the one tied loosely about her waist. Alas, Elizabeth had no means to retrieve the one under her skirt. Their survival rested upon her shoulders, and she was sore to know how to proceed. Without a doubt, Darcy would not be riding in like a knight seeking her favors. Silly as it was, the thought brought a smile to Elizabeth's lips.

"Mrs. Darcy?" The captain murmured in surprise. His gaze landed upon her face, appraising her intent.

Elizabeth shook her head in dismissal.

"Just a foolhardy bit of musing, Captain."

"No whispering!" Their gaoler called in a rough voice.

Elizabeth glanced over her shoulder at Rumbradge.

"I apologize. I simply meant to calm the captain." She returned to her inspection of the wound. "We must staunch the bleeding. I require some sort of dressing."

Again, Elizabeth directed her attention to the man with the gun.

"The captain requires a bandage."

Rumbradge shrugged again, this time as if he held no responsibility in the matter.

"If I do not treat the captain, he could know infection and lose his life."

Elizabeth did not think the wound as serious as all that, but she meant to worry the officer behind the mask.

Rumbradge shook off the idea.

"If the major general does not claim his death in the next few hours, the captain's wound will not matter. As a group, you will die in Fitzwilliam's place, and much to his chagrin, the major general will possess nothing for which to live. Even as we speak, Fitzwilliam receives a message informing him of your abduction. The major general's sense of honor will cause him to act with your benefit in mind."

Elizabeth's chin rose in defiance.

"Yet, if the major general does act with the sense of honor you describe, you would want no more blood on your hands. You made a bargain, Sir, and I expect you to respect it."

Rumbradge's eyes narrow in disapproval.

"The condition of my hands and my conscience is of no concern to you."

As the captor pointed the gun at her, Elizabeth fought hard to quash the panic rising in her chest.

"In my opinion, Mr. Darcy should not encourage your shrewish tongue," Rumbradge remarked with more contempt.

"My husband does not fear a woman of sensibility," Elizabeth protested.

Rumbradge bristled. "And you think I fear you?"

Elizabeth injected her tone with coaxing reasonableness; yet, she meant to speak in earnest, thinking her doing so would rattle the man more than if Elizabeth played the role of subjugation.

"I think you are a well-armed man, who means to use his physical prowess to intimidate me; however, I possess mettle, and I demand you permit me to tend to the captain's wound."

Rumbradge gestured with the gun.

"Look about you, Mrs. Darcy. There is no surgeon available, nor are there medicinals."

Elizabeth bit her bottom lip to keep the words of challenge from slipping out.

"I shall cut a swatch from the tail of Captain Southland's shirt for a bandage and remove the ruffle from my skirt's hem to serve as binding to wrap about my cousin's waist. That is if you will permit me to retrieve one of the daggers left behind on the floor."

Derision returned to Rumbradge's tone.

"I suppose you refer to the weapons you hid from me."

"No woman of merit would wander about London's streets without some form of protection," the countess assured. "True, we did not tell you of our cache, but you offered us few opportunities, and you did search our persons, Sir."

"Meaning the failure rests upon my shoulders," he countered.

Lady Matlock's tone spoke of the countess's contempt.

"Meaning, if necessary, we planned to protect ourselves in a hostile courtroom. However, if the presence of the ancient daggers provide Mrs. Darcy a means to save the husband of my dearest niece then the discomfort of carrying them shall be well worth the bother."

Rumbradge stared hard at each of them before he relented.

"Do not attempt anything foolish, Mrs. Darcy."

Elizabeth stumbled to her feet.

"I am not of an imprudent nature, Sir. Even a woman of less intelligence than I would know a bullet is more efficient than a dagger."

As Elizabeth crossed the room to retrieve the weapon, she wondered what would occur if as a group they would attack Mr. Rumbradge? He held one gun upon them. A single shot volley. Yet, none of them moved because they each feared one of the others would suffer. Shaking off the notion, Elizabeth made quick work of finding the dagger: She did not mean to meet an ugly death. Since accepting Darcy, Elizabeth imagined when her time came, she would be wrapped in William's arms.

Returning to the captain, Elizabeth knelt before him, her back to their captor.

"Bear with me, Captain. We must loosen your shirt."

Southland nodded his agreement.

"Assist me to a seated position," he instructed.

Elizabeth braced the shoulder of his missing arm as the captain shifted to the right so he could lean against the corner joint. With his good hand, Southland tugged at his shirt.

"Done this before," he murmured through several deep breaths. "At one of the battles...the officers...wore nothing but...their jackets. The physicians...required every scrap...of material for bandages."

Elizabeth smiled in encouragement.

"I shan't rob you of a proper presentation."

Southland closed his eyes as she began to cut away the bottom part of his shirt.

"My Anne's dearest cousin...won a fine prize...in you, Mrs. Darcy."

She tore the material into a four-inch wide strip and folded it to cover the bloody gash in the captain's side.

"Press here," she instructed.

Keeping her back to Rumbradge, Elizabeth adjusted her skirt to reach under the hem for the seam of the ruffle. Her every sense noted the officer's steady gaze.

Elizabeth glanced to the captain, whose eyes remained closed. With as much privacy as the situation provided, she hiked her skirt higher to catch a finger hold on the ribbon holding the gun. Elizabeth's eyes remained upon the captain, knowing if he realized what she planned, he would attempt to stop her.

She used the tip of the dagger to cut through the ribbon before squeezing her knees together to prevent the gun from dropping upon the floor. With the dagger's sharpened edge, Elizabeth sliced through the loose ruffle, laid the dagger upon the floor beside her, and gave a tug upon the material. It did not come away from her skirt tail evenly, but it would do.

"I must trouble you again, Captain," Elizabeth said with tenderness as she gathered the jagged-edged strip into her hands. "Just a few more minutes, and I will permit you to rest. Lord Matlock, might I impose upon you to assist me?"

Without turning her head, Elizabeth knew Rumbradge presented the earl a nod of approval.

"First," the officer said with a bit of amusement, "slide the dragger to me. I would not wish to tempt His Lordship to act without forethought."

Elizabeth did as the man suggested. She caught the dagger's handle and sent it spinning across the rough floor, coming to rest a few feet from where Rumbradge blocked the door.

Their captor stretched out his leg and dragged the weapon closer with his foot; yet, Rumbradge never removed his eyes from her. With an upraised eyebrow indicating his mocking attitude, Rumbradge kicked the dagger behind him, sending it skittering across the floor and out into the dark warehouse.

"Tell me what you require, Mrs. Darcy."

The earl knelt beside Southland's outstretched legs.

"Brace the captain as I stretch this cloth about Southland's waist and secure it in place."

Matlock wrapped an arm about the captain's shoulders and eased him forward.

"Not too far," Elizabeth cautioned. "The wound is in the crease of his waist."

Elizabeth leaned across Southland's chest, sending the strip behind him to reappear again in the front.

"Once more," she declared loud enough for Rumbradge's ears.

This time as Elizabeth smoothed the cloth across the captain's abdomen with her right hand, she slipped her left under her skirt to catch the gun in her palm.

Elizabeth noted how the earl diverted his eyes from Elizabeth's exposed legs, but she still required Matlock's assistance.

"Could you lift the captain's jacket in the back?" Elizabeth asked. "The loose threads of the ruffle caught upon a button or a seam, and I do not wish to cause the captain more pain by asking him to tolerate another attempt on my part."

Matlock locked his left arm through Southland's one good one and slid his right arm behind the captain's back.

"Do you feel the end of the material?" Elizabeth asked as she caught the earl's right hand in her left one, before depositing the Queen Anne pistol into his palm. "Yes. There it is," she said with misplaced calm.

A flinch of disbelief crossed Matlock's countenance, but Darcy's uncle quickly recovered his composure. When Elizabeth was certain Lord Matlock had control of the weapon, she pulled the tail of the binding around Southland's waist to tie it over the wound.

"Thank you, my lord."

A slight nod indicated Matlock understood what Elizabeth meant for him to do.

"I shall tend the captain's wound. You should return to the countess and Georgiana."

Elizabeth eased the captain against the wall. She did all she could. Only time would prove whether she made the correct decision.

❧ ❧ ❧

Darcy did not return to the streets where he last saw his uncle and Captain Southland. He knew the two meant to search the area near All Hallows Barking. As he rode, he prayed their "luck" would hold. Somehow, God delivered them from one man's evil.

"Permit me to discover my family in time," he repeated as he set the horse through its paces.

Rumbradge's twin did not deny Cowan's conjectures. Darcy wished he knew the exact directions for Maxen Rhys, but he was certain if Rhys did business near All Hallows Barking, someone would recall the man's extensive scarring.

Reining in the horse before a row of shops, Darcy dismounted. He rapped on the doors and windows of several buildings that showed a light within. At each, he made the same inquiry: Darcy asked for information on Rhys or on the earl's carriage in exchange for a monetary token. He was nearly from coins when a coal cart driver provided Darcy his first tangible clue.

"Yep, I knows him," the man assured. "Rhys delivers wood to one of the Sanfort bonded warehouses on the Thames. Sees him there often."

A few more questions and an extra coin for the man's assistance returned Darcy to his saddle. He was two miles from the building the cart driver described. By his estimate, it was four of the clock, perhaps a bit later. The City and the area surrounding it stirred from its sound sleep. The fact his family had yet to know rest increased Darcy's anxiety.

At long last, he slowed the mount as a line of high-ceiling wooden buildings came into view, and he brought the animal to a halt and dismounted. Dropping the reins to keep the horse in place behind a small shed, Darcy removed the gun he carried in a secret pouch sewed into his jacket. Moving upon silent feet across the grass-covered embankment, Darcy took shelter within the shadows of the first building.

"If the cart driver is correct, the one I seek is the last building of the four," he informed his courage.

Instead of following along the hardened walkway before the dark buildings, Darcy chose the more difficult pathway tracing the back of the buildings. The structures sat upon the Thames' banks.

One wrong move would send him tumbling into the river, but Darcy thought his chosen route would make it less likely someone would observe his approach. He wished Cowan accompanied him; the former Runner would know how best to handle the situation.

It surprised Darcy that no one moved about the area. He thought the buildings would be full of workers starting their days. Perhaps it was a bit earlier than he first believed. Reaching the third building, Darcy cut through the narrow passage between the structures to appear upon the walkway, but he remained within the deep shadows. He stopped to listen to the water slapping the shore and the sounds of the night.

"Where are you, Elizabeth?" Darcy whispered as he examined the area for any signs of Rumbradge.

He scanned the area twice before spotting a glint of light from the moon lingering over a bit of yellow.

Darcy's heart raced. Swallowing hard, he ran bent over toward a grove of trees where he discovered his uncle's coach: His wife was near.

He assessed the coach's condition, although Darcy did not expect to find his family within. Instead, he turned his attention toward the fourth building, which set apart from the other three. He wondered if that fact boded ill will toward those who entered its doors. Taking a circular route, Darcy made his way to the wooden structure.

Finding an unlocked door on the river's side of the structure, Darcy eased it open and stepped into the darkness. He stood with his heart racing, as Darcy waited for his eyes to adjust to the blackness. Even though it was night outside, the moon provided a bit of light to define the outline of the buildings.

However, without windows, the inside of the warehouse remained in total darkness. For one moment of panic, Darcy feared if someone stood within, the person would see him before Darcy could react, but within seconds his vision adjusted enough so he could make out the lines of boxes and mountainous bulges. The scent of fresh cut wood announced the building as a bonded warehouse for the timber business.

At a distance, the sound of something scraping across the floor at the other end of the large stable-like building had Darcy ducking for cover.

What had it been? It did not sound of a rat or small animal. More of a clink of metal. Was someone watching him?

Darcy waited for what seemed forever, unable to convince his legs and arms to move. His eyes searched the open space between him and the place from where the noise sprang, but no other sounds could be heard.

Just as Darcy convinced himself it was some sort of animal, a flicker of light reached his eyes. It was weak, like that of a candle threatening to be gutted by wax.

Uncertain what me might find ahead, Darcy edged forward, careful not to permit his footfall to sound upon the floor, which appeared to be hardened earth rather than wood in this section of the structure. His knee banged against a stack of firewood, and he froze in place, swallowing the curse rushing to his lips, as his eyes searched the weak stream of light, yet, no one appeared.

Easing forward again, Darcy continued his slow progress. Step by careful step across the length of the structure. At length, he could hear the soft murmur of voices emanating from what appeared to be an open door leading to a small storage room.

One voice he identified as Rumbradge, and then he heard her: Elizabeth was alive. The joy of such knowledge nearly brought him to his knees. It was all Darcy could do not to burst into the fray and scoop his wife into his embrace. However, his head warned his heart that Elizabeth remained in peril.

As he wove his way between and around what he could now identify as stacks and stacks of rough cut timbers, Darcy drew ever closer.

"Thank you, my lord. I shall tend the captain's wound. You should return to the countess and Georgiana."

Elizabeth's voice was an anchor to which Darcy attached his sensibilities: Matlock found the ladies, but failed to free them, and Southland suffered some sort of injury in the failed rescue. It was information Darcy would require in order to know success, and he thought it quite ironic his wife unknowingly summarized the situation for him.

Closer. Closer. Inch by ever-long inch. His heart beat so loudly Darcy thought it would signal his approach. *Please God*, he prayed for his wife's life. Every muscle in Darcy's body tightened. He could not breathe.

Five more "infant" steps would bring him into the light to face his wife's kidnapper. *Four. Three. Two.* With a quick breath, Darcy stepped into the portal, his gun pointed at the back of Simon Rumbradge's head, some three feet from the man. The idea of shooting someone thusly remained a foreign thought rattling Darcy's composure.

"Place your gun on the floor," he ordered.

A collective gasp brought his family to their feet, but Darcy avoided Elizabeth's eyes. She was not yet safe, and that fact kept him upon alert.

"Lift your hands slowly," Darcy instructed.

"Mr. Darcy?"

There was a twinge of amusement in Rumbradge's tone.

"What *kept* you?"

Darcy shot a quick glance to where Elizabeth stepped before Southland. He would prefer his wife would remove herself from the line of fire.

"Justice detained me. Cowan and I interrupted your twin's plan for more revenge."

"Twin?" Matlock questioned, but Darcy knew his uncle expected no response. It was a ploy to keep Rumbradge distracted.

"You and Bleddyn wreaked enough evil in the name of retribution."

Rumbradge shifted, and Darcy tightened his grip on the gun's handle.

"And now you think to take me into custody?"

The interloper raised his gun to point at Elizabeth's chest.

"You may wish to rethink your choices, Darcy."

His heart stuttered to a halt.

"I plan to walk away from here, and you will allow my exit, for Mrs. Darcy will walk by my side."

Darcy could not permit Rumbradge to kill his wife, nor could he permit her to leave the room with the man Darcy expected was as much a candidate for Bedlam as was his brother.

"If I am to lose Mrs. Darcy, it will be now rather than later. Just know if you even breathe hard, I will leave your brains upon this floor."

Darcy thought Elizabeth would object to his posturing, but his wife stood taller, shoulders back and smiling, with a knowing lift to her lips.

"I have nothing to lose," Rumbradge declared as tension brought the man's grip upon the gun higher.

Leisurely, as if in slow motion, his finger squeezed the trigger.

Darcy closed his eyes to the scene and felt the weight of the gun in his hand. *Save her*, he prayed, and then the roar of a pistol broke his concentration.

It was much louder than Darcy expected. His eyes sprang open, searching the haze of drifting smoke for his wife's countenance. Then he realized the sound of the explosion came from his left. Matlock stood, arm extended in Rumbradge's direction: A Queen Anne pistol in his grasp.

Rumbradge slumped to the right, his body half in and half from the chair: A small hole in the man's left temple. Darcy shook his head to clear his vision, and miraculously, his wife stood before him.

In three long strides, he closed the distance between them, catching Elizabeth to him, her body soft and compliant against his.

"It took you long enough," his wife chastised as she buried her face into his lapels.

Darcy's fingers ran his hands over her hair and cheek and shoulders, assuring himself Elizabeth did not suffer unduly.

"I prefer a grand entrance," he murmured as he kissed his wife's temple.

Behind him, Darcy heard the earl and countess checking Rumbradge's body.

"He is dead," the earl announced.

Darcy felt his wife slump in weakness, and he caught her to steady her stance.

"It is over," Darcy whispered to Elizabeth's ear. "Know this to be true, Cowan and I captured the East Side Slayer, and no more trouble will follow us."

She nodded her head in understanding, catching his jacket in a tight fist before swallowing her tears. "Permit me to assist Matlock," he encouraged before gently setting Elizabeth from him; yet, before Darcy could turn to access the damage, Georgiana launched herself into his embrace. He held his sister, as he had hundreds of times.

"Everything is well," Darcy assured her. "Cowan is processing the real murderer, and Edward will be released. The nightmare is over."

"But it is not!" the countess declared.

Darcy pulled Georgiana closer, as if his aunt's words might wound his sister further.

"Whatever do you mean, Countess?"

He noted how the room went silent except for the sound of Georgiana's sniffling tears.

"Rumbradge taunted us with the knowledge that Edward was informed of our abduction. My son was told he must sacrifice himself to save us."

"Then we will set a course for New Prison to permit my cousin first-hand knowledge of your safety," Darcy reasoned. "With Cowan's apprehending Rumbradge's brother, the authorities will postpone any execution until the facts can be verified. Meanwhile, Hutchison will present the writ of error to delay the implementation of the verdict."

His aunt's eyes filled with unshed tears.

"You do not comprehend. Edward never planned to face a rope. He asked Georgiana to bring him a gun to claim his own life rather than to be ridden through London's streets in shame."

Darcy cocked a sapient eyebrow.

"Yet, the authorities kept Georgiana from delivering the major general's prize pistol to her husband."

"You *knew?*" his sister asked in dismay.

Darcy brought her closer to him.

"Certainly, I knew. Very little of your life escapes my notice."

The countess's voice broke through the moment of shared assessment.

"You may be aware of your sister's manipulations, Darcy, but not mine. I pressed a gun into my son's jacket pocket when I comforted him after the verdict. Edward has a weapon and a reason to use it either against himself if he thinks we perished because of him or against an innocent in an escape to search out those who killed his family."

Chapter Twenty-Three

Darcy could not recall a time he rode through London's streets with so much chaos nipping at his heels.

"Will it never end?" he asked the rising sun as he avoided the carts clogging the streets leading to New Prison. He prayed he would reach Edward before his cousin acted in a dishonorable manner. If Edward took his own life, all they went through in the previous four and twenty hours would be for naught. The ghosts of the American continent would win.

Slowing his mount to a more reasonable pace, Darcy and the animal sidestepped two cart drivers who took each other's measure when neither would give sway for a choice spot upon the street. As he wove his horse between them, one thought to take him on. Shaking his fist, the burly man called.

"Careful, Guv'nor."

Darcy looked over his shoulder at the man, settling a deadly gaze upon the fellow's ruddy countenance.

"I am rarely rude, but as I hold pressing business at the prison, I would advise you to settle your bloody disagreement and clear the street before I do it for you."

With that, he set the animal into a prancing gallop, the outline of New Prison beckoning him onward. Darcy rode his mount through the open gate leading to the courtyard before anyone could think to stop him. Sliding from the horse's back, he was on the ground and running toward the main entrance.

"Stop!"

One of the guards called after him, but as Darcy had no time for multiple explanations, he prayed no one would shoot him before he could claim admittance. Sliding to a halt before the great wooden portal,

Darcy used his fist to pound upon the door. Behind him, he heard the shuffling of feet coming to a like standstill, but he refused to turn. Instead, Darcy pounded again upon the entrance.

At length, a muffled clank of keys upon the other side announced its opening.

"What be the necessity?" a prison guard demanded.

Darcy brought himself up tall.

"I am Fitzwilliam Darcy. I must speak to my cousin, Major General Fitzwilliam, at once."

"The sun has not yet risen," the guard complained.

Darcy pushed past the man, knocking the fellow's arm from his way.

"Thomas Cowan arrested the *real* East Side Slayer. The authorities in Middlesex have Bleddyn Youngblood in custody."

Darcy assumed Cowan enlightened the local magistrates. For now, all Darcy could do was bluff his way into the facility at an hour long before visitations would begin.

He walked further into the depths of the prison as he explained, "The major general must be informed of the changes in his case."

The officer, who was trailing him, caught Darcy's arm.

"Why the haste, Mr. Darcy? There be some four hours before anyone would move Fitzwilliam."

He eyed Darcy with suspicion.

"Ye wouldn't be the first to attempt to save a loved one before he be hanged."

Darcy half-expected such a reaction.

"May I speak in earnest, Officer…"

"Poplin," the man supplied.

Darcy schooled his features.

"Officer Poplin, Someone supplied my cousin with a gun. I mean to stop the major general from using it."

"Who?" Poplin demanded.

Darcy shook off the man's curiosity.

"The person's identity is not important, but you must believe me. You may keep the major general incarcerated. As yet, I do not expect his release: I simply wish to prevent my cousin from acting in a foolish manner. The truth will prevent his hanging, and he must learn hope survived."

Darcy retrieved his purse from an inside pocket and held it anticipation of bribing the officer. Poplin examined Darcy's countenance before nodding his agreement.

"I will tell Major General Fitzwilliam what you said."

Darcy stepped around the man.

"The major general is more than my cousin. He is married to my sister. We are as brothers. He will demand to hear the news from me. Only I can convince Fitzwilliam his wife and mother desire him to wait."

Confusion crossed Poplin's expression; yet, the officer did not force Darcy from the premises.

"Have you a weapon upon you, Mr. Darcy?" Poplin asked.

Darcy reached into the private pocket where he placed his unused weapon before leaving the warehouse. With a return of his remorse for not acting honorably in Elizabeth's behalf, he handed the gun to the man.

The officer checked the cartridge before returning it to Darcy. Without ceremony, Darcy inserted it into his jacket pocket: He would deal with his culpability in due time; for now, the major general's continued chaotic existence consumed Darcy's thoughts.

"Come along."

Poplin led the way through several passages and up a set of circular stairs to the actual cell area. The odor of sweat and fear filling the air set Darcy's senses reeling. Only a little light dared to invade the high windows, and as it was still early, Poplin carried a lantern.

"Down here," he said as he gestured to a row of cells at the end of a narrow crossing passage.

Coming to a halt, Darcy glanced around at the conditions his cousin endured. If asked, Darcy would admit such restrictions would drive him to Bedlam. Although he viewed the rows of cells from the second storey of the prison, Darcy had not seen where the authorities kept Edward.

Each time he and Matlock called upon the facility, in deference to Matlock's position in Society, the guards brought Edward to them. It was a sobering prospect to consider his cousin's being brought so low.

"Hold the lantern," Poplin instructed as he set the key to the door.

Darcy lifted the light and permitted it to invade the darkness. A cold, damp rush of air chilled him to his bones. His cousin's body rested upon a narrow cot, his right arm draped across his eyes.

"What now?" the major general grumbled. "Am I not permitted my own counsel before I die?"

"It is I."

Edward rose quickly from his makeshift bed.

"Have you come to tell me my wife and mother met a terrible fate? If so, you have no need. A note in the night served that purpose. It took me hours to read it in the moonlight from that bloody window across from my cell."

His cousin gestured in wild agitation.

"If they remain alive, tell whoever took them I welcome my execution, and if they are not, I will welcome it more."

"They are safe."

Darcy set the lantern upon a stool that also served as a table. He knew Poplin lingered in the doorway.

"It cannot be so," Edward insisted, but Darcy noted a glimmer of hope in his cousin's tone.

"I left them, as well as Mrs. Darcy and Captain Southland, in your father's care—so I might bring you the news," Darcy assured. "We found them in a warehouse in Tower Hamlets."

"Are you certain?"

Edward swayed in place, as if relief weakened his knees.

"I embraced my wife and sister. They are a bit bruised, but unharmed. Only Southland suffered a wound, which Mrs. Darcy tended personally. The earl killed their kidnapper."

Edward collapsed upon the cot.

"Who? Over the previous hours since receiving the note, I thought long upon my enemies, but I possess no answer."

Darcy shot a speculative glance to Poplin.

"Rumbradge. The officer we knew as Rumbradge is the twin to Bleddyn Youngblood. He served as the hangman upon the American continent."

Edward scowled and with an equally reluctant glance to Poplin, he sat straighter.

"But Youngblood was tow-headed and with a reddish beard."

Darcy shrugged his answer.

"I have heard of those who use the boiled liquor from the bark of the walnut tree or that of the root of holm-oak or even of boiled alum to change the color of light hair to dark. I once knew a youth at university who used a comb dipped in oil of tartar so he might appear more of the nature of his siblings and not know the label of illegitimate. All I know is Rumbradge, Morgan Pugh, and Maxen Rhys assisted Youngblood to escape his execution. They carried the man's body away before anyone would know Youngblood did not, indeed, die."

"Pugh?"

Edward tilted his head to the side, as if in contemplation. His eyes narrowed.

"I recall now. Pugh volunteered to assist the hangman, claiming a kinship with the executioner. How could an act of violence during the war against American interest play out on English shores?"

"We have time to decipher the enigmas presented by this case," Darcy insisted. "Simply know two things: First, Pugh was the one in the gallery, who called for your execution. I am not certain whether the authorities apprehended him and Rhys of yet, but I hold no doubt Cowan has the situation well in hand."

"How will the arrest of my former soldiers serve me?"

Not even a flicker of his eyes indicated Darcy heard his cousin's protest.

"Secondly, you should know, Thomas Cowan and I prevented Youngblood from carrying out another series of murders. Cowan has the man in custody. Within hours, authorities will release you. We caught Youngblood in the act, and he admitted his guilt before witnesses."

His cousin's agonized gaze met Darcy's.

"It is over?"

Darcy read the torment in the major general's eyes; even Darcy's assurances could not eliminate his cousin's guilt.

"For all intents and purposes. You have many inroads to repair, but you may step into the light if you so wish."

"Tell me what to do," Edward murmured.

"Begin by presenting me with the gun in your pocket. I will never permit you to act the coward."

Darcy paused before saying what was in his heart.

"I shan't be kind in my advice. You were always my dearest companion, but in this matter you acted with sore shame. I gave you my sister's heart, and I expect you to guard it. You are never again to permit Georgiana to know your spoken or your unspoken wrath. You will treat her as your equal. Many think I permit Mrs. Darcy too much sway in our marriage, but my revered father taught me something of happiness while instructing me in my responsibilities. He explained how in a marriage there cannot be two leaders at the same time. Sometimes the husband must lead—must use his strength to protect his wife and children. Other times, the wife must lead, bringing reason and tenderness and succor. You must learn to permit Georgiana her due, or you will deal with me. I wish never to experience such misery again."

Edward grimaced, but he reached into his pocket to hand the gun over to Darcy.

"I would have used it," he announced. "I did not wish my mother or Georgiana to view my execution. However, when the note arrived, my purpose changed. Know this, Darcy, I would give my life to save Georgiana."

Darcy met his cousin's resolve and returned it with one of his own. He stared deep into the major general's soul, gleaning a measure of the man Edward Fitzwilliam had become.

"I do not doubt your devotion to my sister. What I doubt is whether you can learn to love your faults as much as you celebrate your successes."

❧ ❧ ❧

"Is my wife at home?" Darcy demanded when Mr. Thacker opened the door to Darcy House for him.

He spent another hour with the major general, answering his cousin's questions and doling out additional advice before he left Edward to the English legal system. Poplin went about his business after receiving a note informing him Darcy spoke the truth of the major general's innocence. The officer even left the cell door unlocked.

Afterwards, Darcy made a brief call upon Hutchison to apprise the barrister of the changes in the situation. He agreed with the young man that they should proceed with the writ of error as an additional means to clear the major general's name and to shed a light on the irregularities practiced upon this particular occasion.

Then Darcy turned his weary mount toward Mayfair and Darcy House, praying with each step the animal took he would discover his wife at home.

"I believe Mrs. Darcy is in the nursery, Sir."

Darcy closed his eyes in relief.

"Thank Goodness," he whispered. With a deep sigh, Darcy started for the stairs. "Mr. Thacker, please send up hot water for a bath, as well as some breakfast. I am famished."

"Yes, Sir."

Darcy paused upon the steps.

"Has my wife eaten?"

"Mrs. Darcy asked for toast and tea, Sir."

Darcy thought that after going without food for so long Elizabeth required more, but he would speak of his concern to his wife when he saw her.

"And is Captain Southland above stairs?'

"Mrs. Darcy summoned a physician for the captain before seeing to her own needs."

Darcy understood Thacker and the household would view Elizabeth's actions as admirable. The neighbors would soon learn of Mrs. Darcy's kind heart.

"Doctor Nott gave the captain laudanum for the pain. It is my understanding your cousin will not suffer long from his wounds."

"Very good, Thacker."

Yet, Darcy hesitated before mounting the stairs.

"I have one more detail requiring your care."

"Yes, Sir."

Darcy smiled in bemusement. Thacker was a well-rehearsed upper servant.

"Unless Napoleon leads a full army through London's streets, I do not wish to be disturbed for any reason or by any member of my family. I have had my fill of intrigue."

His butler's lips turned up in a like acknowledgement.

"As you wish, Sir."

Darcy turned to climb the last few steps, but a clearing of Thacker's throat gave him pause.

"Yes, Mr. Thacker."

"I thought you should know, Sir, Lige drove your carriage all the way to Rosings Park before Lady Catherine took him to task for being such a dunderhead as to think you would send him to Kent for a copy of your aunt's will."

Darcy frowned.

"Her Ladyship's will? I would not trust such an important document to an unprotected carriage driver?"

Thacker fought hard to keep his expression under control.

"I believe Her Ladyship made a similar argument. I assume Lige's ears will be ringing for several weeks so loud the peal Lady Catherine rang over his head."

What could Darcy say? His erstwhile coachman received a just punishment for his gullibility.

"I will forward my aunt a note of gratitude."

"Yes, Sir."

At length, Darcy made his way to the nursery. He meant to embrace his family, but at the door, he paused to take in the perfection of the scene. A weary-looking Elizabeth sat in the floor's middle, her dressing gown spread out around her legs and a cooing Samuel upon her lap, while Bennet performed a song for his mother's pleasure.

Darcy studied her. Still damp from her ablutions, Elizabeth's glorious auburn hair hung loose about her shoulders. As if sensing his presence, she looked up at him and smiled.

"Your father has returned," she announced as Bennet swiveled about with a smile of mischief upon his lips.

"You hear me, Papa. I sing."

Darcy came to sit upon the floor beside his wife.

"It was an excellent performance. I am quite proud of you." He caught the boy in his arms, burying his nose in the sweet scent of soap lingering on his son's hair.

"I was just telling Lily and Mrs. Prulock that we shall return to Pemberley as quickly as Captain Southland is fit to return to Kent," Elizabeth announced in a tone that indicated she thought Darcy might object. "London's lack of manners is most tiring."

"I play at Pem'ley," Bennet added. "See new horses."

Darcy leaned across his son to kiss Elizabeth's temple. He caressed the boy's cheek, but his attention remained on his wife. All he desired was to return to Derbyshire and spend the remainder of his days loving *his* Elizabeth

"I agree. London holds no attractions of merit when compared to those of Derbyshire. We are of a like mind."

His wife appeared relieved.

"I thought to rest before we are beset with visitors. Will you join me, Sir?"

Her lovely eyes, the ones Darcy once referred to as simply "fine," offered an enticing future, a future he meant to claim with his heart and soul. Darcy could not believe how Fortune had shown on him when he journeyed to Hertfordshire and came away with the woman he loved.

"I ordered a bath, but then I would be honored to share time with you."

Darcy lifted his eldest from his lap before kissing the child's forehead.

"Mind Lily and when we return to Pemberley, I will take you up with me upon Prometheus when I call upon the tenants."

His son stood in awe of the large stallion.

"Yes, Papa." Bennet's eyes grew in anticipation as he scampered to Lily's side.

Darcy ran his finger along the curve of Samuel's chin. The boy's eyes drifted closed.

"And you, my dearest boy, you shall have a new gown for your christening. It is time, young Samuel, for you to claim your place in this family."

"Thank you, William," Elizabeth whispered before resting her head upon his shoulder.

They sacrificed their child's official naming before the Pemberley community for the sake of his sister's predicament; Darcy meant to rectify that slight.

"I will write to Bingley and Jane to request their presence for the ceremony."

"Might we ask Mr. Cowan also to serve young Samuel? I believe the gentleman earned a position of confidence among the Darcys."

Darcy smiled with satisfaction.

"I am certain Cowan will be as teary eyed as I upon the naming of our son." Darcy drew in a deep, fortifying breath. "Know this, Elizabeth," he whispered. "You and our family remain my first priority. My sister and the major general must find their own way. I can no longer serve as Georgiana's defender; she gave her heart to our cousin, and I gave mine to you."

As would any well-trained upper servant, Mr. Thacker deferred the entreaties from Darcy's family until the following morning. During those hours, Darcy renewed his commitment to his wife. When he married Elizabeth nearly five years prior, his loyalties were different; now, he shed the strings, which once bound him.

He and Elizabeth shared intimacies twice—once in devotion, with all the same innocent tenderness they shared the first time they came together and then later with all the urgency Darcy felt when he thought he might not find his wife in time.

"I love you, Elizabeth Bennet Darcy," he whispered against her hair as they drifted off to sleep. "You are my forever."

≈≈≈

The news of the capture of the East Side Slayer dwarfed the story of Edward's wrongful conviction and his release. Darcy read each story before passing the newsprints to Elizabeth.

"It appears," she mumbled as she chewed upon her toast and jam, "we missed some of the details of Mr. Cowan's success. It says Cowan requested that Saunders Welch send men to Liverpool to take Morgan Pugh into custody. Apparently the banker left evidence in let rooms that he meant to return to Wales."

"We can count on Cowan to complete the investigation and to prove Edward innocent beyond any doubt." Darcy studied his wife as she read, and his eyebrow rose in amusement when she reached for another slice of the toasted bread.

Noting his interest, Elizabeth placed her jam-covered knife upon her plate.

"What struck your humor, Mr. Darcy?"

He shrugged in total contentment.

"I was considering how much toast you consumed of late. The only other times I recall your finding toast and jam your favorite food was when you carried our sons. Do you possess news to share with me, my dear?"

A blush rushed to his wife's cheek.

"I did not think upon the possibility," she said through a deep frown. "After all, Samuel is but a few months born."

She smiled that secretive Madonna-like smile of all mothers, as the idea took root in her heart.

"Would you mind, Mr. Darcy?"

"I can think of nothing which would please me more. For now, enjoy your toast and your dreams, Mrs. Darcy."

Elizabeth reached for his hand, and Darcy brought her knuckles to his lips.

"Soon enough, my love."

"Yes," she said so softly if he did not watch her lips move he would not have heard her. The sound of a rap upon the Town house's door interrupted the moment.

"And so it begins," Elizabeth said with regret.

"Only for a few more days, Mrs. Darcy," he promised. "I refuse to permit the lunacy to consume me further."

Within seconds, Mr. Thacker announced Cowan's arrival.

"Please join us, Thomas," Elizabeth gestured to Murray to bring the investigator a plate and pour the man some coffee.

Darcy held up one of the newsprints.

"We were reading of your success."

"I was given more credit than I deserve," Cowan said with a bashful sigh. "We both know it was you who detained Bleddyn Pugh;

yet, I did not wish to bring the story to your threshold without your permission."

Darcy sipped his coffee, a drink for which he had yet to develop a taste, but one he meant to master for many of his business associates swore by the drink. As to his taste, Darcy might "swear at" the drink.

"I am pleased to remain anonymous. The authorities will call later today to take my statement regarding Pugh's capture and his twin's death."

"How did you discover Youngblood and Rumbradge were both Pughs?" Elizabeth inquired.

"Rhys was most cooperative in supplying some of the details we missed. For some time, the man wanted to distance himself from the Pughs, but they threatened to kill Rhys's family. His scars are proof the Pughs would not fail to make good on their intimidation. Rhys is not related to the family—only another British soldier from the same small Welsh village. Bleddyn took the name Youngblood when he claimed his mother's Indian tribe."

"Anything else of import?" Darcy asked.

"A couple of points which I thought would interest you."

"Such as?"

"Do you recall wondering for whom Rumbradge searched among those who crowded about the crime scenes?"

In his mind's eye, Darcy recalled the suspicious behavior they should have investigated further.

"Vividly."

"As we now know, the Pugh twins often switched places during the investigation," Cowan admitted. "Rumbradge was most insistent Bleddyn avoid the scenes when Seimon was serving in his official capacity, but according to Rhys, Bleddyn would sometimes appear in the crowd to see if anyone would notice."

"Then it is possible Bleddyn observed our searches?" Darcy tilted his head in contemplation.

Cowan nodded his confirmation before swallowing the ham he chewed.

"More notably, the sword from the Vaughns' investigation was the one given to Fitzwilliam by Lindale. From what I gleaned, in one of his first encounters in London, the major general had the unfortunate fate to be spotted by Bleddyn Pugh. The cad stole the sword from Fitzwilliam's quarters at the Sephora and attempted to sell it to Vaughn, who collected bits and pieces of war paraphernalia. It was after the pair argued when Vaughn refused the sword because of its inscription that

Bleddyn decided to use it against Vaughn and blame the major general.
By the time Bleddyn disposed of Vaughn, Pugh's madness roared to life
once more. He chose to repeat his crimes from the British front to
create an illusion from which Fitzwilliam could not escape. In truth, the
man is madly brilliant."

"Pugh came close to knowing success," Darcy noted.

"So close that Mrs. Fitzwilliam cut a piece of the hangman's rope,
the one meant for the major general at Newgate, as a reminder of the
major general's folly."

Darcy shot a glance to Elizabeth and his wife nodded her approval.

"My sister in marriage takes a step into her future," his wife
declared. "I am glad of it."

Chapter Twenty-Four

Despite Cowan's assurance that few knew of Darcy's involvement in the apprehension of Bleddyn Pugh, when Darcy escorted his wife to an evening at the opera, people flocked to speak to him and Elizabeth, each offering words of bewilderment and of respect.

"With your new notoriety, I fear, Sir, you may be forced to endure the effusions of my mother soon," Elizabeth whispered as they entered his private box. "Mrs. Bennet has likely called upon every household in Meryton to remind her neighbors you are her favorite son in marriage."

His wife's eyes twinkled with delightful teasing, and even though she chose him as her intended target, it pleased Darcy to witness Elizabeth's good humor returned.

He leaned closer to speak to her ears alone.

"I thought that once Mrs. Bennet viewed Pemberley, I would be elevated in the good lady's esteem."

Darcy kissed the back of Elizabeth's gloved hand.

"Moreover, the only Bennet I care to influence is our son, Mrs. Darcy."

"I am no longer a Bennet, Sir?" his wife asked with an arched eyebrow.

"You, my dearest Elizabeth, are as much a Darcy as was Lady Anne Fitzwilliam. You are the heart and soul of the Darcy legacy. I would be nothing without you."

Engrossed in Elizabeth's closeness, at first, Darcy did not hear the growing applause. As one, he and Elizabeth turned to view row after row of the *beau monde* coming to their feet in admiration.

"I may call out Matlock for his embellishment of the tale of the capture of the Slayer," Darcy growled. "This has my uncle's self-importance written all over it."

His wife took great pleasure in knowing how he despised public attention.

"Would you care to make your bow?" she teased.

"Let us assume our seats. Perhaps that will silence those who do not understand I was no braver than were you, Cowan, or others in my family."

Darcy seated Elizabeth and attempted to smile at those who sought his attention. He whispered as the lights came down.

"I do not merit such accolades. We both know I could not bear to view Rumbradge's revenge; I closed my eyes when the officer meant to shoot you. It was Matlock who brought the hangman to task. I was a coward." A harsh tightening of his throat followed with the confession.

Elizabeth ignored the close inspection they engendered.

"What do you mean? You acted to save me?"

Darcy caught her hand. His private box at the opera was not the place to speak this conversation, but after their unexpected welcome, he and Elizabeth could not leave the performance early. Their unprecedented exit would be construed as poor *ton*.

"I did not respond in time to prevent Rumbradge's ire. You could have died. Do you think I have not relived that ghastly moment a million times in the last three days?"

A catch of regret ripped the words from him.

Elizabeth turned her head to watch a bit of the opening aria, and Darcy wondered if his confession would wedge a chasm of mistrust between them.

"You fired the gun, William," she whispered, at length. "I watched the bullet strike Rumbradge, rattling the officer's composure. In truth, I do not know whether it was you or His Lordship who delivered the fatal strike, but you did act."

"Are you certain? I do not recall squeezing the trigger," Darcy pleaded. The scene played in his mind so often, but never once did he imagine what his wife described. Sometimes, to his horror, the scene ended with Elizabeth's death, the result of his inaction.

"You may ask His Lordship or the countess. They told the authorities of your intervention. Rumbradge's death was not a sight I would ever wish to encounter again. Watching someone die is not a sport for spectators. The scene was so appalling I gathered Georgiana and the countess and moved our party to the open warehouse while Matlock sought out a magistrate."

"I am grieved you witnessed the officer's death," Darcy said through the emotions coursing through him.

In actual fact, while he knew regret at exposing Elizabeth to what occurred, a very male part of his pride celebrated his manhood. He accepted his role in Bleddyn Pugh's detention for what it was: desperation, but over the previous two and seventy hours, Darcy questioned his ability to protect his family.

"I suppose if I thought on it, Officer Poplin would not have returned my pistol if it remained loaded."

Elizabeth's teasing smile returned.

"Has your conceit been restored, Mr. Darcy?"

"No, but my vanity is content," he assured. With a deep sigh of satisfaction, Darcy added. "Let us enjoy the music. This is one of your favorite operas if I recall correctly."

"My favorite opera and my favorite companion. I am a blessed woman," she mocked lovingly.

Darcy brought her chair closer to his.

"Tease all you wish, Mrs. Darcy. I know you are far from immune to my charms."

"You cursed me with a lack of immunity long ago, Sir. In fact, I find being immersed in your 'charms' can be most satisfying."

꒰ ꒰ ꒰

The events of the previous month caused Darcy to question how he felt about his mother's family. Since his father's passing, he trusted the Fitzwilliams to direct his life, when, in reality, they knew no more than Darcy. It was dashed frustrating to have his world so thoroughly usurped.

When his cousin called at Darcy House to ask Darcy to accompany him to speak to General Leigh-Hunt, Darcy thought to make his excuses.

However, Elizabeth cautioned, "You have not spoken to the major general since you left his cell at New Prison on the day of Fitzwilliam's release. You must come to terms with your family, or your life—rather *our* life—will be quite miserable."

"Thanks to my cousin's all-consuming self-pity, I could have lost you," Darcy protested.

Elizabeth rested her palm upon his chest.

"Yet, you did not lose me, and we are stronger for it. Now, join Fitzwilliam in his transition so Georgiana will not suffer."

With a shrug of resignation, Darcy greeted his cousin with polite inquires before they departed in the Matlock coach.

"Mrs. Fitzwilliam expressed a desire to share time with her nephews before we return to Oxfordshire," Edward noted as they waited for Leigh-Hunt to speak to them.

"My door is open. Georgiana does not require an invitation. However, Mrs. Darcy and I will set a course for Derbyshire on Friday morning. Lady Catherine will send a carriage for the captain on Thursday."

Darcy could not swallow the vituperation creeping into his tone.

"Southland is recovering nicely in case anyone should ask."

Edward stiffened in open rejection.

"I sent inquiries and words of gratitude to my former captain."

"Do you not think a visit would be more in accord with what you owe the man?" Darcy accused.

His cousin spared Darcy a sharp glance.

"I assumed I would not be welcomed!"

Darcy withdrew into winter's embrace, pulling himself up tall.

"Even if what you say is true, you owe Southland your fidelity."

"You mean I owe you my fidelity," Edward's voice became rigid with pride.

Darcy shook his head in incredulity.

"You owe my sister your devotion, and until I witness your doing so, I will be less likely to accept what I cannot observe. It is your choice. I simply know I cannot be party to the devastation. Once when I looked upon your countenance, I found determination and a bit of happiness and more than a large dose of honor, but now all I find is self-indulgence and pain, as if you sank into a morass of moral turpitude; and that pain permeates everything you touch. You are not the first to know war's enduring effects. You require a new venture, one that will permit you to place the nightmares of the war years behind you. None of the required changes will be easy, and, as it happens, there are moments I wonder if you will succeed."

"I wonder also," Edward admitted.

Darcy closed his eyes to swallow his growing ire.

"I do not wish to ring a peal over your head; yet, I cannot help but feel the bitter grief of losing my dearest friend." Darcy's jaw tightened. "In truth, I do not know how to overcome the enormous losses." They sat in uncomfortable silence for several minutes. "I always envied you."

The confession came hard, but Darcy thought it important to say the words aloud.

"Your easy manner. The war hero. A man worth emulating. A man with a glorious future."

"And I always envied your sense of person—knowing who you are and how the world views you."

Darcy stared aghast at his cousin.

"You were jealous of my top heavy manners?" he taunted.

Edward shrugged noncommittally.

"More likely your role as Pemberley's heir."

His cousin spoke with practiced lighthearted cheerfulness, but Darcy heard the uncertainty lacing Edward's tone.

"We must begin again," Darcy instructed. "Find our way to a new understanding."

His cousin remained still for what seemed forever.

"I do not know where to start. I look upon my wife's countenance, and I see her fear and know with deep regret I placed it there. God, I wish I never returned from the war. Then Mrs. Fitzwilliam could find happiness with another."

"You must forsake the excuses, Fitzwilliam," Darcy declared in reproach. "You did not perish on the battlefield, but you did bring home the scars of war. Begin there. Find a means to lessen the desolation and celebrate the successes. Concentrate on how you brought salvation to those who knew Bonaparte's oppression. Dwell on what may at first appear to be small, insignificant actions. Find your pride again by enhancing the lives of the less fortunate. During our investigation, Cowan did as such often. Your former sergeant placed Private Walters' feet upon solid ground, and he laid the basis for Mrs. Dempsey to find a better position, one that would allow her to raise her young son away from London's filth. Neither act would be considered world changing, but do not ask either Walters or Mrs. Dempsey to think otherwise: Their worlds changed for the better. Can you not find empathy for others and use that particular emotion to cure your injuries?"

Before Edward could respond, Leigh-Hunt entered, and they rose in respect.

"I apologize for the delay. Please return to your seats," the general announced as he hurried to his desk.

"Thank you, Sir for sending for me. Your continued support under the circumstances is remarkable."

Edward sat very straight.

Leigh-Hunt organized the papers scattered upon his desk in what appeared to be an awkward stall.

"Since we know a resolution to this situation with the Slayer, and the culprit lacks nothing but a date with Destiny, I turned my thoughts to how the Army might remedy what most troubles you."

The general shot a glance to Darcy, as if he would prefer not to speak before him.

"Should I wait outside, General?"

Edward placed a hand upon Darcy's arm to stay him.

"I am grateful, Sir, for your consideration," Fitzwilliam spoke upon a rasp. "Your personal concern for my future humbles me, but whatever choices I make, they will affect Mr. Darcy's sister. I hold no secrets from my cousin."

Leigh-Hunt paused as if deciding whether to continue.

"Very well, Fitzwilliam. I agree your cousin earned our trust; however, I must insist Mr. Darcy keep our confidences."

"Absolutely, General."

Leigh-Hunt nodded curtly.

"I recently held a long conversation with my counterparts at the Admiralty. Much to the Army's chagrin, the Navy beat us to the publication of several journals of their most promising officers. The government hopes to foster the patriotic tendencies of our populace. I initially thought you might be interested in chronicling your service, but I believe it is too soon for you."

Darcy watched his cousin as Edward blanched pale. "We will wait until you feel more inclined to repeat your tales."

Fitzwilliam sat stiffly. Beads of perspiration formed upon his cousin's brow.

"I am not certain, Sir, I could place pen to paper," Edward rasped.

Leigh-Hunt hesitated but a brief moment.

"When the time is right, Fitzwilliam, you will send me word."

The general did not wait for a response. Even Darcy understood Leigh-Hunt meant his remarks as an order.

"More importantly, Vice Admiral Pennington shared another of the navy's initiatives, and I am sore to admit what our naval counterparts developed impressed me. Those of the British Navy recruited former officers who remain on half pay in a different type of service to England."

Darcy noted how Edward's curiosity piqued.

"What type of service, Sir?"

Leigh-Hunt leaned forward in a fatherly stance.

"Nothing such as you experienced previously. Like much of your service there will be many months of inaction. At most, we are speaking of smugglers. Insurgents. Traitors. Those who would defraud or attempt to overthrow the English government from within."

Darcy shot a glance to his cousin. Edward's left hand darted through his hair in distraction, a sign of the major general's anxiety.

"In truth, it is a simple plan, but it is so simple, it is brilliant," the general explained. "The Navy situated several former officers in port cities and the surrounding areas. These men live out their lives as would any British citizen, but they also report any unusual happenings to the appropriate authorities, even upon occasion dispensing with the rebels and thieves themselves. For their service, the government offers appropriate reimbursement."

"You wish the major general to spy upon others?" Darcy demanded in shocked surprise.

"In a manner," the general grimaced with mocked severity. "Perhaps it is best if you learn specifics from one of the Navy's recent recruits. He is a former captain promoted to Rear Admiral of the White after his war successes. He resides in Dorset and would be one of your contacts if you choose to participate in this venture. You may direct your questions to him. Mayhap foster the acquaintance over the next few days. I asked the Admiral to remain in London until week's end so he might be at your disposal."

The general fell silent for several elongated moments.

"Do you wish the man's acquaintance, Fitzwilliam? Keep in mind, beyond Mr. Darcy, you will be working without the knowledge of your family, and you must develop your own contacts and decide whom to trust in your investigations. The venture will require all your cunning."

The muscles in Edward's jaw tightened, but Darcy's cousin nodded his agreement.

"Then, come along."

Leigh-Hunt led them to a room several doors along the hall. Darcy noted the hard slant of his cousin's shoulders. Edward walked as if he was a doomed man, but Darcy thought what the general offered appeared a sensible resolution. His cousin could return to Yadkin Hall and see to Georgiana's future while using the skills the major general developed upon the battlefield to "fight" England's internal wars.

In the small room stood a very formidable man. Years of service upon the sea deeply tanned the gentleman's skin. Menace defined the officer's tall, yet stocky frame, and Darcy thought the gentleman to possess the look of a dark-haired pirate.

"Lord Orland," the general was saying before Darcy came to a standstill, "may I present Major General Fitzwilliam and his cousin, Mr. Darcy. Gentlemen, I am pleased to bring you to the acquaintance of Admiral Wentworth, Viscount Orland of Hanson Hall in Dorset."

He, Fitzwilliam and the admiral executed their bows before Leigh-Hunt continued.

"Fitzwilliam would prefer to learn of our proposal from you, Orland, so I will leave you to discover more of each other." With that, the general rushed from the room as if he feared providing Edward more time to think about the offer might garner a rejection from the major general.

Darcy glanced about them.

"I am here only as an observer, Orland. I mean to permit you and my cousin your conversation. If you will pardon my abruptness, I will find something to occupy my mind over there." He pointed to a sunny corner. With another bow, Darcy retrieved a book and pretended to read.

Edward chuckled in what sounded of practiced society.

"It would appear, Orland, we are to struggle through the awkwardness as if nothing from the ordinary brought us together."

Darcy listened closely to the viscount's response.

"I am often from step in such situations. Perhaps we should sit. I understand from Leigh-Hunt that you received your last promotion in service to Prince George. I suppose that is the reason our superiors thought we might suit in this matter." They sat close, and it pleased Darcy to note Edward's interest continued.

"It was a chance happening," his cousin admitted, but the major general did not elaborate on how he came into the promotion. Fitzwilliam hesitated before asking, "Are you the Wentworth who captured the American ship meant to rescue Bonaparte?"

Orland smiled conspiratorially. "My efforts impressed Prince George, who provided me a once defunct title for my children."

"Are you related to the Wentworth family, that of the Earl of Strafford?"

The viscount appeared amused.

"I am often asked that question, but I fear I cannot claim such noteworthy connections, a fact which remains a sore point with my father-in-marriage. Although I possess a gentleman's education, Sir Walter finds me lacking."

Darcy swallowed his comment; he knew the Earl of Matlock thought little of Sir Walter Elliot. The two butted heads over some property in Somersetshire several years prior. With good manners, Edward also ignored commenting upon the viscount's family.

"Yet, you prevailed."

Fitzwilliam's tone spoke of caution.

"I did. With good fortune as my partner, I won the hand of an intelligent woman, who presented me with a son and a daughter."

"You are fortunate indeed. Mrs. Fitzwilliam and I know parenthood also. My wife is Mr. Darcy's sister," he explained.

"I understand you are the son of Lord Matlock."

The viscount offered an encouraging smile.

Edward responded with a bit of defensiveness in his voce.

"And I assume you heard of my recent difficulties."

To Darcy, it appeared as if a shadow crossed Orland's features.

"I did, but my thoughts were more agreeably engaged. I was wondering why you chose to purchase a commission in the army rather than to earn your fortune in the navy. Does not a second son require his own funds?"

The question caused his cousin to scowl, but the major general had the grace to look chagrined.

"My apologies, Orland. I fear I still reel from the error of my ways. As to my not choosing the navy, I am slow to admit I am not the best sailor. My cousin Darcy would live on his yacht if propriety would not frown upon his choice."

The line of Edward's jaw rippled from exacting control. The viscount marked Edward's struggle.

"Perhaps, if we are to cooperate for the good of England, it would be best if you tell me in your own words of this *error* in your judgment."

Darcy held his breath, waiting for his cousin's response. Would Edward open up to a stranger when the major general refused to speak upon the subject of his service with his dear family? At length, Edward spoke in a harsh whisper.

"The war never leaves me for more than a few minutes at a time. Do you possess such dreams, Wentworth?"

"Aye. Less now than before, but often a sound or an odor or even the quietness, like one experiences before a battle, will bring the desolation of witnessing a man's head blow from his shoulders by a cannonball to my conscious thoughts."

"It is the most excruciating pain I know, and I have no one with whom to share it."

His cousin tried for indifference, but the shield Edward wore as he would his honor knew its first crack, and Darcy breathed a bit easier.

"Do you speak of the horrors, Admiral?"

It was fascinating to observe two men who knew control in every facet of their lives, except one, as they acknowledged their shortcomings.

"Lady Orland traveled with me the last years of the war and possesses some knowledge of the swath war has upon the land and the sea. Many in England know only what they read in the newsprints. They did not witness the terrors of battle. My wife's presence at my side allowed her to accept my occasional reticence."

The viscount spoke so freely of his experiences, Darcy wondered if Leigh-Hunt shared Edward's history with the admiral prior to their meeting.

"Of late, I used my newfound influence to surround my home with men who served me well, choosing those I could trust with my secrets and my life. It would be to your advantage, Fitzwilliam, if you could do likewise."

Edward shot a glance in Darcy's direction, and Darcy pretended not to observe his cousin's speculative expression.

"Mr. Darcy offered similar advice. It seems one of my former soldiers found employment for those suffering from the war's aftermath."

Sorrow marked the viscount's eyes.

"One cannot enter into such an agreement of the soul with the notion of saving the world. Many men served under me in the ten years of my tendency with the navy, but not all who seek my favors are worthy of my notice, now that I am a viscount. A former lieutenant took his orders and now serves as my estate's curate. Several others without a gentleman's education hold laborer positions and those of merchants upon my estate's grounds and in the neighboring village, which depends upon Hanson Hall for its existence. It is not a perfect situation, but I find it satisfying in its simplicity. Moreover, I may call upon these men to assist me with my duties to the Crown."

Orland paused as if weighing what to share.

"Might I make the observation, Fitzwilliam, that it is not healthy to hide your pain? Never speaking of it can only increase the horror. You must no longer mask your hesitation."

Darcy heard his cousin swallow hard and watched as Edward's eyes filled with tears. He knew the major general would not cry—would not show a weakness before another powerful man, although Darcy expected it would assist in cleansing his cousin's soul if Edward did so.

"Sometime in the future," Edward spoke in self-loathing, "would you listen to my stories?"

Darcy waited for the viscount's response. Lord Orland's words held the potential of bringing peace to Edward's door or sending the major general into a chasm of shame.

"I would consider it an honor to serve as your confidant, Major General." No despair. No pity. A simple acceptance. With his confirmation, Lord Orland won Darcy's devotion, and he expected that of his cousin's as well.

Edward acknowledged Orland's kindness with a nod of acceptance and a heavy exhale.

"Perhaps you might provide me with the details of this scheme our superiors concocted. I would be most interested in how you came to claim this role."

For the next half hour, Orland entertained Edward and Darcy with the tale of how Prince George presented Wentworth with a title and property in order to place the admiral in a position to coordinate the government's efforts in controlling the populace. He even included a tale of an unusual find in a Dorset warehouse.

Darcy noted how Fitzwilliam abandoned his earlier trepidation and became fully engaged in His Lordship's tale.

"There is something you do not share, Orland," the major general said when the viscount finished.

The admiral smiled in sardonic amusement.

"I will do my duty to the Crown for it pleases my viscountess to know our children will possess a legacy and a true place in Society; yet, I explained to Lady Orland that I must define the rules by which I engage the King's enemies. My ear will not lead me about as if I am a fool embodied."

Fitzwilliam's features softened.

"I am pleased to hear it. I know Lord Wallingford well, and I cannot say I would care to trust my life to Marcus Lansing's oversight."

The admiral heaved a harsh sigh.

"I should warn you, Fitzwilliam, my opinion of the Earl of Wallingford may be based upon the fact he holds a familiar acquaintance with my wife, which dates to their days in boarding schools in Bath. The earl often refers to the viscountess's 'kind heart.'"

"I am certain you base your contempt on more than a bit of manly jealousy," Edward said with assurance.

❧❧❧

Elizabeth curled into Darcy's embrace. Upon his return to Darcy House, he explained Leigh-Hunt's offer to the major general to his wife.

"Do you believe Fitzwilliam will join the government's efforts?"

With a gentle touch, her hand explored the muscles of Darcy's chest.

Darcy gave a low chuckle. His wife's inquisitiveness knew little rest, and since his speaking of the day's events, Elizabeth insisted upon returning to the topic again and again. However, his body grew warm with desire from her closeness.

"I knew I should not break my promise and inform you of taking the acquaintance of Lord Orland," Darcy chastised in good humor.

Noting Elizabeth's defiant slant to her chin, he added, "The major general will concur, but whether it will be enough to resolve my cousin's inner turmoil, I cannot say."

He ran a line of kisses over his wife's shoulder to distract her.

"The viscountess sounds to be a sensible woman; her acquaintance may prove beneficial in assisting Georgiana to define my sister's role in the major general's healing."

Darcy's fingers traced Elizabeth's auburn curls spread out upon the pillow.

Although she ran her fingers across Darcy's shoulders and down his arms, his wife did not abandon her curiosity.

"And what of those who assisted Mr. Cowan?"

"At Cowan's suggestion, the earl rewarded Mrs. Dempsey with a position upon Lindale's estate and a promise of an apprenticeship for the woman's young son. Tark Hardy refused a like position for he plans to claim Alice Spangler as his wife. Therefore, Matlock presented the pair with a monetary donation toward their future."

"Then all is well with the world," Elizabeth said as she pulled him closer and wrapped her arms about Darcy's neck.

His lips moved to claim his wife's mouth.

"It will be once I convince you how violently I love you," Darcy murmured.

His kiss became more demanding, as images of the intimacies they might share grew stronger.

"I am not so easily persuaded," Elizabeth protested in a husky whisper.

Darcy smiled with ease.

"I adore your challenges, Mrs. Darcy."

He returned her sweet kiss with an all-consuming one. Darcy's heart soared with satisfaction. He would spend endless days loving this particular woman's presence in his life and endless nights simply loving her. Elizabeth was truly his heart.

Finis

Historical Notes

Saunders Welch and the Bow Street Runners

Founded in 1749, the Bow Street Runners were London's first professional police force. The public gave the "Runners" their nickname, but the men involved in the organization never used the term. Formally attached to the Bow Street magistrates' office, the central government employed the men. Working from Fielding's office and court at No. 4 Bow Street, the "Runners" served writs and arrested offenders on the authority of the magistrates, as well as traveled nationwide to apprehend criminals.

Earning the title of High Constable of Holborn, Saunders Welch, a grocer by profession, selected his men from former constables, who were discharged from their duties at the end of their year in office. In 1839, Bow Street disbanded, but it served as the model of increasing professionalism among "police" authorities, as well as establishing state control of London's streets. (Thomas Cowan's character made his first appearance in *The Mysterious Death of Mr. Darcy*.)

Henry Addington, 1st Viscount Sidmouth, Home Secretary

Henry Addington, 1st Viscount Sidmouth, was a British statesman and Prime Minister of the United Kingdom from 1801 to 1804. Elected to the House of Commons as an MP for Devizes, Addington became Speaker of the House in 1789. In March 1801, William Pitt the Younger resigned as Prime Minister, and Addington assumed the position. However, in May 1804, an alliance of Pitt, Charles James Fox, and William Wyndham Grenville, 1st Baron Grenville, took advantage of Addington's inability to manage a Parliamentary majority and drove Addington from office.

Yet, Addington remained a political force serving as Lord President of the Council from 1804 to 1806 and in the Ministry of All the Talents as Lord Privy Seal and again as Lord President in 1807. In 1805, he received the peerage of Viscount Sidmouth.

In June 1812, Addington became Home Secretary. During his reign, Sidmouth countered revolutionary opposition and was responsible for the suspension of *habeas corpus* in 1817 (included in *A Touch of Love*), as well as the passage of the Six Acts in 1819. His term saw the Peterloo Massacre of 1819 (the setting for "His Irish Eve" from *His: Two Regency Novellas*). He left office in 1822.

Ratcliff Highway Murders

The most famous crimes of the mid Regency period were the Ratcliff Highway murders. Two separate incidents occurred, which resulted in seven fatalities. The first took place on 7 December 1811 in a linen draper's shop at 29 Ratcliffe Highway (now called The Highway), one of the three main roads leaving London near Wapping. The first victims were the Marr family: Timothy Marr, his wife Celia, his 14 weeks old son Timothy, and Marr's apprentice, James Gowan. Twelve days later, a second set of murders occurred at the King's Arms, a tavern at 81 New Gravel Lane (now Garnet Street). In that incident, John Williamson, the tavern owner, his wife Elizabeth, and their servant Bridget Harrington knew the murderer's wrath.

After examining many suspects, the authorities arrested John Williams. The courts indicted Williams upon what was purely circumstantial evidence, but Williams never went to trial. On 28 December he used his scarf to hang himself in his cell. Despite Williams' suicide, the court found him guilty. Afterwards, the court ordered his body to be paraded through the streets as proof of the end of the madness surrounding those living in the East Side. The Ratcliff Highway murders served as the impetus for the action of this novel.

Chief John Norton

Playing a prominent role in the War of 1812, the Mohawk Major John Norton (Teyoninhokovrawen) led a group of Iroquois warriors against the Americans and changed the course for British troops at Queenston Heights, Stoney Creek, and Chippawa. Norton's father, taken prisoner during a British attack, was Cherokee and his mother Scottish. His father later joined the British Army and settled in Scotland. Educated in his chosen homeland, John Norton apprenticed to a printer, but, at length, ran away to join the army. Norton knew service in Ireland before being relocated to Lower Canada in 1785.

In 1787, Norton deserted. He traveled in the Ohio region and became involved in the concerns of the Six Nations of the Grand River. In 1794, he became an interpreter for the Indian department. The Mohawks adopted him, and Joseph Brant served as his uncle. He moved to Grand River and married an Iroquois woman.

In 1804, he traveled to England to negotiate treaties for the benefit of the Indians. During this time, the British and Foreign Bible Society asked Norton to translate the Gospel of John into Mohawk. His translation was the first publication of the society.

Norton's journal, published under the title *The Journal of Major John Norton, 1816*, is a firsthand account of the War of 1812, as well as a firsthand account of life among the Cherokees. Norton reportedly left Canada in his final years and moved to Laredo, Mexico. No one knows the details of his demise, or of his whereabouts in these final years, and the mystery adds to Norton's fame.

Isaac Brock

Brock served as a British Army officer assigned to Canada in 1802. Despite the tedium of a wilderness post, Brock took full responsibility for his regiment in Upper Canada (present-day Ontario). His men defended Upper Canada against the United States. While many of his time thought war between England and the United States could be averted, Brock systematically prepared for what he saw as inevitable. When the War of 1812 broke out, his men and the Canadian populace surprised the American invasion forces with quick victories at Fort Mackinac and Detroit. For his forethought, the British government presented Brock a knighthood and membership in the Order of the Bath.

Old Bailey

The procedural activities of the fictional case against Major General Fitzwilliam is based on the real-life case of Richard Ludman, Ann Rhodes, Eleanor Hughes, and Mary Baker in June 1796, as well as the one against Benjamin Tapner, John Cobby, John Hammond, Richard Mills (both the elder and the younger), William Jackson, and William Carter in January 1748. I used the Old Bailey online proceedings to "flavor" the text with the proper legal terms and measures.

Old Bailey Proceedings Online (www.oldbaileyonline.org, version 7.0, 07 June 2014), June 1796, trial of RICHARD LUDMAN ANN RHODES ELEANOR HUGHES, MARY BAKER (t17960622-8).

Old Bailey Proceedings Online (www.oldbaileyonline.org, version 7.0, 17 June 2014), January 1748, trial of Benjamin Tapner John Cobby John Hammond Richard Mills the elder Richard Mills the younger William Jackson William Carter (t17480116-1).

MEET THE AUTHOR

Writing passionately comes easily to **Regina Jeffers**. A master teacher, for thirty-nine years, she passionately taught thousands of students English in the public schools of West Virginia, Ohio, and North Carolina. Yet, "teacher" does not define her as a person. Ask any of her students or her family, and they will tell you Regina is passionate about so many things: her son, her grandchildren, truth, children in need, our country's veterans, responsibility, the value of a good education, words, music, dance, the theatre, pro football, classic movies, the BBC, track and field, books, books, and more books. Holding multiple degrees, Jeffers often serves as a Language Arts or Media Literacy consultant to school districts and has served on several state and national educational commissions.

Regina's writing career began when a former student challenged her to do what she so "righteously" told her class should be accomplished in writing. On a whim, she self-published her first book *Darcy's Passions*. "I never thought anything would happen with it. Then one day, a publishing company contacted me. They watched the sales of the book on Amazon, and they offered to print it."

Since that time, Jeffers continues to write. "Writing is just my latest release of the creative side of my brain. I taught theatre, even participated in professional and community-based productions when I was younger. I trained dance teams, flag lines, majorettes, and field commanders. My dancers were both state and national champions. I simply require time each day to let the possibilities flow. When I write, I write as I used to choreograph routines for my dance teams; I write the scenes in my head as if they are a movie. Usually, it plays there for several days being tweaked and rewritten, but, eventually, I put it to paper. From that point, things do not change much because I completed several mental rewrites."

Other Novels by Regina Jeffers

Jane Austen-Inspired Novels:
Darcy's Passions: Pride and Prejudice Retold Through His Eyes
Darcy's Temptation: A Pride and Prejudice Sequel
Captain Wentworth's Persuasion: Jane Austen's Classic Retold Through His Eyes
Vampire Darcy's Desire: A Pride and Prejudice Paranormal Adventure
The Phantom of Pemberley: A Pride and Prejudice Mystery
Christmas at Pemberley: A Pride and Prejudice Holiday Sequel
The Disappearance of Georgiana Darcy: A Pride and Prejudice Mystery
The Mysterious Death of Mr. Darcy: A Pride and Prejudice Mystery
"The Pemberley Ball" (a short story in The Road to Pemberley anthology)
Honor and Hope: A Contemporary Pride and Prejudice

Regency and Contemporary Romances:
The Scandal of Lady Eleanor—Book 1 of the Realm Series (aka A Touch of Scandal)
A Touch of Velvet—Book 2 of the Realm Series
A Touch of Cashémere—Book 3 of the Realm Series
A Touch of Grace—Book 4 of the Realm Series
A Touch of Mercy—Book 5 of the Realm Series
A Touch of Love—Book 6 of the Realm Series
A Touch of Honor—Book 7 of the Realm Series
His: Two Regency Novellas (includes "His American Heartsong," a Realm series novella, and "His Irish Eve," a sequel to The Phantom of Pemberley)
The First Wives' Club—Book 1 of the First Wives' Trilogy
Second Chances: The Courtship Wars

Coming Soon…
Angel Comes to the Devil's Keep
A Touch of Emeralds: The Conclusion of the Realm Series
The Earl Finds His Comfort
Mr. Darcy's Fault: A Pride and Prejudice Vagary Novella
Elizabeth Bennet's Deception: A Pride and Prejudice Vagary

**For more on how Captain Frederick Wentworth came to his position with the Home Office, read Captain Wentworth's Persuasion.*

order at www.pegasusbooks.net